MERCURY SNOW

A NOVEL BY

TAYLOR R. GRAY

ACKNOWLEDGMENTS

Years ago, I believed writing a book was far too great a task. Grammar and spelling were never my strong suits. Whether it was madness or inspiration, something drove me, and I took on the mantle of author. I want to thank my friends and family for encouraging me throughout the journey.

Thanks to my sister, for allowing me to bounce ideas off of her and for helping me form my story. Her expertise as an English teacher and good sense of plot were tremendous.

To my father, for his attention to detail and his engineering mind. His help in refining my writing and scientific concepts was invaluable.

To my cousin, Cherish, for being my "guinea pig" and providing feedback for the book in its early stages.

To my mother, for continuously encouraging me to keep going.

To my grandparents, for their inspiration and support for my prior works.

To my publishing team at Silversmith Press, for their willingness to take a chance on me.

To my employers for tolerating my excursions into authorship.

Finally, to God for his infinite patience to my belligerence and continued insistence that I finish this book!

DEDICATION

In loving memory of my dear grandfather, my mother's father, Charles Edward Payton 1930–2022. You are an inspiration for my works. May your contributions never be forgotten. Be of good cheer, dear friend.

In loving memory of my dear grandfather, my father's father, Thomas Charles "Doc" Gray 1930–2022. May your strength and dedication be an example. Thank you for your encouragement to pursue my writing career. Until later, alligator.

ISBN 978-1-961093-05-8 (Softcover Book)
ISBN 978-1-961093-06-5 (eBook)

Published by Silversmith Press–Houston, Texas
www.silversmithpress.com

SILVERSMITH
PRESS

CONTENTS

CHAPTER
1

This is it, he thought. *What will they have me do? I hope that I can perform to their expectations. Did I forget to unpack something from the move? Did I lock my door?* He repeatedly clasped and unclasped his hands as he attempted to distract himself by peering out his passenger window at the rows of skyscrapers crawling by. He barely noticed the heavy traffic or the slow progress of the cab as his mind raced with possibilities and questions.

A brilliant light flashed across the dark blue morning sky in his peripheral vision.

"WHOA!" The cab driver shouted as he slammed the brakes and swerved.

Jordin grabbed a hold of the armrest for dear life as he and his briefcase jostled around the backseat. "What!? What's wrong?" He took several deep breaths as he looked around.

"Did you see that?" The driver pointed at the sky.

Jordin peered between two skyscrapers in the direction that the cab driver was pointing. A dissipating white cloudy line, mixed with rays of morning sunlight, spread across the sky.

"What?"

"That thing that zipped across the sky." The driver continued to point, oblivious to the angry honks behind him.

"Oh, you saw it too? At first I thought it was just a reflection of the sun on the window." Jordin wrung his hands.

"Naw. That wasn't no reflection," the driver insisted. "What do you think it was? A missile? It can't be a shooting star in the daytime."

"I doubt it was a missile, we'd still see it traveling. While it's possible to see a shooting star during the day, it's more likely that it was sunlight reflecting off an odd cloud formation or a jet contrail."

"Yeah?" The cab driver turned around to give Jordin an accusatory glance. "How do you know? Maybe it's them aliens people keep talking about on the radio."

Jordin gave the man a reassuring smile. "I'm an astronomer, and a meteorologist. I'm way more convinced that it was a shooting star than anything alien."

"Oh yeah? How's that possible?"

"Large enough or fast objects can enter our atmosphere at just the right angle to burn bright enough to be seen. It's completely natural. I assure you." Jordin glanced at his watch. *Come on, I can't be late. Not on my first day.*

"Hmmm." The driver shrugged. "It ain't never anything interesting." He almost sounded disappointed as he turned back and drove forward.

Jordin breathed a sigh of relief and let his hands drop loosely at his sides.

"So, you're a space man, eh?" The driver asked.

"Yes, sir."

"You heard all that stuff on the radio about UFOs flying around? My kid's obsessed with 'em."

Jordin internally sighed. Outwardly he said, "I've heard a few stories."

"Yeah? What's your take on 'em?"

Jordin shrugged. "It's hard to say. UFO simply means Unidentified Flying Object. If there's anything flying that we don't recognize, it's a UFO I've flown drones and sent weather balloons into the sky only to have someone call the police on it." He began to chuckle. "I wouldn't worry too much about aliens."

"Hmmm. Maybe you're right." The driver nodded. "I've never really believed that little green men could be floating around out there."

"Who says that they'd be little?" Jordin gave the driver a mischievous glance.

The driver turned his head to look back at Jordin. "You know, man. You've got something there. Maybe that's the conspiracy. Why I..."

Jordin lost his focus on what the cab driver was saying as he glanced out the front at the approaching line of stopped cars at a light.

"...and my cousin said that..."

"Watch out!" Jordin pointed forward.

The driver turned his head back to the front and slammed his brakes again. Tires squealed as the cab came to a halt just in time.

Both Jordin and the driver sat there breathing heavily for a few moments. Jordin's hand absently rested on the back of the driver's seat.

"Eh, wouldn't have been the first time. That's what insurance is for, you know." The driver shrugged.

Jordin leaned back into his seat and firmly clasped his hands again. "I'll tell you what. Let me worry about the aliens. Until they actually invade, they're not a problem."

"Hmmm. Good point. Anyway," the driver continued as if nothing had happened, "my kid's birthday is coming up. He's real into space and stuff like that. I'm trying to find something to get him, but everything's so expensive, you know."

"Yeah...I know."

The driver grunted in response.

Jordin collected himself after a few moments. He opened his briefcase and rummaged around, ensuring that the contents weren't too scrambled from the excitement. There wasn't much aside from his thesis paper, a few pens and pencils, paper, and other miscellaneous office supplies. "Ah," he said as he extracted a decal of the NASA space shuttle. "I was given a few of these on a tour of NASA back in college. I'm sure your kid would like it." He offered it forward.

"Hey, thanks man. My kid will love it." The driver accepted the decal and set it on the front passenger seat.

"No problem."

Jordin and the driver spent several minutes discussing various UFO sightings.

A tall skyscraper with a large white dome in the center of the roof appeared ahead as the cab rounded a corner.

There it is. Jordin forgot the conversation and fixed his eyes on the dome. *There's their observatory. Will they let me use it?*

"It's right up here, you can see it now." The cab driver pointed to the dome-topped structure.

Jordin absently nodded, oblivious to the fact that the cab driver couldn't see him. His heart fluttered as they approached.

"Here we are," the cab driver announced as he pulled up to the curb in front of the imposing building.

Jordin nodded and took a deep breath. This was it. It was now time. "Thank you; how much do I owe you?" He asked as he pulled his hands apart and reached for his wallet.

"$23.74," the cab driver replied flatly.

"Here you are and keep the change." Jordin handed the driver a twenty and a ten.

"Thanks, pal."

"Oh, and," Jordin pulled out another twenty, "buy your son a present."

The driver smiled. "Thanks, Space Man."

"You're welcome. Happy to encourage a fellow space enthusiast."

Jordin opened the cab door and stepped out onto the sidewalk, a little shaken but determined. A slight breeze rustled his neatly combed, short black hair. His brown eyes stared up at the towering skyscraper in front of him as people briskly walked by. *I've finally made it,* he thought as he straightened his tie and ensured that his dark blue business suit was properly buttoned. All of those years spent acquiring his doctorate degree had finally paid off. *My first real job. Just don't mess this one up.*

He glanced at his watch. *I'm a little late. I hope they aren't too strict.*

"I suppose I should go in and introduce myself," he muttered as he closed the car door behind him and took a step toward the building.

"Hey, pal," the cab driver shouted after him.

Jordin spun around to see the cab driver pointing, with his thumb, to the back seat of the car. "Oh, my briefcase," he said as he quickly reopened the door. "Sorry about that."

"No problem," the driver nodded.

Jordin grabbed his briefcase and closed the door again, apologizing profusely.

"Good luck, Space Man." The driver waved as the cab pulled away.

Jordin waved back before he turned and strode to the front doors of the building. He briefly checked the reflection of his face in the glass doors for any stray whiskers he might have missed while shaving this morning. A distinctive "new office" smell hit his nose as he opened the second set of glass double doors, taking in the wide-open space he had entered. A large, carved stone fountain, depicting Saint George slaying the dragon, stood in the center of the room. Water merrily splashed out of the dragon's gaping mouth.

He approached the fountain and studied it. The tale of Saint George had always intrigued him. The idea that a mere human could take on such a fearsome creature and win was somehow comforting.

The intricate detail work on the sculpture itself was amazing. A plaque in front of the statue read, *Strive Against the Impossible.*

"May I help you?" The receptionist at the front desk asked.

Jordin snapped back to reality. "Oh...yes, sorry." He walked toward the desk. "I'm Dr. Davidson. I'm supposed to start working here today."

"Oh yes, let me see..." The receptionist scrolled through her computer. "Ah, Dr. Davidson. Do you have an ID?"

"Oh, yes." Jordin reached into his pocket and extracted his wallet. He pulled out his ID and handed it to her.

The receptionist held his ID next to her computer screen, then smiled and nodded as she handed the ID back. She opened a nearby drawer. "I have this for you." She held out a name badge.

Jordin placed his ID back into his wallet and accepted the name badge, inspecting it thoroughly. Part of him couldn't believe it was real. He had wanted his own name badge at a prestigious company for a while. Having one in hand now was surreal. Clear as day in bold lettering next to his own picture was his name "Doctor Jordin Davidson, Astronomical and Meteorological Consultant."

He couldn't help but grin proudly as he held the badge aloft. *Don't worry, Mom, Dad. I'll make you proud,* he thought.

"That will give you access to most places in the building." The receptionist smiled. "Here's a new-hire orientation packet for you." She handed him a large envelope. "This contains a map of the building noting key areas such as our cafeteria, exercise room, conference rooms, etc. It also contains emergency contact information for building security and off-hours assistance if needed."

"Thank you." Jordin smiled back.

"Regretfully, Dr. Wilber will be unable to greet you as he had intended. He instructed me to tell you that your office is room 1305, on floor thirteen. You may use the elevators to your left or the stairs to your right."

Jordin nodded as he opened the envelope to look at the map. He hoped that the observatory would be easy to find and would be open to him.

"Welcome to Planet Mercury Logistics or P.M.L. for short.

Should you need anything, don't hesitate to ring the front desk. My name is Sally."

"Thank you, I'll do that." Jordin nodded as he walked toward the stairs. Part of him thought it odd that no one else had taken Dr. Wilber's place to guide a new-hire around the building. *This is a prestigious company. I'm sure everyone's just busy doing something important.*

"Are you sure you wouldn't rather use the elevators?" Sally called out after him. "It's going to be a hike to get to floor thirteen."

"That's alright, thank you," Jordin called back. He preferred stairs. Something about elevators had always made his stomach churn. Luckily for him, he was in quite good shape. It was part of his daily routine to run stairs. In his younger years, his parents would regularly catch him running up and down the fire escape outside their apartment. In his college years, he had been known to run up and down the interior stairs of the dorms almost religiously. Now that he was in a new apartment in a new city, one of his first purchases had been a stair stepper.

The climb upward was long, but it gave him time to study the map. Directions were not his strong suit, and it would likely be a while before he could walk to his new office by memory alone. In the meantime, he would keep this map with him. He finally reached his floor and turned down the hall.

"1310, 1309, 1308," he mumbled to himself as he walked down the hallway, noting the numbers on the doors. An almost eerie realization came over him as he walked. *Is anyone else around? I've not seen anyone else on the stairs or in the hall.*

"Ah, 1305, that's me," he said as he stood in front of his office door. He brushed off his eerie feeling as he opened the door. *Everyone else must be doing something really important.*

The heavy oak door swung open to reveal an average sized office. The only furnishings were a large wooden desk that sat along the wall to his left and two filing cabinets along the wall to his right. An expensive-looking new laptop computer rested atop the desk. A large mural of the company logo consisting of a blue rocket circling around an image of the planet Mercury with the black letters "P. M. L." superimposed over it plastered the wall behind the desk. Sunlight streamed through a large window on the wall directly opposite the doorway.

Jordin walked in and glanced around. He grinned in satisfaction and said, "This is mine."

"Congratulations," said a wry feminine voice behind him.

He turned to see a tall, thin woman with piercing blue eyes staring intently at him from the office across the hall, blonde hair resting neatly on her shoulders. She was wearing a formal navy blue jacket, white blouse, and a long navy blue skirt.

"Oh, sorry, I'm...," Jordin started to say, but was cut off.

"Doctor Davidson. Our new space man." The woman smiled as she walked out of her office and into his.

"Uh...yes," Jordin nodded, unsure of what else to say. Part of him was relieved that another human being was around.

"Good." The woman nodded enthusiastically. "I'm Doctor Terry, Lauren Terry. I'm the 'astrophysical and biological consultant.'"

"Pleased to meet you." Jordin smiled and stepped forward with his right arm extended in greeting.

"Pleased to meet you too," Lauren said as she looked down into his eyes and shook his hand. "My goodness, you have a strong grip there."

"Sorry," Jordin apologized as he let go and pulled his hand back.

"Don't be, it was a compliment," Lauren replied.

"Well...uhh...thanks."

"Dr. Wilber will be here shortly. In the meantime, make yourself comfortable." Lauren didn't wait for a reply before she walked away and closed her office door behind her.

Taken off balance by what just happened, Jordin laughed. "I suppose I should expect some strange behavior from academics. It's not like I don't have my fair share of quirks." He turned and walked toward his desk.

He almost reached his desk when a loud voice boomed, "There you are."

Jordin turned to see a bald heavy-set man standing in his

doorway. The man wore a denim button down shirt emblazoned with the company logo, black slacks, and heavy, brown, rubber-soled boots.

"Yes, sir. I'm here," Jordin said hesitantly.

"Did you forget?" The man asked with an amused expression on his face.

Jordin was confused. "I'm sorry, I don't know what you're talking about."

"Ah," the man snickered, "I'm guessing you didn't get Mr. Mercury's email."

"What email did he send it to?" A knot formed in Jordin's stomach. Mr. Mercury was the primary owner of P.M.L. The thought of missing something important from one of the most important people in the company his first day made him sick.

"Your P.M.L. one," the man chuckled.

"Well...I...uh..." Jordin waved at his computer, still closed, on his desk.

"Ah typical Mercury. Sent you an email before you've even been given access to email." The man gave him a big toothy grin. "The name's Joseph, Dr. Joseph Wilber. I'm the resident robotics, electrical, and mechanical engineer." Joseph walked forward with his right hand extended.

"Pleased to meet you. I'm Dr. Jordin Davidson. I'm an astronomer and meteorologist." Jordin stepped forward and shook Joseph's hand.

"Welcome to P.M.L.," Joseph said while releasing the handshake.

"May I ask what I missed?" Jordin asked.

"We had a staff meeting in the planetarium to welcome you and introduce you to our new intern." Joseph grinned.

"I...uh...," Jordin stammered.

"Don't worry about it. This is typical. Mercury is a great visionary, but he...lacks certain...interpersonal skills."

"SON OF A!" Lauren shouted as she stomped out of her office. "How many times do I have to tell him to notify me BEFORE the meeting happens that I'm supposed to be there."

Joseph started laughing all over again. "Mercury strikes again. You two have a lot in common."

"He missed it too?" Lauren asked.

"It appears so," Jordin said.

"Typical...typical...typical," Lauren muttered as she returned to her office.

"If it makes you feel any better," Joseph began, "our janitor, Clarence, was conscripted to give the intern a tour of the place."

"Oh?" Jordin raised an eyebrow out of curiosity. "The janitor?"

"Right in the middle of mopping the restrooms." Joseph couldn't help but laugh again. "Mercury just pulled him out and told him to give the kid a tour. It's a good thing old

Clarence knows this building like the back of his hand . . . And just about everything that happens in it."

"I get the idea that Mr. Mercury is a bit eccentric."

"You can say that again." Joseph gave Jordin a friendly slap on the back, surprising Jordin with this sudden, forward gesture.

Jordin brushed it off and continued, "Was he upset that I wasn't there?"

Joseph stared Jordin directly in the eye, his expression darkening. "Yes, he was." Then a wry smile spread across his face. "At least he was until I told him you hadn't started yet."

Jordin thought for a moment. "How often should I expect something like this?"

Joseph snorted. "At least once a week if not more."

"Fantastic," Jordin said sarcastically.

"I'm glad you agree." Joseph flashed Jordin another toothy grin. "I'll be around if you need anything." He turned and left the office, leaving Jordin to soak everything in.

Jordin shook his head as he sat down at his desk. "I better set myself up on the email system," he muttered as he opened his laptop. He continuously clasped and unclasped his hands as he waited for it to boot up, haunted by the thought of his boss angrily firing him on his first day.

The laptop's login screen appeared, allowing him to follow the instructions in the new-hire packet that Sally had given him to access the company network and email.

"Ah...there's Mr. Mercury's email about the meeting..." He sighed as he stared at the email. "I guess I should reply and apologize."

He typed and sent an apology to his boss. For a few moments, all he did was sit there, fiddling with his hands again trying to calm his nerves.

"He hasn't fired me yet," he said after a few moments. "I better get to work. I don't need him any more angry at me than he already is."

He continued following the instructions until there it was before him - the company's information system. He soaked in the wealth of knowledge. P.M.L.'s entire historical catalog of meteorological and astronomical data, collected from around the globe, was now at his fingertips.

"I wish I had this much data when I wrote my thesis," he chuckled.

"I'm glad you like it," snapped a gravelly voice.

Jordin looked up to see a tall, thin balding man in a sharp business suit glaring at him through thick glasses. Gray and white flecks dotted the man's receding brown hair.

"Ah, Mr. Mercury!" Jordin leaped to his feet, outstretched his right hand, and marched toward his boss.

"I'm glad you remember who I am, at least," Mr. Mercury scowled at Jordin's hand, dismissing his handshake offer.

"I...I'm sorry?" Jordin said in confusion. "Is there something that I can do for you?"

"I know it's your first day. So, I will be lenient. But do try not to forget meetings," Mercury scoffed.

Jordin furrowed his brow and retracted his hand. He cleared his throat before speaking. "I apologize, I didn't receive word that I was supposed to be at the meeting until after it was already over. You see, I've just barely set up and didn't have access to the company email until just now."

Mr. Mercury sized up Jordin and glanced at the computer on the desk. He shrugged and said, "Do be more vigilant in the future."

"Yes, sir," Jordin nodded vigorously.

"Your intern is waiting for you in the lab. I look forward to seeing your project proposal," Mercury gave a forced smile and promptly marched out.

"My what?" Jordin said in surprise. "And where's the lab?" No response came as Mr. Mercury had already disappeared down the hallway. "Okay..." Jordin slowly shook his head and returned to his desk. He looked through the information packet. The building map should tell him where the fabled lab was. As far as his project proposal, he would have to figure that out later. Maybe his mystery intern would know.

A ringing noise interrupted his thoughts. A symbol of a phone appeared on his computer with a green "accept" and a red "decline" button. Right below the phone symbol was the name "Dr. Dhar."

"Oh boy, what did I get myself into?" Jordin groaned as he answered the phone. "Hello, this is Dr. Davidson. How may I help you?" His hands resumed their routine of clasping and fidgeting, almost unconsciously.

"Hello Dr. Davidson," Dr. Dhar's calm voice filtered through the computer speakers with a light Hindi accent. "I would like to personally welcome you to P.M.L."

"Thank you, sir," Jordin said.

"Allow me to introduce myself. I am Dr. Dhar, part owner and head of the India branch of P.M.L."

"Yes, I've seen you on the news and on the company website. I'm honored to receive your call," Jordin said as sincerely as he could muster. He already had one owner mad at him. He didn't want to upset another.

Dhar chuckled. "Thank you. I've been looking forward to talking with you. I read your thesis on planetary atmospheres and exospheres. Mr. Mercury and I were particularly intrigued at the proposal of sending dedicated probes to each of the planets to see how they all interact with one another meteorologically."

"Yes sir," Jordin smiled as his hands relaxed on the desk. "It's quite fascinating to see just how each planetary body interacts with the others, especially with weather patterns. Each planet exerts a gravitational influence on the other," he paused, realizing what he was doing. "I'm sorry, you're well aware of all of this."

"Don't worry at all," Dhar laughed. "It's good to hear someone excited about their job."

"I'll do my best to maintain that excitement."

"I'm assuming that you've been briefed on your project, is that true?"

"I've been informed that I need to submit a project proposal and that I have an intern waiting for me in the lab." Jordin grimaced, unsure of how to ask what his project was.

"Were you told what your project was supposed to be?" Dhar's voice sounded concerned.

"Honestly...no," Jordin sighed.

"Unsurprising." Dhar sounded disappointed.

"I'm sorry, I didn't..."

"You've nothing to be sorry for." Dhar cut Jordin off. "You can't help it when other people don't inform you of what your task is. I'll forward you the project details. The basic overview of the project is that we want to design atmospheric probes that can measure weather patterns, even in limited atmospheric conditions. Both Mercury and I were intrigued by your thesis and your idea of measuring and accounting for weather patterns on other planets as well as observing more closely their influence on our own meteorological system."

"That's a huge project to undertake," Jordin said.

"Here at P.M.L. we're dedicated to assisting the scientific community in their endeavors. The data collected from this project would be invaluable. We're aware of the high financial and time risk that this project poses. We want to take this one step at a time. If we can design a system that increases our own atmospheric data gathering for our own planet, we can go from there. Once we prove our concept and design on our own planet, we are certain to gain interest and funding."

"I'll do what I can to ensure that this project is a success," Jordin said positively.

"I believe that." Dhar paused. "I should probably let you get to the lab. I've forwarded you the details that I have. Our team here and our facilities are available to you should you need them. We are currently on the night shift. So, any major requests won't be fulfilled until our main team arrives in the morning."

"Thank you, sir," Jordin said.

"Any time." A clicking noise from the computer's phone program signified Dhar hanging up.

"Well," Jordin thought, "at least one of the owners isn't mad at me...yet." He grabbed the map of the building, then stood and walked out the door. He spotted Joseph walking toward him in the hall.

"Ah," Joseph marched up to Jordin with a grin, "I figured you may want to know where the lab is."

Jordin nodded and smiled in return, "Yes, I'm supposed to meet my intern there now."

"I thought as much. Mercury mumbled something about

it when I passed him in the hall. Let me show you." Joseph made a grand sweeping motion indicating down the hallway.

"Thank you," Jordin said.

"I'm guessing Mr. Mercury stopped by your office," Joseph said impishly as he led the way.

"Yes, he did," Jordin sighed.

"I'm also guessing he growled at you for not being at the meeting and told you to go to the lab."

"He did that too."

"He probably didn't bother to tell you where the lab was or what you and your intern would be doing."

"Well...he did tell me to give him a project proposal." Jordin glanced around at the various other offices and rooms as they passed by.

Joseph let out a chuckle, "Welcome to P.M.L. If we haven't driven you insane in a week, we haven't done our job." He walked up to the elevator and pressed the button.

"Uhhh...," Jordin said nervously. "Do you think we could take the stairs...I...I prefer that option." He paused awkwardly for a moment. "It's good for your health...you know."

The elevator emitted a series of two cheerful beeps as the doors opened. Joseph peered inquisitively at Jordin, then back at the elevator. After shrugging, he said, "Okay. Lord knows I can use the exercise." He patted his stomach then merrily wandered toward the stairs. "As I was saying. Mr. Mercury is...as you said...eccentric."

"I'll say," Jordin agreed as he followed Joseph down the stairs.

"He means well. He's just...scattered. You'll get used to it." Joseph laughed. His laughter echoed around the concrete walls of the stairwell.

"He seemed pretty upset with me." Jordin was concerned that his employment would be cut short, but didn't want to bring up that topic or put the idea in anyone's head.

"Not to worry, he'll forget within the hour that he's mad at you," Joseph assured.

"Well, that's good...I guess."

"Don't worry, he'll find something else to be mad at you for."

"Lovely," Jordin furrowed his brow.

"I wouldn't worry too much about him. As long as you do your job and produce results, he won't get rid of you. It's his way of saying that he likes you. If he isn't mad at you for something, he doesn't care about you."

"Good to know."

"Besides, Dr. Dhar keeps him in line. Get on Dhar's good side and you'll be fine."

Jordin nodded, "Ah, about Dr. Dhar. What exactly does he do?"

"I'll put it to you this way. Mercury is the idea guy, the

guy who gets things started and rolling. Dhar is the one who gets things done. He may be the head of technical services, but he might as well be the head of the whole company."

"Makes sense," Jordin said.

"And...," Joseph grinned, "he's the voice of sanity and reason."

"How exactly does that work considering he is in India and we're here? The time difference should make that difficult, right?"

Joseph snorted, "I thought so once too. But that man's a machine. I'm not sure he's ever slept before. If there is a problem at any point during the day, he's the one calling people to deal with it. In short, he loves to work and is dedicated to his job. Frankly, this place should be called Dhar's Logistics."

"Sounds like he's a good person to know."

"Believe me, your best bet is to get to know him as soon as possible. Mercury's name may be on the building, but Dhar makes it all work."

"Thank you for telling me."

"You're welcome," Joseph chuckled. "I can't tell you how many people I've given this speech to, only to have them ignore me and underestimate Dhar's importance. Most of them only last a week on their own before quitting...or get themselves fired. Dhar and his approval are the key."

"I won't ignore you. Dhar seems reasonable. I'm happy to work with him."

"Good," Joseph said. "By the way, you're a space man." He gave Jordin a sly look. "Did you hear about that surprise meteor shower over Europe yesterday?"

Jordin blinked. "There was a meteor shower yesterday? There's not supposed to be one until...Sorry. No. I hadn't heard. I was in the middle of my move yesterday."

"It's in all the papers. It caught everyone off guard. It's like it just showed up. Do you know how something like that could happen?"

Jordin shrugged as he stepped onto a rough concrete landing and turned to face the final flight of stairs down. "There are a number of small rocks and objects in space. Not all of them are easily tracked. We may have just hit a cluster of them. It happens a lot. Meteor showers and shooting stars happen all the time."

"Yeah." Joseph shrugged. "Makes sense to me. Everyone seemed to make a big deal out of it."

"I don't blame them. Meteor showers can be quite spec-tacular to watch."

The pair had finally reached the tenth floor. "Here we are," Joseph said as he opened the door, revealing several computer workstations dotting the wide room. Many other machines such as lathes, 3D printers, and various cutters lined the walls.

"This is Jimmy," Joseph motioned to a young man in a lab coat that was too big for him. "He's our intern. Just graduated high school."

"Hello," Jimmy waved awkwardly.

"Hello, Jimmy," Jordin said as he offered his hand.

Jimmy clumsily walked forward and shook Jordin's hand limply.

Used to firmer handshakes, Jordin eased up on his pressure on Jimmy's hand. "Your first job?" He raised an eyebrow.

"Yes, sir." Jimmy smiled nervously.

"It's about time you got here," a man with a curly white mustache and blue custodial coveralls said angrily.

"This is Clarence, the head janitor," Joseph said, stifling a grin. "I see Mr. Mercury made you a tour guide."

"If you'll excuse me, I've got a bathroom to finish mopping," Clarence said as he marched out of the door, his heavy boots thumping on the concrete stairwell.

"A good man to befriend," Joseph advised Jordin. "He's rough around the edges, but a big softy. And he knows the building like the back of his hand. Not much goes on here without his knowledge. Rumor has it, he knows everyone's dirty little secrets."

Jordin nodded. "I'll keep that in mind."

"Alright," Lauren said in a huff as she stormed into the lab, "I hope you're all ready to work. I've just wasted valuable time arguing over meeting schedules." She placed a briefcase down on a table and opened it, revealing a laptop and several papers.

"Hello," Jimmy said, nervously clearing his throat.

"Ah, you must be the intern." Lauren pulled her laptop out and powered it on.

"Yes ma'am," Jimmy said.

"It's doctor...we're all doctors here," Lauren quipped back.

"Sorry..." Jimmy blinked.

"You can call me stupid if you like," Joseph joked. "As long as we get work done." He turned to Jimmy. "Don't worry, Dr. Terry isn't a bad sort. She's just had a run-in with Mr. Mercury...again."

"I swear, sanity is in short supply around here," Lauren grumbled.

"I guess we'd better get to work then," Jordin said.

"Okay boss," Lauren turned to him expectantly, "what's our project?"

"Uhhh..." Jordin looked at Joseph and Jimmy waiting for their orders.

"You're the project lead," Joseph said. "Mr. Mercury told us, but I guess he didn't tell you."

"So, what are we working on?" Lauren asked.

"Oh boy," Jordin said, clasping his hands again.

CHAPTER

2

Eager stares bored holes through Jordin as he did his best to formulate his ideas into a coherent thought.

"We need to be able to design probes to study planetary atmospheres and exospheres," Jordin said after collecting himself and finally letting his hands drop to his side. "Ideally, we'll have a probe on every planet of our solar system. These probes will need to be durable and reliable while still sensitive enough to collect the data we need. Our goal is to study the gravitational influences, if any, of every planet on each other's atmospheric conditions."

"Is that all?" Joseph snorted as he chuckled.

"Okay...," Lauren narrowed her eyes thoughtfully for a moment. "We can collect the positional data of each planet and calculate the expected gravitational force. But...how would you know that what you were measuring was as a result of this force, rather than everything else? Also, places like NASA already have extensive studies on planetary atmospheres. Won't we be duplicating work?"

"If we observe current weather patterns, we can establish a baseline." Jordin stroked his chin. "While we do know a lot about other planets and their atmospheres, we don't have permanent probes on all of the planets dedicated to studying weather conditions. The data we collect would expand that field of study greatly."

"Are you saying that we could train our instruments to ignore or filter out major events and only pick up unusual or minute changes?" Joseph mused.

"Yes...I think...I don't know what's possible on the technical side," Jordin said. "If we could do that automatically, that'd be great."

Joseph smiled. "We have sensors that can do that. My team and I just need to know what the goal is and how we plan to accomplish it so we can design something to fit the purpose. You've given us a tall order. Each planet is going to have its own challenges the probes will have to deal with. Plus, if we're measuring gravity, we'll have to track the positions of every single planet with every single probe as well as collecting weather data. Is that what you want?"

"Well...uh..." Jordin paused for a few moments. "We should make our primary goal to observe and report weather patterns and atmospheric particles. If we can do that, then maybe we can do the gravitational calculations ourselves with the data we receive."

"I don't think we're going to be putting a probe on another planet any time soon," Lauren said.

"Not yet, but it gives us a goal to work for. I briefly discussed this with Dr. Dhar. We need to come up with something that works on our planet first," Jordin replied.

Joseph considered this for a moment. "If you want a

proof of concept, we could rig up a sensor array and stick it somewhere."

"What could you make it do now?" Jordin asked.

"What do you want it to do?"

"If we wanted a basic sensor array…" Lauren squinted her eyes and looked at the ceiling. "We could just use data from other sources, pertaining to tracking and positional data of the planets, and send it to the array. We could even calculate the expected gravitational pull outside of the sensors and send it. It wouldn't work well on other planets but it would work fine here with our network."

Joseph agreed. "If all you want are basic sensors, that's simple enough. Where are you planning to put this?"

"Hmmmmmm." Jordin stroked his chin. "We'd need to get it fairly high up to avoid contamination from influences on the surface."

"We could use drones!" Jimmy piped up.

"Maybe…" Jordin took a moment to think.

"A drone would interfere with the data. Its rotating blades are just fans that blow the air around," Joseph said.

"Okay," Jimmy said, disappointed.

"I like the idea though," Jordin said. "We could use weather balloons."

"Are these temporary sensors, mobile sensors, or did you want long term data collection on one spot?" Joseph asked. "Weather balloons are great for what they do. Are they going to do what we need here?"

"Good point." Jordin scratched his head. "We do need a mobile 'probe' at some point. But for now, I'd say let's get a working proof."

"I agree. Weather balloons are a good option later, but not now. We could put stationary sensors on tall buildings," Lauren said with a shrug.

"They'd have to be pretty tall to limit contamination. How high could we get if we built something on top of our building?" Jordin looked up at the ceiling.

"Not high enough to avoid the city contamination. Unless you want to spend millions on a fragile steel structure that goes kilometers high." Joseph said sarcastically.

"What about mountain observatories?" Jimmy hesitantly asked.

Everyone looked at the intern expectantly.

"I mean...," Jimmy cleared his throat nervously, "you want something away from cities and high up that's stationary, right? There are observatories on mountains all around the world. We could install sensors on them. They're already gathering planetary data themselves too. They even observe weather patterns."

"Could work." Lauren nodded after a few moments of silence.

"That's why Mercury accepted your application," Joseph said genially.

"I like it." Jordin nodded in approval.

Jimmy looked surprised. "Really?"

"We'd just have to convince a bunch of observatories to allow us to put even more sensors on their buildings and power them. Lots of paperwork and negotiating." Joseph looked thoughtfully at the floor.

"Places like NASA have a ton of planetary tracking data that's publicly available," Lauren pointed out. "We could use them as a guide, or something to compare our own data to. We could even just use their data entirely. If you want, we could even reach out to them to see if they'd be willing to work with us directly, even if just as a data source. That is, in case we need something that they don't already provide publicly."

"Let's build a baseline sensor for the weather and use what's already available for the rest," Jordin said. "I'd love to work with NASA in the future, but for right now we should make it as simple and easy as possible. We can work up to the rest."

"No sense in reinventing the wheel." Joseph grinned. "We can just take NASA's wheel when we get there."

"If this is what we want to do, I can begin writing up the proposal," Jordin said. He looked around at everyone nodding in agreement. "Oh, I guess I need my computer," he realized. "I'll go get my laptop." Jordin turned and walked out the door.

That went better than I thought it would, Jordin thought as he pulled the map out of his pocket and ascended the stairs. He was glad that Dhar had called to warn him about it beforehand. There were plenty of things to discuss and work out before doing anything, but at least they had a start.

After he returned with his laptop, everyone spent an hour talking back and forth about various ideas and designs. There were a lot of fine details and questions yet to discover and answer. Whether the end goal was possible or not was also in question.

They spent the rest of the day researching. Joseph busied himself by looking up various parts and speaking to engineers about coming up with a design. Lauren began collecting planetary tracking data and reaching out to various observatories for access. Jordin began tracking weather patterns while attempting to start his proposal. Jimmy did what he could to help everyone, but his limited experience and knowledge left him largely relegated to coffee and supply runs.

Jordin looked up from his computer after a few hours. "Hey, Jimmy."

"Yes?" Jimmy looked earnestly at Jordin.

"I need to spend some time on this proposal. Could you start gathering weather data? I'll show you what you need to look for and what I want."

"Sure!" Jimmy happily marched over.

Jimmy cheerfully worked away after Jordin explained the needed data points.

* * * *

"Ah ha!" Lauren exclaimed two days later.

Jordin looked up from his work.

"We just received a response from Chile!"

"What did they say?"

"They'd be happy to work with us on this project. They've sent me access to the data that I requested."

"Are they fine with us putting another sensor array in their facilities?"

"I've not asked them yet. I didn't think it would be appropriate to do so until we knew what we were doing and had approval to do that from Mr. Mercury."

Jordin nodded. "Probably a good idea."

"If they're willing to work with us, we could have access to the largest optical-infrared observatory in the Southern Hemisphere."

"That would be awesome." Jimmy gave everyone a thumbs up, and then awkwardly lowered his hands in embarrassment.

"It would be." Jordin nodded.

Joseph walked through the door, carrying a rolled-up tube of paper. "Okay people," he said loudly, "here's what my engineers cooked up for you." He unfurled the roll onto a nearby counter. "If you like it, I can send you the specs for your report."

Everyone gathered around the counter as Joseph prattled on about the design and what each component would do. Jordin listened and mentally checked off the list of requirements.

After Joseph was finished, Jordin said, "It looks good. It should do exactly what we need it to do."

"I can send you the files to include in your proposal." Joseph smiled.

"Great, I should be able to send it to Mr. Mercury today for approval."

"Let's hope he likes it," Lauren grimaced.

"Be sure to send it to Dr. Dhar too." Joseph rolled the diagram back up.

* * * *

The next morning, Mr. Mercury sat behind his desk, flipping through Jordin's proposal.

Jordin sat across, with clasped hands, staring nervously at his boss. His fingers fidgeted uncontrollably as he silently waited. He glanced down at a newspaper on Mercury's desk. An image of a bright streak across a morning sky caught his attention. *Hey,* he thought. *That looks familiar.* The headline read, *Dozens of daytime shooting stars spotted across U.S.*

Jordin furrowed his brow and leaned closer to read the story. *The shooting star (pictured above) appeared over New York City at seven thirty A.M. the morning of the fifth. This was one of dozens of other daytime shooting star events reported that morning alone. This follows closely after the unexpected meteor shower over Europe the prior day. Experts believe that...*

"This isn't an interplanetary weather probe," Mercury proclaimed as he looked up from the proposal with a scowl.

Jordin brought himself back to reality and straightened in his seat. "Not yet, sir," he said with trepidation, looking his boss in the eyes. His fingers began to fidget and tap against each other more vigorously.

Mercury looked unimpressed. "This is a glorified weather vane."

Jordin grimaced at this interpretation. "It's a first step, sir."

Mercury set the papers down and leaned back in his chair. "Explain."

Jordin blinked and tried to think of the best way to put it. "You see, sir...The end goal is to have an interplanetary probe. However, we can't just start there without building a foundation..."

"I didn't hire you to build houses," Mercury interrupted. "I hired you to go interplanetary with weather probes."

Jordin took a deep breath. He took conscious note of his fingers, which were now wrapped around each other in odd uncomfortable angles, turning his knuckles white. "I understand." He unclasped his hands and forced himself to let them rest at his side. "I want to do that. If I thought I could accomplish that immediately, I'd do it. This is our first step toward that goal. We'll grow up and run later."

Mercury stroked his chin as if reconsidering. "I'm listening."

"I can't guarantee any interplanetary probe would function properly yet. We haven't even built a baseline to test our instruments. I don't want to waste company time building expensive probes and launching them into space with no guarantee that anything would come of it. We need to verify that everything works before we spend all that money." Jordin's efforts to keep his hands motionless were in vain as his nearly unconscious instincts took over, forcing his hands together and writhing his fingers like a mass of wriggling worms.

Mercury perked up at the mention of saving money. "Yes," he muttered. His expression lightened and he picked the papers back up. He flipped through them, peering closely at the specifications and data provided. After a few awkward moments, he set the papers down and looked at Jordin.

"I'm considering it." Mr. Mercury raised an eyebrow. "But I don't want to lose sight of our end goal. I don't want to stop at weather vanes."

Jordin tried to shake his head emphatically and lowered his hands so that his boss would hopefully not see them. "Neither do I. As I said before, this is just the first step in that direction."

"How soon would we be able to move on to interplanetary probes?"

"Hard to say." Jordin racked his brain for the best response. "We'll have to build this first and take it one step at a time."

Mr. Mercury grimaced and shook his head. "I can't afford to have uncertainty with this."

"Building this will answer many of our questions and make our end goal all the more possible," Jordin reasoned.

"And what else will this do for us? Are we just building weather vanes to answer your questions? Everything costs money, you know. My money. And time..."

"Well..." Jordin thought for a moment. "If we can build this and it works, this will be a huge step forward for the scientific community. We might be able to sell it as it is to various meteorological institutions."

Mr. Mercury seemed to perk up again. "We could be on the forefront of scientific discovery?"

"We...could be ahead of the curve on scientific data and information gathering. There's no telling what we'll discover in our own backyard with this."

Mr. Mercury began slowly nodding his head, "Very well. I approve. Carry on."

Jordin sighed in relief. "Thank you, sir." He smiled.

"Just don't disappoint me. If this fails..." Mercury grimaced and shook his head.

"I won't and it won't," Jordin said adamantly as his

hands finally relaxed to his sides again.

"I'll hold you to that." Mercury eyed Jordin suspiciously. He nodded at the door. "You had better get to it."

"Yes, of course." Jordin stood and nodded at his boss before leaving the office. He couldn't help but smile, more out of relief than anything else. *I'll have to tell Dhar that Mercury approved,* he thought. *He warned me that Mercury might not be easy to convince. I'll have to thank him for giving me approval first too.*

Jordin marched into the lab and proudly proclaimed, "He liked it, we're approved!"

"Nice." Jimmy gave him a thumbs up.

"Whoopee, now we have more work to do," Lauren said sarcastically.

"I knew you could do it," Joseph encouraged.

Lauren turned to her computer and pressed enter. "I just sent a correspondence to the Chilean observatory asking for permission to install a sensor and use their facility." She smiled mischievously.

"You knew we'd get approval?" Jordin raised an eyebrow.

"You had Dr. Dhar on your side. It was only a matter of time."

"Fair enough." Jordin walked to his workstation.

Joseph grinned. "I sent the specs for our sensor to my team this morning. I told them to go ahead and start the manufacturing process."

"I'm looking up weather patterns and data according to what you wanted, sir," Jimmy added.

Jordin looked around the room. "Wow, am I the only one who wasn't sure we'd get approval?"

"Never underestimate Dr. Dhar. If you hadn't gotten approval, he would've." Joseph gave him a sly smile.

After reading her computer screen, Lauren asked, "How soon can you get that sensor array built?"

Joseph looked at her intrigued. "It depends on why you're asking."

"The observatory says that they can give us access to the facilities for a week in a couple months."

Jordin blinked in surprise. "Wow, that was a fast response."

"I've been in regular correspondence with them since we started this," Lauren admitted. "P.M.L. has worked with them in the past. That's probably why they responded to us as fast as they did. We already have an inside track with them."

"Oh. Well then. Great," Jordin said.

"I guess we'll have it ready in a few months, then," He said with a look to Jordin. "Are you going to have all the data points you need by then?"

Jordin nodded at Jimmy. "We'll have everything we need by then." He secretly wasn't sure if everything would be ready in time. He knew that any setbacks could severely hamper progress.

"Good," Joseph nodded. "Let's get to it."

CHAPTER

3

"I hope you're not burning yourself out," Dr. Dhar said over the voice program one evening two months later.

"I could say the same to you," Jordin chuckled as he looked out of his office window at the darkening sky. The only other sound was Clarence vacuuming the hall outside.

"We all do what we have to. I can't complain. Are you ready to go to Chile tomorrow?"

"I've got everything packed up and ready to go. I'm just making sure I've got everything." Jordin opened his desk drawer and rummaged about. "These past few weeks have been chaotic. It's hard to believe that we're going tomorrow. The only thing that I need is the checklist that I made...I know I had it somewhere."

"I hope you can find it. Is there anything else you need from me or my team?"

"I think that the last report you sent should be all that we need from you for now." Jordin was somewhat distracted as he looked around his desk and the floor nearby for his list. "Thank you for everything you've provided. You and your team have been invaluable to us. I'm not sure we'd be ready now if you hadn't assisted us."

"We're happy to assist. I'll let you go. Let me know if you

need anything. Notify me when you reach the observatory."

"I'll keep in touch," Jordin said as he peered into his trashcan.

The call ended and Jordin stood and walked to his filing cabinets to search through them. "I had it somewhere…," he muttered.

"I see you've lost something." Clarence stood in the doorway, his mustache twitched as he spoke.

"I had a checklist with a bunch of information I'll need tomorrow," Jordin said as he rummaged about.

Clarence waved a crumpled piece of paper in his hand. "Would this be it?"

Jordin peered at the paper. "Yes, that's it! Where was it?"

Clarence chuckled. "One of my crew found it on the floor by the wastebasket in your lab. He thought it was trash. I saw it and knew better."

"Thank you," Jordin smiled as he accepted the paper. "How did you know it was important?"

Clarence tapped the side of his head. "Not much goes on in this building I don't know about."

"Apparently." Jordin nodded.

Jordin expected Clarence to leave, but the janitor remained, standing motionless, in the doorway.

Jordin shifted uncomfortably. "Is there something else that I can help you with?"

"Have you seen the shooting stars?" Clarence bluntly asked.

"I've seen the newspapers. I watched a few blurbs about them on the news. Why do you ask?"

"I wonder what it means." Clarence's mustache twitched.

"It's just space junk burning up in our atmosphere. It happens all the time."

"Hmmm." Clarence gave Jordin a hard stare. "Maybe. Is this like every other time?"

Jordin blinked for a few moments. "I don't see why it wouldn't be?" He softened his expression. "There's nothing to worry about. From what I hear, they're all burning up in the atmosphere. Think of our planet as having a shield around it. In space, rocks travel at high speeds with nothing in the way. As soon as they enter our atmosphere, the friction generated from hitting all of the particles in the atmosphere causes them to burn up, disintegrate, and slow down. The likelihood of being struck by a meteorite is low."

"Is that the worst that could happen?" Clarence blinked slowly.

Jordin shrugged. "A big enough meteorite traveling at high speeds could destroy a whole countryside. But I wouldn't worry about that. There are several organizations like NASA. that track objects like that. We're more likely to be hit by a car in New York than to be flattened by a meteorite."

Clarence nodded slowly. "You seem to handle Mercury

better than most. I've seen many quit for less already."

Jordin blinked at the sudden subject change. "Uh. Thanks?"

"He's not a bad man. You just have to get past the sharp edges."

Jordin nodded, unsure of what to say.

"Have a good trip. Stay safe." Clarence turned and left before Jordin could respond.

What was that all about? Jordin shook his head. *I hope he's not too worried about meteorites.*

* * * *

The next morning, Jordin stared down at the floor of the airplane and clenched the seat's armrests, his knuckles white from the pressure.

"Hey!" Joseph smiled as he took a seat next to Jordin. "We've got everything loaded up. It's so nice that we've got a company jet. It's not as fancy as Mercury's own private jet, but still nice. I know airport security wouldn't let me bring half my tools with me." He laughed as he looked around.

Jordin tried to sound calm. "Yes...great..." It wasn't the height so much as the vertical movement accompanied by the feeling in his stomach that he hated.

"You okay?" Joseph asked with a questioning glance.

"I'm fine..." Jordin clenched his teeth. He had to mentally force himself to dig his fingertips into the soft cushioned armrests to keep from fidgeting.

"You look sick. Are you sure? It's going to be close to nine hours in the air. If you're sick let us know before it becomes a problem."

"I'll be fine," Jordin tried to assure. "Just get me in the air and level us out."

"Don't worry, that's the goal."

"We are 'go' for takeoff," the pilot said over the intercom. "Taxiing to runway."

The plane moved forward. Jordin tightened his muscles and focused on the sights out the window.

"What's eating him?" Lauren asked from the seat across the aisle.

"He's just plane-sick." Joseph grinned.

Jimmy popped his head over the seat in front of Jordin. "Need a bag?"

"No." Jordin shook his head. He just wanted everyone to stop talking to him right now.

The plane stopped at the end of the runway.

"Runway is clear. Taking off," the pilot chimed.

The plane moved forward at an ever-increasing pace. The scenery outside began to race by.

"Here we go." Jordin closed his eyes and prepared for takeoff. His stomach churned as he felt the plane shaking.

Joseph nudged Jordin. "We're airborne, and still alive."

Jordin opened his eyes and stared at the ground receding below. He deliberately took slow and steady breaths.

After a while, the plane leveled off. Jordin sighed in relief. Now he just had to worry about the landing in another nine hours.

"Should we go over the plan before we land?" Joseph asked.

"Yes." Jordin nodded as he released his death-grip on the armrests only to have his hands promptly clasp together.

The next couple of hours were spent going over the immediate plans upon landing. The staff at the Chilean observatory would have a car and a delivery truck waiting to transport them and their equipment. They would then be given a tour of the facilities and allowed to work with the staff to install the sensor array and begin gathering data. They had a week to test everything out. If this went well, other observatories were likely to come onboard.

After they were done discussing their plans, Jordin tried to get some sleep. He hadn't slept well that night and today would be a long day. He closed his eyes and tried to calm his mind. If he didn't think about where he was, maybe he'd be able to sleep.

*I'll just try to sleep for a little...*Jordin drifted off.

"Hey, wake up." Joseph shook Jordin.

"What?" Jordin looked up with great concern. "What's wrong?"

"Nothing," Joseph laughed, "we're here."

"Huh?" Jordin looked out the window. Sure enough, the plane was sitting motionless on the ground.

"They're waiting to take us to the observatory," Joseph continued.

"Oh...yes." Jordin stood and began grabbing his bags and equipment.

Jordin and his team greeted and exchanged pleasantries with the observatory officials who were waiting for them on the tarmac. After all of the equipment was loaded into the truck, they were off.

Rocky, dusty, desert landscape passed by as Jordin stared out of the car window. The observatory's facilities stood atop a remote hill, awaiting its new guests. The vehicles ascended the roadway and passed through an open gate.

"Welcome," a happy man greeted the guests with a thick Spanish accent as they exited the vehicles, "I'm Dr. Angelo. I'm the director of the observatory and I'll be showing you around."

"Thank you," Jordin stepped toward the friendly man. "I'm Dr. Davidson. Project lead and representative of P.M.L. It's a great honor to be here."

After everyone exchanged pleasantries, Dr. Angelo began the tour of their facilities.

This place is amazing, Jordin thought as he took every-thing in. *There they* are.

Four massive telescopes stood in a row as sentinels of the sky, protected by their rectangular housing. The other smaller telescopes and instruments that dotted the area seemed insignificant in comparison.

His whole life, Jordin had wanted to visit a real observatory. Now he had the opportunity to use one to assist in his project. *Better not mess this up*, he warned himself. If everything went well here, he'd have the opportunity to work in several other observatories.

After the tour, Joseph began directing his team of engineers and observatory staff in unloading the equipment. "I'll let you all know when the sensors are installed," he grunted as he carried a box of supplies. "I hope it doesn't take too long."

"Keep us posted." Jordin said as he and the others walked to the main building that housed most of the controls and computers.

The remainder of the day was spent familiarizing themselves with the facility and listening to instructions on how to utilize the telescopes. Until the sensor array was installed, their official project couldn't start.

* * * *

"You should start getting data feeds from the sensors soon," Joseph announced early the next morning.

Jordin was anxiously looking over his compatriot's shoulder at the mess of wires Joseph was working with.

"Hey!" Lauren shouted. "I'm getting stuff." She pointed at her laptop. "Sensors appear to be working."

Jordin and Jimmy rushed over to look at the data-monitoring program churning away.

"Great!" Jordin said in excitement. "Let's show everyone what we can do!"

"Sure thing, boss!" Jimmy exclaimed.

* * * *

Four days later, Jordin sat, his bleary eyes locked on the monitors. He hadn't slept for a while but he didn't want to stop what he was doing. He had always dreamed of an opportunity like this. The excitement for fully using the observatory kept him going. Outside the window, the moon was high in the sky and the stars twinkled like diamonds.

They had been at the observatory for four days collecting data. By using satellite, telescope, and existing sensor data, they were able to calibrate their sensor array.

"I'm tracking Jupiter now," Lauren said. "Sending you the expected gravitational pull data. Are you seeing anything on sensors?"

Jordin examined the data. Thus far they had been unsuccessful at detecting anything with any certainty. It had been a long few days of tweaking sensor sensitivity and filtering out unwanted information. He perked up. Was he really seeing exactly what he expected to see?

"We're getting data!" Jordin swiveled around and raised

his arms in the air triumphantly.

Everyone else in the room cheered.

Jordin lowered his arms. "Before we get too excited we need to make sure it's accurate. Can we get any orbiting Earth satellites to image and analyze our cloud patterns? We just need data from these locations." Jordin sent Lauren coordinates.

"Getting satellite footage now," Lauren said.

Jordin motioned to Jimmy. "Jimmy, can you verify current weather conditions in the surrounding areas and check to see if something is happening that could affect this?"

"Sure thing!" Jimmy said, furiously typing away at his keyboard.

"All sensors are functioning as expected," Joseph said as he stood behind everyone, reading his own monitor. "My team is reporting that everything is clean. Whatever you're detecting isn't interference caused by dirt nor is it a malfunction."

Jordin stroked his chin. "Widen the sweep of satellite footage. Let's pull up other satellites and see if anything major is happening that could tamper with our data."

"Got it." Lauren nodded, examining the various satellite feeds.

Jordin was optimistic, but didn't want to declare success too early. "I'm saving this data and forwarding it to our team in India. They may be able to verify or spot something that we're missing."

"What is that?" Lauren asked.

"What?" Jordin swiveled his chair around to see Lauren pointing toward one of the monitors. He scooted over to take a closer look at the information on the screen. The satellites in orbit around Earth were certainly detecting something strange.

Lauren squinted. "It looks like something's approaching Earth."

"Is it another glitch?" Jimmy piped up.

"Probably just a simple meteorite," Joseph replied as he walked over to a food cart. He grabbed a sandwich and a cup of coffee. "It'll burn up in the atmosphere like all the others. We just got lucky to see one approaching before it became a shooting star."

"That's odd," Jordin said as he pondered the numbers on the screen. He quickly took control of the panel and focused all instruments on the object. "It's not behaving like a meteor."

"That's what I thought too," Lauren said.

"What do you mean odd? We see meteors approach Earth and burn up all the time," Joseph said between bites of his sandwich. "They don't always act the same exact way. It depends on the angle they hit us at."

"We don't know that this one is going to necessarily 'burn up' yet." Jordin replied mechanically. "It's moving... wait...it's slowing down?" He peered closer at the monitor.

"What?" Joseph walked closer.

"It's slowing down before entering the atmosphere?" Jordin turned to face Jimmy. "Jimmy, try to get any data or readings on this as soon as possible."

"Yes, sir, right away, sir." Jimmy awkwardly saluted before typing furiously away at his computer again. "Just... one question...where exactly is this thing?"

"It looks like it is approaching over northwestern Russia." Jordin turned back and tilted his head to the side as he tried to get his tired eyes to focus on his screen.

"Hey, it stopped!" Lauren exclaimed.

"What?" Jordin blinked. The object, whatever it was, had seemingly stopped its approach just above Earth's atmosphere.

"How big is it?" Joseph asked before taking a sip of coffee.

"Preliminary data puts it between 50 and 80 meters in diameter," Jordin said.

"That could cause some damage if it hit," Joseph snorted.

"Should we call someone?" Lauren asked.

"Get Dr. Dhar on the line," Joseph called out to Jimmy. "Tell him what's going on."

"Yes sir." Jimmy dialed his phone with one hand as he operated his computer with the other.

A series of movements caught Jordin's attention. He turned to look back at the meteorological data screen. A strange weather pattern seemed to be forming over northwestern Russia. He double-checked the weather data. "It looks like there's a storm forming beneath it."

"Is it serious?" Lauren asked.

"I don't know yet," Jordin replied.

Jimmy walked up to Jordin while on the phone. "Yes sir, we will send you the data right away sir." He placed his hand on Jordin's shoulder and indicated for him to follow.

Jordin nodded and followed Jimmy back to his station. He heard Dr. Dhar speaking on the other end of Jimmy's phone. A series of blurry images, as well as a video of clouds rapidly forming, were displayed on the screen. "Is this...," Jordin asked as he pointed toward the images.

Jimmy nodded enthusiastically as he continued his conversation, attempting to explain the situation over the phone.

"That doesn't look like anything," Joseph snorted again. "That's just a blurry blob."

"True, but at least it tells us that something's there," Jordin said.

"Hey, it's gone!" Lauren exclaimed.

"What?" Both Joseph and Jordin rushed back to the monitors.

"It was here, then it was just gone," Lauren explained.

All three stared in disbelief as all indicators and detectors confirmed that the object was no longer there. Jordin turned to stare at the weather screens. All storm activity was vanishing, removing all evidence that anything had happened.

"I want all recorded data to be sent to both the home office and the India office immediately. We need this verified," Jordin emphasized.

"Boss is going to call around to other outposts and organizations to see if anyone else saw this," Jimmy said as he placed his phone back in his pocket.

"What do you suppose that was?" Lauren asked.

"I have no idea," Jordin said. "Are there any indications of impact in that area?"

"I guess we will find out when the boss calls around," Jimmy said.

"In the meantime, I want all the instruments we have to survey the surrounding area. I don't know what that was, but I intend to find out. This could be some new amazing discovery." Jordin stood and marched back to his weather station. He had already forgotten their original project and their purpose for being at the observatory.

"Is there anything we already know about that could have caused this?" Joseph asked.

"It could've just been a meteor, or maybe even an old, decommissioned satellite finally plummeting to earth," Lauren said.

"Meteors don't just stop before entering the atmosphere and I'd think we'd have records of satellites and their orbits," Joseph said.

"There are many stray rocks out in space nearby," Jordin pondered as he swiveled back and forth in his chair. "Several thousands in fact. Many of them are in the size range that we estimated this to be. Is it possible for one to wander close to Earth but then be deflected by the atmosphere?"

"That 'stray rock' as you put it," Lauren raised an eyebrow, "would have to be made of some pretty lightweight and/or porous material to be slowed significantly enough to be shoved back by our atmosphere. Gravity is a weak force compared to other forces, but as slow as that object was moving, it wouldn't have escaped the Earth's pull and gone back into space that quickly. Bouncing off the atmosphere or not, its actions make no sense given what we know."

"Something of that size plummeting to Earth would cause some severe damage." Joseph set his coffee cup down on a nearby console. "Surely, we would've seen something on our instruments had it impacted. And we aren't seeing it anywhere else. So if it didn't impact, and it didn't bounce off, where is it?"

"Maybe it landed," Jimmy stepped forward almost gleefully.

"We just said it couldn't have impacted," Joseph said.

"Maybe it came here on purpose."

Joseph's eyes narrowed. "What do you mean?"

"Think about it, it slowed down before it came to our atmosphere, stopped, then vanished. I may not have my doctorate yet, but I know rocks don't do that. We would've seen it leave and would've known if something of that size impacted. So maybe it knew what it was doing and landed on purpose."

The three doctors stared at Jimmy for an uncomfortably long time.

Joseph looked incredulous. "Are you suggesting what I think you're suggesting?"

"Well...I...uhh...," Jimmy's face turned red as he looked at the floor and backed away.

Joseph suddenly erupted in laughter. "Good. I'm glad I'm not the only one who had that thought."

Jimmy looked up hopefully. "You mean...?"

"Of course, that's always the first thing I think of when I hear of some new space discovery."

"As a biologist," Lauren said, "I'm always hopeful for the opportunity to study biology of other life forms not native to Earth."

"It would be exciting indeed," Jordin said, barely suppressing a smile. "But unfortunately, there always seems to be a natural, non-alien, explanation for these things. Don't worry, when we're finally visited by extraterrestrial life, I'll be one of the first people to want to meet it."

This event showed Jordin one thing - everyone was tired and ready to jump to any extraordinary conclusion. It was time to refocus back to known reality. "We've got all the data on it that we can. We finally have our sensor array working. Let's call it a night and let our array gather data while we sleep. We'll reconvene in the morning."

"Hmmm," Joseph eyed his coffee cup regretfully. "I thought we were going to keep...nevermind."

Everyone agreed and began closing up their workstations. Whatever it had been, it could wait until morning.

CHAPTER

4

Sleep eluded Jordin that night. Wild theories and speculations danced through his mind. What little, intermittent sleep he managed to acquire was infested by dreams of dancing purple marshmallows singing Christmas songs.

When his alarm finally rang, he slowly dragged himself out of bed. The events of last night, as exciting as they were, would need to be put off until the completion of their current assignment.

"Good morning," Joseph welcomed Jordin as he stumbled into the control room.

"Morning," Jordin mumbled, his head still in a fog. "Did you actually sleep last night?"

Joseph shrugged as he gave a wary glance at the coffee on the food cart. "I slept as much as you'd expect. We collected some good data last night from our sensors."

Jordin perked up. "Oh?"

"We have about two hours of good, clean data."

"That's good. What about the rest of it?"

"We started getting a strange interference pattern a few hours ago." Joseph pulled up a graph on a nearby monitor and pointed at it. "See, here's the good data. And this is where the interference started."

"Could it be a malfunction on the sensor or something man-made nearby?" Jordin asked.

"I thought that too. My team and I inspected and reinspected the sensors. Everything's fine. Jimmy showed up before you. He couldn't find anything on weather radars that we aren't already filtering out. For lack of any other explanation, I sent him out with a pair of binoculars and a parabolic microphone to try and see if there's something nearby causing this."

Jordin raised an eyebrow. "Do you think he'll find anything with that?"

"No idea." Joseph shrugged. "But he's not experienced enough to use some of the fancier things around here. I couldn't help him. I wouldn't know what I was looking at. That's your department. He wanted to help, and I had the stuff sitting around. Might as well use it."

"Hmmm." Jordin nodded. "Fair enough." He stared at the graph. "The interference isn't going away."

"No, it isn't. And here's more recent data." Joseph scrolled over to reveal more information.

Jordin's eyes widened in shock. "It's increasing?"

"Very steadily, until this point." Joseph pointed to an area on the graph where the line turned at a sharp angle. Even still, it was trending upward at a slower pace.

"If it were something man-made, I'd expect it to eventually stop or stay consistent. Unless it was some machine coming toward us. If it was a strange weather anomaly, I'd think it'd dissipate by now. Or show some ups and downs." Jordin stroked his chin.

"Now that you're here, you can check out all the meteorological data. Maybe a storm somewhere is causing this."

"I'll take a look." Jordin went to work examining data streams from various weather stations and satellites from around the globe.

"Is there a reason we've got our intern outside, waving a parabolic mic and binoculars around?" Lauren asked as she entered the control room.

Jordin pointed at the graph. "We're trying to find the source of our data interference."

Lauren squinted her eyes and stared at the graph for a few minutes. "Either the other planets exert a far greater force on us than we realize, Jupiter is headed straight for us at insane speeds, or something's wrong." She turned and walked to her computer. "I doubt the planets are misbehaving that badly, but I'll check to make sure."

Jimmy walked in with a disappointed look on his face. "I'm not finding anything," he bemoaned.

"That's okay," Jordin assured. "We're all just as confused right now." He walked to his workstation and began looking up satellite and weather data in the area of the anomaly.

"We've always been able to find the source of interference to verify what it was," Joseph murmured as he looked out a window at the horizon. He turned to look quizzically at Lauren. "Is it the sun? We've been tracking planets and seeing what they do. Is the sun's gravitational pull messing with us now?"

Lauren looked up and shook her head. "No. We're accounting for that. The sun is already one of the most prominent weather generators for us even without its gravitational influence."

"Moon too," Jordin quipped as he pored over weather data.

"Yes." Lauren nodded. "Moon too."

"Okay, maybe it's not its gravity. Could it be heating things up more than we thought?" Joseph watched the sun rise out the window.

Slightly annoyed, Lauren began, "We've already...,"

"Wait..." Jordin waved his hand, "heat may be part of it, but not in that way."

Lauren blinked at Jordin. "Huh?"

"Where did we see that anomaly last night?" Jordin asked.

"It was over Northwestern Russia," Jimmy said.

"Yes it was." Jordin nodded. "And weather data from that area is...acting strange."

"What do you mean strange?" Joseph asked. "Like, it's 'raining when it shouldn't be' strange? Or it's 'raining pianos' strange?"

"It's a lot colder in that area than it should be." Jordin pressed a button to display a temperature graph on the main monitor.

"It's Northern Russia. It's always colder there than is reasonable," Joseph chuckled.

"It's getting winter temperatures right now." Jordin raised his left eyebrow. "But it's summer. And it's only where we saw the interference last night."

"Okay, so that place is setting records." Joseph shrugged. "How does that interfere with us?"

"It doesn't make much sense," Jordin muttered as he stared at the data. "The weather patterns are changing. All of the surrounding areas are experiencing a heat wave..." He pulled up a thermal image of the area and placed it on the main monitor. "It looks like heat is traveling to that area."

Lauren was perplexed. "Okay...Doesn't heat always flow from high temperature areas to low temperature areas?"

"Yes, it does," Jordin said. "But you'd expect to see the area it's flowing toward to warm up, wouldn't you?"

Everyone in the room stared silently at the thermal image on screen.

"So why is that spot, the area where all the heat is flowing toward, getting colder?" Jordin asked.

Jimmy broke the silence that followed Jordin's statement. "Here's a satellite feed of that area." He pressed a button and the main screen showed a series of cloud formations clumping together.

"Is that a storm?" Joseph asked.

"Looks like it's trying to be one." Jordin studied the screen, confused by the video showing all clouds in the area drawing into one point.

"Okay...," Joseph stroked his chin, "how is this affecting us in Chile?"

"You built the sensors. You know how sensitive they are. The changes here are almost imperceptible to us and most other stations."

"Haaa," Joseph began to laugh, "I built something to detect effects from other planets. And yet, I find it hard to believe we're picking up something on our own planet because it's 'too far away.'"

Jordin's phone began ringing. "Mr. Mercury is calling." Jordin clenched his teeth as he accepted the call. "Hello, sir?"

Everyone watched Jordin with bated breath.

"Have you seen the news?" Mr. Mercury asked excitedly.

"I haven't been watching the news here."

"Oh, right, right. Focusing on your job. Good. Keep it up. But I was hoping you may be able to shed some light on something the news is saying."

"I'll do my best." Jordin was a little worried about where this was going. World events and politics weren't his strongest suit.

"I've heard something about a meteorite striking Russia. Now they're having storms. Everyone I know in Russia is being very tight lipped about it. You're in an observatory and have weather instruments there with you. Did a meteor hit us?"

"I can assure you, a meteorite did not impact us. There are no craters and no signs of immediate destruction."

Everyone else in the room looked at each other and exchanged hesitant nods.

"Oh." Mr. Mercury sounded a little disappointed. "I was hoping we could've observed it and been at the head of the information curve on this."

"Well, sir. We did observe the phenomenon that people may be mistaking for a meteorite."

"Oh?"

"We can verify that something happened. We're not sure what. There's an odd weather pattern in the area. I suspect people saw something and are attributing it to a meteorite."

"Interesting. Do you know what it was? Can you explain it?"

"Unfortunately, no, sir. I don't know yet what happened, and I don't have a good explanation. We've sent the data that we gathered last night to our team in India, as well as to our home offices. Maybe someone else can go over it and can find a better explanation. I'll send the data that we have to you as well if you'd like."

"Hmmmmm. I should be able to get it from Dr. Dhar. I was just curious if you had any insights into it. Thank you. Carry on with your good work." The line clicked as Mercury hung up.

Jordin put his phone down and blinked.

"I already sent him everything we had," Lauren said incredulously as she waved her arms in frustration.

"I know," Jordin chuckled. "Sometimes you've just gotta walk people through things. He's a busy man. We're entirely focused on this. He's got a million things to keep up with. He pays us either way."

"You'll have to forgive her," Joseph said, waving a doughnut from the food cart around. "She's been dealing with Mercury longer than you have."

"Whatever," Lauren waved her hand dismissively and looked back at her computer, "as long as he doesn't forget to pay me...again."

"So...," Jimmy said with some trepidation, "do we continue with our project or look at this new thing?"

Jordin looked thoughtfully at Jimmy then to Joseph. "How good is our data for those two hours when we had no interference?"

Joseph shrugged. "You'll have to tell me if it suits your needs. I can tell you it's the cleanest we've had so far. I'm not sure we could make it any cleaner or clearer."

Jordin stared out the window. "We're technically still gathering data we need. It's just dirtied with this new thing."

"If we discover something new, we'd be heroes in our field," Lauren said. She shook her head and frowned. "But then, Mercury would just take credit for it."

Jordin took a few moments, to measure his words. "Science isn't about credit. Science is about discovering new and amazing things. It's about taking us all further than we thought we could ever make it."

Lauren sighed and nodded. "You're right. I didn't join this field to be famous...Who says we can't do two projects at once?"

Jordin turned to Joseph. "Is there a way to separate the data that we're looking for from this new interference, but still keep the new stuff too?"

Joseph shrugged. "Sure. It'll take some tweaking, but we can do it."

"Do it," Jordin said resolutely. "We probably don't have much time left to study it. It's likely to dissipate soon as I don't see how it could continue to increase in intensity where it's at."

"Hey, the interference is changing," Jimmy pointed to the data screen.

Everyone else pulled up the sensor data. Sure enough, the strange readings had leveled off.

"What could this mean?" Jordin wondered.

"I don't know yet," Lauren said, mesmerized by the

screen.

"Let's monitor it throughout the day. Everyone, keep your eyes on weather reports and satellite feeds," Jordin commanded.

Everyone else nodded silently as they combed through their data streams.

Throughout the rest of the day, the anomaly maintained its intensity. However, as night fell over Chile, the sun began to rise over Western Russia. The anomaly began to steadily increase in intensity again. The increase wasn't anything near the spike they had seen initially, yet it was still noticeable.

* * * *

"Yes, sir," Jordin spoke into the observatory's desk phone three days later. The rest of his team and a few observatory staff members were busily packing up while occasionally shooting him a worried glance.

"You had better not be spreading any rumors about this," an angry male voice spoke in a Russian accent on the other end.

"No, sir." Jordin shook his head. "I assure you that we haven't said anything about meteorites, aliens, attacks, or experimental weaponry to anyone. We're just as mystified as you as to the origin of these rumors. Perhaps, if your team and our team were to share data, then we could present a statement to the world about..."

"You have no business in our country," the voice cut him off. "This situation doesn't concern you. Keep it that way. And see to it that you dispel any rumors you hear."

"Yes, sir..." The line clicked before Jordin could finish. He blinked as he lowered the phone back onto the receiver.

Joseph grinned as he set a box of packed supplies down on a nearby table. "Let me guess, that was either a scientist wanting all of our data, a hobbyist wanting to confirm his or her theory, or some government official mad at us for rumors that we didn't spread."

"Either way, that would be about the twentieth of those calls you've taken since we discovered the anomaly," Lauren said as she walked by. "Who told everyone to call us anyway?"

"It was the Russians again." Jordin gave Joseph a wry smile.

"Ah," Joseph chuckled. "The Russians are at twenty-one calls alone. Every other category is still at nineteen."

Jimmy pointed at his computer screen. "Hey, did you all see this?"

"What is it?" Jordin asked.

"It's on P.M.L.s front page. It's a video showing satellite feeds and images we collected. It was put up a couple days ago."

"Of all the...." Lauren waved her hands in the air in frustration. "That explains it. They've told the world we found a mysterious space object and a storm. No wonder everyone thinks aliens have invaded or someone's launched an attack. I swear, we've spent more time talking to people than actually studying anything these past few days."

"I'm happy to share info and dispel rumors. However, I'll be glad to get back home," Jordin said as he closed his workstation laptop. "Maybe we can get away from the craziness."

"Be thankful," Dr. Angelo grunted as he entered the room. "I've got hundreds of people from across the globe knocking my door down begging to be allowed into the observatory."

Jordin grimaced. "I apologize. I didn't expect to cause such a stir."

Dr. Angelo chuckled lightly. "Everyone always wants to come here. They've all got their own projects they want to do. This is just an unusually high volume of requests. We'll manage." He waved around the room as several observatory staff members entered and began assisting the P.M.L. team. "Please, allow me to assist."

It wasn't long before the P.M.L. team exchanged their goodbyes with the observatory staff and entered the awaiting vehicles.

"I could sleep for a week. When we get home, no one bother me," Lauren said as she settled into her seat.

"I'll probably sleep in so late that my wife'll think I'm one of our kids," Joseph said.

Jordin wasn't looking forward to the plane ride, but there

was little he could do about it. "I'll be glad to get home."

On the ride to the airport, Jordin's phone rang. "Ah, Dr. Dhar," Jordin muttered to himself. He hoped Dhar and his team had decoded some of the information. He answered, "Hello, sir."

"I hear you've been having fun," Dr. Dhar chuckled.

"That's one way of putting it," Jordin said.

"Did you get done what you needed to get done?"

"I wish I could say yes," Jordin said mournfully. "We didn't get as much clean data on what we were looking for as I'd hoped."

"I looked at the data you were able to gather. We've got some good stuff here. It's at least a proof of concept."

"I just wish we could've devoted more time to it without being..." Jordin stopped, he didn't know how to say what he really thought without coming across as rude.

"Without being bombarded with phone calls from the entire world?" Dr. Dhar said, amused.

"Yes. It also doesn't help that a strange anomalous event happened at the same time. I feel like I spent more time trying to be a diplomat than studying data since the anomaly's discovery."

"Don't worry. I've been working with Mr. Mercury to direct inquiries to the appropriate channels. He's also come to the conclusion that telling the world where his science teams are will just cause distractions."

"Oh?" Jordin believed he knew how Mr. Mercury came to that idea, but was hesitant to say it. "That's good."

"You and your team have made Mr. Mercury's 'Christmas List.'"

"Is that good?"

"It means he'll send you personal cards every year now."

"Oh...that's good?"

"You may not have gotten the data you wanted. But we're now being flooded with contracts, government grant offers, people wanting to pay to get access to data we've gathered, and a whole lot of publicity."

"That's good."

"From a business standpoint, it's great," Dr. Dhar laughed. "From a practical standpoint, it's overwhelming. However, it's a good problem to have right now."

"I agree."

"I hope you like observing the anomaly."

"It is quite fascinating."

"Mr. Mercury is going to want to redirect you and your team to studying it. I hope you don't mind putting off your original project."

"Well...sir," Jordin wasn't sure how best to respond, "I've been expecting this. And I would hate to miss out on observing a new weather phenomenon. Though I do have to warn you. This anomaly will probably dissipate soon. I see no reason why it would continue to grow much more."

"Good. If it vanishes before you return home, just resume your original project."

"Yes, sir. And by the way, has your team been able to sift through or decode any of the anomalous data yet?" Jordin had been patiently waiting to ask.

"We're still sifting through it. It's not like anything we've ever seen. Our engineers are building sensor arrays according to Dr. Wilber's schematics. We want to see if we can duplicate it or rule out equipment failure or interference. I wish I could give you a better answer. We'll discuss this further later. Have a good trip."

"Thank you, sir." Jordin ended the call and placed his phone back into his pocket.

Lauren raised an eyebrow. "Are we going to be chasing anomalies?"

"Who knows." Jordin shrugged. "Dhar warned me that Mr. Mercury may want us to. However, if it dissipates, then we just continue on our normal project."

"I hope it dissipates," Lauren said with a hint of bitterness.

"And why's that?" Jordin asked.

"Maybe Mercury will leave us alone." Lauren gave him a wry smile.

Jordin looked at her silently for a second. He glanced at Jimmy who was staring out the window watching the world go by. "Maybe. But we can talk more about it later. Let's all just focus on getting home."

CHAPTER 4

Lauren nodded. "Fine by me."

CHAPTER
5

The familiar sound of splashing water and "new office" scent greeted Jordin as he entered the P.M.L. skyscraper.

"Good morning, Dr. Davidson." Sally waved at Jordin as he walked past the fountain. She sat behind the front desk, looking far too happy for this time of morning.

"Good morning, Sally." Jordin nodded.

"Mr. Mercury is waiting for you in the lab for your meeting." Sally grinned.

Jordin paused and blinked at her. "What meeting?"

"Didn't you get the email?" she asked, feigning innocence. "He sent it out ten minutes ago. Your meeting started fifteen minutes ago."

Jordin sighed and closed his eyes. After a few moments he shook his head and laughed. He opened his eyes and looked at Sally in amusement. "Normal day, then?"

"Yes, sir." Sally stifled a laugh. "I have to say, you handle it better than some around here."

"I grew up in Chicago. I've seen it all." Jordin laughed it off as he walked toward the stairs.

He jogged up the stairwell and wondered what the meeting was about. His boss was probably just excited and wanted to know about everything. He entered the lab to see Lauren, looking agitated, sitting at her computer, staring expectantly at Mr. Mercury. Joseph was showing Mr. Mercury a few blueprints and schematics of the sensor array and explaining what each piece did.

"Ah." Mr. Mercury looked up and motioned Jordin over, "Dr. Davidson, please come in, come in."

"May I ask what's going on?" Jordin asked.

"Companies around the globe are asking for our sensor array." Mr. Mercury looked exceptionally pleased. "We were just discussing what we needed to do to make this ready for mass production."

"Okay..." Jordin blinked in surprise.

"Someone...let it slip that we have a sensor array designed specifically to monitor this anomaly," Lauren said in a very measured tone.

Jordin nodded his head side to side. "Technically, it does."

"It's fantastic!" Mercury exclaimed. "This is your design, Dr. Davidson?"

Jordin looked around the room. All eyes stared at him expectantly. "It's all of ours. I just said what it needed to do. Lauren, Jimmy and I retrieved the data while Joseph actually created the design and built it."

"Yes. Whoever came up with it, I like it." Mercury nodded emphatically. "We've got customers lining up to buy it."

"That's a good thing, right?" Jordin asked.

"Very good. You all get a raise," Mercury gestured around the room, "including him." He pointed at Jimmy who just walked in and looked quite confused.

"Thank you, sir," Jordin said.

"Whoopee, another two cents an hour," Lauren muttered under her breath. Fortunately for her, Mr. Mercury didn't appear to hear it.

Joseph turned to "cough" and wipe the smile off of his face.

Jimmy pointed at himself and asked, "Me? What did I do?"

"Whatever you're getting paid, you're getting more of it!" Mercury said then turned back to the blueprints without waiting for a response.

"Yay?" Jimmy blinked.

"Am I correct in assuming that you want us to focus on studying this weather anomaly rather than our original project?" Jordin asked.

"Yes, of course." Mercury smiled and nodded enthusiastically. "Is there anything you need for it?"

Jordin thought for a moment. "I'm not sure. I wasn't expecting something like this. If we had more sensors around the world, or if we could go directly observe it..." He stroked his chin.

Mercury shook his head. "I already tried getting clearance to go into that area. The Russian government has evacuated and quarantined it. No one's allowed near it."

"Might be for the best. It's likely to start dissipating soon anyway. Do they have sensors and scientists studying it? We could work with them."

"Yes, but they aren't talking to us. They keep telling us 'it's a normal pattern that occurs every so often.' Seems to me, they wouldn't have such secrecy and security about it if it were 'normal.'"

"They probably don't want anyone to panic or spread rumors about it. I'm sure things will calm down and we'll be allowed in." Jordin tried his best to see the other side of the argument, but he was incredibly suspicious himself. "Plus," he added, "I can't blame them. If it is something new and exciting, it's their country. It's only reasonable they'd want first dibs. I'm sure other countries would do the same. Also, our foreign relations with them aren't what I'd call friendly right now either."

Mr. Mercury thought for a moment. "I suppose if it is dangerous, they can't just let people run willy-nilly into it. There are reasonable approaches to things." He paused and stared at the blueprints. "Carry on. Do what you can from here. I want these designs finalized so we can begin production within a week."

"Yes, sir," Joseph said with amusement.

Mr. Mercury nodded and marched out of the room, leaving everyone staring after him.

"That was exciting." Lauren shook her head and focused on her computer.

"We all got raises out of it." Jordin raised his left eyebrow and smiled.

Lauren didn't take her eyes off her screen. "If he remembers."

Jordin looked at Joseph who just chuckled and shrugged.

"What was that about?" Jimmy still stood by the door looking confused.

"Hey, Jimmy." Jordin looked thoughtfully at his intern.

"Yes?"

"Could you go to the cafeteria and grab us all coffee?"

"Okay." Jimmy smiled and walked out the door.

Once his intern was out of earshot, Jordin grabbed a chair and pulled it up next to Lauren's desk.

"Can I help you?" Lauren looked at him quizzically.

"Yes, I'd like to understand something." Jordin was rapidly trying to find the best way to say what he had to say.

"I'm going head to my department with this design." Joseph picked up the blueprints and mouthed "good luck" to Jordin before walking out the door.

"What do you want to know?" Lauren narrowed her eyes at Jordin.

"I know I'm the new guy," Jordin said. "But I'm starting to get a picture of how things work. And I think I understand what's going on. However, I'd like to hear it from you. What's it like to work here?"

Lauren scoffed. "You're seeing it for yourself. He charges in like a bull, says a bunch of stuff, then leaves. Half of the time I don't know what he's serious about and what he isn't. If something he says isn't done, he gets mad. If you do what he says but he forgot he told you, he gets mad. It's chaos." She tossed her arms in the air. "It's especially bad for us."

"Why is it bad for us?"

"Other departments have department heads and management chains. The software and mechanical branches function independently from him. Even our IT consulting branch bypasses him entirely and is exclusively under Dhar. We're his 'pet' division. His 'mad idea' branch. Which means we don't have the cushion between us."

Jordin nodded. "How long have you worked here?"

"Five years." Lauren shook her head and sighed.

Jordin looked at the ground, then back at Lauren. "Why are you still here?"

Lauren jolted her head back like she'd just been slapped in the face. "Do I not do good work?"

"You do excellent work," Jordin assured her. "I'm glad you're here. I'm just confused why you're still here if your boss annoys you so much."

Lauren tapped her fingers on her computer. "I don't know. This was a dream job. I mean, it wasn't my first choice. I originally applied to NASA to search for extra-terrestrial life and study the effects of space flight on the human body. But...they...I was too fresh out of university. P.M.L. was the next best thing. They were more than happy to take on a NASA. rejected astrobiologist." She shook her head. "This place wasn't that bad at first. Did you know that P.M.L. used to have a pharmaceutical division?"

"Didn't that branch separate from the company, then get bought out?"

"Yes," she nodded, "I used to work in that division. It wasn't quite what I wanted, or my expertise. However, I had to start somewhere and I was eager to learn. There were...promises of more to come." She paused and cleared her throat. "Sorry."

"It's alright. Keep going," Jordin encouraged.

"Well...when the company broke the pharmaceutical branch off, a lot of us went to work for the new company. Because I have an astrophysics background as well, P.M.L. offered me a new job in their 'Astronomy' division. I thought they were serious." She shook her head and pointed toward the ceiling. "I'd always wanted to use that observatory on the roof. You would've thought that a company with 'planet' in the name would know what it was doing with astronomy."

Jordin thought for a moment as he stared at Lauren. The main reason that he had applied at P.M.L. was because of the rooftop observatory and it was always the first thing he looked at on arrival. If his job would permit it, he would spend all day every day there. Unfortunately, he had yet to step foot into it. His first chance to see it had been the surprise introductory meeting that he had missed. Ever since then, he had been far too busy with his duties. The irony of his astronomy team not using its own observatory was not lost on him.

"Are you okay?" Lauren gave him a quizzical look.

He snapped himself back to reality. "Sorry. I was just...I'd like to use that observatory too. Anyway, what's wrong with the astronomy division?"

Lauren waved her arms around. "Look around you. We're it."

Jordin blinked. "What?"

Lauren scoffed. "You probably thought we were just a team in the astronomy division, didn't you?" She brushed a strand of golden blond hair from her face before she folded her hands on her desk. "This company makes telescopes and equipment astronomers use. We don't do astronomy ourselves. Mr. Mercury wants to start doing astronomy. That's why we're here."

Jordin stared at her hair. *Wow, I've never seen hair that blond color in person before...Why haven't I noticed it until now?* He cleared his throat as he shook himself back and looked around the room at the various manufacturing machinery in the lab.

"Is everything starting to make sense?" Lauren smiled wryly. "The only reason I've stuck around is because Dr.

Dhar both knows and understands what's going on. He's trying to help."

Jordin let out a chuckle. "I always did like a challenge."

"Ha! You've come to the right place then."

"I'd like to ask a favor of you."

Lauren straightened in her chair. "Oh?"

"Feel free to complain to me all you want. I'd appreciate it if you didn't do it in front of Jimmy."

Lauren looked at Jordin sideways. "Is this a disciplinary meeting?"

Jordin flinched slightly. "I don't even know if I have that authority. I wouldn't even know how to do that."

"You're project lead, telling me to stop doing something."

Jordin shrugged. "I'm not writing anyone up for anything. I'm just asking for a favor. I can handle complaints, I just don't want to dampen Jimmy's spirits."

"If I stop complaining completely, Joseph will have to find a new form of entertainment." Lauren grinned slightly. "You know, Joseph used to be just as grouchy as me. He's the head of the engineering department. He has to deal with Mr. Mercury on a daily basis. On top of that, Mercury just loaned him to us to function as part of our team. He has way more work to do without us."

"Hmmmm," Jordin considered. "I guess I didn't realize..."

"There's a lot of things people don't realize around here..."

"So...what changed Joseph's attitude?"

"His kids became teenagers."

"Oh."

"I think he finds Mr. Mercury amusing now."

Jordin conceded, "Mr. Mercury is...scattered."

"You can say that again." Lauren let out a short chuckle.

"Tell you what." Jordin straightened his posture. "I'll make a deal with you. If he bugs you, complain to me. I'll deal with him. Whatever he says, I'm project lead. If he has a problem with you not listening or doing what he says, it's my fault because I'm directing you."

Lauren gave him a side-long glance. "Are you sure? He'll just get mad at me anyway."

"If he wants to fire you, he'll have to go through me first. Deal?" Jordin held out his hand for her to shake.

Lauren squinted at him, then smiled and shook on it. "Deal."

They both stared into each other's eyes as the handshake lingered.

I *never really noticed just how blue her eyes were,* Jordin thought.

The door opened and Jimmy wandered back into the room with four cups of coffee in a carrier. "I hope no one wanted sugar, they hadn't refilled it yet," he said as he set the carrier on a table. "Where's Dr. Wilber?"

"Oh," Lauren said as she hastily retracted her hand. "Thank you."

"I'm sure he'll be back soon," Jordin said as he awkwardly stood to greet his intern. "Thank you for getting the coffee." He walked over to grab one. "Are we ready to study an anomaly?"

"Sure thing, boss!" Jimmy said cheerfully.

"Uh...yeah. Why not?" Lauren shrugged.

* * * *

"Hey, look at this," Lauren said a week later as she pointed at a graph of the anomaly on screen. "It's changing."

Jordin walked over to peer over her shoulder and said, somewhat shocked, "Looks like it's getting bigger." The graph clearly showed expanding cloud cover. "It's been consistently increasing in intensity all week, but the area of the cloud cover has remained the same. Why change now?" He stroked his chin. "Can we cross reference this with the sensor array Dhar's team built?"

"Already did." Lauren switched screens to show a similar graph. "If they hadn't built their sensor array I'd worry that this was just another glitch or something interfering with our data."

The scent of strawberries wafted into Jordin's nose. He thought, *Is that a new perfume she's wearing?*

"What does this mean?" Jimmy asked.

"Huh?" Jordin shook himself back to attention. "Oh, I'm not sure." He checked his computer for meteorological data from surrounding areas. "It's not unusual to see storms forming and increasing over time over large bodies of water. They typically move around and continue to grow. I've never seen a 'storm,' if we can call it that, stay in one stationary spot, as if anchored to the ground...for weeks." He reached over and pressed a nearby intercom button. "Sally, please transfer me to Dr. Wilber's office."

"Dr. Wilber is in the manufacturing plant, personally overseeing things today," Sally replied.

"Oh...please transfer me there then, thank you."

After a few beeps and boops, Joseph's voice came through. "This is Dr. Wilber, how may I be of assistance?"

"This is Dr. Davidson," Jordin said.

"Hello boss," Joseph chuckled, "what can I do for you?"

"The anomaly's cloud cover is now spreading out and increasing in area."

"Oh?"

"How soon are we going to be able to ship more sensors out to everyone? The more we can connect to and collaborate with, the better."

"The truck just left with the first batch of deliveries this morning."

"Okay, thank you." Jordin knew there wasn't much

more that anyone else could do to speed up the process. He hadn't even believed that the anomaly would stick around long enough to see the first sensor array deliveries.

"I'll be over there installing one of these things on P.M.L.'s roof tonight. I was just about to head over there to get things ready. My team is installing one on the roof of our factory here. Though what good that'll do with all the machinery interfering with it...Mercury really wants these things up and running as soon as possible."

"Okay. Let us know when those two come online so we can start cross-referencing what we can. I imagine both the one on the factory and the one on our roof won't have the best quality data, but anything helps."

"You got it, boss." Joseph chuckled as he hung up.

"It's so awkward having him call me boss." Jordin shook his head.

Lauren shrugged. "You are the project lead."

"I know." Jordin considered this for a moment. "I didn't join to be a boss. I joined to study weather on different planets."

"I joined to be a biologist consultant for pharmaceuticals. Then I stuck around to be an astronomer. Here we both are, chasing storms on Earth," Lauren said with a wry smile.

"I joined to do whatever," Jimmy added.

"See." Lauren pointed at Jimmy. "Maybe he's got it figured out."

"And how's my favorite team doing?" Mr. Mercury burst into the lab waving envelopes around.

Jordin calmly nodded at his boss and said, "We're doing fine, thank you."

Lauren focused her attention on her screen and said nothing.

"Fantastic." Mercury walked over to Jordin and handed him an envelope with Jordin's name on it. "Here you are. And here you are." He slid an envelope over Lauren's keyboard before turning and marching over to Jimmy. "And one for you."

"Thank you." Jordin stared at the envelope quizzically. "What are these?"

"Your new paychecks, complete with your raises. Keep up the good work." Mercury turned to walk out the door. He stopped halfway. "Oh, Dr. Davidson."

"Yes?"

"Please give this to Dr. Wilber when he arrives." Mercury handed Jordin another envelope.

"Yes, sir." Jordin nodded.

"Great. I'd love to stay and chat, but duty calls." Mercury marched out the door as quickly as he had entered it.

"Wow, what do you know?" Lauren said in surprise.

Jordin turned to see her holding up a paycheck.

"That's more than two...than I expected."

"See, he's not a bad sort."

"At least he didn't stay too long this time."

Jimmy's eyes lit up as he glanced at his paycheck. "I wish he barged in more often."

* * * *

"Look at this." Jordin pointed to his computer screen. "The monitoring program knows it's there, but I'm not getting any data." He looked at Joseph. The two of them were alone in the lab. Both Jimmy's and Lauren's workstations were closed up for the night.

Joseph was on the phone with his technicians while he hovered over Jordin's shoulder. "We're still not getting data. When we connected directly to it on the roof, it worked. Check to make sure the cables are properly connected to the building wiring." Joseph paused as he listened to his technician on the other end. "No, we see it on screen. We just can't get any data." He listened again for a few minutes, then asked Jordin "You can connect to the one on the factory, right?"

"Yes." Jordin pressed a button to pull up another monitoring program. Choppy data streams flowed across the screen. "That one works fine. Data is full of noise, but we knew that when we installed it. I can even see the one in India that Dhar set up."

"That one works fine," Joseph spoke into the phone. "On the diagram, check part J12. If something isn't soldered correctly, it may be causing the issue...It is...okay. Hey one sec." He looked out the door to see Clarence walk past the doorway and descend the stairs. "Hey Clarence."

Clarence turned and marched back to the door and poked his head into the room, mustache twitching. "Yes?"

"We're having some trouble installing something on the roof. Is there anything that you know of that might be causing an issue?"

"Had a bad air-conditioner. Shorted out some wiring last summer. Boss only replaced what was necessary for the new AC and disconnected the rest. May want to make sure everything you're connecting is connecting to good wires. I kept tellin' him to replace those old wires. Wouldn't be surprised if they're still there."

"Thank you, Clarence," Joseph said.

"Mhmmm." Clarence continued on his way.

"Check our building wiring up there," Joseph said into the phone. "We had an issue with a bad AC last summer. There may be some damaged electrical equipment up there."

Both Jordin and Joseph stared at the screen, waiting. Before long, the graph began to move, indicating that data was being received.

"Hey, we got it!" Joseph said triumphantly.

Jordin navigated around the monitoring program, verifying that all the expected data was now streaming in.

Joseph congratulated his team and ended the conversation. "I was afraid we'd made a bad part." Joseph chuckled. "You never want to have a 50% failure rate on a product you just started shipping out."

"Looks like it's working. The data on these two new sensor arrays is a bit dirty, but that's the nature of where they are," Jordin said.

"I'm sure we'll refine the design over time. We weren't given a lot of time to spend on perfecting it."

Jordin smiled. "It works. Right now, that's the most important thing."

"I'm going to go validate the installation and send my team home." Joseph patted his tool belt and turned toward the door. "Go home, go to bed."

"Don't worry. I'll shut down my workstation and head home."

"Good." Joseph left.

Jordin began packing his briefcase as his laptop shut down.

"Chasing storms?" Clarence asked from the doorway.

Startled, Jordin turned janitor. "Oh. Clarence. I thought you...nevermind." He waved his hand dismissively. "We're observing anomalous weather patterns." He packed his computer into his case.

"Do you know what's causing it?" Clarence asked.

Jordin shrugged. "There could be any number of things

causing it. We're studying it to find out."

Clarence gave Jordin another one of his hard stares. "What are you going to do about it when you find out?"

"Write a paper about it....Publish our findings for the scientific community." Jordin picked up his briefcase.

"What if it isn't what you think?"

"Uhhh. I don't know what to think now. The storm is unusual as it is. I'm sure whatever we discover about it will be fascinating."

"Hmmm." Clarence's mustache twitched. "You're still around. You haven't quit yet. Have you gotten past Mercury's sharp edges?"

"Huh?" Jordin still wasn't used to Clarence's habit of rapidly changing subjects.

"He once paid all medical expenses to save an artist's child. That was before P.M.L."

"That's...good." Jordin nodded politely.

"He's donated to children's hospitals every year since."

"Good to know."

"Good luck on your trip." Clarence turned and walked away.

What an odd man, Jordin thought as he left the lab.

* * * *

"It's a proper storm now," Joseph mused as he stared at

the satellite and radar imaging of the anomaly a few days later.

"It's one of the strangest storms I've ever seen," Jordin said as he observed data streams from multiple newly installed sensor arrays. "We've got heat rushing into the center, but it's getting colder. Storm clouds are forming from the center and spreading out evenly. It's not swirling. It's like everything is radiating out from a single point."

"What's it like under the clouds?" Jimmy wondered.

"Good question." Jordin furrowed his brow. "I wish we could send a team or a probe or contact someone over there. We still can't get anywhere with negotiations."

"They're going to have to let us in sometime," Joseph said. "This thing is getting bigger. At some point everyone, not just one country, is going to be noticeably affected by it."

"Hey, something strange is happening." Lauren pointed to her laptop screen.

Jordin walked over to her computer. Her familiar pleasant scent filled his nose as he took in the satellite feed of the gathering storm playing on her screen. Bright flashes accompanied by odd electric tree-like formations blossomed upward for a few split seconds then vanished. "Ah," Jordin said. "It's now a proper thunderstorm. Those are lightning flashes below the clouds. They look strange above the clouds." He smiled. "Nothing unusual, just fascinating to watch from above."

"This isn't unusual?" Lauren raised an eyebrow.

"Well...," Jordin stammered, "this whole situation is unusual." He stared closer at the screen. "Actually, look at the central cloud formation. That's a cumulonimbus. You expect that in thunderstorms. The clouds around it...nimbostratus?"

Joseph walked over and peered at the screen. "Yep, that there is a storm anvil. It also looks like snow clouds."

"Is it possible to have a thunder snowstorm?" Lauren asked.

"Yes." Jordin nodded. "Colloquially, it's called 'thundersnow.' They're not as common as normal snowstorms or thunderstorms. They'd typically form above large bodies of water such as the great lakes or near oceanic bodies. Northwestern Europe is an area I'd expect them to form in."

Lauren smiled at Jordin. "Wow, I never knew that. I guess that's why you're the meteorologist. Impressive."

"Well...uh..." Jordin nervously cleared his throat.

"But this is Northeastern Europe," Joseph said.

Jordin shrugged. "Maybe it got lost on the way?"

Not satisfied with this answer, Joseph walked back to the main monitors and busied himself with coordinating the efforts to install more sensor arrays around the globe.

"Hey, guys," Jimmy said from his workstation. "I just got reports of seismic activity emanating from that area."

"Great," Lauren tossed her hands in the air, "now the world's shaking itself to pieces. And no one can explain anything that's going on."

"How severe?" Jordin asked.

"It shows that it was a brief quake of about 4.0 magnitude."

"Hmmm." Jordin walked back to his workstation pondering this. He stared at the data streaming in. After a few moments, he realized something was changing. The storm was still growing in intensity, but something was off. He looked at the main screen of the lab. "Guess what?"

Joseph looked up. "I'll bite. What?"

"It's moving...straight south."

CHAPTER

6

Jordin sluggishly trudged up the stairs to his apartment. His stomach growled as the door closed behind him, the plain white walls of his sparse living space coldly greeting him.

He set his briefcase and computer case on his kitchen counter and opened his refrigerator. "Hmmm...leftover chicken noodle soup," he mumbled as he grabbed a bowl out of his refrigerator. "As good as anything else." He removed the plastic covering and sniffed the bowl. The strong meaty, salty, and savory scent filled his nostrils. "Good. I got to this one before it went bad." He chuckled.

As his food cooked in the microwave, he walked over to the one end table that sat beside his only couch in the middle of his main room. Only two things lay upon the end table, a carved wooden sculpture of a flying saucer abducting a cow and a TV remote. He scooped the remote off of the table and turned on his television.

"Sorry," he gave a regretful glance to his stair stepper in the corner, "I'm too tired for that today."

Jordin chuckled lightly as he glanced at the sculpture. "Wonder what you're up to now, Jake?" he whispered. "What would you say if you knew that 'The Space Case' finally got a job in astronomy?"

A twinge of homesickness came over him. While he had seen that sculpture hundreds of times, whether it was the long hours or his recent fitful nights, it gave him a strong desire to see his friends and family again.

He couldn't help but think about how he and Jake had been an odd and unlikely pairing of friends. Jake had been a tall and muscular football player who towered over Jordin's five foot nine inch height. Jordin, though physically fit, was nerdy.

"I wonder if we'd ever have been friends if I hadn't beaten you in that drinking competition freshman year," Jordin mused.

Memories from his childhood and university flooded back to him. "Sometimes I wish I hadn't won." He wrinkled his nose. He wasn't proud of his drinking prowess.

*I wonder how Mom and Dad's liquor store is doing? They never did allow me to help them unload their shipments again after...*He shook his head. *I wish I could make them understand. I was fourteen. The popular crowd picked on me. And Janet...I wanted her to like me. She dared me.* He sighed. "I only got her attention for a couple days after that before I was irrelevant again," he mumbled. "I hope I never have to see that look of disappointment on my father's face ever again."

"Don't worry, Mom, Dad," he whispered. " I know better than to do something like that now. I've got a real job. I won't have to work summers mowing lawns to repay you. I'll make you proud of me yet." He chuckled again as he picked up the wooden sculpture. "At least my alcoholic tolerances gained me one good thing."

The microwave beeped, interrupting his thoughts. He set the sculpture down and opened the microwave and pulled out the steaming bowl. It was too late to run stairs or go to a gym. He would likely just eat, watch some TV, and then go to bed.

The newscasters on the TV screen prattled on in the background as he set his bowl on a tray and carried it over to the couch. He set the tray on the end table and picked up the remote to change the channel. Just before he pressed the button, he froze, eyes glued to the screen. All thoughts of his homesickness vanished almost instantly.

"Leaked footage from the scene of devastation is horrific," the newscaster said. A shaky handheld video began playing. People were shouting in Russian as they ran down the street. Lightning streaked the sky as snow fell. The videographer was running down the street, breathing heavily, clearly in a panic. Loud rumbling sounds rang out in the background every few seconds. Cars honked their horns and careened down the icy streets, trying desperately to get away from something.

The videographer turned the camera back, revealing a terrifying sight. A large dark column of swirling snow engulfed buildings as it approached. A streetlamp shattered and fell over. A building collapsed as it faded from view.

Someone shouted something in Russian, the camera turned to see a man beckoning the camera holder inside a brick building. They rushed in, exchanging panicked dialogue, and closed the door. The scene darkened as the building shook. The sound of falling bricks intensified. Someone screamed, then the video cut out.

"The storm has turned deadly," the newscaster said as helicopter footage of the aftermath played on screen. "At least thirty are reported dead or missing."

A long streak of snow, approximately half a kilometer wide, stretched into the distance, heading straight south. Snowdrifts towered over most humans. Buildings in the path of the snow had collapsed. The further from the center of the line, the better shape the surroundings appeared to be. A long groove, interrupted by large craters filled with churned up dirt, rocks, and pavement ran down the center of the snowy line.

"What the...," Jordin whispered as he stared transfixed at the screen. "Is that a tornado too?"

"Russian authorities have remained silent on the subject," the newscaster continued. "Our sources say that areas in the direct path of the storm are now being evacuated. There's no telling how long this will last or how far it will travel."

Sick to his stomach, Jordin set the remote down on the tray as he sat down and reached for his phone. A sinking suspicion that Mr. Mercury may try to publicly say something came over him as he dialed. He knew Mr. Mercury well enough to know that it would only be a matter of time before Mercury would start making false claims and promises or say something incorrect out of excitement. It would be better for everyone if he walked Mr. Mercury through the facts first.

"Hello Dr. Davidson!" Mr. Mercury said enthusiastically on the other line. "How did you know I wanted to talk to you?"

"Hello, Mr. Mercury," Jordin said hesitantly. "I hope I'm not disturbing you."

"Nonsense, I was considering calling you myself."

"Are you watching the news?"

"No. But I've already had half a dozen conversations with news stations tonight. Sounds like there have been some big developments on the storm. They wanted our input. I told them the appropriate departments would provide better data and insight into this. Do you have that data and insight? I've got several reporters wanting statements."

Jordin sighed to himself. It appeared he was already too late. There was no telling what Mr. Mercury had already really said. He'd just have to watch the news to find out. His free hand began to fidget and pull idly at the couch cushions. "As much as I wish I knew what was going on, I don't have a better explanation. I've sent everyone all of the data that I have."

"Well, I'm sure someone can pull it all together and talk about it. I'll talk to Dhar. He has a better way with words than I do. In fact...," Mercury paused for a second, "let's get him on the line. I was dialing him when you called."

"Okay, sir..." Jordin was getting impatient. He really wanted to warn Mercury about what was going on before he said anything to anyone else. "I really need to..."

"One moment..." Mercury said as the phone made a series of beeps and boops.

"Hello?" Jordin said after a few moments of silence.

"Hello!" Mercury said enthusiastically. "Is Dhar on the line? Are you here, Dhar?"

"Yes, I'm here," Dhar replied, his voice carrying a hint of frustration.

"Good, we've got Dr. Davidson on the line with us too." Mr. Mercury sounded quite pleased with himself.

"We were going to talk before...Hello Dr. Davidson. How are you tonight?" Dhar switched to a pleasant tone.

"Hello Dr. Dhar. I'm well. How are you?" Jordin replied.

"I'm doing well as well," Dhar said.

"I have to apologize," Jordin began. "I've been watching the news and I called Mr. Mercury to warn him about it before the news stations started calling him. I'm afraid I was too late."

"That's alright," Dhar reassured. "Since you've been studying this and you're our resident meteorologist, is there anything that you can tell us about the storm?"

"We've got to give something to the press," Mercury demanded.

Jordin took a deep breath before speaking. "I'm afraid I have some bad news. I need to be honest. I've no idea what this is or what to expect. I've sent you all of the data that we've collected. I knew it was a thundersnow storm, but I never could've predicted the devastation. It's as if an entire storm is concentrated into a one kilometer central area. By the looks of things, there may even be a tornado."

"I didn't even think it was possible to have a thunderstorm while it was snowing," Mr. Mercury interrupted.

"Thundersnow is a natural phenomenon. It's rarer than normal thunderstorms, but it happens. Not to this degree though."

"Do you think it's a tornado?" Dr. Dhar asked.

"I've no idea, to be honest. I'm not seeing telltale signs of tornado activity or formation from above. Yet, wind speeds below the clouds appear to be insane. I'm not sure of anything else that could cause the groove in its wake either. Unless it's a current that blows down and out, sort of like an inverted 'T.' But then the snow is swirling erratically, not based on that pattern."

"In your professional opinion, what would you say this was?" Dr. Dhar asked thoughtfully.

"I'm not sure I can give you that right now." Jordin clenched his teeth. "This isn't like anything I've ever studied or heard of before. By all accounts, none of this makes sense."

"Is there anything that we can do to help figure this out?" Dhar asked. "Like it or not, the world is now looking to us for answers. If we don't know what it is, that's fine. We just need to provide a way forward to figure it out."

"Honestly...," Jordin paused, not liking what he was about to say, "the best way to figure out what's going on is to go to it." He winced. "We need to get one of our sensor arrays in there and people on the ground to observe. There's only so much we can do from here."

"I would've agreed with that before today," Mr. Mercury said in a serious tone. "I still think we should put a probe or something in there. But I can't condone putting people in the path of the storm. Especially my own employees."

"I second that," Dr. Dhar agreed.

"I'm not proposing that we hire someone to stand in the path of that thing," Jordin assured. "This thing is heading on a straight path south. The worst of the storm, as of right now, is affecting an area that's about half a kilometer wide. Maybe there's a three-kilometer buffer zone around it. We could put our sensor arrays and probes in the path and have our people out of its way, watching it pass by. Besides, now that it's moving, it's likely going away from whatever was causing it to form. It's probably going to start dissipating. By the time we get there, it'll have spent a good portion of its energy already. At the rate it's dumping snow and moving, it should only be active for a few days at most. If this thing follows any kind of normal pattern, that is."

"That's still pretty dangerous...but we do need data. The

world is knocking down our door for answers. We need to get them somehow," Mr. Mercury said. "Can you guarantee it's dissipating?"

"I can't guarantee anything. I just don't see how it can continue to grow where it's at." Jordin clenched his teeth. He hoped he was right.

"Every time I've heard you say that it's going to dissipate, it grows. Your data has said that this storm is still growing," Dr. Dhar said in a concerned tone. "It may be only half a kilometer of destruction now. What about when we get there? We could put our people out there thinking that they were safe, then it grows and engulfs them."

Jordin winced again. "We can monitor the rate it grows at. If it stays consistent, we'll have a good idea of where we can be. It may spread out more and snow over a wider area. However, that will likely mean it will be spreading out its energy and reducing the severity of any one place it snows."

"Hmmmm," Mr. Mercury hummed, "we'd still need permission to go there in the first place."

"I think, now that this has gone public and deadly," Jordin replied, "they'll have to let someone in to at least do something. The more we can figure out about this thing, the better we can prepare for it. Right now, everyone's going to be frightened. If they don't let someone in to publicly study it, people will panic." He glanced at the TV The news broadcast had moved on to discussing how beneficial certain pet foods really were. He pressed a button on the remote and turned the TV off.

"Good point. I'll see what I can do," Mercury said.

"I still don't like this," Dhar interjected. "There are far too many unknowns. The danger is very real here. I can agree as far as using mechanical equipment to study this, but I hesitate to endanger anyone. I don't think this thing will dissipate. Show me the data that says it's dissipating and I'll listen. Thus far, everything I've seen says it's just going to get bigger."

"I don't like it either," Jordin said. "But I'm not sure what else to do. We can study it and determine the best way to go about it. We can set up in a place outside of the danger path and ensure that we have either an extraction plan or a bunker to hide in should things go wrong."

"This whole thing has defied known weather patterns to get to this point," Dhar said, frustrated.

"Well, I like it," Mr. Mercury said in a chipper tone. "Let's figure it out."

The phone line went silent for a few moments. Dhar finally sighed. "If this is what we're doing, my team and I will do our best to help. I would only request that we take everything very seriously and use every safety precaution possible. I want everyone out even if it looks slightly bad."

"I'll go myself to ensure everything is done right," Mercury said proudly.

"Okay…," Dhar didn't sound any more encouraged by that statement, "if we can find a place with bunkers that we can easily access should things go wrong...We can't trust any immediate evacuation plans. Helicopters and planes would be unsafe to fly in these situations. Any moving vehicles could be tossed around by the high winds. We also need to do everything legally. I've no interest in getting into trouble with the Russian government or sparking an international incident over this. The last thing we need to do is go in, get ourselves killed, and offend a country. I don't need to tell anyone here how tense the world is now. One wrong move by us and the storm would be the least of the world's troubles."

"I'll start talking to our contacts over there," Mercury said eagerly. "I'm sure we can find a place. We'll do everything by the book. I'm going to have Dr. Wilber start making some probes that can withstand the storm and see what we already have. The sooner we can ship out and do this, the better. In the meantime, what do we tell the press?"

"I'm not sure." Jordin thought for a moment. "Tell them we need to study it further. We need to see it up-close to get a better idea. We're working on getting better answers?"

Mr. Mercury chuckled. "I'll tell them something to keep them occupied. In the meantime, I'll let everyone know that we're traveling soon."

"Actually," Jordin cut in. "I can notify the team. I will inform them of all needed information. That way, you can focus on what you need to do."

"Hmmm, sounds good to me," Mr. Mercury said. "Prepare everyone to travel. Once we get approval, we won't wait."

"Yes, sir," Jordin said.

Everyone exchanged goodbyes and the conversation ended. Jordin set his phone down and stared at his now cold bowl of food. He shook his head and took a bite. It wasn't ideal eaten cold, but he'd manage.

His phone began ringing. "Uh oh," he said upon seeing Dr. Dhar's name. "Hello, sir," he answered.

"I hope you're prepared for what's coming," Dhar said, more worried than angry.

Jordin was also worried. "I hope so too. I also hope I'm not causing too much of a problem."

"It's not you I'm worried about. As much as I don't like it, you're right. Someone who knows what they're doing is going to have to go there to study this thing."

"Believe me, I don't like it either. But to some degree, I think it's necessary. I'm willing to take the risk."

"Is your team willing to take the risk?"

"I'll send them an email tonight to warn them. I'll talk with them tomorrow. If anyone goes with me, it'll be strictly voluntary."

Dhar was silent for a few moments. "Is the world willing to let us take the risk?"

"I...don't know."

"Is there any currently known way that this storm could continue to grow?"

"I may be wrong, but I can't think of a natural scenario that would cause it to keep growing. It's over land, which usually rapidly takes the power away from strong storms."

"Some pretty powerful storms can form and travel quite far over land."

"Very true." Jordin stroked his chin. "Storms need two things: heat and moisture. They're typically caused by rising warm air. In the case of powerful land storms, they can be caused when a mass of moisture-filled air meets a mass of rising warm air. For whatever reason, heat was moving rapidly to this one area. My assumption is that there was likely another mass of air with tons of water vapor. The point where the anomaly formed was likely where these two air masses collided. The storm is now moving away from that point. Even if the air masses travel together, the further over land they roam, the more power will get drained." He paused to take a breath. "All that to say, yes you can get pretty powerful storms over land. However, they tend to die out fairly quickly."

Dr. Dhar thought for a few moments. "You are the expert. I'll cautiously trust you. However, if it starts doing anything you don't like, this trip is over. Understood?"

"I understand."

"Very well. On another note...I debated calling you to discuss this..." Dhar trailed off.

Jordin waited, unsure if he was supposed to say anything or not.

"As Mr. Mercury is going to travel with you and you're project lead...I think it's necessary," Dhar finally said.

"Okay?" Jordin didn't know what to expect.

"Now that he has the idea of doing this and going there himself in his head, it'll be impossible to convince him otherwise."

"If you're worried about his safety, I'll try to convince him to stay as far back as possible."

"I'm going to have a very stern discussion with him. You and your team are going to be the ones in charge on the field," Dhar said sternly. "Dr. Wilber has plenty of field experience working in dangerous situations. When it comes to ensuring everyone's safety, he's going to be in control."

"Okay." A part of Jordin was glad that he didn't have to shoulder that responsibility.

"You'll have control over what's needed to study and gather data. That also means getting results. If we do this and nothing comes of it...," Dhar paused, "we won't be doing something like this again."

"I understand," Jordin said.

"I need to be honest with you. We're a manufacturing company. We make the parts that people use. We are inexperienced in performing scientific studies ourselves. When we originally started our astronomy department, we were only supposed to have consultants for assisting our technicians in designing the tools."

"I've learned some of this."

Dhar chuckled. "I'm sure you've learned more than you're willing to tell me. I'm also sure you had to learn it the hard way. My colleague isn't the best at explaining things. I think the original people in the department were told something else. Once a new idea takes hold, the original purpose is forgotten. Our astronomy department is supposed to be a real astronomy department. Yet, we're sending it to chase storms."

Jordin kept himself from laughing. "I think I understand."

"I wish I could be of more assistance in this matter," Dhar said regretfully. "As your department is the only one we have to deal with this storm, I'm afraid I'd just get in the way. My expertise isn't in storm chasing."

"That's alright. We've got a good team here. I'll be relying heavily on Dr. Wilber for safety guidance in this."

"I have full confidence in you and your team..." Dhar said, still worried.

"Are you worried about Mr. Mercury?"

Dhar chuckled. "He has a tendency to throw his weight around to do things the way that he wants. And the way he wants isn't always the best way. In most cases I can step in and convince him otherwise or change the direction. However, out there, I won't be able to do anything. This is a dangerous situation, and he's been getting..." Dhar stopped.

"Don't worry. I know he can be a handful. Has he always

been this way?"

"This is what I was debating telling you or not. Mercury has always been...enthusiastic...about things. Frankly, it's been getting worse. I'm concerned about him. I'm not there and he can hide it from me when we talk, but I'm certain something's wrong."

"What do you think it may be?" Jordin thought through all of his interactions with Mercury.

"I don't know. A few years ago, he never would've insisted on personally going on something like this."

Jordin couldn't help but feel a little surprised that his boss was telling him all of this. The situation must be worse than he thought. "Is there anything that you want me to do?"

"For now, keep him out of trouble. Make sure he comes back in one piece."

"I'll do my best," Jordin said grimly.

"That's all I can ask."

After the call ended, Jordin shook his head. He needed to inform his team so that they could prepare to leave. He walked to where he'd set his computer case on the kitchen counter and pulled his laptop out. He logged into his company email.

I *wonder how they'll take it?* he asked himself as he typed out an email. *Especially Lauren. I hope she doesn't go ballistic over it.*

CHAPTER

7

"Mr. Mercury called you to his office too?" Jordin nodded his head in greeting at Joseph who was standing outside Mr. Mercury's office door.

"Indeed." Joseph had his typical amused expression as he opened the door and ushered Jordin inside.

"Yes, dear," Mercury said softly into his phone as both doctors entered.

Both Jordin and Joseph took their seats and waited as Mr. Mercury nodded at them. Jordin noticed that Mr. Mercury looked a little more tired and disheveled than usual.

"Don't worry, dear. Yesterday was better. It wasn't so bad this morning." Mercury seemed to sadden as he listened. "I know, dear. Don't worry, dear. We'll figure it out."

Jordin glanced questioningly at Joseph as he idly clasped his hands together. He leaned over and whispered, "Should we be here, listening?"

Joseph shrugged.

"I promise, dear. Everything will be fine." Mr. Mercury glanced at his employees. "I've got to go now. I have an important meeting. We'll talk tonight." He paused for a few moments. "Love you too, goodbye." He hung up the phone and seemed lost in thought for a few moments, Then straightened his posture, his usual demeanor returning.

"Is everything alright, sir?" Jordin asked.

Mr. Mercury smiled. "I have good news. I was finally able to convince the right people to let us in."

"I assume you're talking about going to Russia to observe the storm?" Joseph grinned.

"Yes." Mercury nodded enthusiastically. "How soon can we be ready to go? The sooner we ship out, the better."

"I've already alerted my team to begin prepping equipment," Joseph said. "We have a few spare probes and sensor arrays lying around."

"I'll have to check with the rest of my team," Jordin said.

"Good. Get them ready." Mr. Mercury waved his hands around excitedly.

Joseph was amused. "If we want to do it right, we can have the equipment ready to ship out tomorrow morning. If we do it wrong, we can hop on your jet and go now and pray that we have everything and that nothing gets damaged in transit."

Mr. Mercury looked thoughtfully for a few moments as if he were actually considering the "wrong way." "Be ready tomorrow morning," he finally said. "Can your team manage that?" He looked to Jordin for an answer.

Jordin thought for a moment. "I'll have to check. It's fairly short notice for them."

"Bonuses for everyone who joins." Mercury beamed.

Jordin nodded. "I'll be sure to let them know that."

"Well, what are you two waiting for? Get to it." Mercury dismissed them with a wave of his hand.

Joseph grinned ear to ear as he left. "Yes, sir."

Jordin was a little dazed, but he followed Joseph out and down the hall.

"Meetings with him are always interesting. I used to hate them. Now I quite enjoy them. You never know what's going to happen," Joseph chuckled as he and Jordin walked to their lab.

"I wish I had your attitude." Jordin shook his head.

"He'll either break you or grow on you. Most people break. Which one will it be for you?"

"I honestly have no idea at this point." Jordin smiled. "I'll try not to let him break me."

"That's the spirit. Now, just teach that to everyone else."

"Hey...on a different note," Jordin began, "is there something wrong with Mr. Mercury?"

Joseph burst out laughing. "That's a loaded question. Do you mean besides the usual?"

"Well, yes. I mean, he sounded sad when he was talking with his wife. I mean, I think he was talking to his wife."

Joseph shrugged. "It's none of my business what he talks about with his wife. His personal life is his own."

"True. It's just...nevermind."

"I wouldn't worry too much about him," Joseph cautioned. "He's always got something going on. Just worry about the stuff that concerns you. You'll overload yourself and burn out quick if you try to understand or get involved with more of Mr. Mercury's business."

"You're right. Forget I said anything." Jordin opened the door to the lab.

"Forgotten." Joseph chuckled lightly.

"How long do I have to learn Russian?" Lauren peered at Jordin expectantly as he entered.

"Well..." Jordin glanced at Lauren to gauge her response. He was a bit reluctant to tell everyone how soon their trip was going to be. Not even he had expected it to be as soon as the next morning. He had assumed that big corporations had a lot of bureaucracy and red tape to cut through before something this complex could happen. He clasped and unclasped his hands as he rolled his palms against each other. "Boss wants to fly out tomorrow morning," he confessed.

Lauren looked as if she was going to say something sarcastic, but stopped herself. She glanced back at Jimmy who was at his workstation. She sighed as she looked back at Jordin. "How do you feel about it?"

"Well..." Jordin steeled his expression. "I'm going. I was the one who wanted to go. You can blame me for the suddenness of this." He crossed his fingers behind his back and silently hoped that she would agree.

Lauren squinted her eyes at him. After a few moments, she smiled and said, "Always wanted to go to Russia. Another stamp in my passport."

"Sounds exciting," Jimmy called out.

"Who all is going?" Lauren asked.

"All of us, at least all of us who volunteer, whoever Dr. Wilber needs for his team, and...," he said, shuffling awkwardly as his fingers danced rapidly, "Mr. Mercury."

Lauren wasn't exactly thrilled. "Oh."

"But, I will still be project lead and Dr. Wilber is in charge of safety. Mr. Mercury will just be along to...assist."

Lauren tilted her head to the side, clearly annoyed.

"Boss is also giving bonuses to everyone who goes," Jordin added.

Lauren stopped herself from saying something else, choosing to remain silent.

Jordin wanted Lauren to understand. "It's going to be our best opportunity."

"If you say so..." Lauren considered the big picture. "Very well, boss. I'll go where you go."

"In the meantime," Jordin continued, hoping to move on, "we need to monitor the storm to make sure that it keeps a steady pattern. If it starts deviating or acting unpredictably, we won't go." He turned to Joseph. "Dr. Wilber, as I said earlier, you're in charge of equipment and safety."

Joseph flashed everyone a big toothy smile as he picked

up a clipboard from his desk. "Oh good, I get to babysit everyone."

"Do you think we'll get there in time?" Lauren asked Jordin. She appeared to have resigned herself to the trip. "You seemed adamant earlier that it would start dissipating pretty quickly."

Jordin shrugged. "Not much we can do about that. Even if it's gone, we can at least study the air currents to try and find out why it happened in the first place. If it's still there, it most likely will be much weaker."

"Have you seen the data for today?" Jimmy said in amusement.

"Not yet." Jordin shook his head.

"The storm continued to grow last night, just like it did when it was staying put. It's leveling off now that the sun is going down over there. But it's still moving."

"What?" Jordin pulled his hands apart and marched over. "Show me."

Jordin stared at the data. Sure enough, the storm was still growing.

"Okay..." Jordin mused for a few moments. "Let's monitor it and produce a prediction of what it would look like if it continued to grow over night."

"I'm going to prep my engineering team," Dr. Wilber said as he left.

"How long are we going to be gone?" Jimmy asked.

"As long as we need to be. Not more than a week, I expect," Jordin said.

Jimmy looked concerned. "My college courses start in a couple weeks."

"Oh, are you going to be leaving us?" Jordin mentally slapped himself. He knew that Jimmy was just an intern and internships were temporary.

"Not for good," Jimmy assured. "You guys are paying me to go to college so that I have an official job as soon as I'm done. I'll be here on days I don't have classes."

"Hmmm..." Jordin thought for a few moments. "I'll tell you what then. I don't know how long we'll be gone. I doubt even two weeks. However, we can arrange for you to come back if we're not done yet. Or if you'd rather stay here, I'd understand."

"Are you kidding?" Jimmy exclaimed as if insulted. "I don't wanna miss this. I'll go for as long as I can." He stood and pulled his phone out of his pocket. "I should probably call my parents."

"Go right ahead." Jordin nodded.

Jordin and his team continued to monitor the storm while clearing their personal schedules for a few weeks. Appropriate arrangements and assurances were made so that Jimmy could return early if needed. Jimmy's parents were reluctant to allow their son to leave the country on such short notice, but they agreed after a phone conversation with both Jordin and Joseph.

The storm maintained its intensity and continued to head straight south, never veering off course. By their calculations, it was currently traveling at about twenty kilometers per hour and growing in area by a few meters a day. By the time they would arrive, the storm would likely be traveling close to twenty-five kilometers per hour and have a danger area one kilometer wide. Jordin relayed this information to Dr. Dhar and Mr. Mercury, who ensured that the information was given to the appropriate authorities so those in the path of the storm could be evacuated.

Dr. Dhar expressed severe concern over the news. Both Jordin and Mr. Mercury convinced Dhar that they would act as thought the storm intended to continue increasing in size overnight and they would account for it in their safety procedures.

* * * *

Later that evening, Jordin set his laptop and briefcase on his counter and dialed Dr. Dhar on his phone.

"Hello Dr. Davidson," Dhar pleasantly answered.

"Hello Dr. Dhar," Jordin replied. "I'm returning your call. Is there something I can do for you?"

"I had a chat with Dr. Wilber and Mr. Mercury about safety earlier."

"Okay."

"We've located a town in the direct path of the storm. Russian authorities have evacuated a portion of it in accordance with the data you've sent us. We gave them the data as if the storm were going to continue to grow rather than dissipate. I would've preferred to have evacuated the whole town, but they insisted on only doing what was necessary."

"Okay." Jordin could tell that Dhar was worried. He was too.

"There are storm bunkers in this town and Dr. Wilber has already drafted a plan for positioning of personnel and equipment. Roadways in and out, as well as airspace around the town, will be restricted until the storm passes."

Jordin forced a smile of confidence, more to boost his own assurance than anything else. "Sounds like Dr. Wilber has everything under control."

"As long as everyone follows the plan..." Dhar paused. "You'll all be briefed on the flight there tomorrow."

"I may be speaking out of line, sir. But it sounds like there's still an issue that's bothering you. Is there some way I can help?" Jordin opened his refrigerator to pull out leftovers.

"There's one feature of this town that worries me. No one else was concerned about it. Maybe I'm just worrying about nothing. I'm not a meteorologist. But what I do know about the subject concerns me here."

Jordin's fingers unconsciously tapped against the back of the phone. "Okay...What might that be?"

"There's a lake in the path of the storm. This town is on the other side of it."

"Oh..." Jordin knew exactly the issue now. "So, the storm passes over an open body of water before hitting the town..."

"Exactly."

"How big is this lake?" Jordin set his leftovers on a plate and put it into the microwave.

"I've sent you an email with the town name and the lake."

"Okay, give me a few moments, I'll look it up." Jordin started the microwave and walked over to his laptop. He read the email then clicked on the links to view the town and the lake. The town overlooked a lake that was easily several miles long and a few miles wide. "Okay," he said after staring at the lake for a few moments, "this could be a problem."

"That's what I was afraid of."

"Under normal circumstances, I'd say it's not enough to worry about. However...these are anything but normal circumstances."

"What's your recommendation?"

"We estimated that the danger zone will be one kilometer wide by the time we arrive. I'm hoping they've evacuated more than that though."

"They've evacuated everything within half a kilometer of the danger zone."

"I'd recommend extending the evacuation area to at least one kilometer. So, make it a diameter of three kilometers.

And that's the absolute minimum. If I had anything to say about it, I'd evacuate everything within a five kilometer diameter." The microwave beeped in the background.

"I can give you the extra half a kilometer on either side. I'm not sure if I can give you more. They'll only do it if we get an expert meteorologist's opinion. Now that I have it, I can pass it along."

"I'll take what I can get," Jordin said as he opened the microwave. "Is there anything else I can do for you?"

"Come back alive," Dhar said sternly.

"I'll do my best, sir."

* * * *

That night, Jordin lay in bed tossing and turning. His anxiety over the next few days was beginning to get the better of him. Part of him was also excited. Not many meteorologists had the privilege of being able to observe and study a new type of storm firsthand.

His phone rang, interrupting his restless thoughts. He didn't recognize the number, but decided to answer anyway. "Probably someone trying to scam me to buy a car warranty for a car I don't own," he muttered as he picked up.

"Hello?" he said.

"Is this Dr. Davidson?" a male voice asked in a Japanese accent.

"Who is this?" Jordin scratched his head. Either warranty scams were getting more advanced, or this was someone he should know.

"You need to listen to me very carefully," the voice replied.

"Uh...okay?"

"It's not what you think it is."

Jordin was confused. "What isn't?"

"We've tried to warn people, but no one will listen."

"Warn people about what?"

"You're heading into serious danger."

Jordin was tired and running out of patience. "Right now I'm trying to head off to bed. Don't worry, I've figured out how to sleep without dying."

"The 'storm' won't like you prodding at it." The voice sounded worried.

"What do you mean? How did you get this number?" Jordin asked, getting frustrated. He just wanted to go to bed and this conversation wasn't making sense.

"We're your friends. We want to help. No one will listen to us."

"Okay. I'm going to be honest. I've no idea who you are or what you're talking about. Frankly, all I want to do is go to bed. If you want to help, hang up so I can get some sleep."

"We warned you. We'll do what we can. You're the only

ones allowed in. They've lied to you. They've lied to all of us. You're our best shot at figuring it out." The phone line clicked and went silent.

Jordin shrugged and put his phone down. "I liked it better when they just did car warranty scams." It wasn't long before he drifted off to sleep.

CHAPTER

8

Dark clouds crept over the horizon, sending icy winds before them to herald their approach. The shining summer sun overhead created an odd juxtaposition with the oncoming winter night.

"All systems are up and ready to go," Joseph barked over the radio.

"Not a moment too soon," Jordin said as he stared through his binoculars at the heavy layer of clouds rolling in from the north. He lowered the binoculars and gave a wary glance at the canvas canopy overhead, keeping the biting wind at bay. "I hope this Russian military surplus covering holds up," he muttered.

"Me too." Lauren glanced up from the various monitoring screens.

The two of them were alone on a small hill overlooking the lake, just outside of the northern reaches of town. It was a risky position, but it was one of the best places to see the storm approaching and observe it without any buildings or interference. They were the farthest from any bunker, but Jordin wasn't worried. He had already jogged the distance between their base to the bunker in town a few times and was confident that they could make it if they needed to.

"Everyone do a quick check," Mercury's voice blared out from the radio.

Lauren rolled her eyes. "Oh boy. How many of them are we going to do?"

Jordin gave her a slight smile. "Don't worry. He's just making sure we're all okay. We only had a couple hours to set up. There's a lot to it."

"We would've had more time if he hadn't wasted it trying to get that perfect group photo when we arrived," she grumbled. "And then we had to explain every little thing to the Russians. We could've had everything set up an hour earlier...," she trailed off.

"Just make sure everything you need is set up. Don't let them get to you. It's just you and me here now. Mercury's back there," Jordin pointed back toward a three story brick building in the center of town, "where Jimmy can keep an eye on him. And the Russian military is over there." He pointed to a bunker on a hill to the east a few kilometers away. "The Russians are only watching and waiting to provide assistance if needed at this point."

"You're right," Lauren sighed. "But do you really think the Russians are watching just in case we need their assistance? They weren't polite and they escorted us everywhere." Lauren shook her head. "Whatever. As long as we can do our jobs. All of my stuff is set up and ready."

Joseph chuckled over the radio. "Everything is still good to go. And I still like this old armored van the Russians gave us. We should look into getting one when we get home. We're on the eastern side of town, but with this thing, we can drive wherever needed."

"We're all set up here," Jordin replied. He looked at Lauren. A sinking feeling that the Russians had ulterior motives began to rise in his stomach. "I'm sure everything will work out fine." He tried to assure himself as much as her.

"Town Center watch is up and ready to go," Mr. Mercury said. "We can monitor everything from here. I have access to the town's weather siren. If you hear it go off, get to a bunker immediately. No questions. Hey, Jimmy can you get me...?" The radio cut off.

Lauren scoffed. "He doesn't even know how to use a radio properly."

"He's trying. Give him some credit." Jordin gave her a sidelong glance.

"I know," Lauren said reluctantly.

"Alright everyone," Joseph said over the radio, "this is going to be a close one. I don't want anyone going into the direct storm area. Our automated sensors should be enough. We don't want any heroes here. This storm has already claimed lives. This town is just far enough to be out of the direct path of the storm, but close enough to give us a front row view to this thing. Roads have been closed and most of the western part of town has been evacuated. Our military friends to the east of us won't be able to do much if it gets bad fast. We have no idea what this storm will do as it crosses over the lake, but we need to be ready. We're already going to be experiencing gale force winds here. If it gets bad, everyone get to your respective bunkers. Don't wait. The worse it gets, the harder it'll be to get to the bunker. Do you all understand?"

"Yes, Boss." Jordin smiled then looked at Lauren. "Are you ready?"

"Yes," Lauren nodded. She appeared more and more uneasy as time passed. "I've said so several times already."

"Forward observation reconfirming that we are ready to go," Jordin spoke into the radio.

"Town center base is ready to go," Mr. Mercury said.

"Mobile command ready to go." Joseph said.

Jordin looked at Lauren fidgeting. "Are you okay?" he asked.

"I'm fine...Just..." Lauren paused and thought about what to say. She listened to Mr. Mercury reconfirming that he and his team was good to go over the radio. "I'm not sure why I'm here in the first place. This isn't my area of study."

Jordin nodded in understanding, "People rarely get to do jobs in their area of study. Unfortunately, since you were in the room with us when we first detected this weather anomaly, you have been irrevocably attached to it. If you'd rather wait in the bunker until it is all over, I'm sure everyone would understand. Plus, Mr. Mercury couldn't radio you there. I can handle him if you would prefer."

Lauren thought for a moment before shaking her head. "No. I came here because you all needed help. I'm just as curious about this as anyone else. Besides...," She smiled wryly, "you need someone to help operate all of these instruments."

"Dr. Davidson and Dr. Terry, are you alright?" Mr. Mercury roared over the radio.

"I guess they're expecting another response." Jordin stared with concern at Lauren before slowly raising the radio up to his face and pressing the button. "Yes, sir. We were just getting situated here."

"Good, now we all know our jobs. Let's try to keep radio chatter at a minimum until this is all over," Mr. Mercury commanded.

Lauren flung her hands into the air. "Of all the...He's telling us to keep radio chatter down? Why ask us to confirm and reconfirm millions of times then? How many times do we have to say we're good to go?" She took a deep breath. "At least he's not standing here with us." she muttered.

Jordin placed the radio transmitter down and turned northward toward the approaching storm. "This is a dangerous storm and this is new territory for our company. He is our boss after all. I'm sure he's just nervous and excited. All we have to do is humor him."

"Yeah...just..." Lauren waved her arms in frustration again. "I don't know. After several years of him grinding my patience down...," she trailed off.

"Hey." Jordin turned and gave her a reassuring smile. "It's okay. He's frustrating to deal with. I'll be the guy in-between and try to cut him off at the pass. If you need to rant about it, you can rant to me."

Lauren sighed and shook her head. "I don't know. I mean...I was promised so much with this astronomy gig. When we were at the observatory, that was the first time in years I actually felt like I was doing something useful... something I enjoyed."

Jordin silently listened.

"You know what he's like," Lauren continued. "Inconsistent, loud, forgetful...yeah. It just wears you down after a while."

Jordin nodded.

"I don't know." Lauren shrugged. "Maybe I'm the problem. Maybe I just need to grow up and get over it. Maybe now that you're here, this job will mean something."

Jordin considered her words for a moment before responding, "Your contributions to the project have been invaluable. You were the one who gained us access to the observatory in the first place. I haven't dealt with Mercury as long as you have. However, I know what he's like, so I can't fault you."

Lauren glanced at the approaching storm. "This probably isn't the time for this discussion. We have a job to do. But...thanks for acknowledging me...Boss."

Jordin nodded and turned back to the storm. Waves were

beginning to ripple on the surface of the lake. A chill wind caused the hair on the back of his neck to stand rigid. The distinct watery, fishy smell of the lake filled his nostrils.

Lauren shivered as the breeze ruffled her hair. She pulled her heavy coat and gloves out of her nearby backpack and put them on.

"Hey." Jordin reached into his backpack on the ground near him and pulled out a packet of hand warmers. "It's going to get cold. Put these in your gloves. They'll keep your hands warm. As my mother always said, 'shake 'em, crack 'em, and glove 'em.'"

Lauren accepted the hand warmers. "Thanks."

Jordin smiled reassuringly as he glanced at the thermometer. The temperature was slowly beginning to drop. "I'll warn everyone. Time to coat up." He pressed a button on the radio. "Forward team to everyone else."

"Is something wrong?" Mr. Mercury replied.

"No," Jordin said. "I'm just recommending that everyone put on their winter gear. It's about to get cold, freezing cold."

"Copy, suiting up," Joseph said jovially.

Jordin hastily put on his own winter gear as the light slowly faded as clouds overtook the sun. The faint sound of rumbling reverberated off of the nearby buildings. He raised his binoculars and peered toward the center of the approaching storm.

"Hear that?" Lauren listened intently.

"The thunder?"

"No. Well, I mean, yes I can hear the faint thunder. But listen to everything else."

"What do you mean? I don't hear anything else."

"Exactly....No birds...no insects...nothing."

An involuntary shiver ran down Jordin's spine as he tried to shake off an eerie feeling. He shook it off to concentrate on his observations. "Clouds are coming in low," he said. "I'd say, between 800 and 1000 meters in elevation. They appear to be a mixture of nimbostratus and cumulonimbus cloud formations. The cumulonimbus clouds form the center while the nimbostratus clouds spread out from it."

"Is that good or bad?" Lauren asked.

"I don't know yet." Jordin lowered his gaze below the cloud cover. Flickers of lightning emanated from the center of the storm. A great black wall marched toward them. "Looks like heavy precipitation. Everything below that central cloud formation appears nearly solid." His fingers nervously tapped the binoculars as he studied the wall. He took a deep breath and steadied his hands. "I'd say the worst portion stretches at least one kilometer across. I'd also say...everything within a kilometer on either side will get heavy snowfall as well, but won't have the same intense winds and lightning."

Lauren fidgeted. "Lucky for us, we're not in its path."

Jordin lowered the binoculars and turned to look at her. "It may get bad enough where we are. We'll get some snow for sure." He hastily pulled his gloves out of his pockets and put them on.

"Hey," Lauren said, tapping Jordin's arm, "what do you suppose this means?" She pointed at a seismograph.

Jordin stared intently at the readings. "Intense thunderclaps...maybe..." He shrugged. Both seismographic and sonic reading sensors were picking up the same thing. Heavy pulses occurred at regular intervals.

"It looks like a heartbeat!" Lauren exclaimed.

"Listen," Jordin said, cupping his ear. Through the rumbling of thunder, he faintly heard several dull thuds occurring at the same interval as shown on the instruments. "What in the world could that mean?" He hastily shoved his cold hands into his coat pocket.

"Hey Dr. Wilber," Lauren spoke into the radio.

"Yes ma'am," Joseph replied.

"We're receiving some strange seismic and sonic readings. Are you picking anything up? Do you still have that parabolic mic with you?"

"Funny you should mention that," Joseph said. "I've had mine trained toward the storm. Been picking up some strange sounds."

"Have you been picking up something that sounds like a heartbeat?" Jordin asked.

"Stranger than that," Joseph replied. "I'm hearing that 'heartbeat' but aside from that I'm hearing something that sounds..." Static suddenly cut the conversation off.

"Dr. Wilber, are you there?" Lauren rapidly pressed the radio button. Only static greeted her in response. "Dr. Wilber...Joseph are you there?" She waited a few moments before continuing, "Joseph, Mr. Mercury, Jimmy...anyone?" She shivered from an intense blast of cold air as she watched the thermometer readings continue to drop. The last rays of the sun were enveloped in the creeping darkness overhead. She slowly lowered the radio and stared fearfully at Jordin.

"I guess we are on our own until this is over," Jordin said solemnly. He barely noticed his hands fidgeting in his coat pockets. "Strong electrical storms can interfere with radio signals and power in general."

"Glad we have our coats," Lauren replied sardonically as she hugged her jacket close.

"Don't worry, we'll all get together after this for a round of warm drinks and share stories." Jordin smiled reassuringly. He was trying to keep Lauren calm, but was having a difficult enough time keeping himself from worrying. The mysterious caller's voice kept playing over and over in his mind, *It's not what you think it is.*

The two watched as the storm crept closer and closer. The sound of thunder and the steady thumping grew louder and more prominent. It wouldn't be long before the advancing wall reached the lake. What would happen after that was anyone's guess.

"I wish this was over already," Lauren said. "I never did like storms. As a child, I used to hide under my bed every time lightning was mentioned."

Jordin softened at this. "Don't worry. it's just nature growling at us, trying to show us who's boss. It'll soon pass."

Lauren let out a nervous chuckle as she gazed upon the advancing dread. She shook her head and glanced back at the instrument panel. "Hey, is the storm still moving?"

"I was just about to ask you that." Jordin pulled his hands out of his pockets and lifted the binoculars to his eyes, observing the wall of precipitation. "It looked like it just stopped when it reached the lake."

"That's what this says too. It's not moving...wait, it's moving again...but...that's impossible," Lauren said in disbelief.

Jordin lowered the binoculars and peered at the instrument panel. Sure enough, the instruments were indicating that the storm had just switched directions at a near ninety-degree angle and was now traveling east. He stared back at the storm. The wall was now traveling along the northern edge of the lake. "Something's wrong here. I've never seen a storm avoid water before. It's one of their main ingredients. If it does what I think it's doing...," he trailed off, not wanting to say what was on his mind. His fingers anxiously rapped on the binoculars.

Lauren's voice wavered. "If it goes around the lake...Then

continues south...We're in its direct path..."

"Maybe it'll keep going east now."

"Maybe."

They watched as the wall marched along the lakeside, then approach the eastern end of the lake. They both held their breath. As the storm reached the end of the lake, its center was now directly north of their position.

"It stopped again...," Lauren whispered.

"Keep going...keep going," Jordin muttered.

The storm began to move again. Jordin and Lauren peered at the instrument panel. The data confirmed their worst fears. The very center of the storm was now heading directly for them. A loud wailing siren blared from the central building.

"Time to move!" Jordin dropped the binoculars and readied to run. "We have to get people to shelter. Only the western part was evacuated. Get to the bunker, I'll meet you there." He briskly turned and jogged toward the town.

"Hey," Lauren shouted after him, "I'm not going to the shelter until you do."

Jordin spun around to face her. "Then get as many people as you can into shelters. I'm going to do the same. I'll meet you at our designated bunker." He ran off, not waiting for a response.

People wandered out of buildings in a daze. "Shelter, shelter!" Jordin shouted as he waved at them. He didn't know Russian, but he desperately hoped that someone would understand him. A few of the locals seemed to understand what was going on and began shouting and shepherding people to designated shelter areas.

He ran door to door, knocking repeatedly, desperately hoping that people would answer him. Those who did seemed confused. The sky grew darker as snowflakes began falling. Lightning streaked across the clouds as deafening thunder rumbled. Several police officers and a few of the soldiers arrived on the scene and attempted to aid Jordin.

"You need...get to shelter," one officer grabbed Jordin's arm.

A blinding flash of light followed by a loud boom caused both of them to leap backward. The officer lost his grip on Jordin's arm.

"I have a shelter, get everyone else into one!" Jordin shouted back as he rushed to the next door.

The flakes fell faster.

Jordin nearly slipped but he quickly righted himself. He looked down at his feet. A thin layer of ice coated the ground and was quickly being buried by the continuous snowfall. "Should've brought studded boots," he grumbled.

He slowed his pace so as not to fall yet still continued forward, staying near the buildings and keeping a hand on the rough brick exteriors. All around, people were stumbling and sliding in their frantic rush toward the bunkers. Car tires screeched and loud crashes echoed in the distance.

A horn honked behind Jordin. He turned to see a car carrying an entire family fish-tailing wildly and sliding toward him. The man behind the wheel fought desperately to maintain control but to no avail as the car spun out of control.

Jordin leaped out of the way at the last second, narrowly avoiding the careening vehicle. He fell forward, landing on the snowy concrete. The fresh ice caused him to slide off of the sidewalk into the street where he struggled to get back to his feet.

There was a sickening crash as the vehicle smashed into a brick wall of a nearby building. Lightning flashed overhead. Jordin struggled to get back to his feet as drifts of snow threatened to bury him. Finally, he managed to stand again and stumble toward the car.

"Are you alright?" he shouted, hoping desperately that no one was injured.

The cries of children reached his ears as he approached. One of the doors opened. A mother emerged holding a crying child. Another older child emerged from the back and clung, weeping, to his mother.

Jordin opened the front passenger side. Stunned, A young man looked up at him, a small cut on his forehead.

"Are you alright?" Jordin asked again as he tried to pull the man out of the vehicle.

The man responded in Russian and pointed to the driver.

Jordin peered into the vehicle to see the driver slumped

over the wheel. He felt for a pulse. Thankfully, the man was still alive but unconscious.

An officer shouted something in Russian as he stumbled to the scene.

"This one's unconscious. We need to get him out and these people to a shelter immediately," Jordin shouted over the roar of the wind, hoping someone would understand him.

Together, he and the officer lifted the man out of the vehicle. Another officer soon arrived. The first officer shouted at the second officer. Both officers quickly took hold of the unconscious driver.

"We get to shelter...you follow!" the second officer called to Jordin.

"I have a shelter. You take care of them. I have to make sure my friends are alright." Jordin yelled as he turned and headed back toward his designated bunker.

He struggled forward against the wind. Snow flew into his eyes and stung his face like icy needles. His coat felt like it was trying to drag him backward as it flared out behind him. Snowdrifts taller than him were already plastered against buildings.

"Just a little further," he mumbled. "Should I turn around and go to the other bunker? I don't know where it is. It's too late now. Besides, everyone else will be at this bunker. I have to see if they're okay." He suddenly ducked as a street sign tumbled down the street and narrowly swung over his head. "Maybe I should've just gone to the bunker with Lauren in the first place."

His nose and fingers numbed as he pressed forward.

Did I even do any good? he asked himself. *Did I just doom myself for nothing?*

The central building loomed ahead, the doors to the shelter just beyond it. Other loose objects flew past him. All he could do was pray that nothing would hit him. He leaned forward and trudged on. His boots sank into the fresh snow, building up higher around him with each passing step. Broken fence posts littered his path, barely visible beneath the gathering flakes. There was a loud metallic snapping noise as a nearby streetlamp toppled over and smashed into the ground. Glass shards from the light bulb sprayed out.

He covered his eyes with his hands and peered through the cracks. A large black wall drifted toward him from down the street. This was no wall; a swirling dark vortex of fog and snow devoured everything in its path. Shingles blew off rooftops and buildings began to crumble as they were swallowed by the advancing darkness. A whole building collapsed and vanished into the chaos. The screeching of metal and smashing of bricks added their voices to the cacophony.

He pushed himself to go faster. The bunker wasn't far. If he squinted, he could just make it out.

Above the howling of the wind, crack of thunder, and the siren, an even stranger noise filled the air. It was almost a hum, like thousands of locusts swarming through the air. The ground shook as a loud thudding noise rang out, like a massive object had just crashed to the ground nearby. Oddly enough, there seemed to be a rhythm to the thumps. First a soft heavy thump nearby, followed by a rush of air. Then came the louder, heavier thud from further away.

The doors of the storm shelter were just ahead. He reached out and grabbed the handle. A sudden gust of wind followed by a loud thunderous boom knocked him off his feet. He held on with all his might as he belly flopped onto the ground.

There was no time to focus on the pain. Heaps of snow were already piling onto him. It was now or never. He pulled himself up with all his strength and turned the handle, struggling to open the heavy doors as the wind buffeted him around. The doors creaked as they began to open. Another thud followed by a gust blew the door shut.

"NO!" he shouted as he slammed his fist against the door.

Now was not the time to feel sorry for himself. He strained as he tried again. This time, a force from behind the door helped him. The doors swung open. Lauren and a few other people stood inside.

"Come in quickly!" Lauren shouted as she reached out and grabbed his arm to pull him in.

Jordin held onto the door as he descended into the shelter. The wind, which had worked against his opening of the door, was now keeping the door open. A strange yellowish glow behind him caught his attention. Another sound filtered through the chaos. It was as if several needles were tapping and scraping against the ground.

He turned to see a large dark writhing mass of clouds that seemed to shimmer in a strange yellowish light. As he stared, a large swirling cloud extended and swung out. For a brief moment, he saw what looked like an immeasurably large, six-fingered, clawed hand, cloaked in mist, sweeping toward the central building. It struck the building with a loud crash. Bricks flew in all directions as the building toppled. There was a sudden metallic clang and his world went dark.

CHAPTER
9

Jordin sensed a dim light waving around his head as he opened his eyes. Someone said something in Russian near-by.

"Is he alright?" he heard Lauren ask.

Jordin's head throbbed as he struggled to take in his surroundings. An older woman said something in Russian as she rushed over and motioned for him to lie back down.

"Let me see!" Lauren exclaimed.

He heard her rush over and soon saw her standing over him. "What's going on?" he asked.

Lauren looked relieved. "You're alive."

Jordin winced as his head throbbed. "What happened?"

"The doors slammed shut on your head." Lauren grimaced. "You're lucky it didn't crack your skull."

"The...what?" Jordin looked around then instantly regretted the action as pain shot through his skull. He reached up and felt an old rag wrapped around his head.

He was in a dusty old cellar. The only light emanated from a few flashlights set on nearby shelving. Several people ranging from citizens, police officers, a couple P.M.L. technicians, and a few Russian soldiers sat around the room on the floor. Memories of what had just happened flooded his mind.

"We're in the bunker," Lauren said.

"Where's Jimmy? Where's Mr. Mercury?" Jordin hadn't seen them when he looked around.

Lauren frowned, eyes falling to the ground. "I don't know."

"He said he'd be right behind us," one of the technicians piped up.

"Why are we even here?" another technician complained. "I didn't sign up for this. This is your fault." The technician pointed an accusatory finger at Jordin and Lauren, marching up to them.

"Back off!" Lauren commanded. "No one knew this would happen. He's the one who wanted everyone evacuated and to be as far away as possible!"

"And look where that got us!" the technician raised his voice.

Several of the Russians were murmuring. Many shot angry glances at the P.M.L. crew.

"We all knew this was risky before we came," Lauren growled.

"Settle down, Bob, you're not helping," the first technician said.

"No!" Bob replied emphatically. "I don't care if you fire me. I quit. I'm not risking my life for this. I don't care how much you pay me. I can't spend it if I'm dead."

A commotion at the far end of the room interrupted the argument. A few soldiers and other men carrying shovels and crowbars entered through a small doorway. One of the soldiers said something in Russian then approached Lauren and Jordin. "We've got thick snow and debris over the door. We'll have to wait until most of the snow melts."

"How long have we been here?" Jordin asked.

"Ah, you're awake. You've been out for two hours," the soldier said.

"Do we know if anyone else is okay? Are the other bunkers fine? Is someone looking for us?" Jordin asked.

"When we know more, we'll tell you." The soldier walked away.

"The storm knocked out most communications. As far as I know, no one has been able to reach anyone on cell phones or radio," Lauren said softly.

"Great," Jordin moaned.

"You can't be serious!" Bob exclaimed. "Let me look at it. There's gotta be a way out." He marched toward the opening. The Russian soldier shrugged, handed Bob a shovel, and wished him luck.

Loud metallic clangs followed by Bob's curses filtered into the room from the doorway.

Jordin couldn't help but chuckle. "I guess we wait until Bob is done digging us out."

"I hope we don't have to wait much longer. Someone out there has got to be searching for us. They know this bunker is here. They have to come soon," Lauren pensively said.

Jordin stared up at the gray concrete ceiling, trying his best to hide his own uncertainty. "Don't worry, they'll find us." He glanced back at Lauren. "Anyone ever tell you, just how blue your eyes are?"

"Huh?"

"Uhh..." Jordin blushed. "Nevermind."

"Hmmm." Lauren smiled slyly at him.

Everyone remained silent except for Bob's cursing from the entryway. Jordin's mind wandered back to the mysterious phone call he had received before coming to this town. He couldn't help but think about the strange hand-like cloud formation. Was there really more to this than anyone was telling him? *Of course not,* he thought. *It had probably just been some sort of an optical illusion. Or I'm remembering incorrectly. There's no way any hand could be that large, let alone unscathed by the storm.*

"Hey...did you...nevermind," Jordin said.

"Did I what?" Lauren asked.

"Did anyone call you the night before we flew out here and say anything strange to you?"

"No? Why?"

"Nevermind..."

"Okay?"

"Did you see anything...weird...in the storm?" Jordin carefully measured his words and Lauren's reaction.

"This whole storm is weird," Lauren sighed.

"No...well yes it is...but I mean like..." He paused for a moment. "Did you see anything in the storm that wasn't the storm. Like something in it that was alive?"

"What are you talking about?"

"I thought I saw a giant hand hitting the building before I blacked out."

Lauren looked at his bandaged head with concern. "You hit your head pretty hard. Just try to relax. Hopefully, we'll be out of here soon and can get you to a doctor."

Jordin lay there silently. Maybe Lauren was right. He had hit his head pretty hard, and he had only seen it for a moment. Maybe he wasn't remembering correctly.

A light cough caught his attention. The soldier who had spoken to them earlier was standing nearby.

"I couldn't help but overhear your conversation," the soldier said. "What exactly did you see?"

Jordin thought for a moment. "Nevermind. It was nothing."

"You are the 'storm expert.'" The soldier peered at him suspiciously. "If you have any information, you need to tell me."

Jordin didn't want to repeat what he had said, and look foolish again. "I just saw an odd cloud formation is all."

"How odd?" It was apparent that the soldier wasn't going to drop the issue.

"It looked like a hand…That's dumb, I know, but it did. And it smashed the central building," Jordin finally said.

The soldier squinted at Jordin and appeared to be debating something in his mind. After a few moments, the soldier smiled. "You hit your head alright." He looked around the room. "Thankfully, very few people here know English. The last thing we need is panic or silly rumors spreading around."

"I understand. It's a silly thing to be saying anyway." Jordin smiled back.

"Good," the soldier said with a nod, "be sure not to say that anymore." He turned and walked back to his group where he leaned against the wall, staring at Jordin.

"That was odd," Lauren whispered.

"Yes, but think of the position they're in," Jordin whispered back. "A disaster has just struck the town and they'll be the ones having to clean it up. The last thing they need right now is someone saying crazy things and sparking trouble."

"True, but it's still odd. We were done talking about it. Then he came over and brought it up again."

Jordin chuckled. "Of all the things in this situation that aren't right, that sticks out to you?" His statement was punctuated by a loud metallic slam emanating from the entryway followed by Bob cursing snow and bunkers.

"Fair enough." Lauren nodded.

"Think about it. We're a bunch of Americans in Russia, chasing a new type of storm that no one knows anything about. It just did something we hoped it wouldn't and everyone has lost something here. They may blame us for it. We were supposed to be the experts on this. At least you and the others can blend in. I stick out like a sore thumb here. They just have to look at me to know I'm not Russian."

Lauren thought for a moment and smirked. "Don't worry, if they come for you, they'd have to go through me first."

Jordin laughed. "Whatever happens, we're all in it together now."

"You worry too much," Lauren playfully chided. "Any moment now, someone'll find us and we'll all be fine."

"I hope so." Jordin stared up at the ceiling.

Time slowly ticked by as he lay on the cold concrete floor. Thankfully, his head rested on an old blanket so it wasn't in direct contact with the hard ground. Not many people seemed interested in talking. Even Bob tired of his fruitless endeavor to force the doors open and sat quietly in a corner, glaring at everyone.

Jordin passed the time by imagining patterns in the uneven bumps and nodules in the concrete ceiling. Soon enough, familiar patterns of constellations emerged as he traced them out with his eyes.

"I wish I'd brought a book or something," Lauren mumbled.

"Oh, yeah?" Jordin eagerly latched onto the conversation. "What book would you have brought?"

Lauren waved her hand dismissively. "Oh, I just have a new book series I'm reading."

"What's it about?" Jordin persisted.

"It's just a silly romance mystery series. I'm in the middle of the second book."

"Is it any good?"

"I like it. It's all about this on again off again couple who you never really know if they actually love each other or if it's a convenience thing. He inherited an oil empire and she's descended from foreign royalty. People die and they need to figure it out. I'm just to the part in the second book where..." She paused. "Nevermind."

"Hmmm. Sounds interesting," Jordin said. "I don't remember the last time I read a book that wasn't a manual or a textbook."

"You should. There's a lot more to the world than just bland information dumps." Lauren teased.

"Do you have any recommendations?"

"I have no idea." Lauren shrugged. "You probably won't like the romance stuff. But you're a space man. You might like sci-fi. There's a ton of books that deal with space and weather stuff."

"Hmmm." Jordin tried to nod but regretted it immediately so he remained still. "Maybe someday I'll find a good book to read for fun."

A commotion from the entryway caught Jordin's attention and caused the soldiers and a few police officers to leap up and rush out. One of the soldiers came back and shouted something in Russian. Everyone around began to murmur excitedly. A blast of chill air emanated from the entryway and circled around the room causing everyone to shiver. The air carried an unpleasant damp odor that caused Jordin to almost instinctively wrinkle his nose.

"What's happening?" Jordin asked.

"I don't know. I hope someone's here to save us," Lauren said.

It wasn't long before a familiar figure emerged from the entryway.

"There you are!" Joseph said as he walked in, followed by several other Russian officers and soldiers.

Bob leaped up. "Thank goodness! Now we can get out of here!"

"We're getting everyone out." Joseph pointed back toward the entrance with his thumb. "What happened here?" He hurried over to Jordin, turning to shout something in Russian.

Two soldiers with medical patches on their arms dashed over.

"The door closed on his head when he was getting in," Lauren said as she was ushered aside by the soldiers.

"Don't worry, we've got you now," Joseph assured. "Looks like we've got everyone from our company except for Mr. Mercury and Jimmy."

"I didn't know you spoke Russian," Jordin said as he was lifted onto a makeshift stretcher.

"I don't. I've just learned how to ask for medical assistance." Joseph grimaced. "I wish I'd never had to learn it... Have you seen Mercury?"

"I was hoping you would've seen him by now. He was supposed to be here," Jordin said.

Joseph's expression turned grim. "If they weren't here, there's not much hope of finding them. The central building collapsed." He addressed the soldiers in broken Russian and pointed toward the entrance. A few soldiers nodded and ran out. "That's the tenth time I've had to say 'search the smashed building.'"

"You don't think that..." Lauren gasped.

"I don't know." Joseph shook his head.

The medics lifted the stretcher and carried Jordin out while Lauren helped to steady him. He feared what he would see outside the bunker. The metal doors had been smashed and dented in several spots. Bricks, cement, and rubble lay in piles by the entrance. Snow still blanketed everything. The sound of water splashing to the ground surrounded them. A musty, muddy, damp scent hung in the air. The rapidly melting snow formed pools of slush. Small streams of water ran down the steps of the bunker.

Nothing prepared him for what he saw now. Every build-ing in a one kilometer wide stretch had been completely flattened. Buildings within a kilometer on either side of the stretch were in various stages of collapse. The central building was now a pile of rubble. People of all ages and backgrounds milled about with shovels trying to dig up the last remnants of their lives and livelihoods while holding back tears.

There was an odd juxtaposition of cold snow and devas-tation on the ground and clear blue sunny skies above. No trace of any clouds remained and the warm summer had returned with an unpleasant mugginess. Heat descend-ed from above causing Jordin to sweat beneath his coat while cold air rose up from below, sending shivers down his spine.

The boots of the medics, Lauren, and Joseph sloshed through melting snow and splashed flecks of mud across Jordin's coat and stretcher. An ambulance waited with open doors nearby. They wordlessly carried Jordin to the ambulance and lifted him inside. Lauren hopped in after him. Joseph turned back to assist in the rescue efforts.

A commotion by the rubble of the central building caught Jordin's attention. Joseph and a few others rushed up and began clearing piles of rubble away.

Mr. Mercury shakily walked out from the newly made opening in the rubble carrying someone else in his arms. The expression he wore was one of disbelief, like he couldn't believe what happened. Jordin couldn't quite see who Mr. Mercury was carrying, but he saw the body's arms and legs hanging limply.

A sick feeling formed in the pit of his stomach. There were only two P.M.L. members missing. Both had been in the central building. Mr. Mercury had just been accounted for.

The doors of the ambulance clanged shut, cutting off his view of the outside world. The siren blared and the vehicle started moving. Neither the medic nor Lauren said anything. All his thoughts were dread and doubt.

"This is all my fault...," he whispered.

CHAPTER
10

Jordin lay propped up in a hospital bed. The past twenty-four hours since his arrival at the hospital had been a blur as he wavered in and out of consciousness. He remembered doctors and nurses talking over him in Russian. Now, his full consciousness had returned.

"Your health is good," a nurse said in broken English. "Very lucky. Injury shallow. Recover soon." She smiled and nodded as she walked out of the room.

"Thank you," Jordin said a few moments too late as he was now alone in the room. His head still slightly swam.

Lauren and Joseph entered.

"Hey, you're alive," Lauren said as both she and Joseph took a seat in nearby chairs.

"Barely," Jordin said, his spirits rising upon seeing them.

"How do you feel?" Joseph asked, his face bearing the most serious expression Jordin had ever seen him wear before.

"My head hurts, but otherwise, I'm fine," Jordin replied. "How are you two?"

Joseph stared unblinkingly at him. "Alive."

"I'm fine. Its you, Mercury, and...Jimmy..." Lauren trailed

off.

"What happened? Are they okay?" Jordin tried to sit up but the pain changed his mind.

"The Russian military has confiscated our phones and equipment, anything that could be recovered," Joseph began. "Supposedly, any data gathered will be shared with us. Our objections...were ignored." He paused and looked toward the window. "As for Mercury and Jimmy. They were both rushed to intensive care. Mercury will...recover. Jimmy...," he cut himself off.

A lump formed in Jordin's throat. He feared the worst, but dared not investigate further. An uncomfortable silence descended upon the room, interrupted only by the clock ticking on the wall.

"What happened? How did we get to this point?" Lauren finally asked.

"I don't know," Jordin said softly. "I was wrong...about everything."

"We all were," Joseph said flatly. "When the storm changed direction," he stared off into the distance, "we scrambled to get everyone and everything we could into a bunker. It didn't hit my section of town as hard as it hit you guys. We came out after it passed." He averted his eyes. "I'd been told it was dangerous and deadly...I just didn't expect to see what I saw. It looked like a war-zone, like an army had marched through, destroying everything in its path."

"It sounded like bombs were going off everywhere,"

Lauren said blankly.

"We wanted to come out and help," Joseph continued, "but the military moved in from their encampment and forced us back into the bunker to wait until it was 'safe.'" He gestured air quotes.

"Why didn't they let you help?" Lauren asked. "The last thing you want is to refuse able and willing bodies."

"I don't know." Joseph shrugged. "An hour later, they let us out and recruited us for the rescue effort." He stared up at the ceiling and sighed. "I'm no stranger to death…But… When you go from ruined building to ruined building, trying to find survivors and corpses…" He couldn't go on.

Silence once again descended on the room.

"I wish I could've done more," Joseph finally said.

"You did what you could," Jordin assured.

"We came to prevent this." The anger and agitation was clear in Joseph's voice. "We knew this could happen. You even warned everyone to get out, but they didn't." He wrung his hands in frustration. "I didn't even believe it could happen myself. Sure, I saw the news. I heard this could happen. It's one thing to know what could happen, and a completely different ball game to witness and experience it firsthand."

"That's why this project is so important," Jordin said softly. "The more we know about this, the better. We now know that it can be unpredictable. That makes it more dangerous. I just wish that I had been more cautious. I wish I'd listened to Dr. Dhar. He tried to warn me..." He pondered this, blankly staring at the ceiling.

Joseph peered at Jordin. "So, what do we tell the world? We don't know what it is? We don't know what it'll do? Hope you have a bunker? You think that'll encourage people?"

"I don't know. The best we can say right now is that we'll do what we can. People may not like that answer, but we won't give up...will we?" He looked around the room.

Joseph nodded. "I watched this thing destroy a town like it was nothing. I'm not going to let that go unanswered for." He looked at Lauren who was staring out a nearby window. "What about you?"

Lauren looked back at Joseph incredulously. She shook her head. "Are you kidding? I stuck around P.M.L. longer than sanity said I should've. Now that I'm attached to the storm, it'll have to kill me to get rid of me."

Joseph smiled and nodded. "Good. But what can we do against a storm?" he asked Jordin.

Jordin thought for a moment. "I don't know yet. There are ways to force weather to precipitate. Certain areas will 'seed' the clouds to force it to snow or rain to reduce the overall cloud density. I don't think anything like that would help here. When hurricanes approach, people either evacuate or bunker down. The best thing that we can do is show people what this storm is capable of. Meanwhile, we track it and its path."

Joseph wasn't satisfied. "Aren't we already doing that?"

"Yes, we are," Jordin said. "The reason that this storm is as bad as it is for us is because we don't know much about it. Once we understand it better and know what it'll do, we can better prepare for it in the future. This storm may be devastating now, but we can learn how to handle it."

"You think there'll be more storms like this in the future?" Lauren asked. "I thought something like this has never happened before. What if it's a once in a lifetime, or a thousand years, type of thing?"

"That's something we need to study to find out," Jordin said, pausing thoughtfully. "Even if it never happens again, it's certainly a monumental storm to study now. Frankly, I hope something like this never happens again. As exciting as it is for a meteorologist to discover a new storm, the devastation isn't worth the intrigue."

Joseph scowled. "Let's hope it never happens again."

The door opened and Mr. Mercury trudged in, holding a bag. His face bore a mixture of sorrow, anger, confusion, and regret. A small bandage wrapped the top of his head. Everyone waited patiently for him to speak, but for once, it was Mercury's lack of words that said so much.

Lauren gasped and put her hand to her mouth. "Oh no."

"He...," Mercury struggled to say. "Jimmy...," he took a deep breath, "performed admirably. His family should be proud."

No one knew what to say.

"What happened?" Jordin finally mustered the courage to ask.

Mr. Mercury stared blankly at Jordin. "I don't know," he said after a while. "When the storm turned toward us, I set off the alarm. I ordered everyone to get what they could and evacuate to the bunker. I wanted to be the last person out and ensure everyone else got out first. I made sure the equipment that was left would record and store whatever data it gathered." He paused and averted his gaze out the window.

"Jimmy stayed with me," Mercury continued after a few moments. "I tried to send him away, but he wouldn't go. He insisted on helping me. Everyone else was gone and we were on our way when all power went out. We couldn't use the elevators so we were on the stairs. It sounded like a hurricane outside. The whole building was shaking and rattling. Things were falling over. We made it to the ground floor when..." He stopped, set the bag on a nearby table and walked over to the window.

Mr. Mercury leaned on the windowsill and kept his eyes fixed on the outside world. "I don't know what happened. The next thing I know, I was waking up on the floor. We were trapped by debris. I must have been hit by something and knocked unconscious. Everything was cold and dark. Jimmy was next to me. He...he was trying to keep me warm. He was hurt bad..." His eyes moved to the windowsill.

"He apologized to me the whole time," he continued. "He...apologized to me..." He sighed. "I put him in that situation. I was the one who needed to apologize, not him."

"I'm sorry," was the only thing Jordin could think to say. His own guilt began to eat away at him. Jimmy would still be here had they simply remained in their home office and tracked the storm from afar.

"My whole life," Mr. Mercury said, "all I've wanted to do was make things. I wanted to make life better. I know I'm not the easiest to work with..." He shook his head. "I've been too careless. I tell people to do things and pray it all turns out well. This time it cost more than I was willing to pay."

"You can't blame yourself for it," Jordin tried to assure him.

"Can't I?" Mercury angrily turned. "It's my company. My responsibility. We're here because I wanted us to be here. The safety and wellbeing of my employees is my job. And I failed."

"There's no way you could've..." Jordin began but Mercury cut him off.

"It should've been me alone in there." Mercury turned back to the window. "It took the wrong person. I wanted my legacy to bring hope to the world. How many people do I need to sacrifice to obtain that? Will this be my true legacy?"

The room silently processed this along with Mr. Mercury.

Mr. Mercury turned and motioned to the bag on the table. "I've got enough clout, still, to get everyone's phones back from the military. Call your loved ones. Let them know your madman boss hasn't killed you yet. Put any long distance charges on the company." He left the room leaving everyone speechless.

Joseph stood and walked over to the bag. He picked it up and began handing everyone their phones.

"I can't believe it." Lauren shook her head. "I expected to hear this...Jimmy...but..." She tried to fight back the tears.

"It's the news no one ever wants to hear," Joseph said softly.

"So, what do we do now?" Lauren asked in a shaky voice.

"I'm going to call my family. I suggest you both do the same." Joseph waved his phone and stepped out into the hall.

Lauren stood and took a deep breath. "They're taking the two of us to a hotel soon. We wanted to stop by to see how you were before we left." She warily glanced at her phone.

"Do you have someone you need to call?" Jordin asked.

Lauren chewed her lower lip. "Not really."

"I'm sorry."

"I mean...," she sighed, "I guess I should." She shook her head. "Sorry. I'll let you call your family in peace." She turned and walked out of the room before Jordin could reply.

"I hope she's okay." It was his turn to sigh. "I wish everyone was okay." His own phone sat impatiently in his hands. A faint twinge of guilt and fear came over him as he realized that he would have to call his own parents. "How mad will mom be at me for running off and getting hurt?" he muttered as he turned his phone on.

"Thirteen missed calls," Jordin observed after his phone buzzed to life. "All from my mother." A knot formed in his stomach. "I wonder how many times Jimmy's mother...?" The thought quickened his breathing.

After a few moments, he grit his teeth and suppressed his feelings. "Here goes nothing." He pressed the call button to dial his mother.

"Jordin, is that you? Are you alright?" his mother answered, her voice wavering. "You had us worried sick. How's my baby?"

"Hello, Mom," Jordin replied. "I'm...fine."

"Hey, George, its Jordin!" his mother shouted. "Hang on, I'm going to put this on speaker for your father." A few beeps indicated the transition. "Hello? Can you still hear me?"

"Yes I can." Jordin smiled.

"Can you hear me?" his father's voice filtered faintly through the phone.

"Yes, I can hear you too." Jordin steeled himself for the conversation to come.

"Good," his mother said. "Now maybe you can tell me what the big idea was, running off to Russia and nearly getting yourself killed chasing a storm." Her voice carried both annoyance and concern.

* * * *

Later that evening, Jordin lay in the hospital bed, watching the sun-rays from the window stretch across his covers and fade. A nurse entered the room with a tray of food.

"You, eat." The nurse smiled and set the tray on the table beside him.

"Thank you." Jordin returned the smile.

"How, you feeling?"

Jordin mulled his response over a moment. "Physically, I'm better. Thank you."

"Good." She checked the nearby charts and took a few vitals. "Recover soon." She smiled again and left the room.

"Am I better?" Jordin muttered to the empty room. Floods of emotions overcame him. He didn't know if he should be angry or cry.

"I killed Jimmy. I killed Jimmy," he whispered, the knife twisting. "Had I not wanted to come...had I not insisted..."

He wasn't looking forward to talking to Dr. Dhar about it all. He imagined Dhar angrily saying "I told you so" and "you're fired" over and over in his mind.

He couldn't help but remember the phone conversation that he and Joseph had with Jimmy's parents. They had been reluctant to allow their son to go on this last-minute trip. *Jimmy has to prepare for college. We'll have so little time with him between now and then.* Jimmy's mother's voice echoed in his skull. He dreaded to think about a conversation with them now.

A solid lump of pain, anguish, and sorrow formed in Jordin's heart and spread throughout his body. A young, hopeful life had been snuffed out by his carelessness.

The memory of the "hand" striking the central building continuously interrupted his thoughts. Doubt began to creep over him. Was that really a hand? No, that would be preposterous. And yet...it had struck the deathblow for his intern.

His phone rang. "Oh no," he thought, half expecting it to be Dr. Dhar. The number on the screen wasn't familiar. "Hello?" he answered.

"Hello again my friend," a familiar voice said with a Japanese accent.

"Okay, who is this?" Jordin was angry, sad, and frustrated. However, a part of him was curious. Was this the same person who had warned him earlier?

"Was it what you thought it was?" the voice asked, ignoring his question.

"I don't know what you're talking about."

"You saw something, didn't you?"

"When?" Jordin was reluctant to talk about what had happened with someone he didn't know. However, he couldn't shake the feeling that whoever this was had been right.

"They'll tell you to keep quiet. They won't let you leave. They won't give you your data back unaltered."

"Who won't? What data?"

"You're fortunate to still be alive. I'm sorry to hear that not everyone can say that. I fear more will die."

"If you're talking about the storm, we're doing what we can to figure it out. It is deadly and any areas in its path should evacuate immediately."

"You need to convince them to tell everyone. You need to help fight," the voice emphasized.

"Convince who of what? Fight what? It's a storm. You can't fight a storm."

"Is it? They know what it is. They don't want you to know. You can convince them. You can expose the truth."

Jordin sighed. He wasn't going to get much out of his mysterious caller so he decided to play along. "Okay. How will I convince them? And what am I convincing them of?"

"They released the truth, altered and buried. Your resources can dig it up."

"Where and when did they release the 'truth?'"

"You saw their initial press release the night I first called."

"I'm going to be honest with you. I don't know who you are and you're sounding crazy. Please stop calling."

"Believe who you will. We are friends. We will be watching. Good luck."

The line clicked and went silent.

Jordin laid his head back on the pillow. He was beginning to doubt everything. "Someone please just tell me what's going on," he said in frustration as he clasped his hands together.

CHAPTER

11

The next morning, Jordin awakened to his phone ringing. He groggily reached for it and answered. "Hello?"

"Good morning," Dr. Dhar said. "I hope you're doing well."

Jordin gulped as his free hand gripped the bed covers tightly. "I'm doing as well as I could hope right now."

"I heard about what happened to you. I wish you a fast recovery."

"I'll be fine. How are you doing?"

"I'm not sure...Maybe you can help me."

Jordin grit his teeth. "I'll do my best."

"I've heard a lot about what happened from the news and Mr. Mercury."

"Okay..." A lump formed in Jordin's throat.

"I want to hear it from you. What happened out there?"

Jordin sighed, a lump forming in his throat. "To put it bluntly...I was wrong. About everything. And people are dead because of it."

Dhar remained silent.

Jordin couldn't tell what Dhar was thinking, but he continued. "I didn't think it could get as bad as it did. I thought it would dissipate. I was wrong. You were right to question the wisdom of going there in person."

"Had we not gotten involved, more people would now be dead," Dhar said bluntly. "They evacuated more people than they otherwise would have."

"We didn't have to go there to tell them that. And now Jimmy is...Jimmy...," Jordin paused to choke back his emotions. He was a professional, he would act like one. "Had I known about this storm's aversion to water, I wouldn't have allowed anyone to be in that town during the storm."

"Now we know," Dhar said. "Because of that, towns in the current path, near bodies of water, are being evacuated. I'm not interested in whose fault it is. No one could've predicted what happened. It's admirable that you want to take the blame for it, but I'm not looking to point fingers. Right now, we have a problem. We've lost a member of our company and the world is still looking to us for answers. When this is over we can all sit around a table taking turns blaming ourselves for what happened. For now I need your professional opinion about what's going on," Dhar said sternly.

Jordin blinked and shook his head. He felt as though Dhar had just reached through the phone and slapped him.

"So," Dhar's voice resumed his usual calmness, "in your professional opinion, what is this thing and what can we do about it?"

"Well...," Jordin was still taken aback, but he righted himself, "in my professional opinion, it's way too soon to be able to fully explain what's going on. Most of our equipment and data gathered has been confiscated. I would have to study that more closely. As for what we can do...we need to warn people in the path to evacuate. We now know that bodies of water change the path of the storm. Yet it still travels as straight south as it can, simply moving around water to continue. At least that's what it did with us."

"I can respect that on a professional level. You don't want to speak out of turn and make claims without the data. Outside of any professional opinions, do you have any personal thoughts or theories?"

Jordin sighed again. "I'm not sure...I just don't think...I'm not sure this is what we think it is." His mind wandered to the past two conversations he had with his mysterious caller as well as the "hand" in the clouds.

"In what way?"

"I'm beginning to think that a meteorologist is woefully unqualified to study it."

"What makes you say that?"

"It's not acting like a storm. It's acting...I guess that's the problem. It's acting on its own volition. It's defying weather patterns and all known principles of weather. Almost like...Nevermind. That's way too crazy."

"If it makes you feel any better," Dhar said. "Those same thoughts have crossed my mind."

"Can your team analyze things like videos and photos to see if they were edited or altered in any way?" The more Jordin thought about it, the more he was beginning to believe that his mysterious caller knew something. The phrase, *They released the truth, altered and buried. Your resources can dig it out,* played continuously through his mind.

"Yes, we can," Dhar said.

"Are you able to see what was removed or covered over?"

"It depends. In most cases, no. We may be able to see which sections were altered or find outlines of things that were cut out. However, we most likely wouldn't be able to tell, for example, who was cut out of a photo, only that someone was cut out. Is there something you want us to look at?"

"The news broadcasts showed footage from helicopters of the first event. Is there a way to get that footage and analyze it?"

"I'm sure we can get our hands on it. What are you expecting to find?"

"I'm not sure. I just want to know if anything was altered or not."

"We'll get on it," Dhar assured.

"Is there anything else I can help you with?"

"Be sure to rest up and take care of yourself."

"I'll do my best."

When the conversation ended, Jordin laid back down in

the bed. He didn't know what he expected to find by having Dhar and his team look for altered footage. Part of him hoped they'd find nothing. It would be far easier to reconcile what was happening as just an odd storm rather than accept what his wild imagination was telling him.

Almost before he could set his phone down, it rang again.

"Huh?" Jordin brought the phone back to his ear. "Oh, Jake. How did I forget to call my best college buddy?" He answered the phone, "Hello, Jake."

"Hey, Space Case," Jake said with his baritone voice.

"Hello, Muscle Head." Jordin smiled. "What can I do for you?"

"I hear you went and put yourself in the hospital, chasing a storm. Is that true?"

"Unfortunately, yes."

"Good thing you're a doctor; you can fix yourself up." Jake chuckled on the other end.

"Not that kind of doctor."

"Ah, right. You're a space doctor. Say, are you chasing that big storm on the news? The one that's flattening towns in Russia?"

"Yes, I am."

"Hmmm. I figured as much. That thing sounds pretty serious. How badly did it get you?"

"I hit my head. I'll be fine. I'm expected to recover soon."

"You should be more careful. I'm not there to tackle it for you." Jake's attempts at humor could not obscure his real concern for Jordin.

"Don't worry about me. As soon as I get out of here, I'll tackle it myself," Jordin laughed.

"You still running those stairs?"

"I am. I've got an upper floor apartment and my office is on the thirteenth floor of our building."

"Hmmm. You could probably tackle the storm yourself then. I'm just glad I caught you before your funeral," Jake said with a chuckle. "Your mom called. She was all panicked and worried. I was afraid you were at death's door."

"Not me. It'll take more than a bonk to the noggin to keep me down." Jordin smiled.

"That's the spirit." Jake paused for a few moments. "I've got a big wood working order I'm still working on. But I figured I should call, just to make sure. Is there anything I should know?"

Jordin held his tongue. Jake wasn't the right person, nor was this the right time to talk about Jimmy and everyone else. "We'll have to talk...later."

"Hmmm. Sounds serious." Jake's voice dropped his humorous tone. "I know you'll talk when you're good and ready. You know I'm here, right? If you get hit in the head again...I don't want to be the last to find out. That storm thing is no joke, at least from what I hear. I don't want the next call from your parents to be...Just don't do anything stupid."

"Understood. I'll let you get back to your order."

"Thanks," Jake resumed his lighter tone. "It's two large Victorian style dressers with crown molding on the top."

"Good luck with that."

The pair exchanged goodbyes and Jordin set his phone down on the side table.

A short time later, his door opened and the soldier who had talked to him in the bunker entered, followed by a few nurses.

"The doctor says you're well enough to leave," the soldier said.

This was news to Jordin. "Okay."

"Gather your things. I'll escort you to our facilities."

"Wait...what?" Jordin shook his head. "What do you mean, 'our facilities?' Where's Mr. Mercury? Where's the rest of P.M.L.?"

"They're with us already," the soldier flatly replied. "Your presence is required."

"I'll have to check with the company to see where they need me," Jordin said sternly.

The soldier raised an eyebrow in amusement. "You may confirm with your boss when we take you to him. He is co-operating with us and wants you to join."

Jordin wasn't going to back down. "Then you won't mind

if I call him to verify." He grabbed his phone and started dialing.

"It's your time to waste." The soldier shrugged.

"Hello? Mr. Mercury?" Jordin asked as the other line answered.

"What can I do for you Dr. Davidson?" Mr. Mercury replied.

"Are we working at a Russian military facility? A soldier is here saying that he wants to bring me to a facility and you're there already."

"Yes. We've decided to cooperate with the Russian military and coordinate our efforts. When you're well, we need you here."

"Okay, thank you. I'll be there soon." Jordin hung up the phone and proceeded to get ready.

The soldier led Jordin out of the hospital and into a military vehicle where other soldiers waited. No one said anything during the ride. Jordin couldn't help but feel nervous, especially when they passed by the large chain-link fencing and barbed wire. His head still throbbed slightly but he ignored the pain as best he could.

He was escorted up a few flights of concrete steps and through a set of glass double-doors of a large building in the center of the compound. On seeing them, the receptionist saluted and pressed a button, opening a metal door to the side. Other soldiers and military personnel milled about, paying him no attention. He passed through a large room with several computers, monitors, and work stations where several soldiers pored over graphs and data points.

"Ah, there you are!" Mr. Mercury stood as Jordin entered a conference room.

Mercury, Lauren, Joseph, and all the P.M.L. technicians were here together. Bob looked especially upset about the whole thing.

"I'm glad you could join us," a uniformed officer at the head of the table said, waving a hand for Jordin to have a seat.

"You'll have to excuse me," Jordin said nervously, "I don't know what's going on here."

The officer nodded. "That's what we're all here to find out. Allow me to introduce myself. I'm Colonel Dubinin. You've met my agent, Lieutenant Zhukov." He motioned to the soldier escorting Jordin. "As far as you're concerned, we're now your project leads."

"Okay..." Jordin blinked.

"Please, have a seat." Dubinin motioned again for Jordin to sit down.

Jordin nodded and sat in an empty chair.

"We were just discussing what everyone witnessed at this incident," Dubinin continued. "I understand you have some...unique insights into this, Dr. Davidson. Please, elaborate."

"I'm sure everyone has already told you everything I

could say about this." Jordin had a feeling the colonel was asking about the "hand" he saw.

"Rumor has it, you saw something that no one else did." Dubinin leaned back with a smug look on his face.

Jordin took a deep breath. He folded his hands on the table and did his best to keep them still. "Before the doors to the bunker closed on my head...I thought I saw a giant hand. It hit the central building. That's what caused it to collapse."

"What?!" Mr. Mercury blurted, visibly startled.

Bob threw his arms into the air in frustration. "Here we go again."

Dubinin smirked. "As you can see, Mr. Mercury. Your team is unprepared and untrained for extreme conditions. That's why we decided to take over. You may continue to work with us and we will share data. However, as long as this storm remains in our country, we are in charge."

"That's not very fair," Lauren said angrily. "You all know the circumstances. He got hit pretty hard. You can't judge everything based off that."

Jordin shook his head, tired of all this. He looked the colonel dead in the eyes and said, "You're right. That's a ridiculous thing to say. It's almost as ridiculous as saying a storm hates water...yet it does. It's just as ridiculous as saying a storm can defy all weather patterns and make sudden direction changes on a whim...and yet it does. I don't believe what I thought I saw myself. But...let me ask you this. With everything else it's doing, would a giant hand be much stranger?"

Dubinin raised an eyebrow in amusement. "A man who hallucinates clouds with hands presumes to tell me what is and isn't strange?"

"Alright...," Jordin said to the table, "then kick me off the project. Send me back home. Just give P.M.L. its property back."

Dubinin shook his head. "I'm sorry, I can't let you go back, yet. You helped design the sensor arrays. We need you to train our technicians on how to use these devices."

"So...," Jordin mused, "you're not letting us leave?"

"Not until this matter is resolved," Dubinin said curtly.

"Wait just a minute," Mr. Mercury said, growing incensed. "You don't get to tell my employees what to do."

"Might I remind you," Dubinin peered at Mr. Mercury, "you are on our sovereign soil. Our citizenry has now suffered for your project. You may cooperate or be thrown in prison as American spies and saboteurs."

"You can't do that. It would've been worse without our involvement," Lauren said angrily. "We're helping you. We're not spies."

"Assist us or face charges. The choice is yours."

Mr. Mercury sighed and shook his head. "We already agreed to help you. There's no need for any threats."

"Good," Dubinin smiled and promptly stood. "Follow me

to your new workstations. Cooperate, and we won't have any issues." He marched out the door.

Jordin and the P.M.L. team followed the colonel into the main control room where several other workstations, consisting of a desk, note pads, pencils, and a computer screen, had been set up. Armed guards stood by each station.

"Contact with the outside world will be restricted. You are only allowed to contact your company internal resources," Dubinin commanded. "As we understand, a Dr. Dhar is part owner of P.M.L. You may contact him and him alone."

A soldier pointed Jordin to a workstation where he sat and pored over several data points. Various Russian technicians stopped by to hand him documents. A translator stood nearby to communicate between teams.

Dubinin peered over Jordin's shoulder. "I am impressed, doctor." He snatched a copy of the P.M.L. sensor array blueprint out of Jordin's hand. "Your sensors are incredibly sensitive."

"Dr. Wilber made them." Jordin replied, gesturing toward Joseph as he did his best to ignore the colonel's curtness.

"Regardless, the project is yours."

Before Jordin could respond, a soldier walked up to Dubinin, saluted, and said something in Russian. Dubinin nodded at Jordin then walked away with the soldier without bothering to return the blueprint.

Jordin's phone began to vibrate in his pocket. He pulled

it out to see Dr. Dhar calling him. He excused himself and walked to a corner of the room. A soldier walked up to take his phone, but backed off after Jordin showed him Dr. Dhar's name onscreen.

"Hello Dr. Dhar. What can I do for you?" he answered.

"What have you gotten us into?" Dr. Dhar said immediately. A commotion in the background on Dhar's end made it hard for Jordin to hear.

"I'm sorry? What do you mean?" Jordin plugged his free ear to hear Dhar better.

"We did exactly what you asked us to do. It's caused quite the stir over here." Someone spoke in Hindi in the background, and Dhar responded in kind. "I apologize, they want to make sure I call your attention to this."

"Okay? What's going on? Did you find something?"

"We did..." Dhar hesitated. "We did find digital alterations to the news broadcasts. We removed some...overprints...You need to see this yourself. Sending it to you now."

"Uh...Okay..."

After a few moments, his phone dinged indicating a new message with a video file from Dhar. He opened the file and pressed play. It showed the same helicopter footage he had seen on the news. This time, there was a huge difference.

"He was right..." Jordin muttered. "My mysterious caller friend was right this whole time."

"Can you explain this?" Dhar asked.

"I don't know...I'm going to have to call you back. There's someone who needs to see this."

"Do what you need to do," Dhar said.

Jordin ended the call and turned to look at Colonel Dubinin who was standing with a group of soldiers examining various screens. He stared for a moment, trying to think of how to approach the situation. Another phone went off in a corner of the room. Mr. Mercury dug through his pockets to produce his phone and answer it, waving off an approaching soldier.

Jordin took a deep breath and approached the Colonel. "Excuse me," he said. No one seemed to pay him any mind. "Excuse me," he said louder.

Dubinin paused to leer at Jordin.

"When are you going to tell us all the truth?" Jordin asked.

The colonel turned to fully face Jordin and smirked at him. "About what?"

Jordin motioned around the room. "About all of this."

"You're told exactly what you need to know. Everything else, you tell us. You're supposed to be the 'expert' here."

"I can only help with what I know, and with what I've been told." Jordin stared him dead in the eyes. "My expertise is in astronomy and meteorology. Neither of which are what you need here." He motioned to Lauren. "But maybe that's why you're keeping a biologist around."

"Careful, Jordin," Joseph urged.

Mr. Mercury murmured on the phone in a corner, oblivious to this escalating scene.

"Are you saying you're not an expert on the subject at hand?" Dubinin asked. "Are you admitting to being a fraud?"

"He's not a fraud," Joseph declared. "The man knows his stuff."

Jordin nodded at Lieutenant Zhukov. "When he overheard me say something in the bunker, he was extremely interested...too interested. He could've let it go, but he didn't. He came over and insisted that I repeat what I'd said about the hand. I may have forgotten it all and moved on, but he insisted on bringing it up. Then you talk about it in our meeting. If it's all nonsense, why are you both so concerned about it?"

"Are we not allowed to laugh at your ridiculous statements?" Dubinin said.

"Are you laughing at me, or are you worried that I saw the truth? The truth that you don't want anyone to know?"

Lauren stared at Jordin wide eyed. "Jordin, what are you saying?"

"Maybe you can explain why you released edited footage of the disaster scene to the news." Jordin held his phone aloft and played the video.

Dubinin watched with increasing anger as the helicopter footage played. There, in the snow, alongside the long trench, were footprints. Not any human footprints, but incredibly large, unnatural prints. They had four widespread toes with claws on the ends. Three toes were in front while the fourth protruded from the heel.

Jordin glared defiantly at the colonel. "Is there something you want to tell everyone?"

Dubinin nodded to a few soldiers. All the doors in the room were closed. Locks clicked. Several soldiers moved into position in front of all exits and held weapons at the ready. "What do you think you're doing?" Dubinin menacingly asked. "Are you playing at being a CGI artist now? Are you trying to blackmail us with that obvious fake?"

"Is that why you're locking everything down? You're worried about fakes?" Jordin said unblinkingly.

Lauren worriedly glanced at all of the soldiers around the room. "What's going on?"

"That's no fake," Mr. Mercury said bitterly as he marched to stand beside Jordin. "Our IT department just verified everything."

Dubinin cocked his head to the side. "Is your company conspiring against us?"

"We're trying to help you," Mercury said in exasperation. "But you've been lying to us."

Dubinin folded his arms across his chest. "We agreed to work with your company to help deal with this storm."

"This isn't a storm, it's a creature," Jordin said emphatically.

"What?" Lauren gasped. "That's imposs…"

"I suggest you all forget this nonsense. I'll forgive this incident if you stop now," Dubinin said. "We would prefer to have your assistance in this matter since you developed the equipment. However, we are more than capable of doing this on our own if we need to."

"You knew the whole time," Mercury said bitterly. "I talked with your government, went through all the paperwork, did all the safety measures…and you lied to us." He waved his hands in a fit and paced. "I sent my employees into danger without knowing the whole story."

"I assure you, we did everything we could to ensure your safety," Dubinin stated nonchalantly.

"One of my employees is DEAD!" Mercury shouted.

"Unfortunate. However, as I recall, we were relying on you and your company for our safety measures," Dubinin said with a smirk.

"We can sit here and point fingers," Jordin said. "But the longer we sit here arguing, the further that thing marches."

Dubinin was undeterred. "I have half a mind to throw you all in a psych ward for your own protection."

Jordin peered beyond the colonel to see several maps and diagrams. "Is that why you're deploying tanks? You plan to shoot the storm dead?"

Dubinin glanced to the displays then back at Jordin. "We're planning evacuation strategies."

Jordin narrowed his eyes. "Why are we here?"

"You were intended to help us study the storm and come up with a solution. Something I'm very quickly reconsidering."

"If you didn't want people to know the truth, why would you invite outsiders in? Unless...you're unable to deal with it."

The colonel stayed silent.

"Something tells me you tried to stop it already, and it failed," Jordin continued. "We wouldn't be here unless you were desperate."

"Not desperate enough to keep you much longer." Dubinin turned to his soldiers and shouted something in Russian. A few shouted a response. He turned back to Jordin. "Thank you, your services are no longer needed. We have all we need from you now."

Several soldiers advanced and roughly grabbed the P.M.L. members.

"Now wait a minute, I'm not with these crazies!" Bob shouted as he was cuffed.

"You can't just do this!" Mr. Mercury growled. "You'll hear from our lawyers."

"I look forward to it. Have a nice day." Dubinin beamed and waved everyone away.

Before anyone moved, someone at a monitoring station shouted excitedly. Dubinin instantly redirected his attention and yelled something back and rushed over to a monitor. Jordin studied the monitor. He knew what he was seeing. A strange oval object was hovering just above southeastern India. An anomalous weather pattern began to show beneath it. The object suddenly vanished, and the pattern began to dissipate.

All soldiers, scientists, and P.M.L. members gawked silently at the screen.

One of the scientists at an observation station bellowed something. Everyone turned to take in this new data. The storm they had been chasing had changed direction and was now heading southeast, straight toward where the other object had appeared.

"And then there were two," Jordin's calm voice broke the silence.

Dubinin glared at Jordin then turned back to the screen.

"You can't keep this a secret anymore," Jordin reasoned.

Dubinin dropped all pretense. "Do you know the panic it would cause if we told everyone? How dangerous that would be?"

"I understand and can appreciate what you tried to do. But this doesn't just affect your nation anymore. This thing doesn't care about national borders. You need to tell people."

Dubinin sighed and averted his eyes.

"You could be at the forefront of the world's effort against these. What do you think happens when everyone finds out? When everyone realizes you could've told them? That's an inevitability at this point. You have a choice here. Be heroes, or cowards."

Dubinin glared at Jordin. "Don't presume to preach to me, American."

"You're the one who has to make the choice. It seems to me, now's the time to get as many allies working with us as possible."

The colonel squinted his eyes, locking them on Jordin. For a few moments, neither of them blinked or backed down. Dubinin said something in Russian. All of the soldiers lowered their weaponry and unhanded the P.M.L personnel. "Alright. What do you suggest?"

"Will someone please tell me what's going on?" Lauren asked.

CHAPTER
12

The helicopter rumbled as it flew over the Russian countryside, following a long scar carved into the ground. Grass, trees, houses, and roadways lay in broken clumps beside the long trench. Wide deep craters interrupted the otherwise straight hewn line at recurring intervals. The further north the helicopter flew, the narrower the trench and smaller the craters.

Jordin concentrated on the scenery as it passed by, with Joseph, Lauren, and Mr. Mercury all sat in joining him. Another helicopter contained Colonel Dubinin, Lieutenant Zhukov, and a few soldiers.

Bob and the other researchers remained at the Russian facility. They would work with the Russian teams to gather and interpret data for the duration of the project, however long that would be.

"We've contacted the Indian authorities," Dubinin radioed. "They're going to send their own detachment of researchers. We're giving you first look at it. Surrounding countries have been alerted. So far, everyone is in agreement. We can't let this get out to the public. Everything you see here is strictly top secret."

"We understand," Mr. Mercury replied.

Dubinin droned on. "As this is a secure facility, your phones will be confiscated while you are here. No outside internet connection or contact is allowed. Since we aren't set up to accommodate you and your team at the facility, we will transport you to a nearby hotel in the evenings. Your phones will be returned to you at those times. Be sure to never disclose anything that you are about to see to any-one, not even your families. We will take any infractions of this very seriously."

"I do have a business partner in India. As his country is now also affected, and we at P.M.L. are directly involved, shouldn't we inform him also?" Mercury asked. "He and his team could be a great help to us. He did uncover your altered news broadcasts anyway."

"Given the nature of this project and your relationship, any conversations about the subject with your business partner will need to be monitored by us. We can work with you to determine what is approved."

Jordin followed the long trench-like scar with his eyes to see a cluster of buildings approaching. As they neared, he noticed that it was another military complex comprised of prefabricated buildings with a large canvas tent in the center. The southern ring of heavy fencing and buildings looked as though they had been completely flattened. Another hastily placed chain-link fence ringed the area. Smashed tanks and a few destroyed helicopters littered the ground.

"Oh, my," Lauren muttered when she saw the destruction.

Joseph sat silently taking it all in.

"What happened?" Jordin asked.

"War," Dubinin replied flatly.

The helicopters landed on a pad on the compound's north side. Several soldiers rushed to aid them disembark. Dubinin shouted several instructions then turned to the P.M.L. group. "Follow me."

The colonel led them to a small building adjoining the large tent in the center. Once inside, a soldier in a white hazmat suit directed them to put on their own hazmat suits.

"This might explain." Dubinin nodded at the nearby television screen.

The soldier pressed a button on the side of the screen, playing a video.

Jordin tried his best to put on the hazmat suit and watch the television at the same time, playing security footage from the south side of the building.

The camera's angle showed the central tent, which appeared to be made of a different colored canvas than what was there now. The ground and nearby buildings were blanketed with snow and heavy flakes, making it difficult to make out anything beyond the tent. A myriad of soldiers were suddenly seen running toward the tent.

"This is from that day. You would know it as the day that the storm started moving," Dubinin said. "The electromagnetic interference was affecting communications and growing stronger. As you can see, from the snow falling, the weather was becoming worse and worse. We had just received our orders to...'kill' it."

An explosion rocked the tent on the screen as bright orange flames engulfed the center. Soldiers in flame resistant suits were marching forward with flamethrowers.

Dubinin shook his head. "All we did was make it angry." Dubinin shook his head.

The camera shook and a loud humming noise, like thousands of locusts, emitted from the speakers. The soldiers in the video began to back away. A tank rolled in and began firing into the tent as people scattered. Lightning struck the tent as it began rising upward, lifted from underneath. A loud boom reverberated as the camera shook and rotated to the side, now displaying a snow-covered roadway leading from the main southern gate to the tent.

The whole area began to glow an eerie yellow color as gunfire erupted and people shouted. Tanks rolled across the screen, firing as they went. Scientists in lab coats ran for their lives in the opposite direction.

The ground then shook violently, causing several people to stumble and fall. A spinning helicopter crashed to the ground as a tank rolled on its side and smashed into a building. The camera fell to the ground, followed by a stream of rubble. For the briefest moment, the camera captured a large pale object, not unlike a foot, smash down upon the camera, ending the footage. All went silent.

"We've been unable to contain it ever since," Dubinin broke the silence.

"What is that thing?" Mercury muttered.

"That's what we want you to tell us," Dubinin said grimly.

When they had finished suiting up, they were escorted into the tent, where Jordin was struck by a strange site. Through several scientists and soldiers hurrying around, Jordin saw before him a large, white, spherical object buried in the ground. The whole top had been broken off, leaving only jagged points on the sides revealing a hollow interior.

"Is that an egg?" Lauren gasped.

"How big is it?" Jordin asked.

"We're only seeing the tip of the iceberg," Dubinin said. "Most of it is buried beneath the ground. It's 80 meters long and 60 meters wide. It landed upright, then bored its way into the earth, leaving only this top part exposed."

Lauren gazed wide eyed at the massive object. "How did it do that?"

"It has helical protrusions on the outside of the shell that act like a screw," Dubinin replied.

"Amazing."

"I have to admit," Joseph began to chuckle, "I'd hoped you were all just crazy. Looks like I'm the crazy one here."

Mr. Mercury was in disbelief. "You've had this thing in

your backyard the whole time? We need to analyze this. This is huge. Do you know what it all means? Dr. Terry, you're the biologist. What is this thing?"

"I...I don't know yet. It's an egg...but for what?" Lauren mused.

"Does that mean it's a bird or a reptile?" Mercury said, his enthusiasm starting to build.

"I have no idea. It could be anything."

Mercury marched toward it. "Let's get to it!"

"Stop," Dubinin said as he and Zhukov blocked Mercury's advance.

"What are you doing?" Mr. Mercury asked, annoyed. "You want us to study it, let us study it."

"Are you qualified to do this job?" Dubinin asked.

"Of course I am. It's my company. We're studying it."

"What's your field of study and expertise?"

"Well its...its..."

"Doctor Terry," Jordin said. "Since you're the biologist here, we'll follow your lead. What are your recommendations?"

"I'm going to need a sample of that 'egg.' I need to know what it's made of. I'm going to need all data pertaining to this and the creature. If we can find out what it is, we can better deal with it." Lauren faced Dubinin directly. "I'm going to need Mr. Mercury and the rest as assistants. Do you have an area set up where we can work?"

"Right this way," Dubinin said, motioning toward a group of tables. A soldier in a hazmat suit marched up and saluted. Dubinin saluted and the two spoke in Russian. "You'll have to excuse me," Dubinin said after the soldier was done speaking. "Our forces have engaged the beast in an attempt to slow it down. I'll leave you to it. Lieutenant Zhukov will provide you with anything you need."

Mr. Mercury barely acknowledged Dubinin's departure before marching toward the tables. "What are we waiting for?"

Lauren turned to Jordin. "What do you say, Boss?"

"As far as I'm concerned, you're the boss now. I know nothing about biology," Jordin said.

"You're still project lead."

"Then as project lead, I'm placing you in charge of these... egg studies."

"Whoever's the boss, better go tell Mr. Mercury that." Joseph chuckled, pointing to Mr. Mercury who was standing at a table staring at several tools. "He'll do something strange if we don't hurry up and direct him."

Jordin smiled at Lauren beneath his hazmat mask. "Are you going to be okay directing him?"

"As long as he doesn't act like...himself...," Lauren sighed.

The group took stock of the available equipment on the tables, then Lauren began instructing the team. With Zhukov's help as translator, she gathered data from the Russian scientists who were also working in the area. She was also able to acquire a piece of the egg and a microscope. While she examined the fragment, Jordin, Joseph, and Mr. Mercury pored over translated documents of data that the Russians had already assembled.

"This is...odd," Lauren said as she observed the egg with the microscope.

Jordin looked up from his pile of papers. "In what way?"

"Eggs of terrestrial creatures are often porous to allow for breathing. While this one has little pores, they don't go all the way through. In other words, if this shell fragment is representative of the whole, it has no way of taking in extra oxygen. Which means, either this creature doesn't breathe the same way that we do, or everything it needed was all self-contained within the shell. I wonder if it breathes, how it would deal with the carbon dioxide produced...Does it even produce carbon dioxide?"

"Maybe we're applying Earth logic to something that doesn't follow the same rules?" Jordin pondered.

Lauren shook her head. "I still can't believe that we're literally dealing with aliens now."

"We don't know that." Joseph raised his hand palm outward. "We have no idea where it originated. We just saw the egg above the Earth and then it landed. Missiles we launch end up doing the same thing."

"True," Lauren said, unconvinced. "But something like this? Do you really think it could originate from here without our knowledge? It's not exactly small. I'm sure someone would've noticed it if it had launched from our own planet."

"Who knows?" Joseph shrugged. "I'm just pointing out what we know. The rest is conjecture."

"Whatever it is," Mr. Mercury said grimly, "it's stomping where it shouldn't. I don't care where it came from. I'm going to stop it."

"Yes, sir," Joseph agreed.

"Is there anything else you notice about that egg fragment?" Jordin asked.

"Actually, yes," Lauren said after looking through the microscope and repositioning the fragment. "There are three layers to this shell. The top layer has those shallow pores and rough bumps all over it. However, that layer is otherwise solid. The middle layer has small hollow tube structures. It looks like there are little metal deposits lining the interior of these tubes. I'm not sure."

"Interesting," Joseph said. "Let me see if I have something here." He rearranged a few papers and found one containing what he sought. "Ah, looks like copper. May I have a look?"

"Sure," Lauren stepped back from the microscope as Joseph stepped up and peered through.

"Yep, that's copper." Joseph walked back to his papers.

"Strange...," Lauren said as she looked back in.

"What's on the third layer?" Jordin asked.

"Looks like some sort of a sponge or a cushion material."

Joseph held a paper aloft, as if finding the answer. "Do you know what those are?"

"What?" everyone asked in unison.

"According to this paper, those hollow tubes run throughout the whole shell. Each one is lined with a rough coating of copper and has small amounts of water vapor in them. They're heat conduction rods."

"What?" Mr. Mercury looked inquisitively at Joseph. "What are you talking about?"

"We make them at the shop," Joseph continued. "They're copper tubes with rough, hollow interiors, filled with small amounts of water. They're incredibly good at conducting heat from one end of the rod to the other. It's very easy to accidentally burn yourself with one by holding one end to a candle flame."

Lauren thought for a moment. "Why would a living creature have heat conduction rods in its egg shell?"

"Heat management is a huge problem for space travel," Jordin said. "It's very easy to overheat. Since there's no atmosphere in space, there's nothing to carry the heat away. Radiative heat loss is very inefficient on its own."

"I'm not sure I understand." Mr. Mercury tried to stroke his chin, but his gloves and helmet got in the way.

"Here, in an atmosphere, we often use fans to cool things down. Think about it. We're basically tossing air molecules at heated objects. When the air molecules strike the object, some of the excess heat is transferred to that molecule which is then carried away. Then that molecule strikes and transfers it to others and so on. It's all just spreading the heat out so it's not concentrated. As a result, the object cools down. In space, that can't happen."

"He's right," Lauren interjected as she continued to study the fragment. "Heat will naturally dissipate as it emits infrared light, but the process is slow on its own without a medium to directly transfer the energy to."

"I thought space was freezing cold," Mercury said in disbelief.

Jordin picked up on Lauren's annoyance and spoke before she could, "It is. But if nothing blocks the radiation of the sun, all of that radiation will strike and build up on whatever it hits. And nothing is there to immediately take it away. Think of it this way. The same thing happens to Earth. We just have an atmosphere that can carry heat around. It's a lot hotter during the day when we're facing the sun than it is at night when we're facing away."

Mercury shrugged. "Makes sense, I guess."

"How hard is the shell?" Jordin asked.

"Way harder than any chicken egg," Lauren grunted.

"What's it made of?"

Joseph shuffled through papers. "Silica, carbon, and copper. And some other unknown organic compounds."

"And it's bigger than most houses, with a screw-like exterior," Mr. Mercury interjected. "Plus, we just determined it was completely sealed off, as far as we could tell."

"Exactly." Jordin smiled. "Just think about it. It even has a way to transfer heat around. If ever there was an egg for space, this would be it."

"But...," Joseph considered for a moment, "it's just transferring heat around, not dissipating it. Meaning it could potentially make things even worse. If one part of it heats up excessively, the whole thing or whatever's inside may cook even if it's out of the direct heat."

"True," Jordin said, pausing to think for a moment. "I can't explain it yet. The more we learn, the stranger this becomes."

"The third layer appears to be some sort of a cushion or an insulator," Lauren said. "Maybe that helps regulate internal temperatures too?"

"I guess we just need to keep studying it," Joseph said resolutely.

Jordin noticed something in the stack of papers on the table - a corner of a picture poked out. He instinctively pulled the image out of the stack. A drawing of the whole egg, with a radar map of the egg in the bottom left corner, greeted him. "All of this is underground," he muttered to himself as he studied the screw-like helical protrusions. A line on the page indicated ground level, meaning that approximately seventy percent of the entire egg was underground.

"What's this?" Jordin set the picture on the table and pointed to a rod-like protrusion from the egg that jutted out above the helical wrapping but just below the surface of the ground. The rod appeared to end in rough jagged splinters as if it had been shattered.

"I don't know." Joseph shrugged. "Maybe it was attached to something at one point."

"But what?" Jordin scratched his head.

"Beats me." Joseph raised his hands in confusion.

"There's only one way to find out." Mr. Mercury snatched the picture off the table and held it up to compare to the egg itself. "We'll crack your secrets yet."

CHAPTER

13

"How long are we going to be here today?" Joseph leaned over and whispered to Jordin.

"I don't know." Jordin noticed the sun was no longer shining through the tent.

"Wherever we're staying, do you think they have better food than the bland lunch they provided?"

Jordin shrugged. "I'm just hoping for a clean bathroom."

Before Joseph could respond, Colonel Dubinin marched into the tent. "Have you learned anything?" he asked curtly.

"We're studying what we can," Jordin replied. "Any data that you have could help us greatly."

"I'm not here to work for you. You're here to give us data."

"We've learned that this thing has 'heat conduction rods' in its shell," Lauren spoke up. "It looks like heat, or the movement of heat, is important to it."

Dubinin looked down at the table. "Are these your notes?" He pointed to a pile of papers with handwritten scribbles and figures.

"Yes, we've been documenting our fin...," Lauren started to say before being interrupted by Dubinin instructing a few soldiers in Russian to hastily collect the papers.

"Thank you," the colonel curtly replied. "We'll go over your findings. As you are not part of our military, it is now time for you to leave the base for the evening. We will escort you to a nearby hotel then bring you back at oh seven hundred sharp tomorrow morning."

"Wait a minute!" Mr. Mercury objected. "That thing is still out there. You need everyone working on this as much as possible."

Dubinin gestured to a team of scientists now approaching. "They will replace you until you return."

"Now look here," Mercury pointed at Dubinin. "That thing killed one of my employees. I'm not going to rest until it's dealt with. I don't care if you have to send me after it myself."

"And hundreds of our people have been killed by it," Dubinin said flatly. "We aren't resting. I assure you, everything you've done will be built upon while you are away. You may build upon what you find when you return. You're not useful to us without proper sleep. As such, you are required to go to a designated hotel and rest."

Mr. Mercury shook his head and sighed in frustration, but said no more.

"Colonel," Jordin said, "how are your efforts to 'slow' the beast going?"

Dubinin stared blankly at Jordin for a few seconds. "When

you return, I expect your full attention to your studies."

"I understand that you're reluctant to discuss military objectives with us. However, we both saw it on the map. It turned toward India. The Caspian Sea was in its path. We know how it feels about water. That means it's about to cross the border into either Kazakhstan or Azerbaijan. There are a lot of Middle Eastern countries that are about to be affected either way. What happens here is going to affect far more than just Russia soon."

Dubinin glowered at Jordin but said nothing.

"What I mean is," Jordin continued, "you can't keep everything a secret much longer. I'm happy to work with you to find a solution. However, if there's any data that you can give us to assist in our efforts, the better off we'll all be."

Dubinin shifted and looked sidelong at Jordin.

"Have you found anything that can affect this creature?" Jordin persisted.

"The creature continues to grow. We've fire bombed it and struck it with everything we have, short of..." the colonel stopped mid-sentence and straightened his posture. "It's not even slowing down."

"Is it made of silica, carbon, and copper too?" Lauren asked.

"You saw our best video of the creature itself. The storm surrounding it makes it nearly impossible to see, let alone study. The most we can tell you is that it's a bipedal creature with a long-clubbed tail that it slams on the ground behind it." He nodded toward the entrance. "I suggest you all come with me to the waiting escort. We will translate your notes and be sure to distribute it to relevant parties. To answer your prior question, it's currently heading south along the Caspian Sea border. Appropriate nations have been alerted."

Colonel Dubinin led Jordin and his team out of the tent. After removing their hazmat suits, they were directed to a waiting vehicle.

The hotel appeared to be completely taken over by the military as armed guards screened everyone who arrived. The soldiers returned the personal phones of each P.M.L. members along with a room key.

Jordin sat on the edge of his bed, head in hands. A news-caster on the television in his room spoke in Russian as scenes of destruction unfolded behind her. Towns, cities, roads, and myriad buildings looked as though a giant bull-dozer had run right through them.

In the excitement of everything that had happened, he hadn't really had time to stop and think about everything that was going on. Part of him couldn't believe it. This was an incredibly historic moment. Alien life had both been discovered and had visited Earth. He had been a part of the team that had first noticed it and had been tracking it.

Another part of him wished it hadn't happened. This thing was wreaking havoc wherever it went. Every hour that went by, more people died. Could this thing be stopped? What was it trying to do? Does it even know what it's doing? He wished he had the answers, but he had nothing.

His phone rang. He idly picked it up and glanced at the number onscreen. "Oh, Dhar," he said. He didn't know what to tell Dhar since he wasn't supposed to talk to anyone about what was going on. Then again, Dhar needed to know what was going on in the company.

"Hello?" he answered.

"I hear you've had some excitement over there," Dhar said.

"You can say that again," Jordin grunted.

"How have you been holding up?"

"I'm not sure. It's all too much. I still can't believe it. I wish I could say more, but I can't."

"You can tell me in person tomorrow," Dhar said bluntly.

Jordin sat up straight. "What?"

"Some of us from this office, including me, volunteered to be a part of the Indian investigation team. Since our company has been at the forefront of this, it wasn't hard to convince officials."

"Oh...that's good. We won't have to play phone censor."

"Russian officials may not let you tell me much over the phone, but I'll be there to study the egg in person tomorrow. Then they won't have much of a choice but to tell me."

"Good point."

"We're getting ready to board the plane now. I thought

I'd give you a call to let you know as you are the team leader on this project."

"Oh...I...uh...Lauren is the biologist and I put her in control of the egg studies."

"Then I'll listen to what she has to say, Boss," Dhar chuckled. "We'll be there bright and early. See you tomorrow."

"See you tomorrow."

Jordin put the phone down. "I guess random phone calls are part of the job." He laughed then paused. "Random phone calls..." He picked his phone back up and scrolled through his recent calls. He stared at a mysterious number for a few moments before hitting the call button.

"Hello, my friend," the familiar yet mysterious Japanese voice said after a few rings. "I had lost hope that you would contact us."

"Listen," Jordin whispered, "I don't know who you are or what you want. I'm not sure that I should even trust you with anything. But...you were right...about everything."

"That is unfortunate," the voice said, disappointed. "We were hoping you could have put us at ease."

"Is there anything you know about this...storm...that you could tell me now? Any information would help."

"As you are an eye-witness, you know more than we do. All external data that you have, we have. We uncovered what had been hidden in the broadcasts and have been trying to warn people. If you give us any new information, we may be of assistance."

Jordin realized he wasn't completely sure whether the Russian authorities were listening right now. He cupped his hands around the phone. "Unfortunately, I'm under obligation not to discuss many of the details. However, I can discuss what's publicly available."

"Discussion of what is known often leads to the discovery of the unknown."

"It's growing, heading south, and hates water. Or at least it was heading south. A new...storm is forming above India. The original 'storm' is now heading for it. However, it's still heading south every chance that it gets."

"It travels from the frigid north to the warm Equator. Would it stop there or go to the frozen south? The Caspian Sea is now an obstacle for it to cross. It seeks to avoid the waters."

"Hmmmmm," Jordin pondered.

"Prior to your travels, you released data that showed heat moving toward the storm, and yet the storm itself is frigid."

Jordin squinted. "Yes...," he said with some effort to admit, "it started north, went straight south..."

"What have the Russians done to stop it? And what have those methods gained?"

"They tried to burn it...When they firebomb...it avoids water...heat conduction rods...," Jordin murmured. "HEAT!" he exclaimed, then rapidly looked around before lowering his voice to a whisper again. "It wants heat...and every attack gives it...All this time we thought it was the storm...the storm is a byproduct. It's trying to get out of..." he trailed off, realizing he probably shouldn't be saying what he was saying.

"I believe I understand." The voice sounded optimistic. "You needn't worry. We...how do you say it...play on the same team. What you have given us is invaluable."

"I need to go."

"We will be in touch."

The line clicked and went silent. Jordin hopped up and walked out the door and knocked on the neighboring room.

The door opened and Lauren stared at him, bleary eyed.

"Is there a way for a creature to sustain off of heat?" Jordin asked as he excitedly waved his hands.

Lauren gave him a look that was a cross between "are you serious" and "you woke me up for this?"

"I mean...like plants. They use photosynthesis to 'eat' sunlight and sustain themselves," Jordin tried to explain. "Could something eat heat energy and sustain?"

Lauren was unimpressed. "Plants need more than just sunlight. They just 'eat' sunlight to give them the energy to help break down the nutrients they gain from water and the soil they're in. They don't just sit there eating sunlight by itself."

"Those trenches and craters in the ground...," he muttered. "Silica, carbon, and copper...Could a creature do the same thing, but with heat?" he asked earnestly.

Lauren averted her eyes to think. "I suppose it's theoretically possible. It's all about metabolism and energy usage." She looked back at Jordin and waved her hands. "Why not use heat?"

"Would a creature like that have heat conduction rods inside it to take the heat where it needs to go?"

"You know what, sure. I'll say yes." She blinked at him, continuing to look unimpressed.

"Thank you...uh...goodnight." He smiled and waved. "I need to tell Dubinin." He turned and marched down the hall.

"Okay..." Lauren closed the door.

Jordin jogged down the stairs to the main lobby. A few Russian soldiers stood and held their arms out to stop him as he approached. "I need to talk to Colonel Dubinin." He made a telephone gesture with his hand to his head.

The soldiers said something in Russian and held him back.

"Dubinin...call Dubinin," he said again.

One of the soldiers seemed to understand and turned to shout something at the receptionist. The poor girl looked a little frazzled as she picked the receiver off a phone on the wall and began dialing. After a few moments of silence, she said a few words and then held the phone out.

The soldiers escorted Jordin to the desk where he grabbed the phone and nodded to the receptionist. "Hello?"

"You had better tell me something good," Dubinin's curt voice greeted him.

"I'm going to say something that may sound crazy," Jordin said. "But hear me out."

"Crazy is the new normal around here. I'm listening...for now."

"This thing landed pretty far north. It's heading south, straight south."

"I hope you didn't call me just to tell me that."

"I'm laying out my case. Trust me, there's a point."

"Okay. Don't take too long," Dubinin said, agitated.

"The thing didn't hatch until you tried to kill it with fire. It has heat conduction rods in the shell. It avoids water. All the data points that we observed showed heat moving into the area, yet the storm itself was cold. Every time you attack it, it doesn't slow down. If anything, it speeds up and grows."

"Thus far, all known."

"Don't you see? It's heat that it wants!" Jordin waved his free hand excitedly. He glanced at the receptionist and the soldiers who were staring at him as if he had three heads. He smiled and nodded at them as he placed his hand back at his side.

Dubinin was silent for a few moments. "Explain."

"I don't really understand it myself. But it headed straight for warmer climates. Heat is being drawn in, yet vanishing. Fire hatched it. I suspect the creature itself has a few heat conduction rods inside. Think of it like photosynthesis, only heat-o-synthesis or...whatever you'd call it. All those craters and trenches...it's eating the minerals and...'metabolizing' them with heat."

"You're suggesting that this creature uses thermosynthesis to sustain itself?"

"Think about it...about everything it has done. Every attack you make against the creature just gives it what it wants."

"And how do you explain the storm and the frigid temperatures it generates. If it likes heat so much, why is it freezing everything?"

"I don't know." Jordin scratched his head. "Maybe the storm is just a byproduct. It may be trying to get out of the storm, or find a place where the storm won't be so bad."

"If what you say is true...the storm itself could kill it..."

"If you slow it down...Stop it from moving."

"You may be right, American," Dubinin said. "But it's no longer in our control. The storm has crossed the border into Azerbaijan. It is expected to enter Iran by morning. Joint efforts to stop it have failed. If projections are correct, it will reach its new friend on the southern tip of India within five days. If you're right, we have until then to find a way to exterminate it. No one wants two of these things."

"Dry ice...," Jordin mused. "It's an ingredient in some cloud seeds. People use it to force clouds to precipitate and release built up moisture in the air. Well...it's not the only thing you can use...We can deprive the storm of moisture and potentially reduce the heat flow to it as well."

"Are you recommending this as your professional opinion based off of the information that you have gathered? Or is this a wild theory?"

"What we've been doing against this thing hasn't worked. I didn't originally believe that cloud seeding would do anything. However, I'm now recommending cloud seeding as my professional opinion."

"And if you're wrong?"

"It could make it worse. Yet, firebombs are already doing that."

Dubinin was silent for a few moments. "Alright. I'll pass this information along. However, as it is no longer within our borders, I no longer have direct influence over counter operations. We will discuss this further in the morning. The India team will be arriving. We may have a visit from Middle Eastern dignitaries as well. I hope you're prepared. You'll have to convince more than just me now."

"I'll do my best."

"I hope so."

"Out of curiosity. What happens if we don't stop these creatures within the five days?"

"If we fail here, the world will see a sight it hasn't seen

since the second world war."

A pit grew in Jordin's stomach. He had a feeling he knew exactly what Dubinin was saying. "I won't let that happen."

CHAPTER

14

The next morning, Jordin and his team were hurriedly escorted out of the hotel and driven back to the egg site. On arrival, their phones were confiscated again. They were immediately whisked into a nearby building where several chairs had been set up facing the front of the room.

Colonel Dubinin entered after the P.M.L. team took their seats. "I hope you're ready to present your theory," he said as he walked up to Jordin and handed him a stack of papers.

"Oh?" Jordin was taken aback as he stood and accepted the papers. "I didn't know I was presenting today." The papers crinkled as his fingers fidgeted.

"I know," Dubinin nodded. "I recorded our conversation last night and printed out the transcript." He motioned to the stack of papers. "If you want something to happen, you'll have to sell everyone on it." He turned to look out the door. "They're coming. Prepare yourself." He motioned Jordin toward a podium at the front of the room.

Jordin gulped and nervously stood behind the podium, setting down the now wrinkled papers. He watched the delegation of a dozen smartly dressed men from India file into the room, hiding his clasped hands behind the podium as best as he could.

A familiar face caught his attention. He had seen several photographs of Dr. Dhar before. Dhar was a clean-shaven man in his late forties and wore a smart business suit. His short black hair was neatly combed. Dhar nodded at Jordin and gave him a reassuring smile.

Jordin nodded back.

Murmurs filled the room as delegates exchanged concerned and confused looks. A few moments later, the delegates from the Middle East entered.

When everyone was seated, Dubinin nodded to the soldier at the entrance who closed the door. The colonel then walked to the front of the room and stood beside Jordin. "As you all know," he said. "A grave threat has descended upon us all. Dr. Davidson here has headed a team that has been studying these events from the beginning. He is here today to present his findings and recommendations. After which, you will all be escorted into the egg chamber to study the specimen yourself." He turned to Jordin. "You may proceed, doctor." He moved to stand to the side.

"Thank you." Jordin cleared his throat. "My team and I have been studying the storm created by this creature from the start. We've also witnessed what it can do firsthand. As of yesterday, we've also been studying the egg." He looked nervously at his colleagues. He hadn't had time to run anything past them.

"We believe we have seen a pattern," Jordin said as he shuffled through the papers, relieved at finding the exact picture he wanted. He held the picture aloft. "I apologize if you are unable to see this properly now. I will hand this around the room." He leaned forward and handed it to the nearest person who happened to be a Middle Eastern dignitary.

The dignitary snatched the photo and stared intently at it.

"This is a photo of a cross section of the egg. The central layer of the egg has some odd hollow structures. We believe that they are heat conduction rods as they were filled with water vapor and lined with copper. The outer layer of the egg is bumpy, yet sealed off. The inner layer has a sponge-like consistency."

The dignitary grunted as he passed the paper to the next person.

"We also know," Jordin continued, "that this creature started in the north and headed straight south. On its way, it avoided contact with water. Thus far, all attempts to stop it have failed. It's my belief..." He gulped and looked at Lauren. He had no idea if she remembered their discussion last night or what she thought about it all. However, he knew that he had to present all of the data and theories he had. "It's my belief that this creature may thrive off of thermosynthesis."

The crowd murmured, bewildered by this claim. Lauren winced at the room's reaction.

Jordin took a deep breath and continued on, the palms of his hands rubbing together vigorously. "Think of it as photosynthesis but with heat rather than sunlight. I understand that this may be hard to believe, but consider the facts. It's heading south every chance it gets. Heat is moving in toward it, but then dissipates almost immediately upon reaching it. Every attempt to stop it involves explosions, fire, and well...a lot of heat. Rather than slowing down, it's speeding up. Not to mention, it hates water. Combine all of that with the heat conduction rods in the shell, and...well..."

"How do we know that's what this all means? It could all just be a coincidence," one of the Middle Eastern dignitaries asked.

Jordin sighed. "I don't really know anything. This is all new to me. All I can tell you is what the data suggests."

"This...thing is destroying my nation as we speak," the same dignitary said, standing and gesturing furiously with his arms. "And you want me to trust your guess?"

Several other dignitaries voiced agreement.

"I understand your...," Jordin began but was cut off.

"We came here for answers, not conjecture." Several other dignitaries were now standing and arguing among themselves.

Jordin tried to calm things down, but few were paying attention to him. He barely noticed that Zhukov had entered the room and whispered something to Dubinin. Dubinin then nodded and joined Jordin at the podium.

"Enough!" the colonel shouted.

The noise in the room gradually died down as people directed their attention to Dubinin.

"If his theory is so crazy," Dubinin smiled confidently, "then why did it work?"

The crowd murmured.

"Dr. Davidson and I had a conversation last night. He recommended using cloud seed. While you were arguing over the validity of his theories, we were testing them. The creature has slowed. It is still moving, but we have bought ourselves time to formulate a better plan." He nodded to Jordin. "Continue, doctor."

"Thank you, colonel," Jordin said, relieved as he turned his gaze to his team. "If we can find a way to prevent heat from getting to the creature, or take heat away, we may be able to stop it. If we can't stop it yet, we may be able to slow it down to give us time."

"We still don't know if this is a coincidence or not," the angry dignitary interjected.

"True. We don't. At least, not right now," Jordin said. "But what else has even slowed the creature? You don't have to take my word for it. You are here to study the egg yourself. I encourage all of you to look at the facts."

"How much time has this new cloud seed method given us?" the dignitary asked.

"It was going to reach its friend within four and a half days," Dubinin said. "By our estimates, if we can keep it at this speed, it will now be there within six and a half days."

"And what can we do until then?"

"I suggest that you all begin studying the egg immediately. All known data will be provided to each of your teams." He nodded to Zhukov then turned back to the group. "You will now be escorted into the egg chamber."

The dignitaries spoke in hushed whispers as they were escorted out the door.

"Thank you," Jordin said to Dubinin, who responded by staring him dead in the eye.

"Make no mistake, American. If we find that your theory is false, and this monster has slowed for other reasons; I will be the first to inform everyone. I don't fully believe you myself. However, I believe in results. Thus far, what you have suggested has given us the most promise. I pray you are right. When you and your team are ready, you will be escorted to the chamber." He turned and marched off.

"How did you do that?" Mr. Mercury asked in amazement. "You didn't tell me you knew."

"I must apologize," Jordin grimaced. "I had a thought last night and I got overly excited. I called the colonel to tell him. I didn't think to tell anyone else."

Lauren gave him a wry smile as she approached. "That didn't stop you from asking me strange questions. I thought you had gone insane. Looks like I'm the crazy one. Thermosynthesis...hmmm...who would've guessed?"

"Sorry about that. I hope I didn't wake you last night. I just needed your expertise in biology."

Lauren raised her left eyebrow. "I'm glad it worked out."

"Looks like I owe you something," Joseph chuckled. "Every time I think you've gone nuts, you turn out to be right. When we get back home, I'll take you out for a few drinks, on me."

"Thanks," Jordin said.

"A good speech, if a little unpracticed," Dhar said as he approached.

Mr. Mercury turned around. "Oh, I apologize, I should introduce you. Everyone, this is my business partner, Dr. Dhar."

Dhar made the rounds shaking everyone's hand and exchanging pleasantries.

"I'm glad you liked my speech," Jordin grinned. "I didn't have much time to prepare. I'm happy to finally meet you in person."

"I wish we could've met under better circumstances."

"Me too."

Dhar looked at his team assembled here, almost in disbelief. "I must say, this has been one of the most disruptive projects our business has ever undertaken."

"I apologize," Jordin furrowed his brow.

"No need," Dhar waved his hand dismissively. "Whatever else it's been, it certainly hasn't been boring." He motioned to the door. "We should study the egg. There are a lot of people in the world depending on all of us to provide answers."

"Yes...of course." Mr. Mercury exuberantly marched toward the door.

The soldiers escorted the P.M.L. team to the entrance of the tent where several hazmat suits awaited. The dignitaries and Indian team were already in the process of suiting up, mumbling among themselves.

Upon entering the tent and witnessing the egg, several dignitaries gasped. They all had heard about the egg and how large it was, but few were prepared to actually see it firsthand.

"To think something like this could actually exist...," Dhar said in awe.

"If I hadn't seen it myself, I'd say it was impossible for any living creature to be this large," Lauren said.

"How, on Earth, could something get so large?" Joseph joked as he walked to the tables.

"Earth had nothing to do with it," Mr. Mercury said, completely missing the joke.

Joseph stifled his laugh.

"What's our goal for the day, boss?" Lauren asked Jordin.

"Is there a way to test to see how it reacts to cold versus heat?"

"Get a blowtorch and some liquid nitrogen," Joseph said sarcastically.

"Actually," Lauren replied, "might as well."

"Excuse me!" Mr. Mercury flagged Zhukov down. "We need a blowtorch and some liquid nitrogen."

"I was half kidding...," Joseph muttered.

Zhukov nodded and said something in Russian to a few nearby soldiers.

Jordin and his team settled into their studies. They reviewed the notes from the night shift team as the India team worked at a nearby table. Dhar floated between the two stations, passing data along and trying his best to bring the Indian team up to speed. The Middle Eastern dignitaries wandered among the tables asking various questions and leering in wonder at the giant egg in the middle of the space.

A few soldiers walked up to the P.M.L. table and handed Jordin a blowtorch and wheeled in a canister of liquid nitrogen. Jordin thanked them as they walked away.

"Have you seen the inside of that egg?" Dhar asked Jordin.

Jordin blinked and shook his head. "Not yet. We were too focused on studying this fragment. I didn't even think about it. Seems obvious now."

Dhar chuckled and pointed to a nearby series of metal steps that led to a platform overlooking the egg. A few of the dignitaries were standing on the platform gazing down and gasping.

"We can study this," Lauren said as she peered at the sample. "Dr. Davidson, if you would like to observe the inside of the egg and report what you see, that'd be helpful. This photograph of it," she said waving a picture around, "can only tell me so much."

"Yes, ma'am," Jordin said as he and Dr. Dhar ascended the steps and walked onto the platform.

A few dignitaries were conversing as he and Dhar joined them at the edge. Jordin grabbed the railing and stared down into the cavernous abyss. The Russians had placed a light above the egg that shone directly down into the opening. The jagged shell ringed the hole like serrated teeth giving way to a gaping maw.

Jordin shook his head. "To think," he said, "that's 80 meters deep and it's even wider just under the surface too. This whole area is resting on top of it."

"I hear the Russians had to level this off and do some complicated engineering to keep this area around the egg stable," Dhar added.

"That thing was huge before it hatched. Now it's growing. I hate to think how big it is now, or how big it will be."

"I suppose this means we're no longer at the top of the food chain."

"I guess so." Jordin gripped the railing and gaped down, beginning to feel a bit queasy. Every shift and shake from people walking by caused his stomach to flutter. The realization that they were all over a large pit that could potentially give way at any moment started to make him sick. He tapped his fingers against the railing.

"Are you alright?" Dhar asked.

"The combination of height and motion gets me every time. I'll be fine," Jordin said. "I'm here to do a job. Is there anything in there that stands out?"

"Without going inside, I'd say it's hard to make a determination. Although," he said, pointing down the pit to where the overhead light was dimly lighting up the bottom, "it may just be me, but I expected the entire inside to have that sponge layer. Do you see that patch where it looks like it's missing? There's a mound there and some protrusions."

Jordin squinted. "I think so."

"What are you seeing?" a dignitary leaned in to ask.

Dhar repeated his observation, after which the dignitary loudly requested a pair of binoculars from a nearby guard.

The guard obeyed and spoke into a handheld radio. Before long, another guard ascended the steps carrying two pairs of binoculars. The dignitary took the binoculars and offered one to Dhar who accepted it and thanked him.

"Here, take a look." Dhar handed the binoculars to Jordin.

Jordin peered through them. It was somewhat awkward and difficult to use the binoculars with the hazmat suit goggles, but he managed, observing an odd structure at the bottom of the egg. "You know what that looks like?" he asked after a few moments. He lowered the binoculars and returned them to Dhar.

Dhar put the binoculars back to his eyes. "What do you think it is?" he asked.

"It looks like a whole bunch of pipes came together to form a conical pyramid structure. They've since been broken or separated. I think that's where all the heat conduction rods in the shell lead to."

"And what does that mean?" Dhar asked while studying the structure himself.

"If the creature was attached to that while in the egg, all temperature changes would be very quickly transmitted to the creature. If the creature changed its temperature, that would also be quickly transmitted through the egg." Jordin adjusted his stance as he gripped the railing and tried not to look down.

"You may have something with your heat theory. However, there's something that doesn't make sense to me. I hope you can forgive my ignorance and inform me better."

"I'll do my best."

"If temperature changes are quickly conducted, and it wants heat...then wouldn't the creature have frozen and died in space?" Dhar briefly lowered the binoculars to look at Jordin quizzically.

"A question I've been wondering myself." Jordin furrowed his brow. "Maybe it was in hibernation and the heat of our atmosphere woke it up. The other thing to consider is that in space, while in direct sunlight at these distances, the side that faces the sun becomes incredibly warm. There isn't anything between you and the sun to block its energy. The side facing away can become incredibly cold. However, it's also very challenging to dissipate heat in space without an atmosphere to take heat away. That means, any heat gained or generated could stick around for long periods of time or build up immensely. We also don't know how this thing traveled and where it came from. If it was constantly rotating while traveling it may have kept any side from keeping all of the heat. And the conduction rods could've kept the whole thing warm no matter where it got its heat from."

"It's all very fascinating." Dhar nodded and turned back to observe the egg through the binoculars again.

"That's all just a guess on my part. I've no way of knowing how much of what I just said is true."

Dhar lowered the binoculars and looked at Jordin again. "You've been right about a lot of things so far."

"Not everything." Jordin shook his head mournfully.

Dhar mulled over his response for a moment. "You can't blame yourself for everything that goes wrong then ignore everything that goes right. There's no way either of us could have expected alien monsters. You've been correct enough times to make me pay attention."

"All I want to do is find a way to stop this thing. We should probably tell the others what we found."

"Indeed." Dhar nodded. "If we are to defeat this thing before my nephew's wedding, we should inform the others as soon as possible."

"Wait," Jordin said. "Your nephew is getting married? Congratulations."

"He is. The wedding is in three weeks, assuming my country survives the beast's attack."

"We'd better hurry up then. We don't want you to miss the wedding."

Dhar smiled and nodded as both he and Jordin descended the steps. "I will inform the India team. I may be part of P.M.L. but I am here under obligations from my government."

"Fair enough." Jordin nodded and walked to his table. "Looks like all of the heat conduction rods lead to a single point at the base of the shell. We think that the creature inside may have been attached directly to the rods themselves."

Lauren looked up from her microscope. "Interesting."

"Hey," Joseph motioned to Jordin, "check this out." He held up a piece of the shell.

The shell looked as though it had been dried and cracked. Pieces of it were flaking off like ash as scale pattern scars raced across its surface.

"What happened to it?" Jordin asked in confusion.

"I'll show you," Lauren said as she picked up a fresh shell fragment.

"You need to see this," Mr. Mercury said emphatically.

Lauren grabbed the hose that extended from the top of the liquid nitrogen tank and carefully dripped nitrogen onto the shell. The nitrogen boiled and hissed as it skidded across the surface of the shell and turned into a fog that quickly dissipated.

"The nitrogen rolls off the surface of the shell and doesn't do much, but..." Lauren said, holding the shell fragment on its side, exposing the hollowed tubes, "when you put nitrogen inside..." She dripped a few drops of nitrogen into one of the hollow tubes, then set the fragment down.

Jordin watched as the shell morphed before his eyes, cracking and turning to ash in an ever-spreading pattern. "Interesting...," he said in amazement.

"That's not all." Lauren grabbed the blowtorch and clicked it on. She placed the flame directly to the shell fragment.

Jordin blinked as he saw the shell return to its normal-looking self. "What the?"

"Cold kills, heat heals. Must be something to do with those unknown organic compounds," Joseph said. "You might just be sane yet. Or we're all going insane."

"That means...," Jordin Contemplated, "all the heat rods lead into the shell. This creature may have similar structures. If we can get liquid nitrogen inside..."

"You want us to make it drink liquid nitrogen?" Joseph said.

"We need to get to that other egg," Jordin said. "If this is correct. We could stop the second creature before it hatches."

"How would we get there in time? Most everything is shut down now," Lauren said. "I'm not so sure the Russians would just let us leave now either."

"My private plane is still at the airport where we landed it when we came here," Mr. Mercury said. He looked around the room making mental calculations. "I could fly everyone here," he said gesturing across their workstation and the India workstation, "over to India."

"Okay..." Lauren paused for a few moments. "That still leaves the part where I'm not sure we could just leave yet. Our hosts were very insistent that no one left until this was done."

"Leave that to me," Dhar said. "As this involves my national government now, I'm sure we can apply some influence on what we do." He looked to Jordin. "What exactly do you plan on doing?"

CHAPTER

15

Jordin's eyes fixed upon the floor of the plane, quietly tapping his fingers together. His team, the Middle Eastern dignitaries, the Indian team, a few Russian scientists, and Lieutenant Zhukov all sat on the cushioned seats of Mr. Mercury's private jet. Colonel Dubinin had stayed behind and sent Zhukov in his stead.

Shortly after their new discovery, Mr. Mercury and Dr. Dhar had arranged for Mercury's private jet to pick everyone up at the nearby airport. The Russians had fueled the aircraft and helped place supplies onboard. With any luck, they would arrive at an Indian airport near the new egg in a few hours.

Some of the dignitaries gasped and pointed out of their windows. Jordin glanced up to see everyone move to the other side of the plane to gawk. He gulped and joined them. Sure enough, the storm clouds of the beast raged in the distance. Even from far away, they were intimidating.

Mr. Mercury had intentionally chosen a flight path to allow for a view of the storm. In his words it, "would help give everyone a sense of urgency."

Strange tree-like plasma emissions flashed above the clouds as lightning struck below.

"I hope you're all looking out of the right side of the plane," Mr. Mercury's voice popped with static over the intercom from the cockpit where he sat as copilot. "We're far enough away to not be badly affected by the electromagnetic interference it's giving off. But I'm sure you can tell it's causing a little static on the line here. This is only expected to get bigger and worse. Take a good look at your enemy."

A nearby Middle Eastern dignitary grunted, drawing Jordin's attention.

"To face a storm," the dignitary said, "we must be mad."

"We'll do what we can," Jordin replied, trying his best to sound confident.

"What can man do against his judgment?" The dignitary stared at him intently.

"I guess we'll find out." Jordin nodded grimly.

The dignitary snickered. "I never thought I'd be standing side-by-side with an American when the end came."

"This may not be the end. There's still a chance."

"I hope you're right," he said, smiling. "At least we may face our judgment with honor."

"I'll do what it takes." Jordin motioned around the plane. "We all will."

"A lot of brave people have sacrificed their lives to stop this thing and have failed," Lieutenant Zhukov walked up. "What makes you think you'll be any different?"

Jordin shook his head. "I don't know if anything will change, or if I can do anything to stop this thing. I'm not even sure if anything I've said is correct or just a coincidence."

Zhukov slightly tilted his head to the side and nodded.

"Maybe there isn't a way to stop it," the dignitary said while peering out the window.

"But that won't stop me," Jordin said adamantly. "You won't know if something works until you try it."

"But why you? You're no soldier." Zhukov raised an eyebrow at Jordin. "You study space and planets. The most useful skill you have here is your knowledge of clouds. Monsters aren't your specialty. Why not just go home and let us deal with it? What makes you think you can do anything?"

"Because I'm here." Jordin shrugged. "I didn't get to where I am today by running away from every challenge. My conscience wouldn't let me sleep at night if I abandoned everyone to this thing. Besides, this thing may come for me eventually if it isn't stopped here and now. I'd rather fight it now than later. Maybe I can't do anything. But I'd rather get my teeth knocked out facing the bully than running from it."

Zhukov couldn't help but laugh. "Not going down without a fight. I can respect that."

Everyone grew silent as they watched the storm fade into the distance. The plane veered toward its destination, leaving the storm, and its horrific secret behind.

Jordin knew that this wouldn't be the last time they saw the storm. They were headed toward the new egg and whatever terrifying secret it held. He silently wandered back to his seat and pulled a folder out of the pouch and onto the seat in front of him. He opened the folder and leafed through the pages, his eyes fixating on a new chart handed to him shortly before boarding.

Another minor storm was already beginning to form over the new egg. "This looks similar to what we saw with the first egg," Jordin muttered. "This time, we know what it is, and we only have a few days before both of these storms combine." He couldn't help but feel like a soldier, preparing to make a final stand.

Everyone else gradually returned to their seats and Mr. Mercury wheeled out a food cart.

Jordin closed the folder and placed it back into the pouch. "Isn't this your plane?" he asked Mr. Mercury as the food cart approached.

"Yes, it is," Mr. Mercury nodded.

"Don't you have staff for this stuff?"

"I sent them home. It's just me and my pilot. He's better suited to fly, so I'm your steward today," he said with a grin and a sandwich offer.

"Okay...," Jordin said, accepting it.

Mr. Mercury moved on, handing out various snacks and food items.

Joseph sat next to Jordin. "Dr. Davidson."

"Hello, Dr. Wilber. What can I do for you?"

"I believe I owe you an apology."

"For?"

"I didn't believe you for the longest time. I even thought you'd cracked and gone crazy."

"In fairness, this whole situation is crazy."

"You can say that again." Joseph checked to ensure no one was listening. "I overheard your conversation with the Lieutenant and the dignitary. Between you and me, I agree with you. Now's our best chance to stop this thing. As crazy as what you've been saying sounds, you've been correct more often than not. When we get there, I'll happily do my part. Who knows? Maybe we'll get lucky and down this thing. If not...," he glanced back toward the window overlooking the distant storm, "it's been a pleasure working with you."

"Likewise." Jordin nodded.

Once Mr. Mercury finished handing out food, he rolled the cart back to the front of the plane. "In case you need more motivation," he said as he turned the televisions on.

An American news broadcast played onscreen. "The storm continues to rage on," the news anchor stated as scenes of devastation played behind her. "Cities, towns, villages, and roadways have been completely destroyed." The screen showed a one and a half kilometer wide trail of melting snow. Buildings and roadways in the path had been completely flattened. "The western shores of the Caspian Sea have faced the worst of it yet. The storm is continuing to grow and is predicted to get worse. Iranian leaders are beginning to mobilize evacuation efforts in the path of the storm as it is predicted to head directly to southern India to join with a new storm."

"Thousands are gathering to mourn the loss of friends and family. This storm has left many of them homeless," the anchor said over scenes of people kneeling before walls of pictures of missing people. "The world is demanding answers. One company seeks to deliver those answers."

A video of people boarding Mr. Mercury's plane flashed across the screen. "We were able to grab an interview with part owner and CEO of P.M.L. as he was boarding his plane in Russia to head to India. Here is that clip now."

Then Mr. Mercury appeared, facing the camera next to another news anchor, his plane silhouetted in the background.

"Mr. Mercury," the interviewer began, "the world wants to know what's going on. Can you tell us?"

Mr. Mercury's smug expression didn't exactly hide his love for the limelight.

Joseph quietly chuckled and whispered to Jordin, "He really loves being on camera."

"We here at P.M.L. are dedicated to studying it and providing as much data as we can," Mercury said. "At this time we can't give anything definitive. However, rest assured, we won't stop until either the storm dies down or it kills us."

"Is there anything you can tell us about it?" the interviewer asked.

"We believe that the storm is heading directly toward the southern point of India where the new storm is forming."

"What will happen when the two join?"

"At this time, we still don't know. We are working to try and prevent that from happening."

"It seems a little far fetched to try and stop a storm, don't you think?"

Mr. Mercury smiled. "At our direction, the countries affected have begun using cloud seed. This has already effectively slowed the storm. We are continuing to look into expanding these methods to further mitigate the storm."

"What exactly is 'cloud seed?'"

"It's a mixture of dry ice and a few other chemicals."

"So you're tossing dry ice into the clouds?" The reporter looked into the camera, clearly finding this odd. "Isn't that..."

"Yes, as strange as it sounds, observations and studies have shown that it has prevented some moisture from joining the center of the storm and causing it to grow."

"Do you think you can stop it completely with this method?"

"Hard to say. We hope for the best.

"Okay," the interviewer said, "I don't want to keep you from your projects. Is there anything you can tell us? Anything we can do to help? Anything anyone in the path of the storm should do?"

"Evacuate and get out of the area. If you can't do that, find a concrete bunker. Any donations or assistance in the evacuation efforts can help. People have lost their lives and homes here. P.M.L. is starting a rebuilding fund to help give people their lives back. We will be releasing the details for this project soon. You may donate there or find another charity that is seeking to do the same."

"Thank you, Mr. Mercury," the interviewer said, ending the interview.

The scene changed back to the original news anchor. "There you have it, folks. When we receive the details of the charities we will be sure to spread the word."

The next few news stories shared mostly standard and uninteresting world events.

Lauren walked up to Jordin. "Hey."

"Hey." Jordin nodded in return.

"Before we left, I requested that some of these be stocked on the plane." She held out a box of medication. "I just remembered them."

"What's this?" Jordin eyed the medicine.

"It helps with motion sickness. I know you don't like heights and motion."

"Oh, thanks." Jordin accepted the medication.

Joseph smiled mischievously as he observed the interaction, then turned and looked out the window.

"How are you feeling now?" Lauren asked.

"Fine...as long as I don't look out a window...or think about it," Jordin replied as he crossed and uncrossed his fingers repeatedly.

"My brother used to get carsick on road-trips." Lauren sat in a nearby seat. "I remember that our trips used to take forever. We were always having to pull off to the side of the road and wait a while." She laughed at the thought. "I didn't really understand it at the time."

"I can sympathize with him. I don't really get carsick... unless we're driving along cliff-sides...," he trailed off.

"Just don't try to roll down the window for fresh air," She joked.

"Don't worry, I'll just ask Mr. Mercury to pull over and open the door for me." Jordin grinned right back.

* * * *

When they arrived at their destination later that evening, the sun was beginning to dip below the horizon. Personnel from the Indian military greeted them and assisted in the unloading. Even though Jordin was tired, he knew that time was limited. The storm that everyone had witnessed would arrive in under six days.

The medication that Lauren had provided had helped Jordin through the remaining plane ride. He was feeling far more refreshed than normal after such ordeals. However, he couldn't shake a growing sense of fear and uneasiness. His grip tightened around the handle of his briefcase as he gazed at the gathering clouds.

The setting sun made the clouds glow orange. Their uneven texture made them appear like a puffy quilt over the sky, woven by the sun. "That must be where the egg is." He pointed at its center.

An Indian soldier nodded grimly as he ushered Jordin into an armored transport.

Jordin set the briefcase on his lap and nervously tapped the black leather lid.

"If I didn't know what it meant, I'd say it was beautiful," Lauren said, sitting next to him.

"How do you feel about it all?"

"What do you mean? I don't like any of it."

"I mean...as a biologist, how do you feel about discovering a new species, and then having to kill it?"

Lauren frowned and wrinkled her nose as she stared out the window at the sunset. "I wish there was another way. Unfortunately, we have to do what we have to do. I don't like killing the only known living specimens of a newly discovered species. But it's an invasive species that's destroying the habitats and ecosystems of every other species on our planet. I have to put my desire to study it and its behaviors aside. It doesn't belong here." She let out a drawn out sigh. "Besides, something tells me these aren't the last two of their species. They may have just wandered outside of their own habitat. And if what you say is true, it's struggling to survive with the storms as it is and will only suffer here."

Jordin had never considered this. "I guess that's right. It's suffering and we're suffering." He studied the clouds with a new perspective. "I wish there was a way to communicate with it or find a way to get it off the planet or put it somewhere else. But how many would die before that happened? And we don't even know if it's intelligent enough to engage in communications."

"Life never gives us easy questions," Lauren said.

The military convoy departed, winding its way through the city streets, the buildings soon giving way to fields and hillsides. Clouds overhead grew thicker and more numerous the further they drove.

"Thank you, by the way," Jordin said to Lauren.

"For?" Lauren gave him a questioning glance.

"The medication. It helped."

"No problem." Lauren smiled. "I know how planes affect you. We all need to do our best here."

Jordin nodded in return.

It wasn't long before the convoy arrived at a fenced off area. Myriad prefabricated buildings and tents dotted the compound within.

Jordin peered out of the window at a massive gray-ish white egg poking up through the ground at the compound's center. While the first egg had been impressive, this one was far more frightening due to the gigantic and destructive creature awaiting inside.

An Indian soldier opened the gate and waved the convoy in.

"To think we're so close to something so dangerous," Lauren whispered.

"As long as it doesn't hatch, and it doesn't start snowing...we should be fine." He tried to smile reassuringly, but the sight of the menacing clouds made it difficult.

"Part of me wishes you were kidding," Lauren joked as the vehicle stopped.

The doors opened and everyone was ushered out of their vehicles. They all lined up surrounded by several Indian soldiers as a man in a highly decorated uniform approached to address them.

"Welcome to Vishv Base," the uniformed man said. "I'm General Arya. I hope you will find your stay here both comfortable and productive." The general then went down the line shaking everyone's hand.

"What happens now?" Lauren asked after the general had finished his greetings.

"We get to work," Mr. Mercury said as he walked up. "And we keep working until we stop this monster."

CHAPTER
16

The egg loomed over the base as everyone briskly set up workstations around it. Jordin and Lauren were exhausted but did their best to present their data and findings to the team of Indian scientists.

Joseph shared various specs and blueprints of the sensor arrays and equipment used. As his normal P.M.L. team was now working with the Russians, he would have to work quickly and efficiently to bring everyone on site up to speed with what had already happened.

Mr. Mercury concentrated his efforts on gathering and distributing supplies. He traveled from group to group ensuring that everyone had what they needed. Jordin suspected that Mr. Mercury felt insecure about not having any expertise and wanted to be useful.

Dr. Dhar brought in several members of the P.M.L. Indian branch to assist with data analysis and ensure all computer systems and networks were set up properly.

After Jordin was finished instructing the new Indian science team, he walked over to the structure Dhar had claimed as the "IT and Communications office." He introduced himself to everyone and made the rounds shaking hands. "I'm glad to finally meet all of you," he smiled.

"After you sent us those videos," Dhar chuckled, "everyone wanted to meet you."

Pleasantries were cut short as an Indian solder entered the building. "Senior members are requested in the conference room immediately," the soldier said, meaning Jordin and Dr. Dhar.

"What's this about?" Jordin asked.

"Updates on the monster's status. Please follow me."

Jordin and Dhar followed the soldier to a nearby building. They were led through the front doors and down a hallway to a large room. Several Middle Eastern dignitaries, Indian scientists, Indian military officers, Joseph, Mr. Mercury, and Lauren were already gathered. Lieutenant Zhukov stood at the front of the room next to a large screen, displaying a video feed of Colonel Dubinin sitting at his desk.

"I believe everyone is here," Zhukov said as Jordin and Dhar took their seats.

"As you all know," Dubinin began without any introduction, "Russia, Iran, and India have begun joint military operations against this storm creature. Thanks to the efforts of Dr. Davidson and the P.M.L. team, we have begun seeding the clouds. The creature appears to have slowed. We are continuing to use this method. However, as I'm sure you are all aware, the creature is still traveling to your position. If it continues on the current trajectory, it will arrive in five days."

The colonel paused and glanced at a few papers on his

desk. "I needn't remind you all that, thus far, all efforts to directly attack the creature have failed. If we are unable to stop this beast before it reaches its new friend..." Dubinin furrowed his brow. "I don't need to remind you what has already been authorized."

An Indian officer stood. "Colonel, such an action has not yet been approved on our end. Do I need to remind you of whose soil the creature will be on?"

Dubinin nodded. "We respect India's sovereignty. We wouldn't dream of doing anything to disrespect your nation. As such, we have been working hand-in-hand with your representatives. We want to avoid using such measures as well. However, I'm sure you will admit the situation may soon call for drastic action. I would also like to remind you that this creature invaded our sovereign soil and killed our citizens first. We do not take such an action lightly. We are also confident that if we miss our chance when both of these creatures are together, no nation will be safe. Many in your government agree with this sentiment. Your own citizenry is at huge risk if we don't act swiftly."

"This creature is destroying our towns and killing our people," a Middle Eastern dignitary said, glaring at the Indian officer. "We must do everything we can. You cannot simply refuse our wishes."

"We will do everything we can. I simply object to using such extreme measures as our own citizenry will be directly affected by it," the Indian officer reasoned.

"Everyone is currently being affected and will continue to

be affected until this thing is taken care of," Dubinin said. "We have five days to avoid needing to use these measures. I recommend that you use them wisely."

"We will take every measure to ensure the safety of our own people," General Arya said to reassure the other officer, who returned to his seat. "Russia cannot be the sole decision maker anymore."

"You needn't worry general," Dubinin said. "You will be part of that decision."

The rest of the meeting consisted of various officials arguing with each other. On occasion, a few scientists would present data that Jordin already knew. He began to wonder if this group would be able to do anything together even if a solution were discovered.

When everyone was finally dismissed, Jordin exchanged pleasantries with the P.M.L. team before heading to his designated sleeping quarters. His phone rang before he reached the building.

"Hello?" he answered.

"Hello, friend," the mysterious voice replied. "Do you have any further news?"

Jordin glanced around and ducked between two buildings. "We have five days...five days before the two storms meet," he whispered.

"And what happens when they meet?"

"I fear the worst. Very serious threats have been made by some powerful governments. If we can't solve it here, they will use drastic methods to do so."

"I understand," the voice said with concern. "Worse monsters may be summoned by our own machinations."

"I don't want it to happen either. But I don't know what choice we'll have. One monster is bad enough. If we have two of them wandering around..." Jordin looked up at the cloudy night sky. "The best opportunity to strike would be when they are both together, here."

"You may have a method already," the voice assured. "You informed us about the cold. Have you had any updates?"

"Yes." Jordin decided that the time and need for absolute secrecy had passed. Whoever he was talking to seemed to know everything already. If they only had a few days to develop a solution, they needed as many people as possible helping. Jordin was no longer under direct Russian supervision either, so he decided to take the leap. "They have begun using dry ice cloud seed. It seems to have worked to some degree. The monster has slowed down. Also, liquid nitrogen destroyed the shell when it was injected inside, otherwise it just bounces off the surface. However, heat repaired it. I have no idea if that tells us anything or not. Just because an egg shell is structured in such a way, doesn't mean that the creature is."

"And if it is, what does that mean? What happens when these 'drastic measures' are taken? How much heat is generated by such things? How much heat is generated by most of our modern weaponry?" The voice didn't seem fazed by the direct admission of the monster or the egg.

Jordin stared wide eyed at the dark clouds overhead. A sudden realization hit him. If the monster functioned the same way as the egg, then any "drastic measure" could simply sustain the creature. "If they do...and the creature thrives off of heat...We could feed both of them for a year! We have to cool it down from the inside! The trouble is... we have to find a way to get past the protective outer layer without generating heat." Jordin almost forgot he was on the phone and began thinking out loud, "If there was a way to get liquid nitrogen inside...the creature would freeze quickly. Assuming that it has the same or similar structure as the egg. But that's a huge assumption."

"You have a test subject."

Jordin blinked and narrowed his eyes at the sky. A whole new series of questions hit him. "Is that ethical? I mean... this thing is alive. For all we know, it's just as intelligent as we are. Maybe it doesn't understand what it's doing? It may just be trying to survive and doesn't see us or know that we exist."

"Maybe, my friend. How long would you need to study these creatures to find out? How many people would die before your questions are answered?"

"I know...But Lauren...I mean Dr. Terry and I talked about this a little bit. If there was some way to communicate with them, maybe we could end this all peacefully."

"And if they aren't intelligent enough to communicate?

We would waste our efforts while cities crumble. Even if they are, what happens if they're hostile and learn of us and what we can do? What would stop them from hunting us? Look at the history of humanity. We're all intelligent enough to communicate. And yet, throughout history, the mightier human force has often intentionally wiped out other humans. Who says they wouldn't be the 'mightier force?'"

Jordin sighed and shook his head. "You're not wrong. However, for as many examples of conquest in history, there are also examples of great kindness and beneficial agreements. The strongest groups aren't always the ones that are the most brutal. However, those don't make for good stories, so we aren't as familiar with them. We can't condemn these creatures for unknown motives."

"Very true. And yet, how many have already died due to these creatures? Do we need to know their intent if they are already a threat?"

The image of Mr. Mercury walking out of the rubble holding Jimmy's limp body flashed through Jordin's mind. A bitter knot formed in his stomach. "At the same time, we punish those who murder us whether they intended to or not." He sighed and tossed his free hand into the air. "I don't know the answer. This is all too complicated for its own good."

"Was it easier when you viewed these creatures just as threats that needed to be overcome?" the voice asked in a softer tone.

"Maybe."

"You may not believe me, but I agree with you. We cannot condemn them for an unknown motive, or attribute any to them. Were there any other way, I'd take it. But I cannot sit here and worry about the cleanliness of my soul while people die. Whether the creatures are doing this intentionally or not, we must act in self-defense and preservation, as must they."

"I suppose you're right. We don't have to like it. We just have to deal with it."

"Prepare yourself. You have entered a race. A race against both the creatures themselves and our own world governments. Pray that you cross the finish line first...." The voice paused for a few moments. "You've given us valuable insight. You'll hear from us again soon."

"By the way...who are you?"

"A friend who has seen destruction before and wishes to avoid it."

Jordin shivered, only now noticing the dropping temperature as he spoke. "It may be too late."

"Then we try harder."

The line clicked and went silent. Jordin peeked up at the dark clouds beginning to boil and roll across the sky. The temperature had dropped significantly after the sun went down. "Hmmm," he muttered. "Is it just me or are clouds gathering more quickly over this egg than the first one? On that note, are they still gathering? They should hold steady at night. I'll have to look at the data."

"I see you're making friends on the outside," Lieutenant Zhukov said, stepping from around the corner of a building.

"Oh...I...Uh...," Jordin said nervously.

"Did you think we wouldn't monitor your phones while you were under our care?" Zhukov raised an eyebrow.

"Well...I...," Jordin stammered.

Zhukov stopped a few feet from Jordin, never breaking eye contact. "The night that you called Colonel Dubinin from the hotel," he said, a grin forming, "I had just gotten off the phone with him, relaying everything you'd said to this mysterious outsider."

"I tried not to give anything away," Jordin said sheepishly.

"You broke protocol, and yet...it seemed to serve you well enough." Zhukov tilted his head to the side. "Had you not called Dubinin and had your plans not worked, you would be under 'investigation.'"

Jordin grimaced and remained silent.

"We are willing to overlook certain protocols on your part, as you are a civilian, provided that we get results." Zhukov glanced around to ensure no one else was in earshot. "Besides, we are no longer under Russian jurisdiction here. I neither know nor care to enforce the rules of this base. If talking to this mysterious friend of yours provides solutions, talk away."

Jordin nodded in relief.

"Make no mistake," Zhukov continued, "the colonel and I are not your 'friends.' We are here to do a job. We will do what is necessary to eliminate both beasts. If that is something you are going to struggle with, I suggest you step aside."

"I'm here to do whatever I need to do."

"Good," Zhukov gave Jordin a curt nod and turned to walk away.

"By the way," Jordin said, raising his hand, "do you have any of the data from our sensors on this cloud formation here?"

"The data printouts have been handed to everyone. I suggest you read the packet of information that was at your workstation."

"I was too busy setting up and ensuring the night team had data to read much of it," Jordin admitted.

"The clouds are forming much faster over this egg than over ours. We covered our egg with a tent. I don't need to tell you how warm direct sunlight can be." He turned back around and walked away, leaving Jordin to shiver and stare at the egg.

"That initial spike...," Jordin muttered, remembering the first time that they had detected the strange anomalous storm. "Then it slowed down...You put a tent over it...At night it leveled off. We need to cover that egg!"

He rushed to the main command center hoping to find

General Arya. A guard at the front door stopped him.

"I need to see the general," Jordin said.

"What is it about?" the soldier asked.

"I have vital information about this egg. I know why the storm is gathering more quickly here."

"One moment please, sir." The solider pressed a button on the radio attached to his shoulder and spoke in Hindi. "Name please."

"I'm Dr. Jordin Davidson with P.M.L. Please, this is urgent."

The soldier repeated his name into the radio. Someone on the other end replied in Hindi. "Your escort is on the way. Please wait here."

Jordin waited awkwardly. It wasn't long before the doors opened and another soldier walked out.

"Dr. Davidson?" the new soldier asked.

"Yes."

"Namaste." The escort soldier placed his palms together with his fingertips pointing upward and nodded.

"Oh...uhh..." Jordin muttered as he repeated the hand gesture. "Namaste."

"Follow me please." The soldier spun and walked back into the building.

Jordin followed the soldier down hallways and up a flight of stairs. The soldier opened a door and motioned for Jordin to enter.

This room was a small office with a large wooden desk. The Middle Eastern dignitary who had approached Jordin on the plane was standing in front of the desk speaking to the general seated behind it. Jordin barely noticed the somber mood of the room.

The soldier saluted. "Dr. Davidson, sir."

The general solemnly returned the salute. "Thank you, you are dismissed."

"General Arya, sir...," Jordin began to say as he stepped forward.

The Middle Eastern dignitary emitted an angry grunt and nudged Jordin while making the same hand gesture that the escorting soldier had made earlier.

"Oh...I apologize." Jordin put his palms together and nodded his head. "Namaste."

General Arya smiled and repeated the greeting. "What vital information do you have to report, Dr. Davidson?"

"We need to cover the egg, sir," Jordin said.

The dignitary scowled as the general looked thoughtfully at Jordin.

"Do you have a reason as to why?" Arya asked.

"When we first detected the weather anomaly over Russia," Jordin began, "it was rapidly increasing in intensity. However, its rate of increase was slowed a few hours later. We are seeing the same steep increase here, yet it hasn't slowed its rate. Do you have the information packet on the data collected?"

The general pulled a folder out of a desk drawer and set it in front of Jordin. "Perhaps you could help us understand the data while you are here."

Jordin opened the folder and briskly sorted through them. He felt embarrassed for not stopping by the lab to get his own papers and familiarizing himself with what was most important. "Ah, here...and...here." He pulled two graphs out of the stack and placed them on the desk.

"This graph is what we detected from the initial stages of the Russian storm." Jordin pointed at the graph. "As the data shows here, it was increasing in intensity quite rapidly. However," he said, pointing to a part where the incline appeared to bend and trend upward at a slower rate, "at this point it slowed down."

The general pointed to the other paper. "And is this other graph...our egg?"

"Yes," Jordin nodded, "as you can see here, the rate of increase hasn't slowed down. The only thing that stops it is night-time. On each graph, you can see where it levels off after sundown. During the day, it starts increasing again."

"And what does this mean?" the frustrated dignitary asked, tossing his hands in the air.

Jordin blinked at the dignitary. "It means, this storm over our heads is going to become as bad if not worse than the storm over Russia before...before it hatched."

"How much time do you believe we have?" Arya stroked his chin.

"It took a month before the Russian egg hatched. At the current rate of growth...I'd say...maybe two weeks? That's two weeks from when it landed."

"Hmmm," the general snorted. "In less than five days the big one will be upon us. Even if we didn't have that one to deal with, we'll have our own in a little over a week." He crossed his arms. "Do you know why the Russian egg didn't 'grow' as quickly?"

"I believe so. The Russians put a large canvas tent over it. That blocked the direct sunlight and provided some insulation from the outside world. This thing wants heat, so we need to keep it from accessing heat as much as possible."

"The clouds are blocking the sun as it is. Why would a tent make a difference?" The upset dignitary waved his arms again and turned toward the window.

"The sun emits more than just visible light," Jordin said, peering at the dignitary, and doing his best to ignore the man's attitude and move on. "UV rays pierce through clouds. Some people still need sunblock on cloudy days for that reason. A tent would help shield the egg from those and stop morning and evening sunlight from directly shining on it from an angle. Plus, it's another barrier making it harder for heat to access the egg."

The general leaned back and thought for a moment. "I will rely on your professional opinion, doctor. Do you have any recommendations for the materials? Or any other specifications to reduce the heat to the egg?"

"Unfortunately, I'm not an engineer," Jordin admitted. "However, my colleague Dr. Wilber is. I'm sure he and the other engineers would be willing to provide better solutions. You may even contact Colonel Dubinin in Russia to get the exact details on what they did."

General Arya grimaced. "Thank you for your input. I will instruct our engineers to begin the tent construction immediately."

"Why bother?" the dignitary protested as he twirled around. Sorrow flashed across his face. He quickly righted himself and continued, "The creature will be upon us before this egg hatches. Death comes to us all."

A sudden flare of light streaked across the window illuminating the room in an eerie glow. Thunder boomed overhead. Everyone startled and stared out of the window as small snowflakes began to intermittently fall.

"It's been here, what, approximately two and a half days?" Jordin asked. "It took at least a week for lightning to arrive at the Russian egg. If nothing else, we need to stop the growth of the storm so we can study it."

"I thought you said it leveled off at night," the dignitary quipped, near his boiling point.

General Arya held up his hand and addressed the dignitary in a language unfamiliar to Jordin.

The dignitary took a deep breath and motioned for Jordin to continue. "My apologies. We must all work together now. We're all we have left."

"It does level off." Jordin said, deciding to ignore the dignitary's outbursts and not take it personally. "I need more recent readings. This storm may be a result of everything that happened during the day combined with the lowering temperatures of night. Or there's still enough residual heat in the area for it to absorb."

General Arya pressed a button on his desk's phone, then he spoke in Hindi into the speaker. The response was laced with static pops. When the conversation ended, he said to Jordin, "I've instructed the engineering team to begin immediate construction of the tent and to retrieve Dr. Wilber." He stood from his seat. "Come, let's see why this egg is active when it shouldn't be."

Jordin and the dignitary followed the general out of the door. Two soldiers joined them as they marched out of the building. The outside air had a bitter chill to it. A cold breeze swept falling snowflakes past their faces.

"We should kill this creature now before more...," the dignitary muttered before cutting himself short.

People poked their heads out of windows and guards ogled the ominous sky as the group marched toward the egg, illuminated by an industrial light, causing it to glow menacingly.

Jordin gasped as he saw the surrounding area. Myriad workstations had been set up all around the egg. Each station had a heater churning away. He watched in consternation as a scientist shivered and walked over to a heater to increase its output. What he saw next dropped his jaw in shock.

An entire group in welding masks were busy blow-torching the egg. Jordin couldn't believe his eyes. The pure insanity of it all took his breath away.

General Arya's eyes widened as he began shouting in Hindi. Every soldier and scientist snapped to attention.

The dignitary yelled something in his own language and pointed at a heater.

Jordin frantically ran toward the group, waving his arms to get their attention. "STOP THE TORCHES! ARE YOU..."

The men wielding the blowtorches turned them off and lifted their face-shields, bewildered.

"Turn off those heaters!" Jordin motioned toward the heaters. He dashed forward and unplugged one.

"What are you doing? What's going on?" a Russian scientist asked. "It's cold and we don't have our hazmat suits. We need the heaters."

"The heat is causing this storm!" Jordin shouted.

The Indian officer, who had spoken out in the meetings initiated a heated exchange with the general. Several soldiers scattered, turning off the heaters.

"I warned them," Zhukov said as he approached Jordin from behind. "They wouldn't listen to me. I have no authority here."

Jordin whipped around to face Zhukov. "What happened?"

Zhukov nodded to the Indian officer. "The colonel ordered a complete dissection of the egg. He wants to kill the beast inside immediately to avoid the more 'destructive' methods."

"Couldn't you have told him?" Jordin waved his hands in frustration. "Didn't anyone know? The data is right here. Heat is the enemy. Why of all things would they use blowtorches?"

"Reasonable conversation with a zealot is impossible. I told them to use a drill. The colonel is impatient. The shell is incredibly hard and has self-repairing qualities. The required equipment will take a while to arrive."

Lightning flashed overhead as thunder boomed.

Jordin pointed to the clouds. "The damage they just did is irreversible. Whatever time we thought we had has now severely decreased."

"Had you not arrived with the general when you did, an international incident would have been started," Zhukov said, pulling a pistol from his jacket pocket. "I was just returning from contacting Dubinin to inform him of the situation. He authorized me to take care of the problem by any means necessary." He secured the pistol back in his pocket. "I admire his drive to kill the beast. Yet his methods have caused more harm than good."

Jordin shook his head and stared back at the egg. "Why?"

"Zealous impatience can be very dangerous," Zhukov said with a smirk. "Something your boss needs to learn."

The cloud gatherings became a whole new menace to Jordin. "Everything just became so much worse."

"Have your decisions always been right?" Zhukov raised an eyebrow.

"No..." Jordin couldn't get Jimmy's face out of his mind. Had he not insisted on going to the storm in person, Jimmy would still be alive. Had he chosen a spot farther away from the storm...

"Dr. Davidson," General Arya interrupted Jordin's thoughts, "how much damage has been done? How long do we now have?" He acknowledged Zhukov but kept his focus on Jordin.

Jordin sighed. "We've lost at least a day, maybe more." A snowflake drifted into his eye, causing him to blink. "Everything we do now is going to be harder with the bad weather. The creature may hatch in a week or so, but the weather will get far worse before that happens."

"Will it get too bad to accomplish anything before the other one arrives?"

"I honestly don't know. I'd have to look at the data and observe it for a while."

Arya looked up, then at the egg and shivered. "Is there a way to reverse it?"

"I don't know." Jordin shrugged. "At this point...the only way to stop it or undo everything is probably kill it. Even then, I don't know how it's causing the weather patterns. I don't know if it will still cause the disruptions even while dead."

"Hmff," Arya scoffed. "Here we are, facing an enemy we don't know." He looked Jordin dead in the eye. "And none of us know what to do about it. We're all stumbling blindly in the dark." He addressed Zhukov, "Has your engineering team back home come up with anything? Our engineers are standing by."

"Expect a shipment of supplies and plans soon," Zhukov said.

Arya was satisfied, then looked back to Jordin. "Governments from around the world have begun supporting our efforts. Your own government will be sending troops and supplies." He sighed. "It took an alien monster to bring the world together. Even if just temporarily."

"At least we won't have to deal with this alone," Jordin said.

Lightning flashed across the sky followed closely by a deafening boom.

"General Arya, sir!" Joseph jogged up to the group. "I came as soon as I could. What seems to be the issue?"

Arya nodded to Jordin. "Dr. Davidson can fill you in on the details. We are going to cover this egg and need you to work with our teams to come up with a solution."

"Okay," Joseph said, then asked Jordin, "What are we covering it with?"

"We need to cover it to keep it out of direct sunlight. We also need ways to limit its access to heat."

"Okay," Joseph stroked his chin, "if you want to keep heat away, especially from sunlight, I'd recommend something reflective. There are reflective and insulating materials." He looked at the egg. "I'm guessing we don't have time for the fancy, high quality stuff they use on spacecraft."

"Notify our engineers of anything you need. If we don't have it, we can acquire it for you," Arya said. "If you'll excuse me, I have some housekeeping to take care of." He turned and marched off.

"What happened here?" Joseph asked as he noticed all the unplugged heaters.

"It got cold, so the workers warmed themselves," Zhukov said. "They also decided to dissect the egg using blowtorches."

Joseph closed his eyes and chuckled. "That explains it." He opened his eyes and shook his head. "Looks like we've got a lot to do."

Another flash of lightning highlighted his words.

CHAPTER
17

Jordin awoke the next morning after a fitful night's sleep. He groaned as he removed his earplugs and got dressed for the day, making sure to wear a coat. A light layer of snow crunched beneath his feet as he trudged outside.

Overnight, the engineering teams had draped a large canvas tent over the egg. Wind buffeted it violently, threatening to lift it off the ground. The material stretched and bulged with each gust. Several anchor points appeared to have been replaced, stitched back together, or reinforced.

"Good morning," Joseph said as he and a few others walked by, carrying long poles with canvas between them.

"Good morning," Jordin greeted with a wave. "I see you've been busy."

Joseph smiled. "Not me. I just woke up myself not long ago."

"What do you have there?"

"A sunlight screen. Or at least that's what it's supposed to be. I didn't want to rely entirely on the tent alone, so we made a few screens to block sunrise and sunset. Plus, the tent will inevitably warm up. Blocking as much light as possible from reaching the tent gives us the best chance."

Jordin watched as Joseph and his team walked over to a series of poles with canvas between them already set up. A construction vehicle with a long arm carried a man with a hammer waiting in a basket. The cloth between the poles waved and bulged precariously in the wind. Another team was working down the line of screens and adding reinforcement behind them.

Rays from the rising sun flowed out of the horizon, illuminating the dirty screens. Several buildings helped to block the incoming light. The screens were placed strategically between gaps or in wide-open areas. It wasn't perfect and it didn't catch everything, but it was a start. Hopefully, the tent would provide the remaining protection needed.

Lightning flashed overhead providing an incredibly odd juxtaposition of weather phenomena. The sun was rising over clear summer skies nearby. Meanwhile directly overhead, snow fell while lightning flashed. Each bolt illuminated the snowflakes like diamonds. At other times, the sun would shine through the flakes to make them resemble burning sparks.

The roaring engines of a line of water tanker trucks driving by snapped Jordin back to attention. Each truck appeared to be fully weighed down as they rolled through the camp toward the northwestern entrance. Tightly packed grooves of snow marked the roadway indicating that several other vehicles had passed this way earlier.

"That's a lot of water," Jordin mumbled as the fifth and final truck passed by.

A group of six helicopters rumbled as they flew overhead, heading in the same direction as the trucks. Each of them dangled wooden crates cradled in netting. Jordin could only clench his teeth as he watched the cargo buffet around precariously in the wind. Fortunately, no mishaps occurred.

Wonder what's in those crates? Jordin wondered. An armed guard ushered him through the tent's entrance. Just inside was a rack of heavy coats and gloves. Since the temperature in the tent felt significantly colder than the outside, he gladly layered up.

The egg itself was now almost covered completely in a reflective cloth, snow packed around the base. Someone with a wheelbarrow full of snow nudged past him toward the egg where a group of people began shoveling the snow onto the egg.

Lauren sat at a workstation with a few other scientists, near a large machine that was running several wires to the egg. She motioned Jordin over.

"Good morning," Jordin said.

"I hear you had some fun last night," Lauren gave him a wry smile.

He furrowed his brow. "Just a bit. So, what's this?" He gestured to the machine. A series of wavy lines ran across its screen.

"A heartbeat," Lauren said. "Isn't it amazing? Here, listen to this." She handed him a pair of headphones.

He placed them over his ears. He had to concentrate to

filter out the howling wind and the flapping canvas to parse out a steady rhythmical beat.

"Just think, this is only the top of the egg," Lauren said soberly.

Jordin took the headphones off and placed them on the table. "It's alive alright."

"For how much longer?" Lauren asked.

"We knew it was alive before."

"I know, but...Somehow listening to its pulse...It's a completely new species. Do you know how rare it is to study a new animal in its early stages of life?"

Jordin took a deep breath. Part of him couldn't help but agree with Lauren. However, he knew how dangerous these creatures were to everyone. "I understand," he said gently. "If there was a way to contain these creatures without killing them, I'd do it. But we both know what will happen if we don't do what we can to stop it."

"I know...I just..." Lauren dropped her pretenses. "It's just a baby. It hasn't done anything yet. How can we say it's guilty purely by nature of existing? It didn't rampage across the globe."

Jordin mulled the moral implications of this. "I agree," he finally said, "it's not fair. It's not ideal."

A flash lit up the tent followed by a loud boom.

Jordin pointed upward. "However, I'm not passing judgment on it based on what the other one has done. It's causing problems on its own. Plus, it's showing the same signs and patterns of behavior as the other one. Just because it hasn't rampaged yet, doesn't mean that it never will."

Lauren fixated on the heartbeat lines, obviously dissatisfied with that answer.

Jordin waited patiently for her response.

"I just wish there was another way. I really don't like the idea of killing anything. Had I known...," Lauren trailed off.

Suppressed feelings of anger and guilt began to rise to Jordin's surface. "Had I known, we wouldn't be here in the first place." Jordin turned and glared at the egg. "We're here because I insisted that we go directly into the storm. Jimmy is dead because of my decision."

"You couldn't have known. Who would've guessed a gigantic alien creature was causing it?"

Jordin sighed and turned to Lauren. He adjusted to a softer tone. "No one could've. I understand if you want to leave. None of us expected this. I'm here to see it through no matter what but you don't have to put yourself through this."

After a moment in thought, Lauren looked Jordin in the eye and said, "I said this storm would have to kill me to get rid of me. I meant it. I don't like any of this, but I can't leave now. Besides," she smiled. "do you know how many biologists would kill to study something like this?"

Jordin could guess quite a number.

"There you are," Mr. Mercury said upon arrival, holding

a stack of papers and setting them on the table in front of Jordin.

Jordin realized then that every scientist was watching him and Lauren with great concern. "What are those?" he asked Mercury, trying to ignore the attention.

"This is all the data our sensors gathered from last night." Mr. Mercury pulled a paper off the stack and pointed to a graph. "I heard about what happened. Our graph shows it. Here's the standard evening level off. And here, just a little while later, it starts increasing again. Then here it spikes up."

Jordin frowned as he studied the graph. "That's probably when they started using the blowtorches."

"Blowtorches?!" Lauren blurted. "What kind of idiot would use blowtorches on this thing?"

"Suffice it to say, General Arya took care of the problem and it won't happen again," Jordin said.

"You can go through this data and sort it all out," Mercury said. "Dhar and his team are busy crunching numbers and analyzing things so they can interpret it for everyone else. I need to get back to the supply station. We're expecting a lot of stuff to come in today." He turned to leave.

"What's going on?" Jordin asked.

"Oh, excuse me, you are project lead on this, not me. Since I have no..." Mercury paused out of discomfort. "I've been assigned to supplies. I hope that's alright with you. I'm happy to reassign to where you need me."

"That's okay." Jordin nodded. "If you're needed in supplies, then deal with supplies. What kind of stuff are we expecting?"

"A lot of places around the world are sending supplies. We're getting tons of liquid nitrogen, experimental weaponry, parts to build weapons, and things to stave off heat. That sort of stuff."

Jordin straightened his posture. "Experimental weaponry?"

"Something about liquid nitrogen shots and sprays. I don't know much."

"Is it possible to develop an effective weapon in such a short amount of time?"

"Maybe?" Mercury shrugged. "I hope you're ready. We're going to get a lot of people coming in to build defenses. The whole world is interested in stopping these things here."

"What kind of defenses can you build against something like this?" Jordin asked.

"Beats me. I heard people talking about building moats and setting up cannons to fire these new weapons."

"A moat?" Lauren said in surprise. "What is this, the middle ages?"

"Might as well be," Mercury replied.

"This creature doesn't like water," Jordin reasoned. "If done correctly, we could make a 'fence' of sorts to either stop it or slow it down. The question is, how big is this moat

going to be? And can we build it in time?”

“I don't know,” Mr. Mercury said. “I guess they're just trying everything they can at this point.”

“Makes sense,” Jordin said.

“Are they just going to let it walk all the way here? Why not stop it before?” Lauren asked, worried.

“They're doing what they can to slow or stop it now,” Mr. Mercury said. “But we don't have anything effective yet. We're hoping to have something by the time it gets here. If they can stop it before, then they'll gladly do so.”

“Its arrival is a hard due date for anything we can come up with,” Jordin said as he glanced at the heartbeat monitor. “It's the moment that they'll decide to use far more drastic measures.”

“Exactly,” Mercury smiled and nodded. “Now if you'll excuse me, I have to go see if we've got anything in.”

Jordin stared after his boss. Was it just him, or was Mercury limping slightly?

“That wasn't a bad interaction with Mr. Mercury as far as interactions with him go,” Jordin said.

“Yeah,” Lauren muttered. “He's been preoccupied since we've been here and out of my hair.”

“Even so,” Jordin mused, “he seems...less scattered.”

“You're not wrong. Other people have been ordering him around and giving him directions. Maybe that's what he needs?”

"I don't know." Jordin stroked his chin as he continued to stare at the tent entrance. "It just seems like something's wrong."

"Maybe," Lauren said, her voice wavering slightly. "Ever since Jimmy...he seems to be trying to do better."

"He pulled him out of..." Jordin took a slow, deep breath. "I don't think he's recovered from that."

"Who has?" Lauren asked. "I mean really. You just blamed yourself for it again and I've been putting off how I feel because I have a job to do."

"I don't know. It just seems like there's something else wrong with him." He stared at the papers on the desk without the focus to read them.

Lauren shrugged. "Who knows. You may know better than me. I've spent the past few years trying not to pay attention to him."

"Fair enough," Jordin said absently as he turned to the egg.

"Anyway," Lauren said as she pulled an image out of the stack of papers, "look at this."

Jordin reset himself back to work mode to study the picture in her hand. "It's another rendering of the whole egg," he said, unimpressed.

"Yeah, but look." Lauren pointed at a splintered rod-like protrusion. "It has one of those too. Hang on." She reached down to a backpack at her feet and pulled out another folder. She shuffled through it and produced the rendering of the prior egg. She set the two images side-by-side. "They're both broken in similar ways."

Jordin blinked in realization. "They were connected," he whispered.

"I'm glad I'm not the only one who thought that. The question is; were they connected to each other or something else? And how did they break off?"

"What are those...connections made out of? Are they made the same way as the rest of the egg?"

"I don't know. We just assumed that it was. Why?"

"If they broke off in space...if the connections were internal...the pressure difference would've broken the egg apart," Jordin mused. "All of the water vapor in the egg's heat conduction rods would've been evacuated leaving it useless. These connections must be entirely external."

"Like a growth on the outside of the shell?" Lauren raised an eyebrow.

"Indeed. Maybe its intended to break at some point. Otherwise, they wouldn't be able to bore into the ground separately."

"If they broke apart, there would have been a ton of splinters and space debris around them."

"There was," Jordin said adamantly, locking eyes with Lauren to convey a mutual understanding.

They both nodded in unison.

CHAPTER
18

A commotion erupting outside distracted Jordin from his studies.

"What's all that?" he asked as he stood.

"I don't know. Sounds like a highway outside our door," Lauren replied.

Jordin checked the clock. "Oh, my." The time had gotten away from him. The whole afternoon had passed and evening was already upon them. "I'm going to see what it's all about."

Lauren nodded as she continued examining data.

Jordin walked to the door of the tent and firmly grasped the opening. He knew that as soon as he opened the tent, the wind would try to rip the canvas door out of his hands. After steeling himself, he unclasped the latch and stepped out into the world.

An immediate blast of chill air nearly took his breath away as he peered into the dim surroundings. He hugged his coat closer to his body as a large tank drove past, followed by an assortment of bulldozers, front-loaders, excavators, dump trucks, and backhoes, all accompanied by several marching soldiers.

"What's happening?" Jordin asked the Indian soldier guarding the tent entrance.

"Reinforcements have arrived," the soldier replied.

Lightning streaked the sky, making all of the soldiers appear as ghosts for the briefest of moments. Mr. Mercury and a group of soldiers slogged up to the entrance.

"We've got a truck with supplies that needs to enter," Mr. Mercury said, pointing to an approaching semi-truck with a large crate strapped to its open trailer.

The guard nodded as he proceeded to widen the tent entrance. Jordin and the other soldiers assisted as Mr. Mercury guided the truck through. It took all of them to control the canvas as it flapped wildly around by the winds. After the truck passed through, Jordin and the soldiers closed the tent back up and entered.

"What sort of things do we have here?" Jordin asked as the soldiers placed a ramp onto the back of the truck and began carefully pushing the crate off.

"New drilling equipment, monitors, coolant stuff...that sort of thing," Mr. Mercury said.

Jordin nodded at the soldiers. "I see we've got a few new friends."

"We've got people from Russia, India, Iran, Pakistan, Afghanistan, Iraq, United States, United Kingdom, and even a United Nations task force."

"That's quite the conglomeration. I'd be surprised under any other circumstance if you told me that they were all working together." Jordin smiled.

"The monster doesn't care how we feel about each other. It's going to smash all of us just the same." Mr. Mercury made a sweeping motion to indicate everyone.

"Makes sense to me."

"Where did all this stuff come from? And how did it get here?" Lauren asked.

"They've set up a makeshift port on the coast of the Bay of Bengal nearby." Mr. Mercury waved his hand eastward. "The airport we landed at has been commandeered for our use. Which reminds me. My pilot and I are flying out in the early morning tomorrow to pick up a large shipment of liquid nitrogen from Taiwan. They want to use every plane and resource available to them."

Lauren glanced nervously at the egg. "How much longer do we have until the creature arrives?"

"About four days now," Jordin said.

"Don't worry, I'll be back with what we need before then," Mercury said.

An Indian soldier marched up. "Dr. Davidson and Dr. Terry."

"Yes?" both Jordin and Lauren said in unison.

"Your presence is required at a meeting. Please follow me."

"Lead the way," Jordin said as he and Lauren followed the soldier out of the tent and into a nearby building, into a conference room where several military leaders and scientists from various nations were seated around a large table.

"Please, have a seat doctors." General Arya gestured to the empty chairs.

Jordin and Lauren sat down, with Jordin lowering his hands below the table to hide his fidgeting fingers.

"We were just discussing potential solutions to our problem and we need your expertise," the general continued.

"I'll do what I can," Jordin said.

"Me too," Lauren added.

"Before we begin," Arya said, "have you been able to confirm that our efforts have slowed the buildup of our storm." The wind outside howled and rattled the building.

Jordin grimaced. "The rate of increase has slowed. However, it's still increasing."

"Do you know when our egg may hatch?"

"Hard to say," Lauren shrugged. "Maybe a matter of days to a week. We can't really tell you much more as we don't really know anything about the life cycle of these creatures yet."

Arya nodded. He motioned to the others around the room. "You may ask your questions."

"I read your notes on the shell," a man in an American uniform said. "Were you able to study why the shell reacted the way it did?"

"In what way specifically?" Lauren asked.

"When you poured liquid nitrogen into the shell, it started disintegrating," another man in a British uniform said. "But when you hit it with a blowtorch, it...'healed.' Did you determine if it was truly heat that did this? It could be a reaction specifically to nitrogen or fire."

"I'm not entirely sure," Lauren said. "We used what we had available in the short time that we had it."

"How do we know that anything we're developing is going to do anything?" the British officer asked while peering at her.

"I'm sorry. We've passed along all the data we have. We can continue to study it and let you know."

"We have four days. We can't afford to wait," the American said. "We need to make do with what we have now. Any further information you find can assist us."

The other scientists in the room murmured with agreement.

"I hope you can appreciate why both precision and accuracy are important here," the British officer interjected. "The more we know, the better we can deal with the problem. We could be chasing our tails until new information is presented."

"I agree. However, we have to do something. The Russians are sending egg fragments to researchers around the world. A few fragments will arrive here for our study." the American said. "We can study them ourselves. In the meantime we have to proceed as if what P.M.L. claims is true."

The British officer considered this a moment. "I agree. We have to work with what we have for now. We can't sit here and wait."

"Are we all in agreement then?" Arya asked.

Both the American and British officer looked at each other and nodded. "We will move forward as we have been, operating under P.M.L. and Russian intel," the British officer said, directing his gaze to Lauren and Jordin. "I sincerely hope that you two are correct."

"Now that we have that settled, what do we need to do?" Arya asked.

"Our teams are devising plans as we speak," the American said, looking to a few scientists sitting next to him who nodded at him. "However, there are certain challenges that this presents. Cryo weaponry is very much experimental. We are also at a disadvantage in that we don't know our enemy. We know that it's a living creature and that it's big. We know what its shell is made of and how hard it is. If the creature's skin acts in any way like the shell, it will be challenging to create an effective weapon."

The British officer shuffled some papers around in a briefcase then pulled out a few and placed them on the table. "Our reconnaissance has managed to create an image of the creature through the storm. It appears as though it emits ionic radiation, giving it a sort of yellowish glow. As you may be aware, it also generates high amounts of electromagnetic interference, making it difficult to gain accurate readings."

Jordin examined the photograph in front of him, showing a washed out, yellow, hazy figure in the middle of a gray background. The figure appeared to be a tall, lanky creature with a cylindrical horse-like head, long arms, prolonged legs, and a long wide tail. Several spiky protrusions emanated from its back. The haze in the photo obscured any identifiable features and made it difficult to know what part was the monster and what was an effect of its emissions.

"Is that the creature?" Lauren pointed to the photo.

The British officer nodded. "It's as good of a photo as we can get for now. Though, I'm told we just received new drilling equipment today. Here soon, we may be able to directly photograph whatever's in that egg."

"It looks...strange," Lauren muttered.

"What were you expecting?" Jordin asked.

"I don't know..." Lauren thought for a moment. She asked the British officer, "How tall is it?"

"Anywhere between 700 and 800 meters and growing," the British officer replied.

"How?" Lauren blinked. "That's not possible."

"What do you mean?" the American officer asked. "This is an alien creature. Why should it adhere to Earthly expectations?"

"True," Lauren agreed. "However, there are hard limits to size in nature. The larger something is, the more weight it has to support. Most biological creatures aren't made of materials strong enough to be this large. The only reason whales can be as large as they are is because they're in the ocean and always supported by surrounding waters. Land based creatures of that size would find it hard to move. If they were any bigger than that, they'd crush themselves under their own weight."

"It could be made of something other than what we're familiar with," the American replied.

"Even then," Lauren said while looking at the photo, "there has to be more to it than this. It's far too skinny. It looks like it could fold in half."

"Are you saying," Jordin mused, "that we may not have to freeze it? We could just knock it over?"

"Maybe? Don't take my word for it. I'm just telling you, as a biologist, there's something more going on here. Something's keeping it upright. If we can find what that is...maybe...I don't know. I need a better look at this thing."

"We all wish we could get a better look at it now," the British officer chuckled.

"There might be a way," Jordin thought aloud.

"What do you mean?" the American asked.

"Storms need heat and moisture," Jordin said, folding his hands on the table. "We're currently seeding the storm itself. The cold from the dry ice and moisture loss seems to be slowing it down. If we can seed the surrounding areas to make it precipitate...we may be able to reduce the moisture content available. Thus weakening the central storm." He turned to General Arya. "It's possible to set up ground generators to emit the various gasses needed for cloud seed. We don't have to rely on airplanes alone. You may have to consult your scientists to determine the best mixtures to use."

General Arya pondered this as the other scientists passed notes back and forth.

"We could set these generators up along the monster's path, starting from here," the British officer suggested as he read a note a scientist had passed him. "I'm sure we have the plans for those. Supplies would just be our main concern."

"Are you certain that this would work?" Arya asked Jordin.

Jordin grimaced and shook his head. "No. I can't be certain. It's just an idea based off of principles that I know work for other situations. We already know cloud seeding has an effect. At the very least, it's worth a try."

"Unless anyone can prove otherwise," General Arya glanced around the table, "I say we move forward with that plan. We will instruct everyone to begin cloud seed operations. Keep me informed as to any supply needs. Is this matter settled?"

"Yes," the British officer said. "We will move forward

with these plans. Should our people discover anything new, we will bring those findings forward and act according to the new data."

"Agreed." the American officer nodded.

"Good," the general said. "Now let's return to our discussion on weaponry. What do we have and what do we need?"

The British officer assembled his thoughts a moment before saying, "Our options are limited. We need to penetrate a hard outer shell. However, we also need to reduce heat output as much as possible. We can spray the target with nitrogen or various other coolants. We also have 'cold core' bullets. Their effectiveness is still negligible, as they're experimental."

"We've developed a sub-sonic round with a small canister of pressurized liquid nitrogen inside," the American officer interjected. "As of now, they're in the experimental phase. They're intended to work like a hollow-point bullet on impact and release the stored liquid nitrogen inside the target. Unfortunately, their ability to penetrate through hard substances is lacking."

"If the doctor is correct," the British officer said, pointing at Jordin, "and the creature is 'repaired' by heat, the effectiveness of any such weapon is going to be reduced. The explosion needed to propel the shells, combined with the heat generated from air resistance as it travels, may negate our efforts. That's not even accounting for the heat generated on impact."

"Let's hope that thing can't take a punch," the American said. "Hopefully the force of the strike alone will be enough to do something. As long as we can get the nitrogen in the target, we should be fine. We made it sub-sonic to reduce the propelling explosion and air resistance that the shell would encounter. It will also weaken the impact, but I believe it will be enough."

"We've also developed a few cryo missiles that, upon explosion, will send either liquid nitrogen or dry ice in all directions," the British officer continued. "Tests on these are much more promising."

"Good," the general nodded. "How about our defenses? When will the 'moat' be completed, and how are we going to slow or stop this thing?"

"We've begun digging the moat now. By our calculations, it should be done in two or three days," the American said. "We have a convoy of water trucks driving to and from the coast with seawater to fill it with. If we use salt water, it should prevent the moat from freezing over and allow it to become colder."

The British officer folded his hands on the table. "Traditional defenses may not work here. The creature could just walk over or smash through any wall or fence we build. I'd say, In the time that we have, the cloud seed machines, moat, and several lines of troops and artillery ready to fire cryo weapons, are our best defense."

"Keep me informed. Our supply routes are now up and operational," General Arya said. "Does anyone have anything else that we should all be informed of?"

Jordin looked around the room as everyone shook their heads and said "no."

Arya eyed Jordin's hands suspiciously. "Is there something you would like to tell us, Dr. Davidson?"

Jordin glanced at his hands on the table. To his horror, his fingers were wrapped around each other at odd angles. "Well...It's not much." He hastily separated his hands and let them hang at his sides to consciously keep them still. "We don't have anything conclusive. However, I believe that these two creatures were...connected as eggs."

Arya was taken aback. "What makes you believe that?"

"Both eggs have an external connector," Lauren interjected. "Both of them are broken in the same way."

"We can't confirm that they were connected to each other," Jordin said. "However, there's a strong likelihood that they were."

Arya took this in. "Twins. The elder hatching is coming to assist its sibling. Familial bonds are strong. What happens if we should interfere?"

"We'll be ready," the American said adamantly.

"We have the children. Where are the parents?" Arya looked around the room. "And were there only two eggs in the attachment?"

No one dared to say anything. Jordin didn't even want to imagine what a fully-grown adult of these creatures would look like let alone the possibility of a third egg.

The meeting ended soon after, leaving both Lauren and Jordin to wander back to their respective quarters past several new prefabricated buildings in various stages of deployment. Wind swept snow around them while occasional lightning bolts lit their path. A growing sense of uneasiness filled the air.

Despite this, myriad soldiers with various national uniforms tirelessly carried and set up equipment. Officers of differing armies gave orders to anyone and everyone nearby. No one cared what flag they saluted. Here, they were all intent upon a singular goal.

Even when surrounded by an army, Jordin still couldn't shake the feeling that they were all here alone. The countryside appeared to go on forever. The only movement was from military convoys driving supplies back and forth from the airport and the coast. All surrounding areas and those in the path of the monster had been evacuated. It would be up to them to face the threat.

"I can't help but feel like we're stranded on a remote island," Jordin said. "I know that sounds weird. We've got people and supplies coming and going constantly. But... still..."

"I think I understand." Lauren brushed snowflakes out of her bangs. "Do you think...nevermind."

"What? You can tell me."

"I guess I assumed the eggs were attached to each other.

Maybe they were attached to..." She paused as if she didn't want to finish her statement. After a few moments, she continued, "Do you think their mother is out there...looking for them?"

Jordin shuddered. "I don't know."

CHAPTER
19

Jordin awoke to someone shaking him. He opened his eyes to see an Indian soldier standing over him.

"Huh?" Jordin mumbled sleepily as he sat up and removed his earplugs.

"Dr. Davidson, you are requested immediately at the egg," the soldier said.

A bright flash of light followed by a particularly loud thunderclap startled him. He scrambled out of bed and threw on his coat. The ground beneath his feet rumbled and shook. "What the...?" He staggered and righted himself as the ground settled down.

"Please, hurry," the soldier urged.

Cold night wind blew the door out of Jordin's hands as he opened it to the outside world. Snowflakes swept in, stinging his face like little needles. He had to concentrate to keep his footing and ensure that the wind didn't knock him over. A pit grew in his stomach once he realized he felt this before.

"What's going on?" Jordin shouted over the roar of the wind.

The soldier rushed past, trudging through the ever gathering snow. "Please follow."

Lightning flashes streaked the sky. Snow was now falling at an incredible rate. The ground trembled with every other step. Up ahead, he saw a shimmering yellow glow emanating from inside the central tent. The pit in his stomach grew larger. He dreaded what he would find.

Soldiers shouted as they ran toward the tent. Several tanks, barely visible through the falling snow, drove up and aimed their weaponry at the glow.

As he reached the entrance to the tent, Lauren and another soldier walked up behind him.

"What's going on?" Lauren asked.

"I have a bad feeling that I know what's happening," Jordin gulped.

The sight that greeted them nearly took their breath away. The egg was now glowing bright yellow; its reflective sheet cover had been shaken off. An intense humming noise like thousands of locusts filled the tent. A beam of yellow light shot like a laser out of a hole in the side of the egg. Several people stood beside the hole, broken drilling equipment at their feet. The ground convulsed and the egg appeared to expand and contract as if it were breathing.

Jordin shouted to Joseph who ran up to them, "What happened?"

"They drilled a hole in the egg to get a better look at what's inside," Joseph yelled back. "Looks like that woke it up."

General Arya jogged up to join them. "Our time has run out. If you know how to kill it, now's the time!" He held up a radio. "Tell Dr. Davidson what you told me, Dr. Dhar."

Dr. Dhar's voice crackled over the radio as he spoke, "We're picking up rapid acceleration in intensity on the instruments. All indications point to something in the egg that is ionizing its surroundings. We're getting severe electromagnetic interference. This storm is going to get a whole lot worse soon."

"What do we do now?" Lauren said, watching the egg in shock.

"Uhh, uhh..." Jordin wracked his brain. All eyes were on him. He had to make decisions and fast. "Dr. Terry, get on that heart monitor. Keep us updated on its vitals," he ordered.

Lauren rushed to the heart monitor device and placed the headphones on her head. "Heartbeat is going crazy!"

The egg pulsed and the ground heaved.

"Dr. Wilber, get a pump, hoses, and a bunch of liquid nitrogen, now!" Jordin shouted. "They drilled a hole. Let's fill it with nitrogen!"

"Yes, sir!" Joseph said as he rushed off.

Jordin turned to General Arya. "We're out of options. We need to drown that thing in as much nitrogen as we can and fast. Assist Dr. Wilber at all costs. It's now or never!"

"Understood," General Arya said as he turned and started barking out orders.

Joseph and a group started grabbing lengths of hose and connecting them to a nearby pump. Several soldiers started wheeling containers of liquid nitrogen that had been stacked in a corner over to the pump.

Jordin hustled over and grabbed a container. It was heavier than he expected, straining to drag it to the growing pile by the pump.

Suddenly, the whole tent interior lit up with a blinding white flash. A deafening boom rattled Jordin's bones, standing his hair on end. Everyone startled and gawked at a smoking hole in the roof of the tent. Snow drifted through the opening.

"Did a lightning bolt just...?" Jordin trailed off.

The egg shook violently as a crack appeared where the bolt had struck. Jordin stumbled, trying to keep his footing on the quaking ground as he rushed back to grab another container.

"Heart rate is increasing!" Lauren shouted as the strange humming sound intensified.

A group of soldiers rushed to the hole in the egg, carrying the end of the hose, as other scientists scattered out of the way, shoving the end of the hose through the hole.

Jordin returned with another container as Joseph switched the pump on. Liquid nitrogen began spewing through the opening into the egg. Heavy nitrogen fog swirled around the hose and crept down the egg where it spread its cold tendrils across the ground.

A blast of chill air emanating from the entrance of the tent caused Jordin to look up. A large tanker truck rolled through the widened tent opening, escorted by a few soldiers.

"Jordin," Joseph bellowed, "watch this pump! Keep it going. I'm going to get that truck set up."

"Yes, sir," Jordin yelled back as he stood beside the pump. He had no idea how the machine worked, but he would do what he could.

The pump began sputtering as the stream of nitrogen died down.

"Replace the container!" Jordin shouted, hoping that someone nearby would know what to do.

A soldier swiftly unhooked the empty container from the attachment hose as Jordin held the hose as steadily as he could. He and the soldier quickly positioned a full container and connected it in. Nitrogen began to flow again.

Joseph and a group of people rushed forward with a far larger hose attached to the truck. "Turn off your pump!" Joseph cried out as he readied the truck hose near the hole.

Jordin turned the lever on the pump and the pump died down. Joseph wasted no time flinging the old hose aside and holding the new one to the egg. He signaled to the truck. A large stream of nitrogen burst out of the larger hose.

"HOLD THIS STEADY!" Joseph commanded. Zhukov leaped out of the truck's passenger side and gripped the hose near Joseph. A few other soldiers rushed forward to help.

Joseph handed his position off to Zhukov and ran to wheel the pile of nitrogen containers to the back of the truck.

"Heart rate is going crazy!" Lauren shouted. Her words were punctuated by a series of heavy thumps emanating from the egg that shook the ground.

Jordin stood by the original pump. He wasn't sure what else he should do. If something went wrong with the truck, he wanted to be ready to turn this pump back on. His anxious fingers tapped against each other rapidly.

The shell around the end of the hose began to turn an ashy gray. Spidery fissures emerged outward, spreading across the egg's surface as an ashen wave began to envelop the egg.

"Watch out, it's straining to do something!" Lauren called out.

A loud cracking noise sprung from the top of the egg directly beneath the hole in the tent. Jordin watched as a long, white, shimmery spike plunged through the shell and grew skyward. A blinding flash and a deafening boom startled him backward. Had a lightning bolt just struck the spike?

The shell immediately around the spike began to revert back to normal, pushing back the ashen advance.

"It's a lightning rod...," Jordin mumbled. "IT'S A LIGHTNING ROD!" he screamed while pointing at the spike. "Hey!" He waved down a soldier. "That spike is a lightning rod. We need to take it out!"

The soldier nodded and flagged a few more soldiers down. A dozen of them lined up, pulled out strange looking rifles that appeared to have be from a haphazard system of wires and pipes, and aimed them at the spike. "Fire!" the soldier commanded.

White puffs followed by loud pops erupted from the rifle barrels as the soldiers opened fire. Each bullet impact let out a puff of nitrogen vapor.

The spike began to writhe. Ashen scales formed where the bullets impacted.

"It's in pain!" Lauren yelled.

"It's working...It's actually working," Jordin said in surprise.

Another lightning flash and thunderclap caused everyone to shield their eyes and ears, including Zhukov and the others still holding onto the hose.

"The heat from the lightning is healing it all back," Jordin gasped as he watched the ashen scales fade away. "Keep firing!"

The soldiers continued their barrage. Bullet after bullet struck the spike as it waved around. More soldiers rushed into the tent carrying similar weaponry.

"Whatever you're doing, it doesn't like it!" Lauren cried out.

The ground suddenly seemed to lurch upward, knocking everyone off their feet.

Lauren screamed as the table and the monitoring machine collapsed on top of her.

"LAUREN!" Jordin quickly stumbled to his feet and ran toward her. The ground beneath his feet felt as thought it was breathing, making it difficult to walk, let alone run.

"Dr. Terry!" Jordin yelled as he arrived. He saw Lauren lying on the ground face up with the table covering most of her body, with the large monitoring machine half on the table, half off the table. The top of the machine was mere inches from her head. "Are you okay?" He grabbed the table and tried to lift it.

Lauren grimaced in pain. "Don't."

"It's crushing you," Jordin said with concern. He tried to grab the machine and push it aside.

She winced. "Just my leg. I can still hear its heartbeat. Quit moving it! When you move things, I get static. It's working now. Leave it."

"I can't just let you stay here like this."

"Not my idea of a good time either," she said, trying to crack a smile. "But we've got a job to do."

"We can deal with it. Let's get you out of here." He knelt down beside her as several soldiers ran to her aid.

"For once in my career I'm doing something people care about!" Lauren objected. "You need someone to tell you if it's still alive or not. You won't know without someone here with their finger on the pulse. You move this, you move me, you risk breaking the connection."

A medical officer ran up and put his hand on Jordin's shoulder. "Thank you, we'll take it from here, sir," he said in a British accent.

"But she's..." Jordin began.

"We'll take care of her," the officer assured as a few soldiers ushered Jordin aside. "Take care of that monster. I've got this."

Lauren grit her teeth. "It's getting angry."

Another lightning bolt struck within the tent, but this time the bolt didn't land on the egg.

Jordin stared at the line of soldiers who had been firing. Several of them were on the ground. A smoking hole in the roof of the tent over their heads told Jordin all he needed to know. The egg's lightning rod spike had bent over and was now pointing at the line of soldiers. Gray ashy scales covered its body and flaked off. It had been heavily damaged and seemed angry.

"EVERYONE GET DOWN!" General Arya wailed over a megaphone.

Jordin dropped to the ground, the other soldiers around him dropping down as well. Part of him felt bad for Zhukov; both he and the soldiers at the hose had no choice but to remain standing. Before he had time to finish his thought, a loud boom originated from outside the tent.

Before anyone could contemplate the source of the sound, a sidewall of the tent violently ripped open. A large cloud of nitrogen mist erupted at the base of the spike. The spike and shards of ashen shell tumbled, severed, to the ground.

Wind and snow whipped through the opening. Soldiers carrying stretchers rushed in from the outside to scoop up their fallen comrades.

"It's panicking!" Lauren yelled.

The deep thumps from underground increased in frequency as the ground shook violently. Zhukov and the group of soldiers standing at the egg struggled to maintain footing and grip on the hose.

The top of the shell cracked and bits of it fell away. Yellow light shot out of the newly formed holes like a laser.

"Watch out! It's coming!" Lauren screamed.

A deafening trumpet-like sound blasted from the egg causing everyone to cover their ears to their best ability while staying on task. The blast was followed by a loud cracking noise as the ground beneath the old pump suddenly rose skyward, scattering the pump and several soldiers. Dirt fell away revealing a large, grayish white, six fingered yet thumbless clawed hand protruding from the ground. Gray ashen scales crept up from the base of the hand.

Jordin watched from where he lay. The realization that he had narrowly escaped death thanks to Lauren still hadn't fully hit him yet.

"It's getting desperate!" Lauren shouted. "You're close. It can't hold out much longer!"

Soldiers opened fire on the hand as it flexed its fingers.

The hand turned toward the tanker truck, where Joseph scrambled and leaped away. The driver kicked the truck door open and dove out just as the hand clamped down on the nitrogen tank.

The multi-ton tanker truck was nothing but a toy to this hand as it lifted it up and crushed it. Liquid nitrogen poured out of the tank, dousing the hand in a freezing torrent. The hand tossed the tanker aside and shook violently. People dove out of the way as the truck smashed into workstations and rolled to a stop.

The hand twisted one final grasp skyward as gray ashy scales completely overtook it, then flopped back to the ground, motionless. Everyone stopped and stared. All armed soldiers trained their weapons on the hand. The yellow glow slowly faded along with the humming sound.

"Heartbeat slowing...slowing...slowing...," Lauren said. After a few moments pause, she finally said. "Stopped. It's...gone. It's...dead."

The egg cracked as the whole visible part crumbled and fell inward. Snowflakes that drifted in from the top of the tent became less and less frequent. No further lightning bolts struck. The howling winds subsided. Everything seemed eerily silent.

"The storm is rapidly decreasing in intensity." Dr Dhar's voice came in clearly over General Arya's radio, breaking the immediate silence. "The weather anomaly is vanishing before our eyes. Whatever you did, it worked."

Sunrays crept over the distant horizon. The clouds over-head began retreating. Dawn had arrived.

CHAPTER
20

Jordin trudged through the fast melting slush. The muggy air carried a soggy, wet odor. Sunlight pierced through the dissipating clouds making it much warmer than before. "Guess I don't need this coat anymore," he said as he took off his coat and slung it over his shoulder.

He had been tasked with cleaning up the immediate area around the egg. With everyone's help, it hadn't taken long to clear away the broken equipment.

Lauren and several others had been taken to the medical building, where he was headed now. He hoped that she and everyone else was alright, but he knew some of the soldiers probably wouldn't be. Many had been struck by lightning; others had been crushed by debris or hit by shrapnel as equipment shattered. A few of the soldiers, who had held the hoses, suffered cases of frostbite.

He approached the guard at the door and mechanically identified himself. Another guard escorted him through the building to a long rectangular room reminiscent of a dining hall. A nurse wheeled a gurney out the door as he entered. A body, covered in a sheet, lay motionless on the gurney. The sight struck Jordin dumb as it passed. After a few moments, he pulled himself together and walked into the room.

The long room was lined with beds separated by curtains along both of its side walls. General Arya mournfully watched the gurney disappear from view.

Jordin awkwardly saluted.

"He had a family." Arya nodded toward the door.

"I'm sorry." Jordin didn't know what else to say.

"His wife and child will never know why he was taken from them." The general shook his head and sighed. "I have to write a letter telling them their husband...their father was killed in an accident while studying the anomaly."

Jordin remained silent.

"It's not the first letter I've had to write today. Likely won't be the last by the end of all this." Arya looked squarely at Jordin. "People should have the right to know why their loved ones died. This secrecy is necessary for the situation. But I can't help but feel like the villain."

"Sometimes we need to do what we need to do whether we like it or not," Jordin said softly.

The general smiled and nodded. "We're all here to do a job, no matter how unpleasant it is. All I ask of anyone is to perform to their utmost best."

"I will, general," Jordin said.

"Good, your friend is over there." Arya motioned to a section of curtains. "You'll be happy to note that she's alive." He left the room.

Jordin made a beeline to the curtains Arya had indicated.

"Are you awake?"

"Are you kidding me?" Lauren's annoyed voice emanated from behind the curtains. "After what just happened, I won't sleep for a week. Come on in."

Jordin brushed the curtain aside to see Lauren in a hospital bed, her right leg in a cast propped up by a few straps. She had a few bandages on her face and hands, but otherwise looked fine. The room had a pleasant aroma.

"I see you still have your perfume," he said.

Lauren gave him a sly smile. "You noticed."

"Well...I," Jordin stammered.

"Broken leg or not, I can at least smell nice."

Jordin laughed awkwardly. "So..."

"Another day at the office?" Lauren raised an eyebrow.

"How are you feeling?"

"I can't feel my leg. Which is fine by me. Whenever I do feel it, I don't want to. Other than that, I'm alright. How are you?"

"I'm..." Jordin paused to think. "I'm physically fine."

"What about the rest of you?"

"I don't know." He sat in a nearby chair. "I never thought that my fields of study would be so dangerous."

Lauren tried to force a laugh. "Neither did I. Though...I secretly always hoped to find and study aliens. I guess that's why I went into astrophysics and biology."

"You've certainly been able to do that."

"Indeed. Though, I'm beginning to wonder if I still want to do that."

"I know what you mean..." Jordin shook his head.

Lauren reached out and gently took Jordin's hand. "You're fidgeting again. What's eating you?"

"Oh." Jordin's cheeks flushed with embarrassment as he consciously steadied his hands. "Sorry."

Lauren smiled. "Don't be. What's wrong?" She let go.

Jordin let his hands hang by his side and looked Lauren dead in the eyes. "I'm no stranger to either danger or death. I grew up in Chicago. But I've...never been responsible for it. No one has ever relied so heavily on me for survival before."

"In what way?"

"Everything we're doing is based off of what I've told people. Everyone who gets hurt is because they've been doing what I told them to do. First it was Jimmy, now more people have died, and you've been hurt. I'm project lead. I'm responsible."

Lauren looked up at the ceiling then back at Jordin. "You're not the general. And honestly, our group has only been loosely connected at best since this all started anyway."

"I know...but...they're still basing their decisions on my guesses. And that's what they've been. Guesses. I wish I could say, 'I knew all of this the whole time so listen to me.' But I honestly feel as though I'm just stumbling around. People are relying on me and I have no idea what I'm doing. And they keep getting hurt."

"I don't believe it," Lauren said, shaking her head side to side.

"What?" Jordin blinked.

"This whole time, I've been stumbling around giving them advice and gibberish biology theories. And here I find out you've been taking all the credit."

"Huh?"

"You think you're the only one who has responsibility here? What do you think we're doing when we're not talking to you?"

"That's not what I meant..."

"I've been in meetings galore with them and their science teams talking about this, that, and the other far out possibility. Joseph is running himself ragged trying to invent completely new technologies. We're all to blame here if anyone is to blame," Lauren said bitterly. "I don't think anyone really knows what they're doing. Everything has been a guess. Some have worked, some haven't." She gazed blankly at the ceiling and sighed. "It is what it is."

"I'm sorry."

Lauren sent him an accusatory glance. "Why do you always do that?"

"Do what?"

"Doubt yourself and blame yourself for everything."

Jordin shrugged. "I'm project lead. It's my responsibility."

"Hmmm." Lauren looked back at the ceiling with a distant smile on her face.

"What?"

"Do you know why I didn't go with the pharmaceutical company after it separated from P.M.L.?"

"Because P.M.L. offered you the astronomy job?" Jordin wasn't sure why Lauren was bringing this up.

"That's only part of the story."

"Oh?"

Lauren glanced back at him. "My fiancé was head of the pharmaceutical division."

"Oh," Jordin said softly.

"We had a...falling out and we separated."

"I'm sorry."

Lauren chuckled. "Don't be. It was the best thing for me. He was...manipulative. Everything that went wrong was my fault. I went along with it because...I don't know. I hoped it would get better. I just wanted to keep him happy."

Jordin had no idea what to say, so he silently listened.

"It took me a long time to realize that not everything was my fault," Lauren continued. "Sure, I made my mistakes. I accepted responsibility for what I did, but not for what he did. I wasn't going to let that guilt haunt me, nor would I ever allow something like that to happen to me again."

"Good."

Lauren gave him a wry smile. "Maybe I've gone too far the other way...with Mercury. But...don't do what I did. Don't trap yourself in guilt that you didn't earn. We all have our parts to play in what's happening here."

"Yeah...well...I mean..." Jordin wasn't sure what to say next. "I...I actually did do...," he trailed off.

"What happened?" Lauren asked gently.

Jordin grimaced and looked around to ensure no one else was in earshot, then he leaned in and spoke softly. "My parents own and operate a liquor store in Chicago."

Lauren nodded.

"I used to help them unload shipments and stock the shelves in the evenings," Jordin continued. "I grew up around alcohol and knew what it all tasted like and had been taught to drink responsibly before I ever got my driver's license. Well...," he glanced furtively around, "I was picked on in high school. And Janet...she was one of the popular girls."

Lauren gave him a big grin. "Did little Jordin have a thing for one of the popular girls?"

Jordin sheepishly nodded. "I did. She and her friends found out."

"Uh oh."

"Mmmhmmm. She also found out what my parents did. Well...I'm not proud of it, but...," he trailed off.

"You wanted to impress her?"

"And I did, for two days anyway. I stole a few boxes of alcohol and took them to one of her parties. I was the hero of the evening. For the next couple days, I was in with the popular kids. Then...they asked me to do it again. I didn't want to. So, they kicked me out of the group and I became the target again." He sighed sadly. "Then my parents found out."

Jordin was silent for a few moments before continuing. "There's no amount of childhood popularity that's worth the disappointment and loss of trust of your parents. I worked my summers mowing lawns to repay them."

"Do you still feel guilty about that?"

Jordin nodded.

"Hmmm." Lauren chuckled.

"What's so funny?" Jordin asked, a little perplexed.

"Here we both are, still suffering from bad relationships. You tried to impress a girl who wasn't worth it and I tried to hold onto a guy who wasn't worth it. Did you apologize and pay your parents back?"

"I did."

"I'm sure your parents still love you. Don't do what I did and let it eat you from the inside out."

Jordin took her words to heart. "So," he motioned to her broken leg with concern. "How are you feeling...about all of this monster stuff? I mean, besides your leg."

"Trying to change the subject?" Lauren briefly smiled then sighed, struggling to suppress her emotions. "I thought I'd be fine. I thought I could do it."

"Do what?"

Her eyes glistened slightly. "I had to sit there and listen to it." She hesitated to go on. "I heard its heartbeat. I felt it begin to panic. I felt its fear. I listened to it struggle to escape its deathtrap." She gulped, holding back tears. "I listened to its life fading away. I felt its heartbeats stop. Before it died...it...it gave one last whimper. A final cry for help. Then went silent."

Jordin couldn't help but feel a little guilty. "We did what we had to," he said after a moment of silence.

"I know," Lauren said softly. "There wasn't anything else we could've or should've done. I...I just wish things could've been different."

"Me too." Jordin thought for a moment before asking, "Will you be able to deal with the big one?"

"I'm here for the long haul," she replied. "These things are killing us. I'll do what I have to. Just don't...don't ever hook me up to a heart monitor on one again."

"It's a deal."

The curtain brushed aside revealing Zhukov. His hands were bandaged but that wasn't slowing him down. "Dr.

CHAPTER 20

Davidson. You're wanted immediately." Even with his impatience he still managed to nod at Lauren.

"Okay," Jordin stood.

Zhukov turned toward the exit, with Jordin following behind. The pair walked out of the medical building, through the muddy slush, and into another building. Once inside, they entered a large presentation room.

Several military officers and dignitaries were already sitting and waiting. Dr. Dhar and General Arya stood at the front of the room next to a large screen, featuring Colonel Dubinin attending virtually.. Dhar acknowledged Jordin as he entered, with Zhukov remaining next to the door.

"I believe everyone is here," Arya said as Jordin took a seat next to Joseph.

"As you are all aware," Arya began, "last night, we began drilling operations to attempt viewing what was inside the egg. This awakened the creature within. Thanks to the fast action of everyone here, we were able to put this creature down. Though, not without casualties."

"An impressive feat, to be sure," Dubinin said. "I can tell you that the notice of the creature's death was much needed good news. You may have bought yourselves more time before more drastic measures are taken. I must warn you, such measures are still not off the table while the other creature is alive. The more ardent supporters of such things have been silenced. Their silence won't last forever. That being said, I'm given to understand that you have some bad news."

General Arya nodded at Dr. Dhar. "Please present your findings, doctor."

"Thank you, general," Dhar said as he pressed a button on a remote. The screen changed to show a graph of data. "As you all know, we've been monitoring the original storm closely. This graph measures its intensity and size, as indicated by these lines." He pointed to a pair of lines trending upward. "These have remained steady ever since cloud seed efforts started. However..." He clicked a button and a new line appeared on the graph. The line was fairly flat except for the right side, which turned sharply upward at the end. "This line measures the speed at which the storm is moving. It was consistent until this morning."

Murmurs rolled through the room.

"The speed of the storm has greatly increased," Dhar continued.

"What does this mean for us?" Dubinin asked.

"By our new calculations, the storm will arrive tomorrow evening. We've lost a day to prepare."

"Why would it suddenly do this?" a British officer asked.

"I am not qualified to answer that," Dhar said. "However, I can tell you that the time of the speed increase matches the time of death of the creature in our egg."

"It knows!" a Middle Eastern dignitary shouted. "It knows what we did. It's coming for vengeance."

"It's very possible," Arya said. "We can, at least, assume that it knows something's wrong."

"I can corroborate the speed increase," Dubinin said as the speakers picked up the sound of his shuffling papers. "Our cloud seed pilots report that our trajectories have been off for the past couple hours. They say 'the storm is further along the trajectory than expected.' Instrument readings are showing an increase in speed." He mulled something over before continuing. "They've also reported hearing a loud trumpet-like noise moments before our trajectories deviated. I suggest everyone prepare. You killed a monster before it hatched. Here comes its big brother. I highly doubt it will be as easy to kill. Where are we at with supplies and setup at your location?"

"We are doubling manpower and increasing shift lengths to have more overlap," Arya said. "We have several cargo ships and planes on the way. I will be ordering all non-essential and wounded personnel to evacuate the area immediately."

Arya turned to face Dr. Dhar. "Doctor, I will be moving you and your crew off base to a station in town. Will you still be able to operate?"

"Yes," Dhar said, "as long as we have connections to the data streams. Will you have the strengthened communications antennas up soon?"

Arya asked Joseph, "Dr. Wilber, how close are we to having the communications antenna arrays operational?"

"I believe we can have them up this afternoon. We won't be able to test if they can actually cut through the static generated by the monsters now though," Joseph said.

"How confident are you that we will still have communications operational even when the monster interferes?"

"As confident as I can be right now," Joseph smiled. "I'll run all the tests I can in the time that I have."

"Dr. Davidson," General Arya said, moving on to Jordin, "I will be relocating you to the same off-base location as Dr. Dhar. What do you need to continue your work?"

"With all due respect, general," Jordin said, "I believe that I would be best suited here."

"I appreciate your willingness to assist," Arya said, smiling. "But you are a civilian and a liability in combat."

"You came to me when the egg went crazy." Jordin stood his ground. "Besides, my team and I have been studying the big one the longest. Your strategy and planning is based off of what we've told you. If something goes wrong, I believe I need to be here to assist. Also, as I'm assuming Dr. Terry will be evacuated, someone will need to be in communication with her. She has been invaluable in studying these creatures and may have some insight when we face the big one. As I'm her project lead, I will take her place here."

"The crazy American wants to meet his monster again," Dubinin chuckled. The screen changed back to his camera view. "He makes some good points, general. We've been coming to him and his team. They've been studying this from the beginning. It seems a shame to shut them out now."

"Very well," Arya conceded. "But you will be under my direct command. If you stay, you will assist us in building and readying defenses."

"Agreed," Jordin said.

"I sincerely hope that we succeed," Dubinin said. "I'm not sure how much longer I can keep my analysts sane. Most of your P.M.L. team members here working with us are very helpful." Dubinin couldn't hide his amusement. "However, Bob has been very vocal about his displeasure. We may survive this monster, but he will 'take us all down in court.'"

Arya snorted. "I trust he will have a hard time taking anyone to court over events that 'never happened.'"

"Indeed, general," Dubinin said, grinning from ear to ear.

A commotion outside of the conference room caught everyone's attention. A soldier escorting one of Dhar's P.M.L. crew rushed in and motioned to Dhar for a word. All eyes in the room watched Dhar speak to the pair. Dhar finally nodded and stepped back to the front of the room.

"I have bad news," Dhar said. "We're detecting another storm over Taiwan."

Murmurs rolled through the room.

"Do we have any information on this storm?" Dubinin

asked. He turned and shouted something in Russian to someone off-screen. "Is this another monster storm or just a natural storm?"

"It's still too early to tell," Dhar replied. "The local governments are withholding their promised nitrogen shipments as a precaution."

"We need to send a task force immediately to verify," Arya said, looking around the room. "We can't spare anyone here."

"My business partner Mr. Mercury is already there," Dhar assured. "He was sent to retrieve the shipment. He would be able to investigate."

"Can you walk him through it?" Arya asked.

"I'll do my best."

Arya's expression darkened. "We're on limited time now. I sincerely hope we don't have another egg to deal with. You all know your assignments. Get to it."

CHAPTER
21

"Lauren isn't going to like this," Jordin muttered as he nervously rubbed his palms together. He marched back to the medical facility to assist in the evacuations, as several medical transports drove past him to the building. Nurses and soldiers rolled wounded out on gurneys.

He slipped through the entrance to the medical room. Everyone was too busy milling about to take notice of him as he walked right up to Lauren's curtained-off cubicle.

"Quite the commotion going on," Lauren said as he opened the curtain and stepped in.

"There's been a new...development." Jordin grimaced.

"Oh?" Lauren gave his hands a sidelong glance. "Bad news, I take it?"

"A new storm is forming over Taiwan."

"What!?" Lauren jolted. "We have a third one?"

"No one knows for sure yet. Mr. Mercury is going to investigate. They have supplies that we need. They may be delayed now... or never arrive. If it is a third one, they'll keep the supplies to use themselves."

"Oh, great. Mr. Mercury is investigating...," Lauren said, unimpressed.

"Give him some credit. He really seems like he's trying his best now to do what he needs to do."

Lauren sighed. "You're right. I'm just so used to him... yeah. I'm sorry."

"Don't worry about it." Jordin's hands began to fidget faster. He knew that he had to tell Lauren that she was going to be evacuated. She was already eyeing him suspiciously.

"What else is going on?"

"They're evacuating the wounded," Jordin replied, gritting his teeth.

"I know. Can't hardly think with all the commotion around here. I was expecting it to happen tomorrow." She sighed. "I was hoping that maybe I'd be better by then and I could join you."

"The big monster has sped up significantly. We've lost a day. It'll be here tomorrow."

"Is that what they are? Monsters?" Lauren grunted.

"I...I don't know what else to call them."

"Hmmm...do we know why it sped up?"

Jordin was afraid to bring up the reason. After a brief internal argument, he finally said, "It sped up at the exact time we...killed ours."

"So they were communicating somehow." Lauren averted her eyes to the ceiling, taking this all in. "Its friend stopped talking, now it's worried."

"That's our theory."

A nurse and a few medical assistants entered the cubicle and began unhooking several devices.

"Wait a minute," Lauren objected, "I said I'd be here for the long haul and I meant it. I can still do something."

Her pleas were to no avail. A soldier wheeled a gurney in and placed it beside the bed. He nodded at Jordin and the nurse to assist.

"I'm sorry," Jordin said as he helped lift her out of the bed and onto the gurney. Lauren looked incensed but didn't resist. "I'll be in communication with you. We need your help still. But we need you to be safe."

"What good am I if I'm not here?" Lauren scowled.

"You can guide me through it. I'll send you stuff and you can tell me what you think."

"Am I just supposed to sit in bed twiddling my thumbs and spewing gibberish at you now?"

"Think of it as...we're sending you to a research station." Jordin helped wheel the gurney out of the room and down the hall.

"Just great," Lauren scoffed, "break one bone and suddenly you can't do your job, and everyone babies you."

"We'll be in touch," Jordin said as he wheeled the gurney to a waiting medical transport outside. The medical personnel brushed Jordin aside to take over, lifting the gurney into the back of the transport and ignoring Lauren's protest.

"We better stay in touch! And don't you let that thing kill you!" Lauren yelled just before the doors of the transport closed.

Jordin watched the vehicle drive off, then turned back toward the medical building.

Before taking a step, Zhukov's voice shouted from behind him, "Dr. Davidson!"

Jordin turned to see Zhukov sitting in the driver's seat of a truck. "Yes?"

Zhukov motioned for him to come over. "You're needed at the docks."

"Me? The docks? Why?"

"Get in, I'll explain on the way."

Jordin hopped into the passenger seat, staring inquisitively at Zhukov.

"Lucky for us, you're considered a VIP," Zhukov grinned as he flipped a switch on the ceiling. Yellow lights on top of the truck began to flash. "Should make it faster." He drove the truck forward and maneuvered out of the gates. The bandages on his frostbitten hands didn't seem to affect his driving capabilities.

Several other trucks carrying supplies passed them by, heading toward the base. Other trucks in front of them moved to the side as they approached.

"What's all this about?" Jordin asked.

"You've got a shipment," Zhukov said flatly.

Jordin had no idea what Zhukov was talking about. "What is it?"

"That's what we need to find out. It's quite a large shipment."

"Why do I need to go to the docks? Why is anyone sending anything to me? And how would they know I'm here?"

"They insist that your signature is required to sign off on the shipments. They assure us that it's supplies that will help. As for who it is and how they know you're here, we're hoping you can tell us."

"I have no idea who or what it could be." Jordin shrugged.

"Have you been ordering things from your mysterious phone pals in Japan?" Zhukov gave Jordin a quick suspicious glance.

"I haven't ordered anything." Jordin shook his head vigorously. "I didn't tell them where I was so they couldn't ship me something if they wanted to." He clasped his hands and tapped his thumbs against each other.

"Then we'll both find out what it is and who it's from."

Jordin peered ahead at the passing landscape in an awkward silence. He didn't know what to say and Zhukov wasn't much of a conversationalist.

"Is there a reason we didn't use a helicopter?" Jordin finally asked. He had seen several helicopters going back and forth from the base to the airport. Secretly, he was glad not to be in a helicopter, but he was curious nonetheless.

"I requested one," Zhukov grunted. "It would have been faster. But they insisted that all helicopters were in use ferrying important equipment and evacuating personnel. We can also put a container on the back of this truck much more easily than on a helicopter. I hear it's a few large shipping containers."

"Ah. I guess that makes sense."

"It is what it is."

The two rode in silence for a while.

"So," Jordin said hesitantly, hoping to strike up some more conversation, "how did you get involved in all of this?"

"I go where my country needs me and do what my country asks me to do."

"Okay," Jordin said, followed by more awkward silence. "Do you have a family at home?"

"I do. Do you?"

"Just my parents so far. Well, they're in their own home. I'm alone in my apartment."

"Hmmm," Zhukov sounded incredibly uninterested, "let me ask you something, American."

"Okay."

"How did you get involved in all of this?"

"I don't know, really," Jordin said with a shrug. "I didn't

mean to. I just wanted to study weather and gravitational pulls. This anomaly just...happened while I was in an observatory. It all just came together...I guess."

"Hmmm," Zhukov snorted, "as good a reason as any. Would you do it all again? Knowing what you know now?"

"I don't know...I made some mistakes."

"Would you be willing to go to a foreign land to face an unknown foe and likely die if your country requested it?"

A thought came to Jordin that suddenly made him chuckle.

"You find it funny?" Zhukov raised an eyebrow.

"My country didn't have to ask me to do that. I did it before they could. I beat my own country's soldiers to it. I don't think I'd change that."

Now this, Zhukov found funny. "When this is over. I'll buy you a few drinks. One patriot to another."

"I haven't been to a bar in a while, but I have to warn you, I was able to out-drink everyone in my dorm in college."

"Ah," Zhukov laughed, "good, I like a challenge." He reached into his pocket and pulled out a wallet. He flipped it open and held it out. "My family. To answer your question."

The picture showed Zhukov with a woman and two children. "How old are they?"

"My son is nine, and my daughter is six." Zhukov put the wallet back in his pocket.

"You're a fortunate man."

"Do you have any...family prospects?" Zhukov pried.

Jordin shook his head. "Not yet."

"Something wrong?"

"I've just been focused on university, then getting a job. Now I have to square up my life."

"Hmmm, I thought most people didn't wait to do that."

"Maybe not. But I figured I needed to be able to take care of myself before I tried to take care of anyone else."

This amused Zhukov. "Probably a good idea."

"How about you? When did you meet your wife?"

"I met her while on leave. She worked at a bar in my hometown."

"How long have you been in the military?"

"My whole adult life. Just like my father and my grandfather. Is your father an astronomer?"

"No." Jordin shook his head. "My parents own a liquor store."

"Ah. That explains your alcoholic prowess," Zhukov said with a grin. "Did you not want to take up the family business?"

"Well...no. It never appealed to me to own a liquor store."

"And why not?"

"You deal with a lot of...interesting people. You have to have the right temperament to do that. Plus I've always been interested in space and weather, way more than buying and selling alcohol."

"You don't have that temperament?"

"I can deal with strange people in small doses. But they deal with several daily. Then there's always someone trying to steal something or break the rules somehow. I just don't want to deal with it."

"You would rather deal with Mr. Mercury and alien monsters?"

This good point made Jordin laugh. "I guess so. As long as the monster doesn't want to buy any alcohol, I'll be fine."

"I would hate to see such a beast when it was drunk."

"I wonder if it can get drunk?" Jordin mused.

"A question for another scientist."

"Indeed."

Now Zhukov had a thought that cracked him up.

"What's so funny?" Jordin asked.

"Maybe we would win if you challenged it to a drinking contest."

"Just find a way to communicate with it and I'll challenge it."

"Deal." Zhukov smiled, which faded almost as quickly as it had appeared.

The next few hours of the trip went by with sporadic conversation. Zhukov said very little and never offered up much information. Jordin's efforts to strike up a conversation dried up. Many of his awkwardly phrased questions were met with single word answers or silence. Remarkably, Zhukov seemed more amused by Jordin than frustrated. The lieutenant's constant smirks and grins made Jordin feel a little foolish, like he was a child that Zhukov was babysitting.

"Do you have your ID?" Zhukov asked when they arrived at the docks.

"Yes." Jordin reached into his pocket and pulled out his wallet.

"Good," Zhukov said as the pair exited the truck.

They were led to a nearby stack of large metal shipping containers. A man wearing a company uniform and holding a clipboard approached.

"Are you Dr. Jordin Davidson?" the man asked.

"Yes." Jordin nodded matter-of-factually.

"I need to see some ID"

"Oh, of course." Jordin produced his ID

The man looked at the ID, then handed Jordin the clipboard, pointing to a signature line. "I need you to sign here."

The company name at the top of the document read *Gorilla Whale Shipping Services.* Jordin signed the dotted line then asked, "Do you know what all of this is?"

"Yes, sir. It's yours now," the man said as he grabbed the

clipboard back. "Have a nice day." He walked away.

"Uh...thanks? You too?" Jordin called after him. "Now what in the world is all of this?" he wondered about the stack of shipping containers before him.

"There's a note." Zhukov pointed to a plastic bag taped to the side of a container. "Ah, Japanese. So, it is your friends."

"How did...?" Jordin opened the bag and pulled out a few papers. Japanese kanji filled one side of a page. He flipped it over to see the English translation on the other side. It read, *Dear Dr. Davidson. We hope that this finds you well. We regret that we cannot meet in person. Since our last conversation, we have been hard at work to discover a solution to our problem. As I'm sure you are aware, the nature of this problem has given rise to myriad downfalls for modern solutions. We have developed a few mechanisms that we believe will be useful. All of the parts and instructions have been shipped to you. I trust that you will put these to good use.*

The page was signed, *Sincerely, your friends; I.H. and T.T.*

"Is this...?" Jordin thought out loud, flipping to the other page. He saw several diagrams and instructions. "Wait... They want us to make..."

The metal doors creaked as Zhukov pried them open. He squinted at the contents as if trying to find some secret code. He glanced at Jordin, then at the instructions in his hand, then grinned. "We're going medieval on this monster."

CHAPTER

22

General Arya was surprised by the instructions in his hand. "They want us to build what?"

"We're already building a moat, why not a few ballistae?" Joseph chuckled alongside Jordin and Zhukov in General Arya's office. "It's quite an advanced ballista design. People in the medieval era could only have dreamed of having something like this." He struggled to hold back laughter. "You could just call it 'a giant slingshot that fires huge liquid nitrogen filled arrows' if you want. A cryo-ballista...er cryo-sling."

Arya shook his head. "That doesn't make it sound better."

"To my understanding," Zhukov said, "we're having trouble due to the low heat requirements coupled with the armor piercing requirements."

"I'm not so sure about the armor piercing anymore," Jordin said. "After all, the cryo-bullets we had did a number on the creature."

"That reminds me, you weren't here for the update on the U.N.'s research task force. They've been busy studying the egg and the creature we have." Arya pulled a few papers out of his desk. "We were able to awaken this creature before it had a chance to fully develop its outer exoskeleton. Reports say that it was in the process of forming it when we killed it. There is also some doubt as to how the nitrogen we pumped into the egg affected it. They now believe that the only reason we killed it was because it was still attached to the egg at the base. The liquid nitrogen that entered the channels in between the egg layers appeared to do more than the nitrogen we poured directly onto the creature. We froze it from the inside out."

"So, that means...," Jordin realized.

"We got lucky. The big one won't have the same vulnerability," Zhukov said bluntly.

"Then this might be the perfect weapon," Joseph said. "We don't have any explosions generating heat. The bolt flies at a speed slow enough to reduce air friction. It probably won't even generate as much heat as a sub-sonic bullet. The 'arrowheads' are razor sharp and heavy. So, they stand a good chance of piercing any armor they strike."

"And then what?" Arya asked. "We hit it with an arrow?"

"The whole shaft of the bolt is a liquid nitrogen reservoir. Think about a dozen of our containers welded together. They've even supplied us with the nitrogen. All we have to do is pierce through the creature's exoskeleton and it's designed to rupture that reservoir inside the target."

Arya tapped his finger on his desk. "Do you think it will work?"

"No guarantee of that," Joseph said, shrugging. "But I'd

say high probability. It's better to try than to not."

"How many can we make?"

"Looks like they gave us enough to make three ballist... er...cryoslings with six shots each."

"We have eighteen chances..." Arya said, full of doubt.

"If everything we know is correct," Joseph began. "We only need one shot in the right place and the nitrogen will do its work. However, anywhere we hit it will do some serious damage. It's a big enough target."

"I would rather die knowing that we tried every option we could rather than die knowing we could've tried something else," Zhukov interjected.

"Very well," Arya said, waving his hand dismissively. "Build them. We will tell you where to place them."

Joseph saluted. "Yes, sir."

Dr. Dhar's voice speaking in Hindi came over Arya's radio. The general replied, then said, "Dr. Dhar has Mr. Mercury on the line. There is an update on the Taiwanese storm."

"Hello?" Mr. Mercury said over the radio.

"Report, what is your status?" Arya asked.

Everyone else in the room held their breath, knowing the importance of Mr. Mercury's report.

"Oh, uh...hello general. I'm happy to report that the storm is a false alarm. There is no egg."

All breathed a sigh of relief.

"This storm," Mercury continued, "is completely natural. Actually, its pretty much gone now too."

"That is most welcome news," Arya said with a rare smile. "What does this mean about our supplies?"

"Well," Mercury said, sounding agitated, "our supplies aren't ready yet. The government held onto the nitrogen stock until we could verify what the storm was. Now we know...It's been like pulling teeth to get the nitrogen released to us and loaded. Bureaucracy, you know."

Arya remained calm. "Understood. How soon can you return?"

"I'm not sure. Let me ask someone."

A muffled conversation took place in the background for a few minutes.

"Hello?" Mr. Mercury said.

"Do you have a status update?" Arya asked.

"Yes, sorry. Our arrival back at the base will be delayed until tomorrow evening."

"That's unacceptable. We require you and the supplies back tomorrow morning at the latest."

"Well...," Mercury said, "we could leave now, but we don't have anything. I can't leave without the supplies and I'm not in charge of that. I can tell everyone you need it, but that won't make it magically appear. If you want to shout at the bureaucrats for me, that'd be fine."

Jordin winced. Mr. Mercury was never one for tact.

"Have you and the others been made aware of our new situation?" Arya asked. "There have been new developments since your departure from here."

"I heard you killed the egg. Good job!" Mr. Mercury said. "I also hear the big one is making a grand appearance much sooner than expected."

"Then you understand why we need you and the supplies back before tomorrow evening."

"Yes...yes I do. But there's not much I can do about that. I'll do what I can."

"Understood. Carry on. I will be contacting the necessary parties to try and speed up the process."

"Yes, sir...general sir," Mr. Mercury replied enthusiastically.

As the line went dead, the general closed his eyes, barely able to contain his mounting frustration. He opened his eyes to address everyone. "I don't need to tell any of you how narrowly we've escaped destruction. After two of these creatures, all the world governments are now scared of every heavy breeze. I assume that you all know what they are apt to do if left to stew in their worry. I will send Mr. Mercury's report to all concerned." He looked at Zhukov. "Be sure to inform your superiors."

Zhukov nodded, and Arya returned it.

"You all know your assignments. Get to it."

Jordin spent the rest of the day assisting Joseph and the engineering crew in building the cryoslings and setting up various other defenses. The death of the egg creature and Mr. Mercury's bittersweet news lifted everyone's spirits, but this was short-lived. The sense of impending doom now hung heavily over the base.

As the sun began to dip below the horizon, Jordin ascended the metal staircase of the northwestern watchtower. The tower was little more than a metal platform on stilts covered by a steel pyramid-shaped canopy. There were no walls, only a railing around the platform to prevent accidents.

The soldier normally on duty here was nowhere to be found, likely called away to help with other tasks.

Now that efforts were winding down, Jordin knew the soldier would be returning to his post soon. Until then, this was probably one of the few places and times where he could go to be alone and collect his thoughts. He was physically and mentally exhausted from a day of hard work and he knew that tomorrow would be even harder. He was too tired to pay attention to the height and slight wobble of the structure.

Once at the top, he walked to the northwestern edge and leaned on the railing to survey the scene. The cold metal chilled his hands to the bone as he tightened his grip so as to steady himself. A wide moat with a small retractable bridge wrapped around both the northern and western sides of the compound. Lines of tanker trucks dumped their saltwater payloads into the moat and drove away, making room for the next line of trucks.

Tanks and artillery installations were positioned outside of the base behind the moat, serving as the primary forward defenses. Other cannons and tanks were scattered around the base. Engineering crews had rapidly installed cloud seed machines along the countryside to the northwest.

The wide rolling landscape sent a chill down Jordin's spine as the sun began to set, its last rays reflecting off the moat waters. Ignoring the height and wobble of the tower, and knowledge of the terrible threat steadily marching toward him, the view would be calming and relaxing.

Soldiers rolled two of the cryoslings below, each one standing ten meters tall and twenty meters long. Twin prongs that could fold out to hold the elastic firing rope ran along the sides. A long channel in the center contained a trap door that, when opened, revealed the bolts beneath, equally as long.

All they needed to do to load a shot was to open the trap door and pull the firing plate and the elastic bands back. A bolt would then pop into place. Once fired, they would simply pull the plate back again to reload.

The firing methodology was a combination of elastic bands and magnetic rails. By pressing a button on a panel at its side, the elastic bands would start pulling, the firing plate and an electromagnet would activate, pushing the heavy iron plate even faster. The bolt in front of the plate would be thrown at great speeds over long distances, at least in theory. Jordin had watched engineers assemble and successfully test them with other objects.

The whole device had been shipped pre-wired and incredibly modularized. All that the engineers had to do was follow the instructions and fit each piece together.

I should probably thank our mysterious benefactors, Jordin thought.

He pulled out his phone and began dialing.

"Hello, friend," the familiar yet strange voice greeted him.

"Hello. Were you the one who sent us the cryo-ballistae parts?"

"I assume that they have arrived."

"Yes, they have," Jordin said gratefully.

"Good. I regret that we had so little to send. If we had more time..." the voice said, not finishing his thought.

"That's fine," Jordin tried to reassure. "We weren't expecting anything to begin with."

"May they serve you well."

"I'm sure they will. I was calling to thank you for sending them."

"You are most welcome, my friend."

"I'll let you know how they work." Jordin gazed out over the landscape uneasily.

"Are we correct in our understanding that the egg has been dealt with? The anomaly over your position has vanished."

"Yes, it's dead."

"Encouraging news. We have a chance yet."

"I can confirm that liquid nitrogen inside the creature is fatal."

"As it would be for us as well."

"True. I suppose I'm not saying anything that we couldn't have guessed."

"We would have turned to fire as our solution were it not for you and your team. Then we would have surely failed."

"I'm sure someone would've discovered it had I not."

"Perhaps," the voice mused, "yet we do not have to find out. What could have been is not what has been or will be."

"Can't argue with that."

"We also see that the original creature is moving faster now. Is that true?" the voice asked in concern.

"Yes," Jordin frowned as he began pacing, "it's unfortunate but true. It will be here tomorrow night."

"I don't envy you, my friend."

"It is what it is. I chose to be here."

"Stay strong, friend. We watch in anticipation. Our only regret is that we cannot stand with you in person."

Jordin carefully considered his response. "Look," he finally said softly, "we got lucky with the egg. We only stood a chance because it hadn't fully developed yet. It was the egg structure itself that enabled us to kill it. I've no idea if what we're going to do here will work. I've been wrong with this before and people have died. If I'm wrong this time, I won't be around to warn anyone. You know what could happen if we fail here. You know what people will do. I may be wrong about how to kill it, but if I'm right about what it feeds on...I dread to think of what these drastic measures may cause."

"Understood."

"I may not come out of this. If I don't, someone needs to learn from this. Someone needs to delay these drastic measures until there's no other option. Someone needs to find a way to stop this thing. It doesn't need to be me. I don't think I'm even qualified to be where I am now. I could be leading everyone to their doom."

"We stand ready to pick up the fight. Even should you fail, your efforts will give us valuable information."

Jordin sighed. He reflected upon all his past conversations with the mysterious caller. A sudden realization came over him. "I don't know who you are, but thank you. Everyone gives me credit for discovering its susceptibility to cold. Yet, I only thought of it after talking to you. You probably knew the whole time and just led me to the answer."

"We simply question what is known in order to discover what is unknown."

"There's no way you could've designed, built, and shipped these cryoslings in the time since I 'discovered' the cold weakness. You told me it wasn't a storm. You're the one who put it in my head to check the news broadcasts for editing. And you held my hand as I stumbled around looking for its weakness. Who are you? I.H.? T.T.? What do those initials stand for? And how did you know all of this? And why did you choose me?"

"Someday, you may understand. Reality is far stranger than we know."

"If I make it out alive, I'll owe you one."

"Victory is the only payment needed."

"I'll do my best."

"We know you will. Farewell, friend."

"Wait! I need to know who you...," Jordin tried to ask, but was too late. The line clicked and went silent. Jordin placed his phone back into his pocket as he returned to the railing to observed the cryoslings below. *Who are you?*

"Prepared for tomorrow?" Zhukov said from behind him.

Startled, Jordin turned around. "Yes...er...well...I think so."

"I hope your friends know what they're doing. It sounds like we've based everything off of their input." Zhukov was baiting Jordin, but before he could respond, they both heard heavy clunking on the metal stairs leading up to their position. Joseph emerged from the stairwell carrying a few boxes.

"Ah, good, you two can help me," Joseph grunted upon

seeing Jordin and Zhukov. He set the boxes on the floor by the railing. "I've got binoculars, telescopes, and communications antennae."

A ladder suddenly propped itself up against the outside of the tower. Another engineer ascended the ladder, carrying more antennae and wiring.

"Will the communications work through the static?" Zhukov asked as both he and Jordin helped Joseph unpack the boxes.

"As far as I know, they will." Joseph motioned toward the telescopes. "Set up those standing telescopes so they face northwest. These binoculars need to be up here somewhere so that people can grab them and use them at will. I'll be helping him set up the antennae on the roof," he said, pointing at the engineer climbing the ladder.

Jordin was already tired of setting things up, but he helped Zhukov place the telescopes. He knew everyone else was equally as tired.

After everything had been set up, Joseph flipped a switch on a metal box he had wired to the antennae on top. "Northwestern watchtower reporting in. I repeat, northwestern watchtower reporting in. Can you hear me?"

"We can hear you, northwestern watchtower," Dr. Dhar's voice replied.

"Good. Please inform General Arya, this watchtower is wired up to receive, transmit, and boost the signals."

"Will do."

"Moving on to the next tower." Joseph flipped a switch and sighed. "At least this one worked the first time." He chuckled. "Now I'm worried it'll break when we need it. Oh well, on to the next one." He and the other engineer left Jordin and Zhukov alone again, taking the ladder with them.

Zhukov peered through a telescope. "I hope you like the view from up here."

"It's not a bad view. I'd like it better if some big monster weren't headed for us," Jordin said.

"Getting...how would you say it...cold feet?"

"No. I said I'd stay. I'm staying."

"I've been instructed to drive you off base into town to join Dr. Dhar and the others if you wish," Zhukov said, still peering out the telescope.

Jordin blinked and remained silent.

"The general is very generously giving you another way out," Zhukov continued. "Were it up to me or Colonel Dubinin, you wouldn't have another opportunity like this. I wouldn't squander it if I were you."

"No," Jordin shook his head, "I'm here to stay. You can drive me off base and to the airport when the creature is dead."

Zhukov straightened and turned to Jordin, studying him. Then a slight smile crept across his face. "Good. I wouldn't want to owe a drink to a coward." He gazed out over the landscape.

"Besides," Jordin said with a shrug, "these communications haven't been tested against this monster's interference. If that breaks down, I'd be in the dark the whole time if I wasn't here. My theories could fail and everyone could die and I'd not know it until it was too late. I can't risk everyone's lives by just hoping that I'm right and hoping that these communications will work. Who would I be if I told everyone that they had to risk their lives listening to my theory if I wasn't willing to do the same? How trustworthy would I be?"

Zhukov nodded as he continued to take in the landscape.

"You can give me a gun and I'll shoot the monster myself if I need to," Jordin continued. "I didn't grow up or gain a doctorate in my field by running away from challenges."

"Well said," remarked the Middle Eastern dignitary from Arya's office as he ascended the metal steps. "My own thoughts exactly." He joined Jordin at his side. "I've already argued with Arya about this myself. This foe ravaged my lands. I'll not retreat from it if it can be stopped. Anyone who stands with me, against it, is an ally. I will write a formal complaint to my government should his request be denied."

Zhukov turned and smiled in solidarity. "I'm glad you could join us." Zhukov bowed slightly to the dignitary. "It saves me the trouble of tracking you down to inform you. I've requisitioned cryo-rifles for the both of you. As you're both staying, you will need to defend yourselves."

"Good," the dignitary said emphatically.

"I won't deny fellow patriots their opportunity to join us in arms against our common enemy." Zhukov walked to the stairs. "The general expects both of you to report atop this watchtower tomorrow at 14 hundred hours sharp. You are both to observe and report any changes in theory. If things go poorly, you are to evacuate in an escape convoy."

A white vapor began emitting from the cloud seed machines over the countryside, creating a dull hissing noise. Jordin and the dignitary exchanged knowing nods.

CHAPTER
23

Jordin barely slept that night. He knew what the day would bring. In his dreams, he was constantly running from a freezing tornado that was unrelenting in its pursuit.

He awoke early the next morning, already exhausted. It took a strong internal push for him to lift himself out of bed. Part of him hoped that maybe if everyone just pretended it was still night and kept sleeping, the monster would never come.

"Irrational, silly...," he mumbled as he mechanically readied for the day.

The air around the base was filled with tension. Soldiers, engineers, and the few remaining scientists somberly went about their last-minute preparations. Whatever didn't get done today, never would be.

He spent the morning assisting the soldiers in carrying weaponry, ammunition, and supplies to artillery encampments. Barely anyone spoke to him as he mimicked what the others were doing without being asked.

When noon arrived, he sat in the outdoor mess hall with the soldiers.

"There you are," Joseph said as he wandered over with a food tray and sat next to Jordin. "I almost thought you'd left."

"Not yet," Jordin said. "I've been supplying the artillery with munitions."

"Ah. I've been finishing up the communications installations."

"How's that going?"

"As well as you could expect when you install experimental technology that hasn't been fully tested yet," Joseph said with his signature chuckle.

"That well, huh?" Jordin took a bite.

"I warned them about all of this. But that's just how it goes. As long as we accomplish our goal in the end, right?"

"I suppose so."

"Have you had a chance to check out those cryoslings yet?" Joseph took a sip of his drink.

"Not really. Not up close, at least."

"You should. For something based off of medieval technology, they're fairly advanced."

"I did read the instructions and I saw them tested. I bet people back then would've killed to have an electromagnetically assisted ballista," Jordin laughed.

"It would've outperformed anything in that day. I'm beginning to believe it'll even outperform what we have today."

"Really? That seems...odd to say. I mean...they're nice

looking machines. But are they really better than an artillery cannon?"

"Under normal circumstances, no," Joseph said. "For just about every application you could think of, an artillery cannon would be far better. However, in this instance, the ballista may just be better." He pointed with his fork at the ballista in the center of the camp.

"What makes you say that?"

"It's very hard for modern weaponry to not rely on heat in some way. Whether through explosions, massive amounts of force generated on impact, or from air resistance. These ballistae may be perfectly suited for what we need. They'll have enough impact force to pierce the exoskeleton, but not enough to generate large amounts of heat in the process."

"I guess we'll find out."

"Indeed." Joseph nodded vigorously.

The roar of jet engines echoed across the landscape from a squadron of jet fighters flying overhead, heading northwest. A little while later, a fleet of larger, slower-moving planes with nozzles trailing behind their wings followed.

"That's our cloud seed squadron," Joseph said as these planes flew by. "If they're activated...that means it's getting close..."

Jordin shivered at the thought and concentrated on his meal.

"You okay?" Joseph asked.

"Don't worry." Jordin shook his head. "I'm fine...I'm just...nervous is all."

"So am I." Joseph sighed and pulled his wallet out of his pocket. "I'd be lying if I wasn't afraid that I might die. But I'm more worried about them." He opened his wallet and pulled out a picture, setting it on the table. "Who takes care of them when...if I'm gone."

Jordin examined the photo showing Joseph with his arms wrapped around a woman and his three teenage children, two boys and a girl, all smiling.

"They all want to go to college. But they need someone to pay..." Joseph chocked back tears. He cleared his throat and continued, "Emily is this close to getting her braces off." He pointed at his daughter. "I was looking forward to seeing her first smile without them." His eyes remained fixed on the photograph.

"Don't worry," Jordin assured. "We'll get through this. You'll see your daughter smile. And the rest of your family too."

Joseph scooped the photo up and returned it to his wallet, his usual light demeanor turning thoughtful and serious. "I'm here to face this thing now so that she doesn't have to later....So that none of them have to. As long as I can assure their survival, that will be enough for me."

Jordin thought about his own family. He wasn't married and didn't have any children, but he had parents. The thought of this monster rampaging through Chicago and killing his mother and father was enough to make his own blood boil. He knew that Joseph was right. If they failed here, then this thing wouldn't stop anytime soon. It may hate water now, but who knows where it may end up in the future.

"If stopping this thing here protects your family, then I promise you, I'll do whatever it takes to stop it." Jordin held out his hand for Joseph to shake. "It'll have to kill me first."

Joseph nodded and firmly shook Jordin's hand. "If we survive this, my family and I will owe you one."

Zhukov interrupted before Jordin could respond. "Dr. Davidson."

"Yes?" Jordin said, turning to the approaching Lieutenant.

"You'll be happy to note that expanded cloud seed efforts have started since last night." Zhukov pointed to the sky. "Our cloud seed squadron has just begun their operations as well."

"That's good...what does that mean?" Jordin asked.

"We are now seeding a wider area."

"Has it done anything?"

"Yes. The storm hasn't slowed, but it has spread the precipitation over a wider area."

"And what does that mean for us?"

"It will start snowing sooner, but it won't be as heavy.

And we can also see the monster directly now."

"That's...good?"

"That remains to be seen. You may wish we hadn't revealed it to the world."

Jordin couldn't help but look northwest. Buildings and a fence blocked his view, but he could still imagine a terrifying beast lumbering over the landscape.

"Don't forget to report at the northwestern watchtower in an hour and a half," Zhukov ordered before promptly turning and walking away.

"You're stationed at the northwestern watchtower too?" Joseph beamed. "That's where I'm stationed."

Jordin couldn't find the words to respond.

"I guess that means we'll have a perfect view of it and everything."

"Lucky us...," was all Jordin could manage to say.

After finishing lunch, Jordin marched back to the supply hut. On his way, he passed by the tent in the compound's center. The sides and top of the tent featured lighter colored patches, serving as scars, reminding everyone of the hatching event. Several scientists and soldiers in hazmat suits entered and exited the tent, carrying containers with samples. They loaded the samples into the back of an awaiting truck. More heavily packed trucks drove away from the scene out of the base.

The lights within the tent cast an eerie shadow of a giant clawed hand protruding from the ground. Jordin shuddered at the sight. He knew that the giant hand within was tiny compared to what was coming.

He glanced at the large cryosling sitting, not far from the tent, near the center of the compound. The other two slings were positioned outside the compound as backups to the artillery cannons. He felt small compared to the machine. The thought of his own tiny insignificance washed over him as he realized just how small the sling was compared to what it was built to stave off.

He shook himself back to reality and entered the supply hut. From there, he assisted soldiers in carrying supplies to their destination. He tried his best not to think too deeply about what was about to happen as he followed the soldiers out of the compound's main gate.

After a few supply runs, a chilly breeze made him shiver. He set his box of supplies down next to an artillery cannon and checked his watch. "Oh...I'm supposed to report..." he mumbled as he dashed back to the main entrance of the compound.

He ascended the stairs of the watchtower to see Zhukov, Joseph, the Middle Eastern dignitary, and a few other soldiers already positioned, looking out over the landscape. Joseph was busy setting up a telescoping camera on a tripod.

"I'm glad you could join us," Zhukov said in amusement as he handed Jordin an odd looking rifle. The weapon's sleek design included a lower chamber with several coils around it. The barrel and sights looked as though they had been hastily taken from other weapons and placed atop a cobbled together mishmash of tubing and cooling chambers.

"You should've seen the look on your face when you realized what time it was," Joseph laughed as he turned away from the camera.

"Sorry," Jordin sheepishly said as he took the weapon from Zhukov.

"You're here, that's all I care about," the dignitary said.

Zhukov pressed a button on the radio box. "Northwestern watchtower personnel present and accounted for."

"Acknowledged," Dr. Dhar's voice replied. "Connecting directly to General Arya."

The line buzzed briefly before the general's voice crackled over the radio. "Northwestern watchtower, your orders are to observe and provide strategical information and recommendations. Dr. Davidson, are you prepared?"

Jordin gulped before he stepped forward to say, "Yes, general."

"Good. Dr. Terry will be in direct communications with you. You are to relay her information relating to the creature itself and how it reacts. Do you understand?"

"Yes, sir!" Jordin awkwardly saluted.

"Lieutenant Zhukov."

"Yes, General," Zhukov replied.

"You are to translate what our civilian VIPs say into tactical orders. Do you understand?"

"Yes, sir."

"Everyone else, provide as much tactical support as possible," Arya commanded.

"Yes, sir," the others said in unison.

"Good," Arya replied.

The radio went silent. Jordin slung the rifle over his shoulder and cautiously walked to the railing. He peered out, eyes fixed on the horizon. He rapidly tapped the cold railing with his fingers.

"Nervous?" Zhukov asked.

"A little bit. This isn't the first time I've been in the monster's path. But last time, I just thought that it was a storm. Now I know what it is."

"You faced it before and survived. We are honored to have you stand with us," the dignitary said. "We stand together."

"Let's hope I don't have to dig any of you out of a snow bank again," Joseph said while adjusting the camera's focus. "Though I guess I'll be buried with you this time."

"Any word from Mr. Mercury?" Jordin asked.

"Last I heard, he was in flight back here," Zhukov said.

"Let's hope he gets back in time."

"It may already be too late," Zhukov said flatly.

"Why?" Jordin asked.

"Feel that breeze?" The lieutenant motioned around with his gloved hand, bandages still showing around his wrists.

Jordin shook his head. As far as he was concerned Zhukov was either incredibly tough or a machine. He wondered if his own hands had been completely frostbitten if he could still do half the things Zhukov was doing.

"The cold winds of death herald our foe," the dignitary said as he removed one of his gloves to feel the wind.

"How close is it?" Jordin whispered as a chill ran down his spine, his fingers tapping more furiously.

"We'll be able to see it on the horizon within two hours," Zhukov said, suppressing all emotions.

Jordin joined the rest in staring at the horizon.

"Tell me," the dignitary broke the silence, "Dr. Davidson."

"Yes?"

"What was it like, to face the beast head on?"

Jordin considered his response. "Like rushing into the apocalypse."

The dignitary nodded gravely. "What should we expect?"

"Winds strong enough to carry you away. Snowfall so thick it appears as a solid wall advancing toward you. Ground tremors...humming...an eerie yellow glow...and a hand." He motioned back toward the tent. "A hand like that one, but far bigger."

"The creature is visible now. The weather effects won't be as strong as when you faced it," Zhukov pointed out.

"Nevertheless," the dignitary said, "we face a mighty foe." He gazed out over the landscape. "I will not retreat from such a devil. If I am to die, then I will die. And then I will be reunited with the family it took from me."

Jordin's heart sank. "It killed your...I'm sorry."

"I appreciate your condolences. However, all I need is this creature's death or my own."

"We will all work to kill this thing," Zhukov assured.

Very little else was said. Soldiers milled about, readying the last-minute preparations. The air felt somber and heavy. Everyone knew what was coming, yet everyone seemed to ignore it while completing their tasks.

A little while later, Jordin heard, or thought he heard, a strange thumping noise in the distance. "Hey. Do you hear that?" His whole body froze as he listened, half hoping he was just hearing things.

Everyone fell deathly quiet to listen. Sure enough, a dull, distant, rhythmical thumping rolled over the landscape.

Zhukov handed Jordin a pair of binoculars and pointed at the horizon. Jordin gulped as he placed the binoculars over his eyes.

Dark clouds drifted over the horizon, growing larger and closer by the moment. Flashes of lightning flickered in the boiling mass. A strong, frigid breeze pierced him.

The base's siren began blaring. "Everyone to your stations now. This is not a drill. I repeat, man your battle stations now," General Arya's commands crackled with static.

Jordin's heart pounded in his chest. This was not the first time hearing a siren as the storm approached. He did his best to suppress the past's unpleasant memories.

Soldiers rushed out to their stations and readied their weapons. The prongs on the end of the cryoslings swept outward with a whooshing sound before clicking as they locked into place. Their internal generators hummed as the metal plates slid back, putting tension on the firing bands. All three slings clicked in unison as their respective bolts popped into place.

"Attention all personnel," General Arya's announced over the communications, "prepare for hostile approach. We are the last line of defense. Failure is not an option. You all know your tasks."

Zhukov pulled a coat off a pile slung over the railing and handed it to Jordin. "Here."

Jordin accepted the coat and took a deep breath, preparing himself. Their foe had arrived.

CHAPTER
24

The familiar dark clouds poured over the sky as the temperature rapidly dropped. All of the summer heat was sucked away to fuel the oncoming nightmare. An absence of noise from the natural world made the countryside seem menacing. A light snowfall advanced toward them. Thunderclaps, once distant, boomed louder and closer. A rhythmic thumping shook the ground.

"I see it...," Joseph whispered as he peered through a telescope. He quickly switched to his camera on the tripod and attempted to focus it.

"Dr. Davidson, you have priority on telescopes," Zhukov said as he motioned for a soldier using another telescope to move aside.

Jordin handed the binoculars back to Zhukov, dreading what he would see as he looked through the telescope's eyepiece. The sight nearly took his breath away. His heart felt as thought it skipped a beat. Every fiber of his being told him to turn and run. However, he knew he must stand firm. He couldn't abandon everyone, not now.

Zhukov flipped a switch on the radio. "Northwestern watchtower, reporting enemy sighting. Please establish communications with Dr. Terry."

"Acknowledged," Dr. Dhar replied.

"Attention!" General Arya's voice boomed over the loud-speakers. "Enemy is in sight. Prepare to engage. I repeat, prepare to engage."

"Dr. Terry here," Lauren's voice sputtered slightly over the radio. "What are you seeing?"

Jordin was transfixed in awe at a gigantic creature that seemed to rise out of the ground on the horizon. The lumbering creature's head brushed the clouds as it marched. A yellowish glow around it highlighted its monstrous form. Its skin appeared to be gray, yet still shimmered and reflected the light. The creature's frame seemed slim and slender, yet tall and imposing. Its cylindrical horse-like head protruded forward. Air rushed in and out of numerous narrow, nostril-like slits that served as the creature's mouth and nose. Three dark orb-like eyes bulged out on the sides and the top of its face glared their direction menacingly. A black circular indentation lined with a reflective obsidian-like substance lay atop its head.

Three massive, translucent, shimmering sails, framed by spiky bone structures protruded from the creature's back. Two large wing-like limbs protruded from its shoulders. The wings appeared to be made of the same shimmering translucent material as the sails. Its two long arms reached to the ground where massive thumbless six fingered claws swung by its side, translucent webbing connecting the creature's arms with its body. Its long, thin legs rooted in outspread feet, three clawed digits in the front and one in the back, protruding from the heel. A long, wide tail, with several spiky, millipede-like legs, dragged behind the creature, the tip of which was a large, round, bony nodule that smacked the ground between the creature's footsteps.

With each slam, the tail would curl under the creature, sweeping piles of loosened materials under itself. The tail would then wrap itself around the rubble pile while the protruding legs rapidly tore the material asunder like needlepoint teeth.

"Is that how it eats?" Jordin muttered, transfixed by the mesmerizing glow. "Hello?" Lauren radioed. "Are you there?"

"Dr. Davidson," Zhukov placed a hand on Jordin's shoulder, "report. What do you see?"

"Sorry," Jordin refocused, and tried his best to describe the beast as he saw it.

"I'm recording this as we speak," Joseph said after Jordin finished his description. "Command, please verify you're getting this?"

"We're getting your feed now," Dhar said. "There's static interference, but we can see it. Though I wish we didn't. Forwarding it to Dr. Terry."

"Oh...my..." Lauren gasped upon seeing the image on her end. "I'd hoped you were joking about your description."

"What can you tell us?" Zhukov asked, his patience growing thin.

"This thing is huge. How tall is it?" Lauren asked.

Joseph squinted through the camera and pressed a few buttons. "Easily 850 meters tall. Give or take a few."

"Dr. Davidson," Zhukov wasted no time in continuing the conversation, "you mentioned something about eating."

"Ye...Yes." Jordin shakily pointed a finger at the creature. "Every time it smacks the ground with its tail, it curls the loose debris back into itself and the...legs on its tail...chew...it?"

"It eats dirt and rocks?" Joseph wondered.

"I have no idea," Jordin said.

"It would explain some things..." Lauren mused. "It's been growing rapidly. Nothing grows without something to grow from. A creature of that size would've starved to death if it had to rely on meat, vegetation, or even just heat itself by now. There's nothing on earth that could sustain it for long. If it ate the minerals itself...it could have an endless supply everywhere...It may have even toppled over or frozen to death by now if it had to stop to...graze with its mouth on its head like other creatures. Amazing..."

The closer the creature came, the louder a humming locust sound grew. With every passing second, snowfall swelled around them.

"Is there a way for us to exploit its eating?" Zhukov asked. "We could plant nitrogen canisters in its eating path."

"It would get liquid nitrogen inside the creature," Lauren said.

"But it's smacking the ground and chewing it up outside its body first," Jordin sighed, disappointed that idea wouldn't work. "Anything we currently have would be smashed and broken up. All liquid nitrogen or coolant would be lost before it entered the creature." He pointed toward the tail. "Watch, the ground it's eating is covered in snow. But every time the tail curls, snow and water flings out. If we knew this beforehand, we may have been able to make something to exploit its eating."

"I'll make note of that and pass along...Just in case," Dhar's voice crackled.

"Any other recommendations?" Zhukov asked.

"Those sails...those wings..." Lauren pondered. "Previously, I've wondered how this creature could remain upright. It should collapse under its own weight. Those webbed protrusions could be keeping it upright. Think about it. There's enough wind force from the storm to blow buildings over. It could probably provide some significant lift."

"Are you certain?" Zhukov asked.

"No, but do you have a better idea?" Lauren replied.

"Are you telling me that those are its weak points?"

"What about those big eyes on its head?" Joseph asked. "Heads are always good targets for anything."

"I've got some data from the U.N. team what they found in the egg," Lauren said. "They say that the eyes are covered over and coated in a thick, translucent, obsidian-like substance that's just as hard if not harder than the exoskeleton. In other words, the thing is wearing armored goggles."

"We need a soft target so we don't waste ammunition," Zhukov said, impatiently tapping his foot.

"The webbing on its sails and wings," Lauren noted. "Those are the thinnest and weakest points on the creature. Destroy the webbing, and you just may cause it to fall over. It won't have anything to catch the air currents."

Zhukov flipped another switch on the radio. "Target the wings and sails. They are keeping the creature upright."

"Acknowledged," Arya said.

"Attention all units, target the creature's wings and sails," Arya's voice boomed over the speakers.

Zhukov flipped the switch back.

"Shouldn't we always be in communication with the general?" Jordin asked.

Zhukov raised an eyebrow. "He has to coordinate everything and deal with everyone else. Do you really think it wise to make him listen to civilians shouting and babbling this whole time?"

"Oh..."

Artillery cannons and tank turrets whirred with aim adjustments and prepared to fire. Everyone remained silent as they leered with grim determination at their advancing enemy. Each rhythmical smack of the creature's tail seemed to synchronize with Jordin's heartbeat. He felt as though someone had just lit a bomb fuse and everyone was watching it burn down.

"Are you ready?" the Middle Eastern dignitary asked, as he glared at the advancing monster.

Jordin glanced back at the dignitary. "It killed my intern, and countless others. I won't let it kill anyone else. It's our turn now," he said grimly.

The dignitary liked the sound of that. "Good."

The roar of jet engines flying in from behind caught Jordin's attention. He leaned out and looked up to see a squadron of fighter jets fly out toward the creature. The jets fired several missiles in unison then peeled off. The missiles wobbled and began winding erratically through the air. Several missed their mark entirely, exploding in a white fog on impact. The lumbering monster didn't seem to notice the few that struck it as it continued, unfazed.

"Forward artillery, open fire!" General Arya commanded over the loudspeakers.

Loud booms echoed over the landscape as the artillery cannons fired. Misty explosion clouds peppered the creature and the ground around it. As with the missiles, the gargantuan beast tread forward as if nothing was happening.

"I thought we were aiming for the wings and sails?" Jordin said in annoyance at the sight of sporadic explosions.

Zhukov flipped a switch on the radio. "Concentrate fire

on wings and sails. Current firing pattern is erratic."

"Acknowledged," General Arya replied. "Field is reporting interference with targeting systems and highly chaotic winds surrounding the target. They are switching to manual targeting. However, they also warn that, at current distance and height of requested target, accuracy will be impossible."

"Acknowledged," Zhukov said as he flipped the switch back.

"Great...it has its own natural defenses against projectiles," Joseph bemoaned. "An exoskeleton wasn't good enough for it. It had to get its own weather system too."

Snow began falling more heavily around them as the clouds completely blocked out the sun. Their primary source of light was now the glow of the creature itself, along with lightning flashing around them. Several bolts struck the sails protruding from the creature's back.

"That's it," Jordin said. "That's how it's surviving the cold. It's sustaining on lightning generated by the storm."

"It's using lightning to metabolize the minerals it's eating?!" Lauren exclaimed, somewhat impressed.

"It's probably the best heat source that it can find," Jordin replied.

"It's an electric powered monster," Joseph chuckled.

The jets circled back around and fired more missiles at the creature. Several missiles struck its shoulders at the base of the wings. One of the jets flew past the creature's face. The monster waved and arm in front of its face, shook its head, and emitted a sound that sounded like colliding hurricanes.

"It thinks jets are annoying flies," Jordin muttered.

A heavy, cold blast of air suddenly roared past them, kicking snow that had once been on the ground into everyone's face.

"Whoa," Joseph said as he dusted snow off his camera lens, "tell your jets not to fly past its face. That thing snorted and nearly sent us flying."

Zhukov radioed the general to instruct the jets to avoid flying directly in front of the creature's face.

The roar of cannon fire nearly drowned out the thunder as the creature grew closer and closer, seemingly unaffected by the relentless assault.

"All remaining artillery units, fire," General Arya commanded.

Explosions poured from behind the watchtower as the cannons within the base began firing.

"It's getting pretty close," Joseph said. "Nothing seems to be working."

Jordin no longer needed the telescope or binoculars to observe the creature, and the droves of explosions pounding base of the creature's wings and sails. "You're striking the most heavily armored parts."

"Strike the webbing. That's the part that's catching the

air currents," Lauren said. "You don't have time to sever its wings."

Zhukov relayed the message. The cannons adjusted their aim and resumed firing. Nitrogen clouds soon began erupting across the creature's wings.

"That's doing something!" Jordin said excitedly as he pointed at several holes that had formed in the webbing.

The creature emitted a deep rumbling grunting noise that sounded like two mountains dragging across one another and lifted its wings even higher. Lightning bolts struck the claw-like protrusions on the end of its wings.

"What the..." Jordin watched in disbelief as the holes in the wings closed up. "It's just undoing everything we did."

The jets circled back and fired another salvo of missiles. This time, several missiles struck the creature's head and eyes. The creature shook its undamaged head and turned its attention to the flying jets. Its eyes began to shine a bright yellow as the glow of the creature became more intense and the sound of humming locusts intensified.

Lightning was now striking more frequently as the jets peeled off to circle back for another run. A lightning bolt suddenly struck one of the jets, sending it careening out of control. It exploded into several pieces into the ground.

"We warned you about the head!" Jordin said. "You just upset it, now it's fighting back!" Two more jets crashing into the ground punctuated his words.

The remaining fighter jets turned to leave the area.

Strong gusts of wind battered them, rendering their flights far more difficult now.

Jordin's world went completely white for a split second as a deafening boom nearly knocked him off his feet.

"Good thing I put that lightning rod on our tower," Joseph chuckled as he helped Jordin steady himself.

"That was close," Jordin said, trying not to sound panicked.

"It lashes out with its wrath. Why do we not show it the full force of ours?" the dignitary asked. "Fire the slings!"

"Yeah, why aren't we firing the slings?" Jordin asked. "The creature is almost to the moat." He gripped the railing as the tower shook. Every footfall and smack of the creature's tail now caused the structure to shake. He tried his best not to look down at the ground three stories below.

"Do you really think something like that will work?" Zhukov asked.

"I have no idea, just try it!" Jordin shouted back over the ever-increasing roar of the wind and humming.

Zhukov gave the order. The sling on the left flank angled itself and fired.

Jordin watched the bolt wobble through the due to the severe winds. To his disappointment, the bolt missed completely. "That's a miss. Try again! Hurry!"

The right flank sling fired as the left flank reloaded. The bolt struck the creature in the left leg, where it remained, quivering. Gray, flaky scales formed and crept over the creature's body originating from the bolt. The creature emitted a high-pitched grunt that sounded vaguely like rending metal and stopped in its tracks.

"It's working!" Jordin shouted. "Keep firing!"

The creature looked down at its leg. It groaned again as the left flank sling fired once more and struck the creature's right leg. The enormous beast looked from leg to leg, then peered at the slings. It straightened up to its full height and emitted a sound resembling a trumpet blast. The ground tremored as it stomped forward, heading directly for the left flank sling.

Soldiers scattered, repositioning themselves to fire their weapons while the slings reloaded and fired again. The creature grunted in pain with each bolt's impact, the liquid nitrogen injecting itself like a poison.

To everyone's dismay, the moat didn't even faze the creature as it simply stepped over it. Soldiers leaped out of the way as a large foot came crashing down on their position, crushing several artillery cannons in the process.

The beast swiped its right hand in a scooping motion, digging into the ground. This lifted the left flank sling, and anyone unlucky enough to be caught in the mayhem, into the air and tossed aside.

Chaos erupted as solders and tanks began wildly firing while withdrawing from the creature.

"Should we move?" Jordin asked as he gawked up at the

towering monstrosity, now too close for comfort.

The creature turned its gaze back toward the base, fixating on the large central tent.

"I refuse to retreat from this creature!" the dignitary said as he raised his weapon to aim.

"Hello? Hello?" Mr. Mercury's voice popped over the radio. "Is anyone there?"

"Yes, we're here!" Jordin shouted.

"We're on approach with the supplies. What's your status?"

"It's too late, I repeat, it's too late. Enemy is here. We won't be able to get the supplies in time," Zhukov said.

"Oh...that's too bad," Mr. Mercury replied, dejected.

The ground quaked and the tower swayed as the creature resumed its leisurely walk toward the base.

"I've got a plane full of liquid nitrogen. Sounds like you could use it," Mr. Mercury added.

"Unless you've got a way to get that nitrogen past an exoskeleton, it's of no use to us now," Zhukov said.

"Oh..." Mr. Mercury went quiet for a few moments. "We've got an idea that just might work," he said. "We've got the coordinates of the monster from Dhar. We've heard some reports of what's happening on our way. Seems to my pilot and I, our plane is quite the massive projectile. We're jammed full of liquid nitrogen. I'd hate for it all to go to waste."

"No!" Zhukov said. "You've no idea if that'll work or not. And you'd just kill yourselves for nothing. Those supplies can be used later."

"We're setting auto-pilot and jumping out over the airport," Mr. Mercury said. "Good thing I keep parachutes in this contraption. Oh, and we're venting remaining fuel. Minimizing the fireball and all..."

"Disengage! I repeat, disengage!" Zhukov shouted.

"Too late, over airport now, let's go." The line went silent.

"Stubborn American..." Zhukov muttered.

The beast smashed the ground with its tail causing another shudder.

"Mercury's aircraft is entering airport airspace now," Dhar said. "Side door is open. One is out. I see a chute. One remains. Wait...door is closing...Wait...I only see one chute. What's going on? Attention...Mercury aircraft. Report. What are you doing?"

Zhukov sighed.

"Hello?" Mr. Mercury's voice came back over the radio.

"What do you think you're doing? Land or jump now!" Dr. Dhar bellowed.

After a series of pops and static, General Arya commanded forcefully, "Mr. Mercury. I'm ordering you to jump now."

"Wait, what's happening?" Lauren chimed in.

"At least follow your own crazy plan, you silly...," Zhukov

trailed off.

"This creature messed with my plans for the last time," Mr. Mercury said.

"Mr. Mercury...sir," Jordin began, "what are you doing?"

"We all know that the winds surrounding the creature would knock this plane off course," Mercury said. "There's no way to guarantee these supplies get delivered where they need to go unless someone is here to make sure they get there."

"Of all the...," Dhar grumbled.

"Nonsense! Jump or land now," Arya ordered

"We need you at P.M.L.," Jordin reasoned. "Why do this? Why take away the idea guy behind everything? You've so much to live for."

"It beats withering away like a husk on a bed," Mercury replied.

"What? What are you talking about?" Dhar asked.

"A few months ago...," Mercury started to explain.

The ground convulsed and soldiers shouted over the boom of cannons and gunfire.

"I was diagnosed with a terminal illness," Mercury continued. "I was given a year to live. That...that really put things in perspective. When I started P.M.L., I wanted to do things that helped the world. I spent my whole career making tools to help other people change the world. I realized I never changed it myself. So, I went looking for something I could do. Some lasting way we could contribute to the world. That's when I read your paper, Dr. Davidson. I thought...maybe for once we would be at the forefront of discovery. We would set the standards. We would lead the world. We wouldn't hand it off to someone else to discover. We would do it."

The approaching jet engine roared closer in the cloudy skies.

"My legacy would be one of discovery. I wouldn't have to play second fiddle to someone else anymore. But then...," Mr. Mercury paused. Jordin watched Mr. Mercury's jet burst out of the cloud layer and barrel straight for the monster. The plane wobbled as it struggled to maintain course through the gale.

"I got carried away in my own delusions." Mr. Mercury audibly choked back his emotions while straining to maintain control of the aircraft, several warning sirens blaring in the background. "I didn't realize how much it would cost. You never know what your legacy is going to be until you carry the lifeless corpse of one of your own employees out of the wreckage. I don't need to discover anything anymore. My own self-worth isn't worth the lives of those I sacrifice to obtain it."

"He'll deflect off the creature's wing..." Jordin muttered. He turned to the radio and shouted, "We need to take out the wings...If you can get to the base of one of them....you may be able to...to..."

"Understood," Mr. Mercury said, his voice shaking from

the turbulence. Several alarms were now blaring as the plane itself shook violently. Lightning flashed around it.

"Make a path..." Jordin whispered to Zhukov.

The Lieutenant nodded. He flipped a switch on the radio. "Attention, left flank cease firing. Right flank, fire the sling; we need to turn the creature. Get its attention." He solemnly flipped the switch back.

Cannon fire on the left flank died down as the right flank picked up the slack.

"You crazy..." Dr. Dhar struggled to say. "It's been an honor."

"Take care of the company. It's all yours now," Mr. Mercury replied.

The right sling fired and struck the creature. It emitted a grunt and began turning, seeing the approaching jet and rapidly turning its head toward it.

"You killed the wrong man the first time, FREAK!" Mr. Mercury shouted. The jet flew under the creature's left wing and arced upward at the last minute. There was a loud boom as the jet struck the base of the creature's wing with full force. The plane vanished in a gigantic explosion that was soon replaced with a white nitrogen vapor.

The creature howled as its skin filled with flaky gray scales. The wing separated from its body and crashed to the ground. It stumbled forward, managing to stomp on the right flank sling. The sling by the tent fired, striking the creature in the abdomen.

Jordin watched as the creature began tipping forward, its body looming directly over the base. "We should move NOW!" he shouted as he and the others turned to run for the stairs. Out of the corner of his eye he saw the dignitary shouting and firing his weapon at the creature.

The tower lurched and tipped as the creature's body brushed it. Jordin fell forward, landing on the unforgiving metal floor. He scrambled to grab hold of anything he could as the tower fell backward into the base. His body slid and slammed into the railings. His entire world tumbled as he rolled over, arms flailing to the snow-covered ground below.

Before he realized the pain coursing through his body, the metal tower came crashing down upon him. All he could think to do was cover his face with his arms and huddle into as small a ball as possible. Metal struck all around him, kicking snow into his eyes.

CHAPTER
25

Jordin was curled in a ball, eyes shut. The ground shivered and the sound of buildings crumbling to their foundations surrounded him. Soldiers screamed, seemingly from every direction. Gunshots and explosions erupted wildly.

"Everyone alright?" he heard Zhukov shout.

Jordin opened his eyes and scrambled back to his feet, careful not to strike his head on jagged metal. He ignored the pain as best as he could. Zhukov was dusting the snow off himself not far from Jordin.

"Never better," Joseph said as he stood and shook the snow off.

"Assistance please." The dignitary lay on his stomach in the snow, half his body beneath the mangled metal structure. A slight tapping noise from beneath indicated that at least one of the soldiers was trapped entirely.

Zhukov, Jordin, and Joseph struggled to lift the rubble. They managed to raise it enough for the dignitary to crawl out and in turn, assist them in pulling the trapped soldier out of the mess.

The soldier's legs were scraped up so badly that he could barely pull himself out of the rubble pile. He pointed back into the heap where his comrade-in-arms lay eerily still.

Joseph propped the soldier up while Zhukov crawled in to take the other soldier's pulse. After a few moments, the Lieutenant emerged and shook his head.

Jordin felt sickened at the prospect. He had little time to dwell on what had happened before an explosion went off above his head. White, misty nitrogen vapors wafted by his face.

"Let's go!" Zhukov ordered as he climbed out of the wreckage, then helped Joseph carry the soldier out. Myriad explosions rocked the area.

As soon as they cleared the tower's wreckage, Jordin's breath was nearly taken away. The creature lay on its hands and knees, stretched out over the base. Several buildings had been crushed. Its head waved back and forth over the central tent. The cryosling at the center of the compound was still standing but part of it appeared severely damaged. Nitrogen explosions peppered the creature's back as the remaining artillery installations fired as rapidly as they could.

Soldiers crawled out of wrecked buildings while others ran to them. Tanks drove beneath the creature's chest firing wildly. Several lines of soldiers opened fire with their cryo-rifles. All semblances of order and command were lost. Most of the communications and the speaker systems had been knocked down by the creature, leaving everyone to fend for themselves.

Wild winds made it difficult to hear what anyone was saying as a heavy snow accumulated.

"We need to find the general! We need to get everyone to regroup!" Zhukov yelled over the roar of the wind.

"We're so close to victory!" the dignitary shouted back. "Why retreat now?!"

"We aren't retreating, we need a more advantageous position!"

"That sling by the tent!" Joseph shouted. "Looks like it's damaged. If we can get that to fire now, we could finish this thing!"

"I agree!" Jordin exclaimed. "We need to get that up and running again!"

Zhukov looked at Joseph and Jordin. "Fine, do it!" He looked at the dignitary and nodded at the soldier. "I need you to help me. We can't leave him here."

The soldier opened his mouth to say something but Zhukov interrupted, "You're coming with me, that's an order."

The dignitary looked at the sling, then at the creature. He scowled and said, "Very well," taking Joseph's spot.

"GO!" Zhukov howled as he and the dignitary began carrying the soldier through the maze of rubble.

Joseph dashed toward the sling. "Come on!"

"Careful!" Jordin called out as he followed. "You're going to go directly beneath it!"

The ground rumbled as the creature raised its right hand.

"WATCH IT!" Jordin wailed. Both he and Joseph dove behind a rubble pile.

The creature grabbed the tent and pulled it upward. Metal tent stakes and poles flew in all directions as it was ripped out of the ground and tossed aside.

A pale, dead hand covered in gray scales lay limply beside the large, cracked egg. The once massive hand now seemed minuscule compared to its older sibling.

The creature gaped at the lifeless hand, then into the cracked opening of the egg.

Joseph scrambled forward to run again.

"Wait!" Jordin called out to no avail, grumbling as he stood and ran after his friend. "You'll get yourself killed." Both of them were now directly under the creature's body. *If they kill it or it lies down completely...we're dead*, he thought.

The creature blared a low, mournful sound not unlike that of a whale's call. Its yellow glow shifted to blue and the humming noise decreased to a mere whisper of what it had been. Its head lifted skyward and intensified the wailing.

Jordin stopped dead in his tracks and froze as the creature shifted. The ground beneath him wobbled. He stared in horror as the creature lowered its head and turned it to the side, its left eye locking directly on Jordin.

*If I don't move...*Jordin hoped desperately that the creature would just ignore him.

The creature growled deeply as the ground convulsed violently. The blue glow of the creature shifted to a ruby red. A crimson light, surrounded by the obsidian blackness of the creature's eye, fixed upon Jordin with a piercing gaze.

The humming noise returned with a vengeance. This time it sounded as though millions of angry hornets were descending. The clouds overhead grew darker and began to swirl intensely.

"Oh..." Jordin whispered as a cold sweat ran down his forehead. He reached for the rifle strapped to his back. "I guess you see me." He steeled himself. "But I won't back down." He raised the rifle and aimed it at the creature's head. "NOT FROM YOU!"

A blinding flash and a deafening boom caused Jordin to cover his ears, the rifle dropping to his side. He had little time to consider what had happened before there was another flash, then another, and another.

It was as if a dam had burst in the clouds. Lightning poured down like water, striking the creature over and over again.

Jordin fell to the ground in agony, shutting his eyes and covering his ears.

After a few moments, the lightning grew more distant. He cautiously opened his eyes to find the creature standing back up, its massive body rising skyward.

Jordin picked himself up and took in, mouth agape, the gargantuan monster before him, now glowing in an evil red light. Its lopsided form was no less threatening or imposing. Lightning continued to strike it over and over, brushing away the cracked gray scales on its shoulder. The explosions from shells and missiles that peppered its body seemed insignificant.

The monster stood to its full height, lifting its head and remaining wing skyward. Its piercingly loud trumpeting sound shuddered Jordin's bones.

That sling! he thought as he turned to run after Joseph. *Either we kill the monster, or it kills us.*

As he ran, he heard the creature make a deep inhaling sound. Jordin glanced back, noticing a funnel of clouds rushing into the creature's nostrils. "Oh...great...," he said as he dove behind a mound of snow collected around a remnant of a pillar from what used to be a barracks.

The creature leaned forward and burst forth a mighty gust of air from its nostrils, sweeping its head across the base. Hurricane force winds blew snow, canisters, people, and rubble away like paper.

Jordin huddled down as snow enveloped him. A tank flew by overhead, crashing into one of the only buildings still standing. To his horror, its roof peeled off and the walls disintegrated.

When the winds finally died down, he extracted himself with great effort from the snow. Once free, he peeked out from behind the snow bank.

The monster was now leering down at the cannons and soldiers still firing from the artillery lines. It raised its left foot and sent it crashing down. The ground quaked upon impact. It whipped its tail around and sent it crashing down on another artillery installation. Over and over again it stamped its feet, targeting anything that moved.

Jordin stumbled toward the sling, desperately hoping that Joseph had made it there and could fix it. Several other soldiers rushed for the sling as well. Every stomp of the creature's foot and every slam of its tail took his feet off-balance as he ran, causing he and other soldiers to stumble and fall. He finally made it to a rubble pile next to the sling and huddled behind it with a few soldiers. The firing button was a mere twenty feet from his position.

Joseph and several other engineers worked away, pulling debris out of the sling's mechanical systems and trying to repair any damage. No one dared interfere with them.

A squadron of jets zoomed overhead, loaded with fresh weaponry. Jordin cautiously peered over the rubble after them as they fired, striking the creature's shoulder. Several shells ripped through the clouds above the creature, continuously barraging its back from above.

The monster growled and waved its arms to swat them away, but the jets were too fast. Whatever was shelling it from above the clouds was out of its reach. It arched its back and trumpeted a wretched howl into the clouds.

A new torrent of lightning began striking the creature's back, just below the shoulders, over and over again. As lightning poured down from above, the creature stomped the ground and slammed it's tail down repeatedly chewing up the landscape. Two, spiky protrusions began rapidly growing from the lightning impact points. The protrusions were comprised of several jointed segments, not unlike fingers. The lightning bolts continued to strike the tip of the spikes as they grew.

Jordin gasped as he saw the protrusions grow above the creature's head and curve over to point forward. From its joints sprouted several other smaller spikes, translucent webbing connecting them.

"What's it doing?" Jordin asked.

The creature stopped stomping its feet and tail and pointed the protrusions skyward. A ruby red glow started from the base of the spikes and ran all the way to the tip. The world suddenly lit up in a brilliant red glow as two crimson lightning bolts shot out of the protrusions.

A mangled burning husk of a gunship plummeted through the clouds and shattered into millions of pieces on the ground.

"Lighting rods...in reverse!" Jordin yelled. "Watch out!"

The monster turned its gaze to the jets. In another red flash two jets exploded mid-air. One by one the pilots perished. With the annoying flies out of the way, its eyes turned to the ants below, vaporizing an artillery cannon and its surroundings in an explosion from a red bolt.

"ONCE I FIX THIS, SOMEONE NEEDS TO FIRE IT!" Joseph shouted.

The sounds of screams and gunfire swirled all around Jordin as he looked back at the sling. A bolt popped as it sprang up into place. Fog from the liquid nitrogen inside the great missile rolled off its sides as ice crystals formed on the outside of the canisters. It had already been damaged and had a slight leak in one section. If the sling mechanism couldn't be repaired soon, the nitrogen would leak out entirely, rendering the shot useless.

A building near the sling lit up in a red flash and exploded. Jordin covered his head with his hands as dirt, snow, and rubble hailed around him. Flash after flash hit the surroundings, each one kicking up more dirt and debris.

"What happened to the cannons?" Jordin asked after realizing he no longer heard any cannon fire.

Another red flash illuminated his surroundings. Several nearby soldiers fell. That blast had been close. Too close. He turned back to see the great creature, bathed in its red glow of rage, turn to direct its wrath toward a group of fleeing soldiers. "We're all that's left...," he whispered.

"I GOT IT! FIRE IT, FIRE IT!" Joseph shouted as he and the other engineers around the sling scrambled to extract themselves from the tangled mechanisms.

Here goes nothing, Jordin thought. The soldiers around him nodded and readied their weapons. Together they ran out from their cover and headed directly for the open firing panel. Only one person needed to make it. All that had to be done was press the button. At this range, the sling couldn't miss. *This one has to do it. It's pretty hurt now...right?* Jordin tried to reassure himself as he ran.

There was a sudden bright red flash as he was thrown backward off his feet, the soldiers falling or tossed aside.

The creature had noticed them.

Snow, rubble, and several remaining metal containers flew in all directions. Jordin lay on his back clenching his teeth. All of his muscles ached. A sharp pain rippled through his spine. The dark sky broiled above him. He blinked snowflakes out of his eyes as the sheer amount of them buried his body.

A bright red glow began to envelop the right side of his vision. The world grew strangely silent even with the ever-present hum of the creature and the wind whistling by. There were no screams, no gunshots, no cannon fire, not even any thunder. No one else stirred nearby. Had they really been the last few people left? Were the others dead? The soldiers had been closer to the blast than him.

He turned to see creature looming over him. It leaned forward, placing its hands on the ground. Each palm struck the earth causing a violent puff of snow and a minor quake. Jordin locked eyes with the monster. Its eyes burned with an intense anger and hatred. Slowly, the creature raised the two lightning rods and directed the points straight at him. Its mouthless face seemed to contort into a wicked smile.

Jordin struggled to stand but to no avail; the pain was too great. He could only move his head, so he looked around and noticed several metal canisters in precarious positions nearby. The explosion had sent one into the control panel. It rested, leaning against the panel at an awkward angle. The red fire button was just beneath it. If there were some way to dislodge the canister, it would fall directly onto the button.

He kicked at the nearest canister and immediately winced in pain. The canister inched away, toward another. Snow continued to accumulate around the canisters, threatening to bury or anchor them down. "Not today!" he shouted as he kicked again. The canister dislodged and smacked against another one. The other canister tipped over and landed on the canister resting on the panel.

To his dismay, the fallen canister simply bounced off and rolled away. He grimaced in pain; each kick had been increasingly more painful and difficult. All he could do was lay there staring up at his would-be killer. "I guess it will be today," he whispered, then he laughed painfully. "To think, I almost thought Saint George really could kill the dragon. This is what I get for believing a fairy tale."

The lightning rods began to glow red. Crimson bolts climbed between the spines at a slower than normal pace.

That thing is going to kill me, and enjoy every moment of it. Jordin gripped his rifle and grunted in pain as he aimed it at the button. *Not if I can help it.* He pulled the trigger. The gun clicked. Its canister hissed as a white mist sprayed out. "Ha," Jordin tried to chuckle, "how like life." He struggled with the weapon, trying to pull its strap out from under his back. *If I can throw it...*He hissed in pain, trying to unhook the tangled strap from the gun instead, but his efforts were fruitless.

The pain in his spine grew unbearable at every movement of his arms. The thought of tossing a snowball at the button crossed his mind, but he couldn't will his hands to grasp the snow. He gave up and lay helplessly, staring the monster in the face. "I'm sorry...for everything...," he whispered.

A sudden loud crash rang out. Jordin saw a large pile of debris topple onto the control panel. The rolling canister had bumped into a twisted metal rod that had been supporting a debris pile, bringing the whole thing down. There was a loud whoosh followed by a snap as the sling fired. Air and snow rushed past his face. The missile whistled through the air, leaving a trail of nitrogen mist as it barreled toward its target.

The missile sailed straight through the creature's leftmost nostril. Startled, the creature stood back up, shaking its head, its lightning rods firing wildly upward. Gray flaky scales spider-webbed across the creature's head. A heavy nitrogen fog drifted out of its nostrils. Lightning struck over and over again, trying to fight back the advancing scales but it was too late. Poisonous, frigid nitrogen had done its job.

Jordin watched as the red glow subsided, replaced by blue. The creature arched its back as it gazed up through the clouds. The humming noise changed from angry buzzing to an almost mournful wail as it stumbled forward. Slowly, agonizingly, the creature fell to its knees. It caught itself with its hands as it toppled forward but its strength steadily drained. It would be only a matter of time before its arms gave out. Jordin realized the creature's head would fall on his position.

"Guess it's going to be mutual," Jordin said as he closed his eyes and grit his teeth. "So be it. I did what I had to do. I only wish I could tell my parents I loved them...one more time."

"JORDIN! JORDIN!" Joseph's voice strained over the air as running footsteps crunched through the snow toward him.

Jordin opened his eyes to see Joseph, a gash in his forehead, run to his side. "No, run away," Jordin pleaded trying to wave off his friend, unable to lift his arms. Joseph dashed to a nearby soldier and checked his pulse, not finding one while surveying the area for other life.

"Nope!" Joseph said as he scooped Jordin up and sprinted away. "It fried my engineers and your soldier escort. I'm not letting it take you too!"

A rush of air and blasts of swirling snow overtook them as they ran. The huge shape of the falling monster grew closer and closer. Ground tremors made running difficult, but Joseph pressed forward. A final loud thud and violent rush of air knocked Joseph off his feet. A swirling mass of kicked-up snow enveloped them.

The snow gradually subsided over what felt like an eternity. Both Joseph and Jordin lay in the snow ogling the huge creature in a heap before them. Its blue glow grew fainter until it vanished entirely. Likewise, the humming sound subsided until it was silent. Both doctors lay there unsure of what to say. All was quiet. Neither of them had realized how overbearing the humming noise had been until it was finally gone. The silence now seemed unnatural, but it didn't stay that way for long. Faintly, in the distance, the sound of several approaching helicopters echoes over the landscape.

A beam of sunlight from the setting sun broke through the clouds. The storm was dissipating.

"Well...," Joseph finally said, "what do you tell the family about this?"

"A skiing incident?" Jordin chuckled through the pain.

"In Southern India, during the summer? Away from the mountains?"

The two of them lay there laughing in the snow as the roar of the helicopters grew louder and louder.

A horn honked and tires screeched to a halt nearby. "You crazy Americans..." Zhukov shouted.

The Lieutenant, the dignitary, and General Arya leaped out of the vehicle and rushed toward them. Arya pulled out a flare gun and fired. A green flare sailed upward and lazily drifted down. A display of various other flares erupted across the scene of destruction.

"We did it..." Jordin coughed.

"Don't speak," Zhukov said.

"We avoided 'a sight the world hasn't seen since World War II,'" Jordin sputtered.

"Barely," Arya said. "Well done."

"And so David fired his sling at Goliath," Zhukov said

with a chuckled.

"Give me a sword. I'll cut its head off." Jordin forced a laugh that made him cough. He looked at Joseph and struggled to speak. "You'll...see...Emily smile." He lay his head back down in the snow, faintly hearing Joseph say, "Don't worry, you'll see your family too," as he slipped away into unconsciousness.

CHAPTER
26

"The devastating march of the storm has finally stopped," a news anchor said, on the television. "But it isn't without great sacrifice." The broadcast aired images of the destructive path the storm had taken in a side square.

"Sources tell us that the storm was finally stopped due to a unique formula of cloud seed gasses. These gasses were developed in a joint effort between P.M.L., India, Russia, and the U.N. They reportedly discovered the formula just in time. Though, not soon enough as it would seem. Enigmatic P.M.L. part owner and CEO, Trevor Mercury," the screen changed to show a picture of Mr. Mercury, "as well as several researchers and soldiers perished in the line of duty. The new full owner and CEO Dr. Dhar gave an impassioned speech at the memorial to the fallen."

The screen changed to show Dr. Dhar standing next to a monument with General Arya and Colonel Dubinin sitting in the background. "I only regret that we didn't act fast enough," Dr. Dhar said. "Many brave men and women sacrificed their lives to combat this deadly storm."

The camera panned across the monument. Several names had been etched into the stone face. A table displaying pictures of the perished stood in front. Tearful family members were walking up and placing flowers and lighting candles next to the images of their fallen loved ones.

"We now know what these storms are and how to combat them," Dhar continued. "Their sacrifice allowed us to fight the storm and win. Our futures are now secured. We at P.M.L. are dedicated to continuously monitoring for other such storms. We have also joined with dozens of relief organizations to assist those who have been displaced or lost loved ones due to this catastrophe."

The camera scrolled past the pictures of Jimmy and Mr. Mercury. Jordin did his best to remain composed as he watched from his hospital bed. His injuries were severe. His spine had been fractured in multiple places. The full body cast in itched and made it difficult to concentrate.

"You don't need to subject yourself to this," Lauren said as she hobbled into Jordin's hospital room on crutches, her right leg in a cast.

Jordin smiled. "Hello, Dr. Terry."

"Hello, Dr. Davidson. Seems like we've been in hospitals a lot lately."

"I guess it's just part of the job."

"Who knew astronomy was so dangerous?" She looked down at her crutches and laughed. "Did you get your medal yet?"

"Medal?"

"I guess you haven't heard. We're going to be getting some sort of medal. I don't know much about it. I guess we're honorary soldiers now or something."

Jordin mustered a laugh. "I'd just as soon forget about the whole thing. Get me back on my feet. That's all I want."

"Yes, but I guess getting a medal looks good on your resume."

"That'd be awkward to explain. Hey, you got a medal? What for? Oh, I fought an alien monster." He painfully chuckled as he tried to readjust.

"I suppose it's good to have just as a symbolic thing."

"I suppose. Say, were you going to put it on your resume? I mean...nevermind."

Amused, Lauren said, "You know how I feel about P.M.L. Especially...." She trailed off and looked out the nearby window.

"I guess it's your choice," he said.

She looked back at Jordin. "We'll see...In the meantime, they want me to study the remains of the creatures."

"Exciting." Jordin smiled.

"Most biologists would kill for this opportunity," she added.

"How do you feel about it?"

Lauren blinked at this loaded question. "I can still hear its heartbeat."

"I'm sorry."

"Don't be. We did what we had to do. And now those things can't kill anyone else."

"That's true."

"Though...," she paused for a few moments to collect her thoughts, "I can't help but wonder...Could we have communicated with them?"

Lauren's question sparked a memory. "Maybe. It communicated quite clearly to me without having to say anything."

"Oh?"

"I never thought something could hate me as vehemently as it did. It stared me in the eyes..." he remembered, unable to go on.

She shook her head. "We may never know."

"Even if we could communicate," Jordin said, "I'm not so sure it would've turned out differently. Maybe it would've been worse. It ignored us until we caught its attention. Then it sought to obliterate us all."

"But that was after we attacked it and killed its..." Lauren sighed. "Had we not done this, hundreds or thousands... maybe millions more would've died if two of them were given free reign to stomp around our planet."

"What's done is done. They're gone now."

"Those two are." Lauren walked to the window studied the sky. "I find it difficult to believe that only two of these creatures exist. Wherever they're from...I have to believe there's more. Who knows how many are coming this way now, or will find us in the future."

"I have no idea." He tried to shrug but realized he couldn't move his shoulders. "I have to think that this was just a fluke. I don't believe this environment was to their liking."

Lauren cracked a smile. "I used to look up into the sky and wonder if we were alone in the universe. I got into astronomy in hopes that someday I'd see or discover extraterrestrial life." She turned back to look at Jordin and contemplated her words mournfully. "Now, I know we're not alone. And that terrifies me. I hope that we never come across aliens again."

"Maybe they're all thinking the same thing."

"Maybe." She gazed at the sky a few moments. "Do you want to know a secret?"

"Okay?"

"When I was a child, my bedroom was on the second floor of the house. I'd climb out of my window at night and lie down on the roof, staring up at the stars. I did it because it was my only escape."

"Escape from what?"

"From the roof, my brother couldn't find me to torment me and I couldn't hear my parents arguing in the next room."

"Oh...I'm sorry," was all Jordin knew to say. His relationship with his family and history with them hadn't been so bad. He didn't have any siblings to argue with and his parents had always largely gotten along.

"Don't be," Lauren softly said. "It's ironic that my escape ended up bringing me face-to-face with alien monsters." She focused on a gift for Jordin on his bedside stand – a carved wooden sculpture of a landed flying saucer with its front door open and a ramp leading down to the ground, where a likeness of Jordin stood on the ramp, waving with two antennae on his head and wearing some sort of a space suit. A plaque on the bottom read, *To Space Case. Get well soon. From Muscle Head.*

"What's that all about?" Lauren asked, motioning to the wooden sculpture.

"Oh." Jordin chuckled. "It's a long story. It's from a friend from college."

"Hmmm." Lauren cracked a smile.

"About work...," Jordin hesitantly began, "whatever you decide is up to you."

"I guess we'll see."

"By the way," Jordin said. "Remember when you told me that I should start reading a book for fun?"

"You mean when we were in the bunker?" Lauren asked.

"Yes. Open the drawer of the stand."

Lauren opened the drawer, the sight inside delighting her. She pulled out a book.

"The nurses have been reading that to me for entertainment," Jordin said. "It's sci-fi, all about monsters and superheroes and the like."

"And how do you like it?"

"It keeps me entertained. I guess I'll eventually need a bookshelf for my apartment."

Lauren set the book back in the drawer. "Let's hope you can get one, soon."

* * * *

Jordin hobbled through the front doors of P.M.L. two months later, his carrying case slung over his shoulder. He had been bedridden for far too long. His broken spine was mending but the doctors had warned that he might never fully recover. The hospital had tried to loan him a wheelchair but he refused. Nothing was going to keep him down forever. The back brace cast he wore restricted his movement, but still enabled him to get around.

The familiar sight of water splashed merrily down the sides of the lobby's fountain sculpture greeted him. He peered into the marble eyes of the dragon, then at the knight. "Well George," he whispered, "it is possible for mere humans to slay the dragon after all."

"It's a nice fountain, isn't it?" Sally called out from the front desk.

"Oh." Jordin nodded at her. "Yes, it is."

"It was hand chiseled and given to us by one of Mr. Mercury's Japanese business associates."

Jordin returned his gaze to the fountain with a newfound appreciation. "Hand made...well done," he muttered.

"Welcome back, Dr. Davidson. I wasn't expecting to see

you so soon," Sally said with a smile.

Jordin returned the smile and hobbled toward her. "I wasn't going to let you all have fun without me."

"I'm sure things will be more interesting around here now. How's your back doing?"

This subject was touchy to Jordin but he decided to be polite. "Well, it's still there. Supposedly, it'll be in one piece soon."

"That's good news. Hopefully, it won't be much longer before you're back to your old self."

Jordin gazed back toward the fountain wistfully as his mind returned him to the hospital. The doctor's voice saying that he may never fully recover and need a cane in the near future echoed around him. "Oh...," he began, "don't worry about me." He smiled at Sally. "It took an alien monster the size of ten skyscrapers to do this to me. I think I'll be fine." He laughed, then clenched his teeth after realizing he probably shouldn't have mentioned aliens to Sally.

"Well, from what I hear, I should see the other guy," she chuckled.

Jordin breathed a sigh of relief. "At least I'm the one up and walking." His expression turned serious. "But I wasn't alone. I just happened to be in the right place at the right time. It could have been anyone. Heck...I didn't even press the button. Rubble did."

Sally grew somber. "According to Dr. Wilber, if you hadn't been there, no one would've come back. We're all glad you were there. I'm sure that Mr. Mercury..." Just saying his name made her speechless.

"Better men than me didn't make it out alive," Jordin said, before brightening. "But we're here now and I've still got a job to perform. The data collected from all of this will be fascinating to examine."

"It's good to have you back."

Jordin nodded in appreciation, "It's good to be back. By the way, do you know which one of Mercury's Japanese associates made that sculpture?" He motioned toward the fountain.

"I'm sorry, sir. Mr. Mercury never revealed the specific name. Not even Dr. Dhar knows. I asked him." She winked. "It's from someone that Mr. Mercury knew before he founded P.M.L."

"Too bad. I wonder if they do miniature sculptures. Saint George and the Dragon was always my favorite story as a kid. I used to pretend I was saving a village from ..." He stopped before he said something even more embarrassing. "Nevermind. I guess I better get to work."

Sally reassured him with a nod. "You know, Mercury used to donate to a traveling company that performed a play about Saint George and the Dragon. They'd put on shows at children's hospitals."

"Hmmm. There's a lot I didn't know about Mercury."

"He wasn't a bad sort, once you got past his sporadic chaos," Sally said mournfully. "By the way." She reached into a drawer behind the desk and pulled out a box of motion sickness medication. "Dr. Terry left these here for you."

"Oh." Jordin blinked in surprise as he accepted the medication. "Thank you."

"Don't thank me, thank her."

"Is she here? I mean, does she still work here?"

"I'm sorry. I can't discuss employment status."

"Oh." A pit formed in Jordin's stomach. He had a feeling he knew what that meant. "Thanks anyway."

"No problem. Is there anything else I can help you with?"

"That's all for now, thanks." He turned and hobbled toward the stairway. When he reached the stairs, he stopped and peered at them, following the winding stairway up with his eyes. He nervously patted his brace and looked over his shoulder toward the elevators, then down at the box of medication in his hand.

"Are you sure you wouldn't rather take the elevator?" Sally called after him.

"Uh...yes...I...uh...yes of course," Jordin stammered as he awkwardly walked toward the elevators, shooting Sally a nervous smile as he passed. He didn't relish the thought of riding the elevator but he didn't seem to have much of a choice.

Should I take the medication now? he asked himself as he pressed the elevator button. *It won't help me in time. I don't have a glass of water. I'll have to take it later...for when I'm leaving.*

The elevator beeped merrily as the numbers on the display counted down to meet him. With a final series of rapid beeps, the elevator doors opened wide.

You faced down a gigantic space monster. Why are you scared of a little elevator? He steeled himself and marched, as best he could, into the waiting carriage. This wasn't the first time he had ridden in an elevator, but he still didn't like it. He leaned against the wall as he pressed the button for floor 13. After another series of rapid beeps, the doors closed.

"Here we go," Jordin said as he closed his eyes, clenched his teeth, and gripped the railings tightly. *I'm not getting sick. I'm not going to let this silly machine win.*

The floor moved beneath his feet. He felt as if his world were rocking back and forth. Merry beeps told him when each floor passed. Finally, after what seemed like an eternity, the elevator came to a stop with a jolt. The rapid series of beeps informed him that the door was opening.

He slowly pried his eyes open as the elevator doors parted, revealing a familiar hallway. His shaking hand let go of the railing and he hobbled out of the elevator into the hallway. The elevator beeped happily as it closed behind him.

"Well, that wasn't so bad," he muttered to himself as he walked down the hallway toward his office. Then he laughed. *Airplanes are worse. I'll have to get used to that elevator. It'll be how I get to my office for the foreseeable future.*

Everything in his office was just as he left it months before. He took a deep breath as fond memories of time spent with coworkers returned to him. With a sigh, he walked to his desk where he placed his carrying case and the medication box. He then opened the shades to let in the warm light, and surveyed the streets below.

"Well, I didn't expect to see you so soon," said a friendly voice behind him.

Jordin turned to see Lauren standing in the doorway. He was glad and relieved to see her here, the pit in his stomach vanishing. After their last conversation, he wasn't sure if she was going to stay at P.M.L. He smiled and nodded at her. "I have a job to do. Besides, I was getting bored laying around all day."

Lauren smiled and returned the nod. "It's been rather dull around here without you. Joseph has been trying to keep things interesting, but I already know all of his tricks."

"I'm glad I can be so interesting. I'm also glad to see you still here. I was half-expecting not to see you ever again. What have I missed?"

"I guess I just don't know when to quit." She gave him a wistful smile. "You haven't missed much; everyone has been focused on studying the creature's remains as well as examining the data. I'm sure you'll catch up quickly."

"Thanks for the medicine. It did help on the plane." He tapped the hard body cast. "I'm going to need it if I'm riding the elevators now."

"No problem." Lauren gave him a mischievous grin. "I didn't want you throwing up in our elevators."

Jordin chuckled slightly. "Me neither."

An awkward beat passed between the pair.

"So," Jordin began, "how have your investigations been going? Hopefully, I'll be able to assist in examining its effects on the weather."

Lauren lit up. "Fascinating. We've determined that the big one was a male and the one in the egg was a female. We're only guessing. They have similar yet different bone and body structures, much the same way human male and female structures are different. Did you know that the creatures were comprised largely of silica deposits? And their circulation system is fascinating. They don't have blood, but rather use hollow tubes with water vapor to circulate temperature."

"So, it was just like the egg?"

"Yes, but to a different degree. And the skeletal structure is unlike anything I've seen before. It's more like a carbon fiber system with supporting musculature and a tungsten core. That humming buzzing noise was because they have little insect-like wings all over their bodies the same way that we have hair. It was all flapping in unison, quite rapidly too. And did you know that they had a functioning solar panel on their heads? There are tons of other organic compounds that no one has even begun to understand yet...but you probably don't care about biology as much..."

Jordin chuckled, "That's alright, I know I can go off about weather patterns. It's all fascinating to me. I'd love to read your report and your findings if you would let me. I'd be happy to share my findings as well."

"You may have to wrestle the military for it," Lauren mused. "They've been obsessed with the creature. Most of the world militaries have taken bits and pieces of the monster for 'study.' They're particularly interested in the shell." She shrugged. "Oh, by the way. When you are up to it, Dr. Dhar wants to speak with you about hiring another intern...," she said carefully.

Jordin's mood turned somber. "I know. Dhar and I talked a bit yesterday. We didn't finish our conversation. I'm just worried that ..." He leaned against his desk, unable to continue.

"I'm sorry, I didn't mean to..."

"It's alright. We need to move on with our lives. I realized when I came back that I'd have to continue to do my job, no matter how hard it would be. I'll talk to him again today."

"Take your time," Lauren said. "It took me a while until I could call Dr. Dhar boss." She gazed out the window blankly. "We ran ourselves for a week while he was at his nephew's wedding. We still sort of do. He's really busy with everything else."

"Speaking of Dr. Dhar," Jordin said with a smile,. "he and I both agreed that our astronomy division should have access to our rooftop observatory whenever we please. I've been given authority to grant access to whomever I wish."

Lauren perked up. "Oh?"

"I'll be there tonight. The cafeteria will have dinner ready and waiting for whoever joins me. Care to join?"

Lauren gave him a sidelong glance. "You kidding? Of course I will. It's about time we used that telescope."

"Good." Jordin smiled again and nodded. "I'll see you there....And I'll let the cafeteria know."

An unspoken, awkward yet exciting tension passed between them.

"Oh...uh," Lauren jolted herself back to reality, "it's good to see you back. I wish you a speedy recovery. If you need anything else let me know. Joseph should be here soon. He had a meeting this morning about who knows what."

"It was about how I'm tired of having meetings about things rather than just doing the things," Joseph boomed from the hallway before appearing and sporting a big toothy smile. "Well, well, well, Dr. Davidson returns." He strolled inside to shake Jordin's hand.

Jordin was relieved to see Joseph as he shook it. "And how have you been?"

"Just peachy," Joseph chucked. "I've had more meetings and more work than you could shake a stick at. I swear, these alien invasions are more trouble than they're worth."

Jordin agreed. "Let's hope they aren't habit forming."

"Indeed, indeed."

Lauren giggled. "Another meeting about meetings? That's the third one this week."

"I swear, these big corporate and government types are more obsessed with talking about data than getting the data. I suppose large monsters make anyone nervous, but come on. Just let me do my job," Joseph bemoaned.

"I'm sure everyone is just trying to cover their bases," Jordin said.

"That's true. But it's frustrating to deal with." Joseph beckoned to Lauren. "Well, we should probably let the good doctor get settled in. We owe him some time to get back into the swing of things. He did save us all, after all."

"I was just telling him that he could count on us for anything he needs," Lauren said.

"Yes of course. We're here if you need anything," Joseph replied.

"Thank you. I think I'm fine for now. I'll let you know if I need anything," Jordin said.

Both Lauren and Joseph left the office.

"Hey, thanks for the meds...again," Jordin called after Lauren.

"You're welcome," Lauren called back.

"I didn't save..." Jordin began, but trailed off. "Well, I'd better get back to work...but first," he said as he opened his shoulder bag and pulled out a framed photograph. He then hobbled to the wall by the window and placed the picture on a single hanging nail.

The picture was a company photo that Mr. Mercury had insisted on taking as soon as they had landed in Russia to commemorate P.M.L.'s momentous involvement with the "weather anomaly." Mr. Mercury's confident face smiled back at him. Jordin's eyes moved down to find Jimmy's eager, yet fearful expression. Lauren and Joseph both had forced smiles saying, "why are we taking this photo?" His own expression in the photo was one of confusion. At the time, he hadn't understood Mr. Mercury's obsession with taking the perfect photo.

"Don't worry, you two," Jordin said aloud to the images of Mr. Mercury and Jimmy. "We won. You helped bring the monster down." A twinge of sadness washed over him. "I should've died in Russia. I got lucky. 'There, but for the grace of God'..."

"...go I." Clarence's gruff voice interrupted his musings.

Jordin turned to see the janitor standing in the doorway.

"How can I help?" Jordin asked, a bit taken off guard.

Clarence walked to the window and took in the view. "Most people don't know what happened, do they?"

"Excuse me?"

"According to all official statements and news broadcasts, it was just a new type of violent snowstorm. They omit most of the details."

Jordin nodded. He wasn't sure if he should discuss what actually happened with Clarence. Something told him that the old man already knew everything anyway.

Clarence twitched his mustache and glanced at the photo. "The government named this new storm."

"Oh? What did they name it?"

Clarence turned to look Jordin dead in the eye. "Mercury Snow."

"Appropriate."

"Maybe. They don't know what you did. Very few do. Maybe they should've named it after you."

"I didn't really do..."

Clarence cut Jordin off, "A pebble dropped in the right place on a mountainside can cause a rock-slide further down. If a man drops that pebble, didn't he cause the slide despite not pushing the boulders himself?"

Jordin wordlessly contemplated this for a moment.

"This came for you," Clarence finally broke the silence and pulled an envelope out of his pocket and, handing it to Jordin.

"What is it?"

"No idea." The old janitor said nothing more as he left the room.

"Okay..."

The envelope was addressed to Dr. Jordin Davidson with no return address or stamp. He opened it and pulled out a decorative certificate. The border had an intricate hand-drawn serpentine dragon twisting around leafy vines. A holographic sticker seal adorned the center. Another hand-drawn image of Saint George and the dragon took up most of the space beneath the sticker.

"Is that...?" He looked closer. Saint George looked an awful lot like himself. "Must be a coincidence," he muttered.

Below the image was a line of Japanese kanji, under which were the words *Strive Against the Impossible*.

Two signatures in the bottom right corner caught his eye.

"You two...You were the ones who made the fountain... You were calling me...You sent the slings...But how did you...?" The empty stamp location on the envelope taunted him. Then an idea occurred to him. He looked toward the door. "How did Clarence get this and not Sally? How did it...?" He realized he could always ask so he leaned against the wall and pulled his phone out of his pocket. He dialed a familiar number.

"I'm sorry, the number you have dialed is no longer in service," a robotic voice greeted him.

"Ha," Jordin snorted. "I guess I'll never really know for sure." He put his phone back into his pocket and reread the certificate. "Thank you, friends," he whispered. "No one knows that you were the real heroes. Someday, I'll figure out who you really are and give you the proper credit. Maybe Clarence can tell me."

Jordin shook his head at the thought. "I'll try to talk to him later." Taking in the group picture again, a wave of sadness washed over him as he hobbled back to his desk and sat down. What to do next? It would prove difficult to move on at first. He would never forget those who didn't return.

"To think," he said, "this all started because I wanted to put weather probes on other planets." He chuckled to himself. "I wonder if anyone else even remembers our original project. Will we ever get back to it?"

His phone rang – a welcome distraction. Dr. Dhar's name appeared on the caller ID.

"Now, back to work." Jordin took a deep breath, smiled, and answered the call.

THE END

www.ingramcontent.com/pod-product-compliance
Lightning Source LLC
Chambersburg PA
CBHW071147020726
47502CB00002B/301